I0542501

139: IN EVENING

2nd Edition

Aden Ng

ISBN (E-book): 978-981-09-9905-6

ISBN (Paperback): 978-981-09-9904-9

To my teachers of Teo, Quek, and Hong.
For building me up, bringing me forward, and tearing me down.
Respectively.

CHAPTER ONE

Coming Evening

"The best thing about dreams is that fleeting moment, when you are between asleep and awake, when you don't know the difference between reality and fantasy, when for just that one moment you feel with your entire soul that the dream is reality, and it really happened."
- Unknown

2 months earlier,
03:45 P.M.

Price stood at the store window, gentle snow falling atop his baseball cap. His golden, cat-like eyes staring back at him from the reflection. Smell of sewage floated up from the drains, of rotting eggs and flushed away feces, the lovely smell of the city. Boots and jacketed, with his school bag hanging lazily at the side, Price watched as the newscaster continued her report from the store television. The newscaster was a redhead, and he liked redhead. Not just a preference for them, but a full blown sexual attraction. His entire porn collection consisted solely of redheads.

The newscaster reported, "It seems the illness that causes death inducing nightmares has spread. Reports are coming in of more and more fatalities throughout the world." He raised up his energy bar and took an uninterested bite. "The CDC have officially named the phenomenon, the Vashmir Pandemic, known more colloquially as Suicide In Nightmare, or Sin. Locally, there have been but thirty-six known cases of Sin, but that number is expected to rise over the following weeks."

He gave a derisive snort. "Sucks to be them." He took the final bite of the energy bar and unceremoniously tossed the wrapper on the ground.

"World's unfair," he said aloud.

"As the number of cases rise, so have the demand for the controversial sleep-aid drug, Somnidin. The drug is known to be highly addictive, but continues to be the only medication so-far that is capable of combating Sin."

With a final glance at the television set as the newscaster went on to cover celebrities, Price whistled as he walked off. A police car, horns blaring, lights flashing, zoomed past him, leaving a trail of dust and lines of light in its wake.

Thinking he had nothing better left to do that day, Price decided to follow, jogging after the fading car, jaywalking across as a passing motorist honked him fiercely.

"Asshole!" Followed after.

The city was filled with shortcuts and he darted into an alleyway to cut off the pursuit at the next junction. He made a mental note though that if the car went past the block, he was not pursuing it further. No point in wasting his energy just to satisfy his curiosity.

Luckily for him, the police car came to a stop at just the turn of the corner. Joining the ranks of a ring of other law enforcement vehicles surrounding a pharmacy, the spinning lights of red and blue turned the streets into a dizzying disco. The perimeter of the scene was fenced off by impromptu yellow tapes. Like talismans, they warded off the crowd that had gathered. Shivering officers stood behind them as guards in the freezing temperature, forced to put on a professional front despite the cold.

From the passenger's side of the newly joined vehicle, a bald, burly, coat wearing man stepped out.

"Ugh..." Price voiced his displeasure. The man was as ugly as he looked brute.

Then, from the driver's side, a woman stepped out. Slender, tall, flowing red hair, and long-legged in grey pantsuits, he inadvertently wolf whistled as she stood.

The female heard him and shot him an angry glance that made his heart skip a beat in fear. But he wondered how a woman as sexy as that ended up with a man as ugly as a troll.

The pair headed towards one of the officer standing guard. From where Price stood, he could just hear the female ask, "What's the situation?"

"Attempted robbery, detectives," the officer replied. "One suspect, armed with a shotgun. He's got a hostage."

"Robbery?" the male detective replied. "At a pharmacy? What drug was he trying to steal? Ritalin? Xanax?"

5

"Somnidin," the officer answered. "The man says he has Sin but doesn't have the money to buy the medication."

As the officer and detectives continued to discuss the situation, Price caught sight of a man in the crowd opposite him. A man in a sleek onyx suit, black bowler hat, and sharp sunglasses. He stood unwavering, intently writing into a small notebook in his hands. Price thought he might be a reporter, but the lack of the boisterous personality of one made him think otherwise. After staring at the man for a while, Price puffed over-dramatically, turning his attention away and back to the pharmacy.

But nothing happened. No gunshots or screams or shouts. The robber did not storm out with a ransom demand like they do in movies. No red-dots aimed menacingly at the building. No SWAT team busting down doors. Just a long period of silence and bored tension that hung in the air with the snow. A couple of people within the crowd let out a contagious yawn.

Price clicked his tongue in frustration. "This is lame. I'm going home."

Just as he said that, the loud echoing blast of a gunshot rang through the streets and the crowd jumped. The police scrambled, cutting through the barricade and running towards the pharmacy, guns drawn. Another shot and the glass window of the pharmacy shattered. The crowd started screaming and dispersed, running away from the scene in which they had recently given their rasp attention. The two detectives ran towards the danger at flank.

Price stood in the midst of the chaos, unmoving, stunned by the events that are so quickly unravelling before him as crowds rushed to pass him. He did not turn to look when a man walked up beside him, did not even give him full attention when he started to speak.

"Makes you wonder, doesn't it?"

Price mumbled a meek reply. "Wonder about what?" Opposite him, the man in the bowler hat and suit continued to stand his ground, a lopsided grin on his face.

"Just what kind of nightmare these Sin victims are having that makes them desperate enough to kill."

Price turned, only to be faced with air. The man that had been talking to him had seemingly vanished without a trace. The only thing left in his wake were the screams of the crowd and the falling snow.

CHAPTER TWO

Yesterday, Tomorrow, Today

"All the things one have forgotten scream for help in dreams."
- Elias Canetti, Die Provinz des Menschen

14 days earlier,
11:45 A.M.

Seventeen year old Timothy Kleve, student of Ridge Valley High, sat alone at the corner-most lunch table, poking at his chunky bean paste. His maroon hair, a natural coloured gift given to him by his late mother, neat and swept to the side, dangled its bangs in front of his eyes. It irritated his eyelashes but he felt too down in the dumps to raise his hands to swipe it away.

Tim wore an odd combination of black jeans with sandals and a tattered hooded t-shirt. A dress sense laughable in the fashion centric age. Most of the time, he just picked the first set of clothing he sees in his closet, and owned only one set of formal-wear. To him, there were no reasons to alter his looks and comfort for the viewing pleasures of others.

"Why so gloomy, kid?" A body sat opposite him, setting a tray with a tuna sandwich and salad down on the table.

He knew of only one person that called him 'kid', even though said person was only a month older. "Lost the spot for the team this year," he replied.

"Too bad man. " The guy bit into his sandwich. "Naybe yo'll cat a chansh nesh yearsh." His friend never could close his mouth when he ate.

"I don't know dude," Tim said, finally looking up. "I mean the seniors– Whoa! What the fuck happened to you?"

Clay Barber had a black ring around his left eye and a partially bloodied tissue stuffed up his right nostril. Tim found it somewhat impressive that whoever hit him was able to grant a darker colour to ebony skin. Clay's parents both had early whitening of their hair, something he inherited at a young age, which he often got teased for. Coupled with his 'never back down' attitude, Clay had gotten into his fair share of scuffles. He kept his hair in a buzz cut, which made him look like he was simply wearing a white beanie when viewed from a distance. He wore a black 'peace' shirt with khaki shorts and sandals, never really having liked long clothings as he sweats easily. He didn't care much for sports either. As such, he had a thin figure which made his clothes droop over his body like a shower curtain.

Despite Clay's injuries, Tim could not help but crack a grin. "If I didn't know better, I'd say your whole body's bruised."

Clay swallowed the food in his mouth and pointed with his sandwich, bobbing it at Tim as if it was a pencil. "That's racist and you know it."

"You don't care and *you* know it."

Clay chuckled. "Yeah."

"You do look like shit," Tim continued mockingly. "More than usual I mean. Who's it this time? Basketball? Soccer?"

"Wrestling club."

"Ouch," he winced at the imagined pain. "Your pride will be the death of you, man."

"Yeah." Clay half bit into his food again but paused to yawn.

"History's up next. We all know how you love that." He pushed his tray of beans away. "Take a nap then."

"Yeah." Clay took a small bite, pulling at the lettuce from between the bread. Tim watched as his friend stared blankly at the sandwich, the crisp lettuce crunching as he reeled it in with his bites. Something about his action felt serene to Tim, but he could not put a finger on why he felt that way.

Clay swallowed softly. "I'll sleep then."

14 days earlier,
02:58 P.M.

The ringing of the clock tower bell signalled the end of the day, and on that day, the end of the week as well, for Tim felt that the week ends on Friday, starts on Saturday, and ended Sunday again. Towards the end of the class, Clay had quietly stepped out of the classroom and had yet to return.

Tim packed his book into his sling bag, grabbed his belongings and picked up his club gear, which included his air rifle. Ever since the renovations to the storage room started, air rifle club members had been asked to bring their equipments home. A possibly misplaced trust in their responsibleness and slight fear of the shootings that had taken place in recent times.

He headed to a girl seated in the far back corner next to the window, directly across from his seat. "Hey Stella, where's your brother?"

The girl looked up through her oval glasses and from the horror novel she was reading, Vrykolaka. With strawberry blonde hair and a ceramic pale skin, Stella Barber was Clay's adopted sister.

"Aren't you always with him? Why are you asking me?" She readjusted her glasses, straightened the collar on her white shirt and smoothed the crease out of her chequered red and black plaid skirt.

"I haven't seen him since lunch," he retorted. "And we're not always together."

She replied with an exaggerated snicker. "Right..." she raised her hands to stretch, her long, pony-tailed hair waving behind her, and gave a veiled yawn. Bending back, her small breasts raised out in front of her, her white bra outlined prominently by her white shirt.

Tim felt the temperature rise and his cheeks heated up, no doubt as red as an apple. He turned away from the sight. "Y-yeah. I can't keep tabs on him all the time."

"And I'm supposed to?" She stopped stretching and turned back to Tim. Noticing his blush, she could not help but grin. "Oh? Little Timmy getting aroused?"

"Am not," he snapped back, which only caused her to giggle daintily. "You know, people say you're all soft spoken and nice, but you're actually a devil, aren't you?"

She replied with only a smile. "He said he wanted to wash up, so I'm guessing the bathroom's where he is." Opening her book, she went back to the bookmarked page. "Maybe he fell asleep on the can."

"Maybe he slipped and hit his head on the sink," he added.

"Maybe he's vomiting blood into the toilet bowl from food poisoning."

"Or maybe he's fine."

"Maybe he got murdered."

"You're getting more disturbing by the day. You should stop reading those books."

He saw the corner of her mouth form into a smile. "Bye Tim. Tell brother to hurry it up. We're having pizza tonight."

He turned and headed for the door. "Okay, okay. See you later Stell."

Closing the classroom door behind him, he stepped out into the nearly empty hallway. Most students had already left, and the remaining stragglers had their shadows and reflection stretched across the waxed ceramic floor, silhouetted by the light from the glass front door at the far end of the hallway. Someone slammed a locker and the echo rang through the long chamber. The sounds of footsteps and squeaky shoes were sparse and inconsistent. A waft of after-school sweat hung in the air.

Tim headed down the familiar hallway, the lights overhead flickered on, rolling out brightness in his way like a red carpet. A dozen lockers after a gossiping pair of girls were the bathrooms. Males on the left, females on the right.

Because the girls are always right. Clay once said.

Clay's voice bellowed into the hallway. "Why don't you suck my dick, ass-face!"

"Fucking kid!" came another familiar, gruff voice. Something large slammed into the bathroom door, causing such a commotion that people from down the hall turned to search for the source.

Going against the general rule of not heading into danger, Tim burst through the door and inhaled the smelled of ammonia and cheap lemon soap.

The lanky red-headed Joseph stood tall in front of him. The shorter, and brutishly muscular Horace, crouched in the corner, rummaging through Clay's bag. Joseph was breathing heavily, his fist clenched, and a flaming rage lit his brown eyes. Both wore the school's Air Rifle Team's black and blue lined jacket.

"Tim?" Clay's voice croaked.

Tim turned to find his friend slumped down against the wall beside the urinal, next to a dirtied mop and its bucket. Both his nostrils were bleeding this time, as was his forehead. He grinned at Tim's shocked expression, showing that he had also chipped a tooth yet kept his callousness.

"What the hell? You all right?" Tim stooped down in an awkward attempt to treat his friend's wound, only to have his hand held back.

"I'm fine," Clay insisted as he tried to get back on his feet, though he still leaned on Tim for support.

Tim turned to face his seniors. "I don't know what Clay said this time, but this is too much."

Joseph took a single step forward. "Not your business, Timmy-boy. 'Sides, this ghoul started it."

"No smoking in the toilet," Clay coughed out. That's when Tim noticed the cigarette butts in some of the basins.

"Shut up, Clay."

"These kids jumped me after my shit."

"You said it while on the can?"

"What can I say, I really hate the smell of smoke."

Tim turned to Joseph. "You guys beat him 'cause he asked you to stopped smoking? Are you high?"

"Hey Joe," Horace called out. "Look what I've found." From Clay's bag, the bulky teen took out a bottle of pills.

"Hey!" Clay pushed himself towards the two seniors. "Don't touch that, man."

"Aw... what's the matter?" Horace teased, though his voice sounded more like a vicious growl. "Tough guy can't make it without getting high on his drugs?"

"Yeah, exactly." Clay sounded desperate, a tone Tim had never heard him use before. "Now give it back."

The seniors laughed, and Joseph took the pills from Horace's hands. "You know what," he said, tauntingly shaking the bottle. "I'll flush it. Much better idea. Teach ya to mess with us."

Action and reaction. A primal urge for survival. Tim called it instincts, something which he had a truck load of. Clay broke free from Tim's support and rushed the seniors with the mop. The bucket sloshed against the wall as he unsheathed. He swung the cleaning tool over his head and brought it crashing down against Joseph's skull.

Joseph dropped to his knees in a yell of pain. The head of the mop snapped in half. Blood splattered across the floor. He dropped the bottle of pills and it rolled under the sink, uncapping and spilling its contents across the tile floor.

Clay dove for the bottle, dropping the broken mop handle in the process, clawing for the pills in panicked fervour.

Horace, the lumbering goon, took the chance and grabbed the broken mop handle, and, with the sharp end, swiped at Clay's head, drawing blood.

The younger teen griped in pain but managed to roll aside to dodge a second swing. Joseph got to his feet and stumbled to deliver a stomp to Clay's stomach, forcing Clay to curl up into a fetal position to protect his face as Horace joined in the onslaught.

Joseph, his head bleeding, shouted, "Fucking freak! I hope the nightmare gets you," he too the weapon from Horace and raised it to hit but was stopped by the touch of a cold steel barrel to the back of his head.

"Put down the stick," Tim warned, pushing the barrel of his black

11

pump air rifle a little harder against his head. "Diabolo pellets. You know what these thing can do at close range."

Horace, despite his thuggish appearance, backed up against the cubicle door, a rare look of genuine fear in his eyes.

"You gonna shoot me for not putting you on the team?" Joseph asked.

"No," Tim replied calmly. "I'm gonna shoot you for beating up my friend."

Slowly, Joseph raised his hands. "Okay. Okay," he said, slowly turning to face the door. Tim circled him, putting himself between Joseph and Clay. "But you can kiss your chance of making the team next year goodbye too."

"I'll take that chance." Tim gave a nudge with the barrel and Joseph stumbled a step forward before walking out. Tim gestured for Horace to follow and the thug gave a fierce glare before leaving.

Lowering his rifle, he turned back to see Clay sombrely picking up his pills. Despite his oversized shirt, he looked really small. A large portion of the pills had been crushed in the fight and he was sure more had been kicked into corners of the bathroom better left unexplored by human hands.

Tim bent over to pick up a pill by his feet. He examined the pill and carved into it was the letter 'S'.

The action froze Clay in mid movement. He looked up to his friend with eyes full of worry, like a child who got caught taking cookies out of the jar. Tim finally understood the full weight of the bags under Clay's eyes.

"Somnidin." Tim looked to Clay on the floor and thought of tales, myths and legends of fallen gods and felled titans, the demise of those who were once mighty. "You have Sin."

CHAPTER THREE

Normal

"Sometimes, there is absolutely no difference at all between salvation and damnation."
- Stephen King, *The Green Mile*

14 days earlier,
09:44 P.M.

He never really understood the process in naming places. There were no flowers on Rose Avenue and no bridges at Connectors Estate. Ridge Valley was nowhere near a ridge nor a valley. Instead, it was located near the sea where it froze each night. The swing set chains squeaked from years of use as the three teens swung in a rhythm that made it so that none of them would be at their highest swing at the same time. A cool breeze blew through the empty park playground, carrying with it the scent of the sea. White lights floated upon old lampposts, eerily hanging sparse across the park. Floating fairies in the dark.

The group took comfort in rubbing their toes in the playground sand at the nadir of their swing. Stella especially, humming *Colours of the Wind* in bliss. The moon was a sharp crescent in the sky, flanked in all directions by stars. Dogs' barks echoed through the neighbourhood followed by a long, pitiful howl.

Clay's cuts had been cleaned up though he was still bruised at places. To their parents, the siblings gave the excuse that they had revisions to do at the library and lamentably missed pizza night. Tim was the first to break the peaceful silence.

"You have Sin."

"Yeah," Clay replied.

"Do your parents know?"

13

"Just Stella. And you now, I guess."

They fell back to mute. With the crickets singing, the swing chains squeaking, their feet kicking the sands, and Stella's musical hum, the night turned into a peaceful rhythmic orchestra.

Tim broke the silence again. "People with Sin dies."

Stella stopped humming.

"I'll be fine," Clay replied. "As long as I keep taking the medication, nothing will happen."

"You barely have enough for the week."

"I'll get more tomorrow."

"And what if the stock runs out?"

"It won't run out."

"If."

"I'll find a way."

"If there isn't a way?"

"You're starting to sound like Stella."

The girl chimed in, "Not even close."

Again, the trio entered a sort of silence, minus Stella's musical hum. Slowly, the brother and sister pair slowed down their swinging. Clay sat still and tried to bury his feet in the sand. Stella's were barely brushing against the ground.

Tim swung higher and higher. The wind rushed around his face on each descent, parting his hair, his troubles, his weariness. It was a physical lullaby. With thoughts on Clay's illness, his position on the air rifle team, and his impending return home, he took the short respite from life in full.

Stella switched to singing a song to the tune of the Christian hymn, *'Will the Circle be Unbroken?'*. Her voice carried loud and clear through the empty park.

Tim felt his worries floating away. No Sin, no seniors, no loneliness. He closed his eyes to rest, kicking off each swing based purely on his instinct of descent.

Long ago far on a prairie, where the sun raised with the night.

Tim felt the smile that spread across his face. With each swing, the rush of the descending wind got stronger, cooler, calmer. Clay always said his sister's voice was magical, and he was right. The girl had an aura of tranquillity about her that shined such finesse and serenity that she could probably diffuse a bomb by her mere presence.

Where the moon rose with brightness, did the world slept through all time?

From the corner of his eye, he could see Clay leaning his head back

14

against his spine, eyes closed, enjoying her light tune.

Will the circle be unbroken, by and by, by and by? Is a better home awaiting, in the sky, in the sky?

The wind felt cooler somehow, as if it was trying to lift him from the swing and into the unending sky.

Lost alone in the forest...

He breathed deeply, the fresh air sparking his heart and mind.

Which men built with tools and hands.

The crickets stopped cricking and the dogs no longer barked.

When the heaven scrapes starts falling...

Another rush of wind as he swung back up to the zenith.

Will we rise or all descend.

Tim's eyes flashed open as the freezing gale rushed into his back. He was falling. Falling through a wide, open, endless blue sky that stretched across him as far as his eyes could see. There was no sun, no stars, no moon, just an infinite blue. Falling through the clouds. Falling through the atmosphere. Falling through the sky with the wind on his back, gushing past his ears in a roar.

Will the end of all be coming...

A female voice – soft, doleful, ethereal – continued the song. He searched for the source. Around him were others who were falling from heaven, scattered at varying distances. An old lady in a floral dress. A teenage boy in a baseball jersey and a cap. A middle-aged woman in a business suit.

live and died, lived and die?

A young boy in a school uniform. A fat man in a stained white sleeveless shirt and shorts. An older, well built-man in farmers gear. A young girl in a white dress. All of them, falling through the vast, empty sky. He wondered if there was something for them to land on after the fall. He tried to turn to face the ground but his body felt sluggish, sleepy, rejecting his attempts to move. A shooting star cuts across the sky.

Dreams of fire, salves of healing...

The girl in the white dress. Tim focused onto her. She was smiling, her lips moving a second out of sing with the song. Her long snow-white hair trailed and covered her face.

Are one thy...

He could hear the waves of the sea.

Are one thy?

He hit the ground, though not as hard as he had expected. The crescent moon, with its blade sharp tail, hung in the Ridge Valley night sky, stars all around. He felt the sand at his neck, cold to the touch. It felt like the world was a blur, moving fast, and when he stayed still he swore he could feel the Earth spinning on its axle.

"You all right, kid?" Clay and Stella's heads popped into Tim's field of vision.

"What happened?" Tim sat up groggily, his back aching. He stretched to massage the outline of his spine.

"You fell out of the swing, idiot, that's what happened," Clay replied.

"Must have fallen asleep."

"Is my voice that soothing?" Stella added seductively.

Tim didn't reply, for he was too focused on remembering the dream he had. He recalled a sad and lonely voice echoing through the back of his mind. A drip of water in a hollow cave. He ran his fingers down his spine again, feeling the vertebrae. He remembered the fall from far above the heavens. He remembered the hymn. He remembered the people around him. He remembered hitting the water. He remembered the pain. He remembered breaking his spine.

13 days earlier,
00:03 A.M.

One of the common problems with living by the sea was how fast metal rusted. Bikes, machines, buildings. Not one spared from the slow encroaching wrath of time. So it surprised Tim that he tried to push the door to his apartment home as slowly as he did, since he knew the hinges would shrill despite the speed. Somewhere in his mind he held hope that just once the door would open silently.

He winced with each creak, even as he stepped over the threshold and locked the door behind him. With the curtains of the lone window drawn and facing an unlit alleyway, the only source of light was the red glow of the power light of the old CRT television that watched him as a demon would in the dark.

The three room apartment was where Timothy and his father Joshua lived. It was small, with the kitchen and living room squeezed into the same 140 square feet. The singular stove, refrigerator and kitchen sink shared the space with a two-seater couch and a coffee table where the odd stains marked late night dinners and rushed breakfast. They had a single bulky 21 inch CRT television that sat on a plastic storage box for entertainment, and a lone cactus plant won long ago from a carnival game as decoration beside it. Two doors sided the set.

Sliding his sandals under the shoe rack, he made his way to the furthest of the two doors, the floorboards creaking under his light steps. No light seeped from the cracks of his father's room as he passed it. He felt safer, knowing that the chances of his father being out working late or asleep was high. He took the next step with confidence.

The door to his father's room opened and the bright yellow light flickered on.

His father stood with his back to the light, poised like a priest to a sinner. His short golden hair, messy, glowed like a halo. His arms were folded in disdain. Even though he simply wore an unimposing set of white sleeveless shirt and grey boxers, Tim could feel his father's overwhelming presence.

His father spoke in a growl, "Where were you?" Tim timidly turned to his father.

As a construction worker, Joshua Kleve was a naturally muscular man that always seemed to exude a debilitating presence of rage. His rugged face had forever been distorted in a frown for as long as Tim could remember. His amber eyes, yellowish in the dark, were catlike, stalking the figure of his son.

Joshua asked, "Have you got any idea what time it is?"

"Twelve, dad. It's not that late," Tim replied, his head down, not daring to meet his father's gaze.

"You've got any idea what's going on out there right now? How dangerous it is? Where were you?"

"Just out with Clay and Stella."

"Oh, that makes it okay then," his dad replied sarcastically.

Feeling that his father had just taken a stab at his friendship, he found the rage within him to fight back. "Yeah, that makes it okay."

His dad slapped him across the face with enough force that Tim stumbled back. "Don't you dare talk back to me!"

Tim's first instinct was to rub his wound but held back, not wanting to give his father the sense of satisfaction that it hurts. In the darkness, his arms limped at his sides, numbed by the emotional turmoil. He boiled with anger. "Or what? You'll beat me again? Like all those times when you were drunk?"

He could tell his father had lost his tongue. The yellow eyes widening in recognition. Silence grabbed the man and wouldn't let go.

Tim nodded in the dark. "I thought so." He turned and headed for his room.

He heard his father call out softly behind him. "Where do you think you're going?" A feeble last attempt at discipline.

17

"Where I'm safe." He slammed the door behind him. He heard his father slam his door as well. Like father like son.

His room was small, fitting only one desk against a bed that doubled as his chair, a small cupboard above his desk as his closet. The room had the cosy standing space of exactly two people with the door closed. One of the small comfort was that he had his own bathroom to the immediate left of entering which was equally small. It meant he need not see his father as often as otherwise. A single cord on his table was connected to and charging his cell phone, a simple mobile that could only call and send messages, capable of storing a total of 20 contacts if the names were not too long. Its special function includes a built in torchlight and the ability to be used as an unbreakable projectile. The only electronic he owned.

He had books, but not many. Most were loans from the library. A total of five stacked into the nook between his desk and the wall and half a dozen scattered across the desk. A single lone novel leaned against the windowsill. Outside the glass, he had the amazing view of the brick wall of the neighbouring apartment. But for a full half hour past noon and midnight, he could see the sun and moon respectively through the cracks in-between the roofs if he leaned his face against his bed frame.

Sitting at the foot of his bed, he had his air rifle disassembled and laid bare across the rest of his mattress. Meticulously, he cleaned each part with a cloth, dabbing them with a layer of oil from a small bottle. He found the process therapeutic, something to focus on other than life. Once done, he reassembled the gun, checking the safeties, the firing mechanism, and the smoothness of the moving parts.

He pumped his gun, pulled the cocking lever, leaned the stock against his shoulder, aimed at the wall, and let off a click. Everything was working. Everything was smooth. "Everything's normal."

CHAPTER FOUR

Somnidin

"If God dropped acid, would he see people?"
- Steven Wright

13 days earlier,
07:34 A.M.

"Morning, Stell," Tim announced as the door opened, newspaper in his hand.

"Morning," she replied with a smile. "Thanks for the paper."

"Least I could do," he crossed the threshold into the house and left the paper on the living room table as he always did. He had been picking up the weekend paper for the Barbers since the postal services had stopped their weekend deliveries earlier that year. "Where's Clay?"

"He went to the pharmacy to get more Somnidin."

Breakfast at the Barber's had become a weekly routine for Tim. When Gordon and Matilda Barber learnt of how he ate cup noodles every weekend when his dad went to work, they invited him over.

The Barbers lived in a small colonial style cape cod, one of many that lined the coastline. They had a small sheltered patio as their dining area from which they had a view of the sea. The calm waters stretched out over the horizon, cutting the edge of the round world like a floor of lapis. From where they stood, it would not have been hard to imagine that the world was indeed flat.

He was alone with Stella when they stepped onto the deck of the patio, him dressed in khaki shorts and the same white hooded shirt from the day before. The girl wore denim shorts and white sleeveless top. She had another of her horror novels in hand.

"Did you guys tell your parents about that?" he asked.

19

"About what?"

"You know, Clay and his Sin."

"It's rare that we don't get any wind in the morning." She sat down on one of the chairs and opened her book.

"I don't think it being a little less windy will surprise me after last night," he replied, taking a seat himself.

"Really? We're a city by the sea. Not even a little bit curious?"

"I'm not gonna die from there not being any breeze."

"You could get heat stroke."

"I'm not even sweating!"

"Maybe you have hypohidrosis."

"You're a really negative person you know?" He paused and surveyed the surroundings. To his annoyance, he was a little intrigued by the lack of wind. "Wait, you're trying to change the subject."

He saw the corner of her lip lift into a small smile. "Maybe."

"And what subject might that be?" Matilda Barber, Stella and Clay's mother, stepped out from the living room with a tray of pancakes in hand.

Tim spun around in his seat, slightly surprised by her appearance and thanking luck that she had not heard the whole conversation. "History," he said, covering up.

Matilda was in her late thirties. Like her son, her hair was white, though she kept it fluffed and frilled instead. Her skin was lightly freckled which drew similarities to chocolate chip cookies. She wore a flowered dress with a yellow apron. "Well, it's a good thing Clay's at the library. He'd just fall asleep," she jabbed at her son's dislike of the class.

Stella looked away from her book to smile at her mother. "He'd fall asleep at the library."

The woman laughed and set the food down on the table. "Right. Wait awhile and I'll go wake your dad," she turned to leave.

"Uh... Mrs. Barber?" Tim called out. She spun on her feet, as if dancing. "Thanks for breakfast again."

"What did I say? You don't ever have to thank us. You're family," the woman replied with a smile before heading back into the house.

Once he was sure Matilda was out of earshot, he turned to Stella. "You lied to your mother?"

"About?"

"Clay. Pharmacy. Library," he punctuated each word for effect.

"I didn't lie. He's going to the library after to borrow a book for me," she replied, not once looking away from her novel.

"So what now? You're just gonna lie for him while he's sick?"

Stella placed her book on the table faced down. "I'm getting the paper," she announced matter-of-factly and went into the living room.

Though it seemed no different from all the other peaceful weekend start, Tim could not help but feel distracted. His best friend had Sin, the Vashmir Pandemic. Nobody affected by it had been known to survive.

Maybe he's different.

He wanted to think that. It would be nice if Clay was the hero in all the pandemic movies that had taken over the movie theatres. The immune protagonist who would go on to save the world with a vaccine. But life was never like the movies. He remembered his mother screaming when he was a child, his father shouting, and how he prayed for the Power Rangers or Superman to come and save him from the nightmare.

A speedboat came into view, cutting across the calm ocean, its wave slicing the sea like a plough through snow. There was no wind. Something else nagged at Tim aside from the breeze-less day and lack of modern heroes. Something he missed. Something he saw. Something he didn't want to know and ignored, as he did with all the horrible things in life. He ignored.

"Tim," came Stella's frantic voice from behind.

He stood from his seat, suddenly aware of what he had missed. The headline which he had only glanced. "Yeah?" He turned slowly, the bold headline sprang out at him like a jack-in-the-box.

SOMNIDIN SHORTAGE
PHARMACY OUT

Stella's glare was both fierce and worried, as were her words. "Where's my brother?"

At night, Smith Street was considered the red-light district of Ridge Valley. Though those who were more familiar with the area such as the police and frequent bar-goers would know that the labyrinth of alleys behind the street was where the real action lay. With over two dozen bars and rented apartment hotels, the shady underground business goes on 24-7. The interconnected backstreet made illegal activities hard to trace and sting operations difficult to navigate. Over time, the police had turned a blind eye to Smith Street and its dealings, for the rewards no longer justified the risk or trouble. Occasionally, patrols were sent around the area, but even then, it was mostly a show to calm the public.

Clay walked down the streets in his over-sized green 'SKI HAVEN' shirt that covered him like the leaves of a tree. He kept his hands in the pockets of his capri, hiding what he had inside by giving the illusion of bulk. He also wore shoes instead of his usual sandals.

He headed for Highway Pup. Its neon sign had been turned off with the first crack of dawn. A sign on the tinted glass doors read, 'No patrons under 21 years'. Another said 'Closed'. He entered anyway.

The inside of the bar reeked of alcohol and vomit. Dim incandescent lamps hung around the walls of the room, their lights barely penetrating the smoky interior. Two burly males in black leather jackets were knocked out cold in a corner booth and another man in a crumpled suit leaned asleep against one of the centre tables. The bartender was the only one still awake, wiping the cleaning cloth over the marbled surface of the bar table under the only white lamp in the otherwise dark establishment. His white shirt and black vest crisp and stainless. His blonde hair neat and combed back, as if he had just showered and dressed.

Clay walked up to the bar and the tender looked up. "We're closed, kid. And aren't you a little young to be here?"

Clay walked up to the bar, "Cut the crap. Where's Adam?"

"You know the rules. Appointments only."

"Make an exception."

"How about a no?" The bartender put the cleaning cloth away. His attention now entirely on Clay.

"How about I call the cops?"

"Go ahead, I've got nothing illegal here."

Clay grinned sinisterly. "I'm so glad you said that."

He took a brown paper bag from his pocket and threw it at the wall. An explosion of white powder burst upon impact, filling that portion of the room with a white cloud.

"What's that?"

"Make a guess."

"Is that coke?"

"Make a guess," he said again. Clay pulled out his phone, dialled the number, and set the phone to speaker. The ringback tone echoed. For some reason, the sleeping bodies suddenly reminded him of corpses in a crypt, mummies ready to jump him.

"What if I shoot you?"

The tone stopped and a woman picked up the line. "Nine-one-one, what's your emergency?"

Clay could feel his grin widening. "Try it."

He and the bartender exchanged glares, neither blinking.

He knew the man did not keep guns with him. The bar was used as a front to direct 'customers' to the real black market and was the first line of defence against police raid. Keeping anything against the law would have defeated the purpose of the patsy establishment.

"Fine," the bartender finally relented, turning his eyes away to the powder on the floor.

"Fine what?" Clay said.

"Hello? Is anyone there?" the operator asked.

"Room thirty-nine. Hotel Uno."

"Sorry," he said to the operator. "Wrong speed dial." And hung up. To the tender, he taunted, "Now was that so hard?"

The sun was above the horizon line by the time Clay left the bar. The streets were quiet and empty, with only a couple of cars parked nearby. Hotel Uno was located behind the Irish bar two blocks down. A desolate-looking, greying and moss grown building, Hotel Uno was slated for demolition later that year.

Clay walked down the streets towards the hotel, a red sports car zooming past him, its engine roaring even as it turned at the junction with its wheels screeching, vanishing with the corner. There was no wind. He headed down into the alleyway and entered the street to the building. The white paint was peeling and moss had spread to a large part of the structures' base. He went through the entrance and an electronic bell rang his presence.

The lobby was of meagre size. Aside from the one reception counter that took up half the room, there was a small common area with a few couches. Past the reception was the forked corridor that led to the first floor rooms and the elevator up. The receptionist, a bald man, did not bother to look up from whatever it was that had his attention on his desk, which suited Clay just fine. Clay passed the counter and called the elevator. The door opened immediately. He entered and hit the third floor button. Ryan Cabrera's *On The Way Down* played in through the elevator radio.

Exiting on the third floor, he found himself in a single long corridor that extended both left and right. A copper plate screwed into the wall in front of the elevator directed him left to room 9. The door was ajar so he pushed into the smoky room.

From the entrance, there was a bathroom to the right before the room opened up to the living room. The blinds of the room were drawn, but enough of the morning light shone through to dimly light the area. The room had no couches, tables, or television. Instead, dozens of cardboard boxes stacked up almost to the ceiling. A lone desk was placed in front of the window, where the light silhouetted Adam's figure. Clay closed the door behind him.

"Clay Barber," came the voice of Adam. "You continue to intrigue me, kid." Adam had two bouncers with him, neither which Clay recognised. The two men stood to with their arms folded, their only acknowledgement of Clay's presence was their intense stare.

"What's up, Scarface?" he greeted the muscular African American with a prominent scar running down his cheek. To the equally muscular but smaller sized Mexican, who wore a sleeveless shirt that showed off his heavily tattooed arms. "*Tatuage Hombre*," he mocked in an accent.

Adam stood from his seat at his desk. The man in his early forties was not what was expected of street dealers stereotypes. He carried an air more akin to that of crime lords. He had his onyx hair styled back, shimmering with the result of probably dozens of hair products. He wore a crisp black suit and tie with a maroon inner shirt. Though his face was rough with the residues of early fights, he did not look thuggish, but rather, wise.

"You blackmailed a bar you knew was ran by a gang and waltz uninvited into a drug den. Insults two man twice your size without batting an eye." Adam was skilled in keeping his voice almost monotonous, making it hard to catch if he was either impressed or angered. "If you didn't have Sin, I'd say you have a death wish. What brings you here?"

"I need more Somnidin." Clay locked eyes with the older man.

"Stock's low, price's high. I've got lots of bidders and I highly doubt you can match them."

"Then name a price."

Adam walked up to Clay, staring down at him, their eyes never leaving each other. "You're something else kid. You stare eye to eye with men twice your age, twice your size." He pulled back his jacket to reveal a pistol at his belt. "Men that are armed. But I think you knew that. Walking like you've got no equal in the world. I could use some runners like you. Open a shop at your school, cut you a profit, and all the Somnidin you need."

"Not interested. Now, price."

"Pity. Give a kid like you a few years, you'd go far in our 'business'," Adam gestured to his goons with his head. From one of the boxes, Tattoo took out a bottle of the medicine and handed it to his boss. "Five hundred per bottle. On the spot."

"Discount."

"Oh, you're desperate. First time I'm hearing you beg. Maybe I'm wrong about you. Six hundred."

24

"I see how this is," Clay said, stepping away from the man. In one swift motion, he reached under his over-sized shirt and from his belt, pulled out a Model 24 'stick' grenade. He wrapped his fingers around the fuse cord. "How bout this? Drugs, or we die."

CHAPTER FIVE

The Last Good Day

"We fear violence less than our own feelings. Personal, private, solitary pain is more terrifying than what anyone else can inflict."
- Jim Morrison, interview with Lizzie James

13 days earlier,
08:15 A.M.

On a good day, things go according to plan. On a good day, you get to use a packet of body powder as cocaine. But good days never lasts. From the corner of Clay's eyes, he could see the tattooed henchman reach for something round his back. Clay tightened his grip on the fake stick grenade, all the while staring down Adam the drug dealer. He knew he would need to react faster than they could shoot.

"The bartender called, you stupid kid. The coke? Just baby powder," Adam replied, a smirk across his face. "You can't scare us with the same crap."

"Wanna bet?" Clay replied defiantly.

Adam laughed. "Kill him."

Clay pulled the cord, igniting the homemade sparkler ignition, burning the potassium nitrate and sugar mixture stored in the head. The false cap on the tip of the grenade popped open, releasing a burst of pink sparks, producing large streams of smoke as it did. He saw the shock on Adam's face, lit up by the sparks. The man reached for his gun, and Clay expected the other two would do the same. He threw the smoke grenade at the drug dealer who jumped to the side. The smoke quickly filled up the room as Clay pulled his shirt over his nose and charged straight at Adam, tackling the man over the desk. Two gunshots rang behind him.

He felt the silk of Adam's suit and yanked at it. The man stumbled

26

back into him and Clay jumped onto his back, swiping away the dealer's gun and wrapped his arms around his neck as tight as his underdeveloped muscles allowed. The smokescreen had completely enveloped the room and he could hear everyone coughing for clean air as they choked on the nauseous sulphur.

Another gunshot echoed in his ear, followed by the clatter of shattering glass while Adam fell to his knees, clawing away at Clay's arms. A hand grabbed hold of the back of Clay's shirt and with a strong pull, separated him and the drug dealer, flinging the teenager halfway across the room.

Clay stone-skipped across the floor, slamming back first into the opposing wall. He scrambled to his feet, ignoring the pain in his spine and oriented himself to the murky source of light which was where the windows were. With his hand out front, groping like a sex offender, he searched to the right of him and sure enough, felt the form of the cardboard box that the tattooed henchman had taken the drugs from. He reached in, grabbed two handfuls of the bottles and stuffed them into his oversized pockets.

"Find that bastard!" he heard Adam snarl through bouts of coughs.

Time's up. Clay turned towards the door, letting out an unwitting cough despite his makeshift mask. Wading through the smoke, he smashed into the familiar soft body of a human.

Then he felt the cold steel of the gun slapping across his neck. For a moment, he thought his heart had stopped beating, his legs about to collapse from the shock.

The pistol discharged right next to his left ear. The recoil smashed the gun into his temple, the bullet sent splinters from the wall cutting across his face.

His ears ringing, head spinning, and face bleeding, his legs buckled and he started to fall. He reached out with his hands, felt the floor, felt himself spinning, turning and tumbling across it. Miraculously, he got back onto his feet, stumbled forward with hands outstretched, felt the handle of a door, and yanked, swearing that if it was the bathroom, he would stick his foot up the devil's ass.

He bumbled forward and stepped across the threshold...

...into complete darkness.

He almost vomited from the sudden change in environment and his physical condition. He swallowed hard so as to not puke from the bile bulging against his throat. His ear no longer ringing, his head no longer spinning, his face no longer bleeding, Clay wished he was back in the room with the three homicidal gangsters.

Surrounded by shadows, he stood in complete darkness. He raised his hands out in front of him and could barely see past his elbows, the entire area was surrounded by a veil of shadows. Turning on the spot, the ground beneath him felt as soft as dirt. The darkness was disorienting and he felt like throwing up again.

Clang.

The sound of an aluminium bat hitting the non-existent baseball. The invisible crowd started cheering. He stood in the darkness, listening, waiting. He wasn't going to run. Not any more.

The cheering got louder and louder, slowly rising. Horns and trumpets started blasting and the noise reached a deafening level. The ground vibrated from the noise, but Clay stood his place, not even raising his hands up to cover his ears as he did so many times before. He was ready to go down swinging.

Something tugged inside him, a pressure squeezed lightly on his heart and lungs.

"You're out!" The rough, cracking whisper came from behind him.

Clay spun in place, saw the silver outline of the bat coming right at his face, and he fell, face-flat onto the carpeted and brightly lit hotel corridor floor, his head jerked violently back, sending a sharp pain into his neck from the strain that snapped his concentration back to him.

The ringing in his ear was back. And so was the bleeding and the headache. His heart beat faster than he ever felt before, trying its hardest to force its way out of his chest. He did not know how long he was out for, and it was not the time to find out. Thick grey smoke poured out the room like an avalanche along with shouts of obscenities from Adam.

Clay got to his feet, legs shaking, and vomited. His spew splashed across the floor, the taste of bile and backwash lingering in his mouth. His nose watering and leaking. His stomach constricted in a grappling match with his intestines. He was glad Stella wasn't there to see him.

"Get that fucker!" Adam yelled from the room.

"Oh...he's pissed," Clay groaned to himself. He made his way in as fast of a jog as possible to the elevator, one hand over the spot where the gun smacked him and another over his wrestled belly. The elevator doors opened immediately upon calling, for which he thanked a god. Which god though, he wasn't sure. Robbie William's *Rock DJ* played over the elevator radio.

The door slid opened and Clay stepped into the lobby. He barely saw it coming. The bartender's punch came from around the corner. Clay only managed a feeble attempt at a block as the older man's strike broke through his guard, connecting with his jaw and sending him spinning to the ground once more.

Sprawled on his back, disoriented, stomach clenching, head spinning, face bleeding, ear ringing, Clay mustered up enough gumption to spit a ball of phlegm, bile and blood and all, at his attacker's crisp white shirt.

The bartender reacted with a crooked smile and a glint of sadism in his eyes. From his back, he pulled out a gun and pointed at Clay, only to be blindsided by a two-by-four across his face as he did Clay with his sucker punch, crumpling to the floor like Jenga blocks.

"What?" Clay huffed out a genuine cry of surprise for the first time that morning. He tilted his head to see Stella in denim shorts and yellow shirt, holding the plank of wood in her hands, staring at the now unconscious bartender.

She turned to her brother. "He's kind of hot," gesturing to the older man.

"Stell? What the hell are you doing here?" He tried to push himself up but a sharp pain shot up his neck and stopped him. He lay back down, groaning in pain.

Stella knelt down beside him and gently lifted his head until he sat up straight. "Saving you apparently. What were you thinking?"

"You shouldn't have come. It's dangerous here."

"Yet here you are." With a huff, she slowly got him to his feet. "And your breath smells bad."

They stepped over the bartender and headed for the door as fast as he could manage but stopped as the wooden door swung open.

Tim raised his air rifle at them. "Out of the way," he growled.

With what strength he could, Clay pushed his sister away and ducked to the side. Tim squeezed off a round, his rifle letting off a loud clack, the metal pellet producing an audible smack as it hits the receptionist square in the eye. The man let out a yelp of pain.

Tim stepped towards the man, whose eye was now bleeding, and smashed the butt of his rifle across the head. The man flopped to the ground, his groaning ceased.

Tim turned to his friends. "Let's get out of here."

13 days earlier,
08:42 A.M.

By the time their legs gave way, the trio had ended up laying sprawled across the tarmac in an empty outdoor parking lot by the docks. A passing ships' horn blasted the morning and a flock of crows took flight from the one tree at the street corner.

Panting heavily, his legs aching, Tim forced himself to stand, his body heating up with impatience, needing to move. He walked on the spot in circles, hands at his hips as he took deep breaths of air, his air rifle in its bag on the pavement.

Clay got to his feet, albeit much slower. Most of his blood had been washed away by the sweat from their long escape and had stained his shirt with patches of brown along the collar. The bandages from the day before had peeled off, leaving ghastly marks across his face. He limped over to Tim, Stella finally sitting up.

Tim stopped walking and turned to his friend. "That was too close, asshole."

Once they were near, Clay drew his arm back and punched him across the jaw. "What the hell were you thinking? Bringing my sister here?"

Stella jumped to her feet and bear hugged her brother from behind, her thin arms holding him back. "What are you doing?" she cried out, but Clay ignored her.

Tim stumbled back but managed to keep his footing. He threw Clay a fierce glare as he pushed his jaw till it gave a thin crack to stretch away the pain. "Good to know you're not a complete idiot yet."

"Don't make me punch you again, kid."

Stella released her brother and stepped between them. "Look, I chose to come, okay? Even if Tim had tried to stop me, I would have nutted him."

Clay started to calm down, staring at his sister, his fury fading away. "Still, you shouldn't have come. It's...it's reckless for you to have come."

Tim stepped forward. "Oh, and it was totally safe and not reckless whatsoever for you?"

"You don't get it."

"What don't I get? Huh? You went out of your way to find trouble with drug dealers and gangsters. For what? Some shitty meds? Fine, you're sick. I get it. We can get you to a bloody hospital."

"Shut it, kid!" Clay shouted, his voice echoing into the neighbourhood, the empty docks playing back the recording. "You don't fucking get it. To go through each day afraid to just – just to close your eyes. The meds ain't a godsend or nothing. They just let your body sleep. Your mind's still awake. Mentally, I've not slept for over a week."

Tim couldn't bring himself to reply. It was that moment he realised just how much he had been escaping the situation, how much he had downplayed the severity of his friend's condition and how little knowledge he had of the Vashmir Pandemic. The morning sun rose from the sea, shading half their faces in light. He could see now, the sharp and focused mania that glowed in Clay's eyes, the bruises and cuts highlighted and sunken into his skin.

"And when my mind gets too tired, when I can no longer stay awake," Clay looked away from Tim and into the sunrise. "I sleep and go to these...places. And these people, these things, chase us around like pigs. Trying to kill us. And the doctors, they all say it's in our heads, but I know its not. There's no way it is. We feel the pain, like, actual pain that lingers even after we wake and the injury's gone. And the experts can't help. They still think it's some mass hysteria shit. And we have to fight to survive."

"We?" Tim asked.

Clay looked to his sister. She held his hand in hers, gently rubbing at the creases. "Stella has it too."

Tim felt sick. He spun in a circle, looking for something to lean against. "When? How?"

With her back turned, Stella replied, "Three days ago."

"Is it-"

"No," Stella cut in. "As far as we know, it's not contagious."

"But the odds, the two of you, both having it! I mean, isn't it supposed to be a one in a million thing?"

"There's a support group online," she said.

"Useless bunch they are," Clay said, spite in his voice. "All they do is give advice of how to tell family members and write wills. A lot of them outright gave up. Many hiding cause they're 'fraid of being ostracised."

"Morbid place," she said. "But everyone thinks the government's covering up the numbers and deaths to prevent panic until they figure things out. Things don't really add up."

Tim was pacing around his small circle now. He wanted to go home to his dingy little room and argue with his father till birds could fly to space and the sun turned green. "What's the number?" he asked.

Clay exchanged glances with his sister. "We think it's about one in ten thousand, maybe less. But the number's definitely increasing."

Tim stopped in his tracks, staring out at the open parking lot, back to his friends and deep in thoughts. "These things that are trying to kill you, what do they look like?"

"According to everyone on the support site, it's always the same seven people-things. Hunters, they call them. They're definitely not human," Clay explained, looking slightly distressed as he did so. "Mine is a guy in a baseball uniform. Looks like a teenager. Name's Smith."

"You know his name?" Tim replied, surprised.

31

"Yeah. It's on his uniform. No team name though," Clay surprised Tim again with a sudden enthusiasm in his voice. "I thought maybe he exists. Like outside of the dream. Might help us stop this. But the most common last name, one of the most popular sports in the world, over a hundred years of history, it's not easy. So far, I've got squat"

"That's why you needed the Somnidin," his mind started connecting the dots. "You needed more time."

Clay nodded in confirmation. "That, and Stell needs them too."

"What about you, Stell?" Tim turned to her when mentioned. "What's chasing you?"

"Huh? Well, a girl actually. It's kind of flattering," her voice was nebulous when surprised, like what he'd imagined a voice would sound like if it was in space. Distant and dreamy. It was a rare sight from her. "She has the whitest of hair. Like snow, really."

A memory came to the forefront of Tim's mind. "A white dress," he said instinctively.

"Yeah, how did you know?"

"I don't really know..." Waves of memories bombarded him at once, some of which he did not think he's actually remembering. Others he recalled as dreams from long ago. He waded through it all, desperately searching for the source of the girl in the white dress. He stood on the spot in a trance.

"Tim?" Stella called out. He could barely hear her, her voice a distant echo.

"Dreams of fire," he said in a monotonous voice.

"Hey, kid?" Clay called. His friend stepped forward, face-to-face with him, but Tim couldn't see him.

"Salves of healing," the verses came to mind.

Images of the sky filled his thoughts. A single flash of white, and a fleeting image of the girl with the hair of snow and the dress of whitest white.

Smiling.

CHAPTER SIX

Long Walks

"In extraordinary times, the ordinary takes on a glow and wonder all of its own."
- Mike A. Lancaster, 0.4

12:12 P.M.
13 days earlier

Tim left the Barber's just past noon with a fresh change of clothes he kept at the household whenever he stayed over; something which he had been doing with increasing frequency. Clay kept his rifle on the promise that he'd return it the next time they met. In a black shirt and cargo pants, he was thankful that the day was cloudy and that the wind had returned.

"Tim!" Stella called out as he crossed back onto the walkway. She jogged up to him and hugged him. "Thanks."

"For what?" he asked, returning the hug.

Pulling apart, she gave him a peck on the cheek. "For saving my brother," she said and ran back inside.

As the door closed behind her, he wondered if he really saved Clay as she had said. His friend was still affected by the Vashmir Pandemic; tied to a time bomb ticking away to his death. Tim walked away from the house and headed in the direction of the city. He wanted to do a lot of walking. And thinking. And Brooding.

05:37 P.M.
13 days earlier

Even before the park entered his field of vision, Tim could hear

33

the commotion that resonated from the place, echoing and reverberating through the concrete jungle of high-rises and skyscrapers of the city centre. A Ridge Valley Police Department blockade of cars and plastic barricades walled the cross junction to the city hall. Vehicles honked and drivers blasted verbal assaults across the road as the traffic refused to budge. Traffic jams were rare sights in a small city like Ridge Valley, the line stretching passed the junction behind him; disappearing into the maze of buildings. The late afternoon sun reflected blindly across the skyscrapers' windows.

A crowd had gathered at the blockade. Though noisy and vulgar, they were not the main source of the commotion that had first captured Tim's attention.

Tim approached a lady in a black and white skirt suit who stood a short distance away from the main group.

"Hey," he greeted when they locked eyes. "What's going on here?"

The Caucasian brunette replied with a small shrug. "Some kind of protest is going on in the park and city hall. Cops have the whole of forty third up to Golden Heights blocked off."

A loud roar of dissent from the park captured their attention and the group at the blockade were temporarily silenced, though they built-up to resume their shouts and swears at the police soon after.

"Not gonna make it back to the office at this rate," she turned around to leave, but not before giving a final piece of advice to Tim, "I wouldn't stay here if I were you. Might be trouble round the corner, looks like."

"We want the truth! We want the truth! We want the truth!" The protesters began to chant in unison, their deafening demand amplified through the alleyways, rumbling windows and bursting eardrums.

Curiosity was both a blessing and a curse. He had lived in Ridge Valley his whole life, exploring many parts of the city, suburbs, and outskirts with Clay. Including parts of the underground sewage tunnels. He dodged into a nearby alley and located a manhole cover. A steel bar jutted out from a dumpster. He used it to pry open the cover and climbed down the ladder into the sewers, taking the steel bar with him. The stench of a city's wastes and run-off burnt his nose.

It was in the darkness of the sewers where he was grateful for his cheap phone with the inbuilt one-bulb LED flashlight. Though nothing as bright as the camera flash in most smartphones of the day, it served its purpose, lighting up a couple of feet of path. He readjusted his bearings towards the direction of the park and followed the angling road, taking slow steps to avoid slipping on the mossy patches on the concrete. The sewage stream flowed and slushed down the channel, sided by pathways on both flanks.

Dust fell from the ceiling as the protesters let out another loud cheer. The ground trembled as the group above began stomping their feet in unison, drumming their stand into the concrete. He found a ladder opposite a cross-junction stream, probably emerging out into the streets of the protest if his sense of direction proved right. Crossing the metal beam bridge, he climbed the ladder with his phone in his mouth. Jamming the steel bar into a corner niche, he leaned his weight into it. The opening process was slightly harder from below ground and by himself. He broke a sweat just as the metal cover popped open. He pushed it aside and climbed up into the light of 43rd Street.

Most of the main roads were empty, with the few parked cars and bystanders who came out from the surrounding buildings to view the commotion. The protesters were gathered in the park, though many spilt off the walkway onto grass patches and some even to the streets. All faced the marble-white City Hall building and courthouse across the other side of the park from where Tim stood.

"Fucking curiosity," he seethed to himself as he faced the sheer magnitude of protesters, noting that it might have been prudent for him to run.

From outside the crowd, he tried to make sense of the shouts and picket signs, but none of the boards were facing him and the voices combined into a slurred roar. That's when he saw the familiar golden hair, standing a short ways into the main crowd. Charging into the protesters, Tim pushed aside men after women without hesitation nor difference, a sudden rage swelling up within him. He reached the golden haired man, grabbed his shoulder, and spun him around.

"What the hell?!" Joshua exclaimed, only to be doubly surprised to be facing his son. "Tim? What are you doing here?"

"I should be asking you that, *dad*," he punctuated the end of the sentence with sarcasm. "You're supposed to be working. But you're here doing what? Wasting time on some hipster protest?"

"It's not like that."

The shriek of a woman filled the air, drawing the attention of father and son. They turned to the direction of the source and saw smoke rising with the flickering of flames in the reflections of the windows of the buildings around them.

"Run." He grabbed his son by the hand.

Tim pulled away from his father, flicking his wrist violently. "I don't need your help!"

They stood facing each other as more shouts and screams erupted from the main group of protesters, a few of which had started to scatter past them. But for that moment, despite all the noise, their world went silent and felt infinitely small, consisting only of themselves and the space between them.

His father's face contorted in a disfigured mixture of sadness and rage. "What did you say?"

"I don't need your help," Tim reinforced. "Never will, never did."

He turned away from his father and ploughed into the crowd, his father calling out behind him but Tim ignored it, the noise from the outside world pouring back into his ears the further he went. Police sirens did nothing except add to the noise. Tim made it to the streets where the less violent protesters were escaping into the alleys. Riot police moved in from the extending junctions where the blockades were, riot shields and batons in hand, tear gas flying into the crowd leaving trails of smoke as the mob turned violent. Eager men and women charged head first into the oncoming law enforcement, clashing body with plastic sticks and polycarbonate shields.

Tim decided not to stick around for the aftermath and made his way with the other fleeing protesters, disappearing into the concrete jungle as the setting sun bathed the streets in a sea of red.

09:13 P.M.
13 days earlier

His head buried in his arms, wrapped around the playground swing set, Tim pondered the fragility of life and the suddenness of changes to his otherwise familiar day-to-day before reprimanding himself for being an 'emo fuckwad'.

"Have you seen the news?" The sand did not shuffle as Stella approached, almost as if she floated across it to him. "Riot at City Hall."

"I know. I was there," he replied, not looking up. "And so was my dad. Not working."

"Do you know what the protest was about?" She did not sound shocked at his presence there and Tim had long since given up on figuring what made her as calm as she was, unwavering in composure in almost any situation.

"Nope. The riot started when I got there. Didn't really have the time to find out."

"Aren't you curious?"

"Curiosity is bad. For all I know, it's just about getting a pay raise."

36

"Maybe it's a plot to overthrow the government."

"Maybe they were shooting a movie."

"Maybe everyone were actually terrorists trying to start a war."

"Maybe it was nothing at all."

"Maybe they were starting a violent revolution or uprising."

He chuckled. Their exchanges, though weird, were always fun and uplifting for him.

"Hey, Stell?"

"Yeah?" she replied, her voice soft and caring.

He thought for a moment on how to phrase what he wanted to say. "I don't know what normal is for me."

"Your life *is* pretty weird," Stella replied. From the corner of his eyes, he could see her settling down onto the swing next to him.

"My mom died because of my dad; And he's a useless bum now. My best friend gets into a fight every other day with people older and stronger than him. I'm barely an adult and yet I spend my free time exploring sewers and back alleys instead of, I don't know, shopping; And we just stood up to armed-to-the-teeth gangsters and drug dealers twice our age with nothing but baby powder, sparklers, and a toy gun. And got away with it as if we just went out for breakfast or something. I walked straight into a protest turned riot and I don't feel like it was anything out of the ordinary for me. And you are, well, you."

"What's that supposed to mean?" she pouted.

He laughed. "It means you're unique."

"Oh." She sounded less surprised than happy. "Well, you're pretty unique too, don't you think?"

Slightly stunned, he took awhile to respond. "Never thought about it like that. But I don't think unique is the word to use here."

"Another thing then," she said.

"What?"

"Has it sunk in yet?"

"What has?"

"That we have Sin?"

As if she could read his mind from the silence in the air, she stood up from her seat, dusted herself, and floated off before he could answer and he realised he did not know what he would have said either way. Tim looked up and watched as she walked away into the darkness of the park, never once looking back to him. He buried his face back into his arms.

37

CHAPTER SEVEN

The Barn

"Alone. Yes, that's the key word, the most awful word in the English tongue. Murder doesn't hold a candle to it and hell is only a poor synonym."
- *Stephen King, Salem's Lot*

The red 1957 Ford Thunderbird drove along the small bumpy road, sided by thick towering fields of wheat that swayed as the car drove by. The path was small, barely wide enough for the size of the vehicle, the crop randomly clipping and folding under the fender mirrors. The field seemed to go on forever with the path closing behind him. A farmhouse began to grow over what could be seen over the field, its mossy shingles appearing first, with the second floor slowly materialising soon after. He eased on the brakes, slowing the car down as the crop began to thin out and the rest of the old Victorian styled building seeped through the stocks like light through a blind.

Tim pulled the car up the muddied driveway of the house which was sided by an equally tall barn. The red paint of the latter had faded with time and had mostly peeled off above the door, giving the building a muddy brown hue, the timber beneath dark and rotting. He turned off the engine and stepped out of the car onto the path, his shoes sinking into the mud. Dark clouds were coming in from the horizon beyond the farm. Surrounded by an endless wheat field, he only had one choice left. The wind began picking up speed as he headed for the house, the field swaying and dancing, the stocks bending over as if bowing to him.

The bevel kitchen protruded out of the house. Planks were nailed to the windows and what curtains could be seen through were drawn. Some of the glass windows were cracked while others were discoloured with moss and age. He tried to peek through the cracks between the boards but

38

found the blinds closed as well. He went to the main door, once painted white, and hammered at the aged wood.

"Hey! Anyone in there?"

When his call wasn't answered, he stepped back out onto the muddy front yard. "What's the point of coming all the way here then?"

He thought about going back to the car and driving down the road until he found an inn or another place to stop for the coming storm.

"Where was I going anyway?" he asked himself, the question suddenly coming to him.

A soft musical humming came from the barn, catching Tim's attention. He turned and headed towards the barn, shouting over the wind as it picked up. "Hey! S'anyone there?"

As he got closer, he realised the dark colour of the barn was not solely because of the wood. Hundreds of cockroaches had made their home in the creaks and recesses of the building, crawling up and down the walls, squirming with each passing second.

Approaching the barn door, he made sure to check the texture of the wood near him to identify which parts were infested. Even then, he only pushed the right of the large double door open with his foot. The hinges were rusted and the door heavy, creaking loudly like the constant scratching of a chalkboard. He cringed from the sound but kept pushing, half a dozen roaches dropping from the archway. He managed to open the door large enough for him to fit through, feeling disgusted but relieved. The humming was louder and he could identify it as female.

Stepping through the threshold, the stench of horse manure immediately attacked his nostrils and he had to cover his face with his arms, his eyes watering. The barn was dark with barely enough light from the outside to give a shadowy outline to the inside. From what he could see, it was a two story barn with two stables and a workbench on the ground floor with a staircase leading up. A soft blue glow emitted from the second floor. The humming seemed to be coming from above. He started for the stairs.

"Will you play with me?" Tim spun on the spot as he heard the young boy's voice.

The child in his school uniform stood a distance in the darkness in front of one of the stable.

"W-what?" Tim asked.

"Don't you want to play with me?" the boy asked. Though his eyes were set in Tim's direction, they did not seem to see him so much as into him, piercing his soul.

"I...I don't really have time to play." Tim found himself stepping away.

"That's a shame," the boy said, his voice echoing endlessly. "Do you want a mommy?"

"What did you say?"

"Cause I have a mommy."

Tim blinked and a woman appeared beside the boy. Dressed in a yellow shirt and white frilled skirt, her long maroon hair slid behind her shoulders, her bangs neat and straight, her eyes a shining green. Miranda Kleve looked as alive as she was years ago.

"Mom?" A flash of lightning lit up the room. After having adjusted to the darkness, the light was blinding, forcing Tim to close his eyes. The roaring thunder followed and when he looked again, the boy and his mother were gone.

He found himself breathing hard, his heart pumping with neither fear nor excitement. A general rough beat that followed no rhythm. Tim felt the trickle of a tear roll down his cheek.

Somehow, the humming managed to find its way to his attention again and he turned back towards the stairs. The tune followed that of *Will the Circle be Unbroken*. His heartbeat slowed back down, calmed by the mesmerising sound. He headed up the stairs into the soft blue light.

The second floor was where the hay bales were kept. Stacked against the walls and up the ceiling like bricks, he felt as if they would tumble over and crush him if he went any closer. The source of the light and sound was a white figure at the far end, with its luminosity shining bright enough to repel the darkness.

"What am I doing?" Tim said under his breath. He approached the figure with hazy steps.

As he closed in, the figure became prominent. Lying on the ground seductively, her legs were bent and angled out of her dress, showing the curvatures of her thighs. Her dress was loose and smooth, showing more skin through peeks and gaps. Her petite body and small breasts were outlined clearly by the clothing. Her light skin almost melted together with her dress. Their eyes locked and her humming ceased, her irises a smoky grey.

She smiled mischievously. "Do you want to fuck me?"

"W-what?" Tim was stunned by the question.

She began to crawl on her hands and knees towards him, raising her hips and sliding across the air like a snake. Her white dress seemed longer than her body as she moved closer, dragging to the sides of her but not impeding her movement. She reached out to him, lightly holding onto the back of his thighs as she slowly raised herself against him, with as much of

40

her body brushing against his as possible without leaving eye contact. He felt his manhood erecting, bulging against his pants as she wrapped her hands around his neck, bringing them face-to-face, her continuing to rub herself against his crotch.

"Do you want to make love to me?" she replied to his previous question.

Upfront, she was beautiful, her cheeks lightly freckled and her ghostly eyes entrancing. Even as she seduced him, her face held a sense of innocence and cuteness, looking no older than he was.

"I..." he tried to reply but found himself at a loss for words. "I...no. I'm here for...for..."

She leaned herself into him, forcing Tim to support her weight. She was almost feather light. He could feel her breasts and nipples rubbing against his chest through their fabrics. She drew her face closer, their noses touching, lips barely millimetres apart.

He couldn't think. He tried to think of his previous sentence but something else clicked in his mind. "What...am I here for?"

Shelter? No. Before shelter. His mind raced. Though still enticed by the girl, he was capable of clear thoughts now.

Her breath on his lips, "Carry me out," she said.

He did just that, lifting her by the back of her knees and armpits as she wrapped her arms tightly around his neck, gently leaning her head into his shoulder. He had no trouble carrying her, her weight no heavier than that of a large soft toy.

"I want you. Outside. Hurry," she whispered urgently. He headed for the stairs.

Zoot. Zun. Zoot. Zun.

The sound of a saw.

Zoot. Zun. Zoot. Zun.

Cutting something.

Zoot. Zun. Zoot. Zun.

Descending the steps, another stroke of lightning lit up the interior for a split second. An elongated shadow stretched out from behind Tim. He could feel the presence and swore he could feel the colours of rage and hatred emitting from it, piercing his body in tiny needles. If there was a way to physically feel fear, that was it.

"Come. Faster," she whispered.

He reached the bottom of the steps, the ground muddier than he remembered it to be with the air smelling of humid rust. Though no footsteps followed behind, he knew that someone, or something, was there. And whatever it was had a killing intent that he felt in his bones. Making his way to the door of the barn, he thought his legs might give way, not to the weight of the girl, but to the fear that whatever creature chasing him has brought.

But he made it across the threshold and out under the torrential rain. The wind swept droplets across them, as sharp and cold as ice. A middle-aged woman stood in front of him, dry despite the downpour. Her neat, long, fire red hair effortlessly still in the rough storm. She wore a black office blazer over a crisp white shirt and a matching black knee length skirt with onyx high heels. She seemed to be in her early thirties, her figure slick and slender, her skin smooth and powdered, her chest tight but endowed.

"Sign here," the woman said, holding out a briefcase with a piece of paper and pen over it. Words began to slowly form on the paper in what looked to be the format of a contract. "Sign here. And you can have anything you want."

The girl in the white dress hugged Tim tighter, drawing impossibly closer than they already were. It felt as if every inch of their body that could make physical contact was making it, her face snuggled into his shoulder, her cheek leaned into his neck.

And in a surprising change of tone, no longer seductive, she asked, "Are you awake yet?"

Zoot. Zun. Zoot. Zun.

"No," he replied. A bolt of lightning cut across the sky, blinding Tim for a split second with its flash. The business woman disappeared from where she stood.

Zoot. Zun. Zoot. Zun.

"I'm definitely sleepin." He spun around, twisting his legs like a dancer. It wasn't hard to hold onto the girl for she clung tightly to him. Even with one hand raised against the man with the straw hat, they held together. The rusty saw came slicing down on his arm and he felt the cold steel cutting through it. He was sure he let out a scream but it was drowned out by the rain.

All he could see was pain. All he could hear was fear. All he could taste was blood.

CHAPTER EIGHT

Quoting Strangers

09:22 A.M.
12 days earlier

Screaming all the way into the sun, Timothy Kleve woke up under the late morning rays. Grasping frantically at his arm, he breathed a sigh or relief to find out it was still intact. However, the area above the elbow tingled with aches as if he pulled a muscle. He stretched it, hoping for the pain to go away. As he did so, he realised he was still at the playground. Passerby stared at the mad screaming teen that slept on the bench.

He swung his leg over the edge of the seat, rubbing his face as his body slowly warmed up. Though it had not rained in the night, his body was drenched in sweat. His heart beat at an unevenly fast pace and his lungs stung with each breath.

Checking his phone, he found eight missed calls from his father and two from the Barbers' house. He deleted them all. A woman and her son walked past the bench, hand in hand. The boy, a look of curiosity. The woman, a look of disgust.

He needed a library.

10:34 A.M.
12 days earlier

Ridge Valley Central Library was the largest and most extensive library in the county. Built at the same time as the founding of the city, the building had undergone multiple extensive renovations over the decades, eventually relocating entirely across the street of where it first stood. An office building had since replaced the original site. The library, a five story

43

building of modern architecture, complete with glass rooms, rooftop gardens and uncountable automated doors, served approximately 10 people a day, most of them lost on their way to the nearby shopping mall.

The sliding doors opened seamlessly, letting out a short puff of cool air-conditioned breeze. Immediately passed the threshold and the EAS Gates, the reception table appeared from behind a right turn. At the desk, typing single-mindedly into the computer was Howard Galloway. The librarian, with messy, soot black hair and dark eyes unfailing, did not seem to even notice Tim walking in.

Tim stopped at the front of the desk. "Mister Galloway," he greeted.

The man looked up from his screen, his eyes slowly focusing on Tim before widening in surprise. "Timothy! Ah hah!" He stood from his seat excitedly, arms opened wide. Leaning across the desk top, he pulled the teen in for a hug which was warmly reciprocated. "I haven't seen you in years! But I'd recognise those eyes and hair anywhere!"

"Am I really that noticeable?" Tim replied with a chuckle. Despite being in his late fifties, Howard Galloway had a face no older than the turn of thirty; If not, younger than when Tim last saw him. Tight and sharp chinned, had the small scars that adorned his skin not been there, one could not think the man had any more life experience than that of a young adult.

"Yes! Wait, no! Depends. I mean you do kinda look like crap. And I haven't seen you in so long. I saw Clay yesterday, and Stella every other week, but you! You fell off the face of the Earth you did." The librarian had an uncanny energy. He turned to rummage through the stack of newspapers on a stand behind him and shoved the front page of the days' *Ridge Valley Daily* in Tim's face and asked, "This is you isn't it?"

Tim had to back off a step before his could read the headline. "Protest Turns Riot. I must say, big news, but not my style," he lied.

"What? No!" the old man looked at the front page again and heaved exaggeratedly before turning the page. "I mean this!" He shoved the second page at him, forcing Tim to take another step back.

SMITH STREET DRUG RING ARRESTED

"How is this me?" he lied again.

Howard pulled the paper back and placed it on the tabletop. "Because the drug dealer specifically mentioned a kid named Clay Barber."

"Could be any Clay Barber."

"I only know one who could pull something like this off."

44

"We're kids!"

"Did you three not pull out the spark plugs of every single bulldozer five years ago when they were tearing down the old library?"

"There's no proof of that!" Tim waved the accusation away dramatically. "Why are you still here anyway?" he changed the subject.

"I told you, I can't go home so I'm stuck here. Might as well be in an interesting place."

"You've been saying that for eight years. Besides, we're in Ridge Valley! What's so interesting about a port town?"

"City."

"What?" Tim replied confused.

"Port city. It isn't exactly a small place any more. We've got skyscrapers, suburbs, districts, law firms, and drug dealers. All we're missing is a strip club and this place's a bona fide city."

"Fine. Port city. It's still Ridge Valley. Nothing interesting here."

Howard looked towards the newspaper, pointing to the articles with his eyes.

"Almost nothing."

The man sighed. "My dear boy, the interesting part's just beginning. But enough chit-chat. I'm guessing you're here for some reason."

As if snapping back into reality, a sense of urgency overcame Tim. "Yes. I need everything you have on the Vashmir Pandemic and lucid dreams."

"You know you could easily find those stuff on the internet."

"No computer."

"You should get one."

"No money."

"Get some of that while you're at it then."

"No job."

"Also get one of those. I hear they're all the rage," Howard started walking towards the door of the archive to the side.

"Where are you going?"

The man stopped and turned to him, a glint of focus and what Tim felt was a look of concentration crossed his scarred face. For a split second, the man looked his age. "There's not much published scientific research on Sin. Most of what you'll be looking for would be news articles. I'm getting the digitised copies for you from the archive."

"Okay. Thanks, Mister Galloway."

"No problem." He continued towards the door but stopped again to

45

quickly point at his computer. "You can print out a list of books with lucid dreams from there. Just check the tags."

As the librarian headed into the room, Tim walked around the desk and sat at the computer. A document was opened on the screen, the first chapter from another one of Galloway's many unpublished works of writing. Underneath the chapter title was a quote by Ralph Waldo Emerson from Prose and Poetry.

"Every book is a quotation; and every house is a quotation of all forests, and mines, and stone quarries; and every man is a quotation from all his ancestors."

He read it with slight confusion, though not for its meaning, before minimising the page and bringing up the library's search engine. Typing in the tags 'lucid', 'dream' and 'sleep', he hit enter which brought up 13 results. Only 9 of which were not on loan.

After printing out the list from the printer underneath the desk, Howard Galloway returned from the back with a red flash drive in hand.

"Why did you add that quote?" Tim asked as he got up from the seat, gesturing to the file now back up on the screen.

"Why? Lots of books have quotes."

"I know," Tim replied matter-of-factly. "I'm just wondering, since I've always found them to make the author look like some college wannabe know-it-all."

"That's where your mind gets narrowed my boy!" the older man replied enthusiastically. "Quotes are crackers of knowledge from people across time and space, preserved in words. Bits of history and wisdom passed down in bite-sized pieces for our lazy brains to chew on. A single quote can explain the entire meaning behind a story despite its length. People don't have to remember what I write as long as they can remember what knowledge and feelings I'm trying to convey. The quotes are like summaries. If they can just remember the quote before it, then my job is done."

Laughing, Tim asked, "So what are you writing anyway?"

"This? It's my biography. Nothing as interesting as compared to your life though."

"My life's about as eventful as watching paint dry."

"I know. Exciting right?" the man did not seem to have caught the sarcasm. "Maybe you'll let me write your biography next?"

"If you do, don't add any stupid quotes."

Grinning mischievously, Howard replied, "I'll have one for each chapter."

CHAPTER NINE

Threshold

"I demolish my bridges behind me... then there is no choice but to move forward."
- Firdtjof Nansen

03:39 P.M.
12 days earlier

Tim rubbed his eyes as they dried in the air-conditioned reading room. He was cornered by white walls, tables and chairs, with a one-way mirror that showed the library interior as the only source of other colours.

VASHMIR OUTBREAK KILLS THOUSAND

"I'm the dumbest asshole on Earth," he whispered under his breath as he leaned back in his seat.

SIN OUTBREAK: PRESIDENT REMAINS CALM

For the last two hours, Tim had combed through dozens of articles and skimmed through four books on the Vashmir Pandemic. Scribblings on a notepad had statistics of numbers and words circled and crossed off. The newspaper directly in front of him was one of the most recent. On the front, splattered across the entire top half of the page, wrote:

SIN FIGURES COVER-UP

After a knock on the door, Howard Galloway, the librarian, slid into room. "You've been in here past lunch, my boy. Aren't you hungry?"

47

With his pen, Tim tapped on a page of one of the opened books. "Continuous usage may cause mania, fatigue, and addiction," he mumbled to himself.

"What?" Howard walked over to the teen, leaning over his shoulder.

"Somnidin. The miracle drug against Sin," he recalled yesterday's news that reported a shortage of the drug in the country.

Howard placed a caring hand on Tim's shoulder. "You okay?"

"One third," Tim said, more to himself again. "One third of the world is estimated to die from Sin by the end of the month. And if Clay is right and this is a cover up, even more people are not going to make it to that date."

Howard picked up the notepad the teen was writing on. Flipping the pages, there were several graphs that plotted the number of infected against the time since Vashmir Commons's death in different states and countries. He looked to the newspapers and books where keywords and figures were circled across the pages.

"Tim, this is...very...very detailed," the man set the pad down. "But kind of obsessive. And against the rules of drawing on library property. Still, one third of the world is kind of a long stretch, don't you think?"

"The rate of increase has been accelerating," Tim buried his face in his arms. "The next two weeks will be the steepest increase. After that, half the world will be walking corpses."

"Look," Howard pulled up a chair beside him. "I know you're a sharp boy but–"

"Sharp?" Tim sprang straight in his seat, looking at Howard for the first time in the conversation. "If I was so sharp it wouldn't take me so long to make the connection. If I was so sharp, I would have paid more attention to the world going to shit! If I was so sharp, why...the fuck...did I not act sooner?"

Silence fell between the two. Their eyes crossed, but Tim felt neither compassion nor confusion from the man. Instead, it looked as though the librarian's eyes were filled with a sort of pride.

Howard broke the air. "Someone you know have Sin?"

Tim clicked his tongue and turned away from the librarian.

"It's not your fault you know."

After a short pause, he replied, "I know."

"This is too big for you. There's nothing you can do."

"I've got to try."

"Good. It wouldn't be fun if you didn't," Howard said, much to Tim's surprise. The man got up from his seat and headed for the door. "You're a sharp boy Timothy Kleve. Maybe you've forgotten it, but you used to be able to make the connections between things faster than anyone I've seen. You just need to remember why you forgot."

Tim watched as the door closed behind the man. Turning back to the piles of information on the table, he wished Howard wasn't so cryptic all the time. Then he remembered Clay and Stella, and from there, his father. Then he cried for he remembered his mother.

07:22 P.M.
12 days earlier

Clay sat on the couch in his living room in grey shorts and a white shirt, his laptop on one side of the armrest. Newspaper clippings, magazine articles, and his father's tablet covered the wooden coffee table. He could hear Stella preparing the drinks in the kitchen, the light clinking of ceramic plates and teacups setting the slow tempo.

He shuffled through a series of websites before picking up one of his notes and comparing the details, before letting out a frustrated sigh and putting the paper back down. He zoomed out of the mind-map that was opened up on his tablet and swiped away one of the notes attached to a box titled 'schools'.

From the kitchen, Stella floated out with a tray of two teacups and a steaming floral ceramic teapot. She wore a red-white striped long sleeve pyjamas and matching bottoms, her strawberry blonde hair combed and flowing freely.

"You really should rest," she said, setting the tray down on a lone empty corner of the table before sitting beside her brother and pouring them two cups of tea.

Clay smiled at her. "I know. But I feel like I'm so close to making a connection here," he leaned back into the cushion, resting his head against the angled seat. He glanced grimly to the two pill bottles of Somnidin on the table. One for himself and the other for Stella. He redirected his attention away to his sister. "Any luck with Tim?"

With graceful movements, she separated the cups for his and hers, nodding slightly as a reply. "He just texted me. He's on his way home now."

"That stupid kid, making us worry like that." He picked up his cup and sipped from it before quickly sticking his tongue out to cool after being burnt by the steaming hot drink.

"Careful, it's hot," she said with a mischievousness grin.

"Yeah, I got that!" he replied with a joking snap.

She smiled gently, scanning the data sprawled across the table. "What do you have so far?"

"Next to nothing," Clay placed his cup down with a cling. "I've crossed all baseball teams in half the country that wears the same uniform colour, home or away. There's five different Smiths, two of them coaches, one girl, and the other two looks nothing like the guy. There has to be a link. What if I can't find it in time? I'm not as good at this research thing as Tim."

Stella lovingly kissed her brother on the cheek and rested her head on his shoulders. "You'll find it. You're my brother."

He chuckled at the comment. "That's not a very good argument."

"On the contrary. It's the best in the world."

08:32 P.M.
12 days earlier

Standing outside the apartment door, Tim stared at the cracks of the frame where light from the inside was seeping out. His father was home, probably with a mouthful for where Tim had disappeared to. He held his key in the keyhole, contemplating whether to turn it when the door swung open from the inside, the rusty hinges calling as it did so. His key, having slid out of the lock, held in his hand, hung in the air limply as Tim stared at his father, golden hair backed by the bright interior light, sloppily dressed in his white sleeveless shirt and shorts. Tim began to wonder if that image of his father, backed by a holy glow, was ever going to fade.

For a second, Tim thought his father was going to explode in rage, but the man instead spoke calmly with nonchalance, a look of relaxing daze that he did not think was possible from such a rugged face. "You had dinner yet?"

Stunned at the lack of bulging blood vessels and thrown furnitures, Tim shook his head without a word.

"I got takeout." His dad gestured into the apartment before heading back in. Tim followed warily.

On the coffee table were two cartons of Chinese food, one already opened. His dad sat on the couch and un-muted the television and ate his share of the noodles with a fork. Tim took a seat on the floor and took the unopened box in hand. Opening it, he found it too contained noodles. He broke apart the wooden chopsticks and began eating while watching the show, slurping with each mouthful.

When the shows' protagonist stubbed his toe on a chair and began cursing and knocking things over, the man let out a laugh. "Hah. Ain't that the truth."

Tim quietly watched the show and could not help but smile.

As they slowly ate and the night grew deeper, Tim, for the first time in years, felt at home. The clock on the wall ticked into the next hour.

"We should do this more often," his father said. "Maybe once a week? I could come home early and–"

"Dad?" Tim cut in.

He could hear his father's breathing stopped, the soft shuffling of utensils digging through the cardboard box had ceased.

"Yeah son?"

"I'm still angry at what happened to mom." Tim paused, the ensuing silence between them drowned out the television where the protagonist ripped his pants while riding a bike. "But it's not your fault any more."

He could hear his father snort through his nose, perhaps tearing up. Perhaps with a noodle sticking out like people in cartoons. Tim continued eating, speaking through the remnants of noodles and meat in his mouth, never turning to look at his dad. "That night, when mom died, I blamed you. If you weren't drunk, she wouldn't be driving. That was my reasoning," Tim finished the last of his noodles and placed the empty carton back on the table. "But it wasn't your fault. I just wanted it to be. I needed it to be, to make sense of it somehow. But I realised, with the things that have been happening lately, I was just being selfish. I've been that way since mom died, I knew that. But I *know* it now."

"Tim. About yesterday, that protest–"

"I know," the teen cut in again. "You weren't skipping work. I've figured out the details. Read the stupid newspapers. And no, we don't have to talk about it. Nothing we can do now."

"Okay then," was all his dad could say.

"We should go on a vacation sometime," Tim said matter-of-factly.

"Yeah."

"Maybe visit mom's grave together one of these days."

"She'd like that."

Tim got to his feet and went to his room.

"Son," he said, stopping Tim at the threshold. There was a pause as he attempted to form the words. "I... I love you."

Without denying or accepting the words, Tim silently closed the door behind him.

CHAPTER TEN

Fight or Flight

"You cannot be a hero without being a coward."
- George Bernard Shaw, John Bull's Other Island

Tim watched as the piece of white cloth inched closer to his arm. Seething through his teeth, he nervously voiced, "You know what? I don't think this was such a good id-OOOOWWWW-my god! That really hurt!"

Getting angry, the girl with the white hair and dress yanked the knot of the makeshift bandage tighter, causing Tim to yell out in another round of pain, squirming in his seat. "Maybe if you'd stop moving and acting like a baby, it wouldn't hurt so much!" Her voice was musical but slightly sharp like a violin.

"Maybe you'd like to try getting your arm cut off?" She pulled again at the snappy reply, his following wail akin to that of a whimpering dog.

The twilight sun shone its orange glow into the classroom, birds chirping musically outside the whitewashed windows. Tim sat in the centre of the classroom on the desk in a puddle of his own blood that had faded into the light The girl of white tied the final knot in his newly acquired stump of a right arm. Surrounding the pair were dozens of empty desks, and to the front, a chalkboard with the phrase 'I will not be late' repeated over and over again in different handwritings.

Raising what was left of his right arm, which had been sliced clean off from the elbow down, he stared at the blood that slowly pooled under the makeshift bandage. "My shirt's the same," he said nonchalantly, ignoring the stinging pain.

"What?" the girl asked, confused. She leaned lightly against the desk next to and facing him.

"I'm wearing the same shirt as last time," he turned his attention to his black shirt and cargo pants which he wore in the day, completely forgetting about the fact that he was one arm lesser than before. "I'm assuming I'm dreaming again. I changed my clothes before I went to bed so I guess I can assume the last time I was asleep was like a save point?"

"Wow..." the girl stared at him, her eyes wide opened. Her greyed out iris reflecting the orange sun. "At a time like this you can notice your clothes?"

"Yeah, maybe I'm a little short in the attention span department but–"

"No, no!" she waved her arms protesting his misconception. "It's a good 'wow'. Really. You're observant, that's a good thing here."

"Pfft, you're just saying that," he replied, slightly embarrassed.

The girl leaned across to him, forcing him to attempt to slink away. She followed relentlessly until he could no longer retreat in his seat and her entire torso rested against his. The fabric of her dress felt thinner than silk and she brushed her chest against the bare skin of his one good arm. Her face an inch away from his, their noses touched at the tip.

Her voice echoed operatically as she spoke with a seductive tongue, "Why? You don't trust me?"

A haze seemed to engulf his thinking as he tried to stammer out a reply. He opened his mouth to speak but only let out a soft wheeze. He noticed her dress was shorter and tighter than he had previously noted, the skirt barely covering her thighs. He found his heart beating hard against his chest at the girl's erotic movements and the tightening bulge in his pants. The girl let out a small, gentle, flower-sweet breath against his lips and he fought the urge to lean in and kiss her.

She retreated back, and as suddenly as the lustful cloud engulfed him, it dissipated. His thinking cleared up as she settled back onto the desk, crossing her legs with a sly smile across her lips. Her dress was longer now, wrapping splendidly around her ankles.

After composing his breath, Tim tried to sit up straight again but forgot his missing right arm, slipping as his invisible appendage attempted to grasp the edge of the desk. Falling off the desk, he managed to land on his left shoulder, receiving a sharp pain on impact.

The girl laughed loudly. A tomboyish laugh right out of an anime character.

With grunts and huffs, Tim managed to push himself off with his one arm. The floor was stained with his blood from the impromptu medical treatment and so was the desk he sat on. The girl's snow-white dress remained unstained.

"You could have helped me," he slowly got up, balancing his weight precariously on one arm.

"Why? It's more interesting to watch you squirm."

"Well, you've helped me so far." His tone was more serious now as he gained momentum in the conversation. "I 'woke up' and there you were, bandaging me and all that. When I was panicking and screaming from the pain, because, you know, lost an arm and all that. You calmed me down. You bandaged me. Why?"

The smile faded from her face, an action that for reasons unknown to Tim, saddened him. "You managed to figure out it's a dream on your first try. At the barn, before you got, well, you know," she nodded towards his arm. "You said you were asleep. Most people survive the first time by instinct and figure things out on the second or third try. Some even on the day they die."

"You say most?" he asked. "There are others?"

"A few, yeah. About one in a hundred or so."

"Do you help them like you did with me?" even as he said it, he wasn't quite sure what sort of 'help' she had provided him, merely following a gut instinct that she did.

As if ashamed of herself, she looked away from Tim and down at her feet. A few quiet seconds passed before she softly let out, "No."

"Why me?" He gave her no time to recover from her reply.

"It's complicated," she snapped back, force in her voice.

"I've got time."

"No you don't." This time, she did not give him time to compose a comeback. Her stare was as ice cold as the scream that suddenly pierced the air around them.

"What the fuck?" Tim bolted to the windows to get a look outside for the source of the shriek. However, he was overwhelmed with confusion when the school grounds ended at the gates. The ground floor was an empty dirt courtyard. No trees nor markings decorated the landscape and nothing moved in sight. The walls surrounding the school were spiked with metal barbed wires, the only relief of the fort-like defence was the single metal gate of the entrance. Beyond that, marmalade tinged clouds stretched far into the horizon of where the streets should be.

"I'm not the only one here," the girl said. "There are those like you. But there are also those like me."

Zoot. Zoon. Zoot. Zoon.

The sound of a saw slicing into wood. The hair on Tim's nape stood at attention, the temperature in the room dropping drastically as his skin stung from an unexpected dry and piercing cold.

He turned back to face the girl as she said, "You should run."

Zoot. Zoon. Zoot. Zoon.

He waved his finger at the girl. "You owe me an explanation."

The back door of the classroom slid open with a loud slam, the chirps of the birds, wherever they may be given the lack of any living things outside, instantly died. Behind the threshold to the corridor stood a man in a white shirt under blue overalls, with a straw hat covering his eyes and a piece of straw in his mouth. The classic farmers' look. Bulked up and heavily scarred, his arms were akin to that of a rough tire. Cuts and bruises ran down the visible skin, barely hidden by the ragged arm hair. His beard was short and scraggly, with what looked to be pieces of red meat caught between them. The man held a rusted crosscut saw, which Tim assumed was the same one that sliced off his arm. The dried blood that plagued the edge of the tool sent shivers down his spine, no doubt part of them his own.

Zoot. Zoon. Zoot. Zoon.

The sound played even though the saw wasn't cutting anything. An auditory hallucination echoing in his head. He was reminded that bones made the same noise.

The teen bolted for the front door, his adrenaline sky-rocketing in the process. He felt his face burn red and his body began sweating, even though he had moved barely five meters across the classroom. He wasn't tired or worn out, but felt energetic. He was unsure why until he attempted to open the door and noticed his hands trembling.

Fear had engulfed him, his body moving on instincts, which can be bad when attempting to perform an action that required immense precision. Like opening a door. His sweaty hand slipped on the handle, again and again, before finally grabbing the metal bar and flinging the barrier open. He turned and glanced as the Sawman strolled through the aisle, his crude weapon clinking against the metal desk legs as he did so.

Zoot. Zoon. Zoot. Zoon.

The girl in white had disappeared from the classroom. Rooted in his spot, Tim stared at the approaching 'man' in fear and awe. Towering almost two heads taller, the Sawman was perhaps the most intimidating being Tim had ever faced. Even though the man's eyes were hidden, Tim could not help but feel as if he was being summed up, scanned from head to toes.

Zoot. Zun. Zoot. Zoon.

It was not the time to hesitate. Forcing himself out of his trance, he sprang out into the corridor, but his feet could not find any ground to grip. The floor was there, ceramic tiles and all, but his feet phased through them, seemingly cut off. Time seemed to slow for him, his right feet lingering behind in the classroom, teetering between the invisible line that separated it and the false grown.

And he fell. Through the floor. Whirling and spinning as his mind made feeble attempts to grasp the seemingly solid surrounding. His legs completely phased into the ground, followed shortly by his body and arm. Finally, as his face melted into the floor, he managed one last glance behind him to see the Sawman standing over him at the doorway of the classroom, 'I will not be late' repeated in white on black behind him.

CHAPTER ELEVEN

The Diner

"Worthless people live only to eat and drink; people of worth eat and drink only to live."
- Socrates

The diner was barely half filled with patrons having their breakfasts. Scents of scrambled eggs and bacon floated out of the kitchen and marinated the room. The establishment had a 1960s theme to it. The black and white ceramic tile floors were waxed to the point of reflection. The red leather upholsteries of the booth seats etched into the background with the clinking of utensils. Tim sat on one of the stools at the bar, watching his remaining hand on the grey marble counter top confusingly. His newly acquired stump of a right arm stung with pain, but not enough to be at the forefront of his mind.

"Can I take your order?" The girl in white stood on the opposite side of the table. She leaned her elbows on the counter with her cheeks on her hands, so that her face was parallel to his.

He stared into her grey eyes, attempting to re-grasp his situation, then shifted his gaze over to the familiar Street 99 Diner. "I used to come to this place with my mom and dad. But this place closed down years ago."

"I wouldn't know," she replied dreamily, "It's not my memory."

He turned back to her. "Memory? Isn't this a dream?"

"Dreams, memories. Past, future. They're really the same thing here."

"What does that mean?"

Her smile turned into a grin. "Come on, make a clever deduction or something. Like Sherlock Holmes!"

Annoyed at her reply, he turned his attention away from her and towards the booths of the diner. He registered that at least four booths were filled, though he could not seem to focus on the individuals within them,

57

his eyes darting away from direct sight, only gazing at them from his peripherals as if his eyes were introverted beings.

"Dreams are our conscious minds working in sleep," he recalled the theories and speculations on dreams he read at the library that day. "It draws on memories and senses to create images."

Her smile was wide, from ear to ear. "Mmm-hmm," she said as she gleefully watched him go through his thinking process.

"And memories can sometimes be mistaken for visions or things happening in the present, like Déjà vu." He felt as if he was starting a rusty old car, the engine that was his mind whirring in creaks. The pain of his stump clouded his thinking. He turned back to the girl. "So... this dreamscape is based on my old memories?"

She clapped happily as he reached the conclusion. "Bravo! I am genuinely impressed."

"Wait," he stopped her celebration. "But that barn from last night, I've never been there before."

"Of course not. You're not the only one asleep now, are you? Sleep is just a way for your consciousness to view all the could, should, would and have been in your life. Like–"

"Alternate universes?" he cut in.

"Whoa, you are really good," she replied, genuinely surprised.

"It doesn't make sense. How is this possible?"

"Don't know."

"Who are you?"

"No idea," she turned to investigate her nails which were all well kept and bone white. "But you should run."

"What?" just as he said that, the bells that signalled a new customer rang as the double doors swung opened. He spun in his seat, only to see his father, golden haired, wearing a brown polo shirt, black and white chequered shorts and sandals standing at the archway, scanning the diner.

"Dad?" Tim voiced, but the man seemed not to hear him.

Joshua Kleve headed for one of the empty booths and sat down. One of the other waitresses, a woman with long maroon hair, approached him with a menu in hand to take his order. From where he sat, Tim could not see her face.

In a rare display, his father smiled. One so toothy and full of joy Tim almost could not recognise the man. "Hey there, nice seeing you again." his father's voice boomed in his mind loudly as if it were amplified by a speaker.

"Don't know why you keep acting surprise," the woman replied. Tim felt he heard that voice before, but with the murkiness of the situation, he could not quite put a finger on it. "You come here pretty much every day."

"Well, the food here is something worth living for." Tim had always thought his father was a terrible liar.

The waitress giggled. "Then that would make you a very simple man."

"How so?"

"Well..." The waitress placed an arm on her waist and another under her chin, apparently in thought. "I've always thought the worth of a person was less what they're willing to live for and more what they'd die for."

"I never took you for a hippy," Josh joked.

"Shut up," the waitress said laughingly, pushing his shoulder.

All of a sudden, Tim felt the hair on the back of his neck stand. His father seemed to be continuing his conversation with the waitress but Tim could not hear Josh's voice, with the man sounding distant, like he was talking from the end of a long tunnel. The teen turned back to the counter to find the girl in white gone like before. In her stead was an old lady.

The woman looked to be in her late 70s, her face wrinkled and skin dried, though she had the look of a caring Grandmother with her soft smile. Her hair was as white and curly as cotton candy, lips weathered and cracked. Wearing a red-white floral dress, her plump body looked to be more accustomed to the seat of a rocking chair or floating around the kitchen baking cookies than to be serving in a diner.

The Grandmother asked, "Hungry?" before sliding a plate with a sandwich on it across the counter to him.

"Uh...no thanks ma'am, I'm fine," as Tim said it though, he found his hand picking up the sandwich and taking a bite from it. "Phwat thergh fook?" he spoke through the chewing.

"See? You are hungry." The kind tone suddenly felt malicious, echoing in his ears as he noticed for the first time that her eyes were black, like her eyeballs had been replaced with onyx beads. "Here, have some more."

He stuffed the rest of the bread into his mouth, the fresh lettuce and succulent ham engulfed his sense of taste. Almost as soon as the bread left the plate, a bowl of fries were pushed in its place. Even with just one hand, he was stuffing his mouth at such a speed he could no longer talk through the mash of food built up.

Stop!

He tried to think, but the taste of the food was overwhelmingly delicious. Every bite seemed to excite his senses like an orgasm of the tongue.

The old lady smiled, her grin showed her missing half her teeth. "Eat up now, boy."

Saliva drooled from the corner of Tim's lips, his stump of a right arm swung desperately to stop the binge episode that had taken him. He didn't choke. Couldn't choke. The food slid down his throat with such ease it burnt his lungs.

Cake. Tarts. Sushi. Noodles. His eyes watered as dishes after dishes were served by The Grandmother, always smiling, her eyes black as the night staring at him with broken teeth. His waist stung as his belt tightened around it. No. His stomach was expanding against his pants. Head spinning, ears ringing, Tim wanted to hurl but the constant consumption prevented him from doing so.

I gotta move or I'm gonna die!

His muscles were tensed from the pain of the experience, his mind dizzy from his senses being overloaded. His surroundings blurred as he was about to pass out when his feet slipped from the footrest, knocking against the wooden back board of the bar.

It's moving?

Without thinking further in the how, he raised his legs against the backboard and pushed his seat away from the table. Food spewing from his mouth as he fell. He landed hard on his back with a loud slam, painfully swallowing down a large chunk of food as he attempted to gasp in pain. The ringing in his ears continued to annoy him.

No time. Move! His mind screamed.

Scrambling to his feet, Tim took a quick glance around the diner which had emptied out during his struggle with the force-feeding granny. Between coughs and biles and spits of phlegm, he bolted for the door, tackling it open with such force that the glass cracked on impact against the rubber stopper.

Out on the streets, he hobbled to the closest lamppost for support and vomited over the pavement. His nostrils dripped, eyes leaked tears, and his throat burned with stomach acid. Looking back to the diner, he saw The Grandmother slowly walking out from behind the counter, humming a distorted tune of the nursery rhyme *There Was an Old Lady who Swallowed a Fly*. Panicking, he darted out into the road, the ringing in his ears growing louder.

He looked right. Looked left. A red sports car. Yellow headlights. A blaring horn. The sound of tires screeching.

06:45 A.M.
11 days earlier

Tim lay on the floor of his room, his shirt drenched in sweat. His blanket had been kicked into a bundle in the corner in the night and his heart was beating light drums at a rock concert, chest rising high with each heavy breath. His ears were still ringing. He was unsure how long he stayed on the floor. Once his heart slowed, he realised the ringing in his ears were that of his alarm clock which automatically stopped.

When everything in him had calmed down, he surveyed his surroundings, only to find nothing out of the ordinary for his closet-sized room. He breathed in deep to calm himself and swung his body forward to sit up. A sharp pain flashed into his ribs, forcing his body to tense and his back to arch in agony. The pain was so great, he could have sworn he was hit by a car.

CHAPTER TWELVE

Evil Hound

"Like as the waves make towards the pebbled shore, so do our minutes hasten to their end."
- William Shakespeare, Sonnet LX

07:09 A.M.
11 days earlier

Even from his window with a brick wall for scenery, Tim could tell it was a misty morning. He changed into a fresh pair of blue jeans and a long brown sleeved cotton shirt. Beads of dew rolled down the fogged up glass, the colour of the neighbouring bricks slightly desaturated with the mist, the scent of earth floated even within the enclosed room. With a short glance over outside, Tim picked up his sweat-stained pyjamas and dumped them in the laundry basket in his bathroom. He looked for his air rifle but remembered he had left it at the Barber's.

"You can't do that!" His dad shouted from the living room.

Stunned in place, Tim stood silent as the echo from his father rang throughout the apartment.

His father continued again, this time in a softer voice. "Yes, I'm aware that I was on medical leave." A short period of quiet again. "Yes, I was at the protest, but that doesn't mean–"

Curious, Tim grabbed his school bag and quietly opened and stepped around his door. In the kitchen, his father, still in his grey boxers and white shirt, stood facing the fridge, holding the house phone to his ear. Tim could see the man's veins bulging around his neck and tightening fists.

"Look, please, I need this job or – No, I understand but – The protest wasn't about that!" he raised his voice with the last line, punching the fridge door with his left hand. "Look, boss, just give me another chance. I swear to you it won't –" he was cut off for the last time it seems. For awhile, Josh stood there, unmoving, save for his trembling hands.

Suddenly, with a loud roar of anger, he threw the phone against the kitchen wall, the small appliance shattering into dozens of pieces, its shrapnel travelling as far as to tap Tim lightly in the cheek. Burnt out and exhausted, Josh slammed his hands against the counter top, leaning into them with heavy sighs and deep breaths.

Tim didn't move, standing in his spot observing his father, hands still on the handle of his door. The clock on the wall ticked itself away and after what seemed like hours, he finally, gently, closed his door. The soft click as the metal slid into place caught his father's attention in the dead silence of the room.

As he wandered into view, Tim said, "I'm going to school now."

Josh slowly scanned the room for a moment, as if trying to locate the source of the voice before finally meeting his son's stare. "Yeah. Stay safe," he said, having calmed considerably.

Tim couldn't hold his gaze and awkwardly looked away. "Yeah," he replied, before making his way to the main door, taking care not to step on any of the broken pieces of the electronic. After he had put on his sandals, he said, "Watch your step." Before leaving the apartment.

07:55 A.M.
11 days earlier

Waxed ceramic tile floors stretched the dim light of the sun that shone from the school's entrance. Tim's footsteps echoed into the empty corridor of the high school with each passing second. He could count a total of six students in the hallway, sluggishly dragging their feet as they headed for their lockers and classrooms. An eerie veil of despair seemed to hang throughout the building.

He crossed the notice board that acted as the announcement board for the sports groups in the school. A notice with large, black, and bold lettering was pinned over all the other notices.

ACTIVITIES CANCELLED
UNTIL FURTHER NOTICE

It didn't require any special skills of deduction for Tim to know something was wrong that day and it would not be a normal school day. Confident in his deduction, he headed straight for his classroom without stopping by his locker to pick up his books. Despite it being just two minutes to the start of lessons, he only saw one teacher on his way to class. Just as he reached the door of his class, old Mrs. Harway, with her frilly grey hair, smiled grimly as she passed, only meeting his stare for a split second before nervously turning away. He turned to watch the older woman's silhouette melt into another classroom further down before entering his own just as the bell rang.

The classroom, including Tim himself, had a total of eleven students. He locked eyes with Stella who sat at her corner seat, and she nodded for him to go over.

Tim crossed glances with his classmates. Some of the more studious ones continued to pour through their textbooks while the rest shifted uncomfortably in their seats, smiling weakly when Tim greeted them.

He reached Stella's desk and asked, "Where's Clay?"

Playfully annoyed, she adjusted her green cardigan, which she wore over a white shirt, and smoothed out the creases in her jeans before replying, "What? No, 'Hi Stell.' or 'How's it going Stell?', just straight up 'Where's Clay?', is it now?"

He sat on the empty desk beside hers, sarcastically replying, "How are you Stell?"

"Meh, could be better," she replied with a shrug.

"So, where's your brother?"

"Hookie. Not that it really matters considering our numbers." She looked grimly around the near empty class as did Tim. "I don't think our teacher's coming in today either."

"Any announcements?" he asked, a sinking feeling growing in his gut.

"Mary said the principal is holding a meeting with the school board right now." Mary was the student body president and one of Stella's friends. "From what she said, it seems like one third of the school are confirmed to have Sin. Maybe more."

I have Sin too, he wanted to say to her. He swallowed hard, instead saying, "That's a pretty high number"

There was no point in worrying her further, and knowing Stella and her brother, Tim was sure they'd share their Somnidin with him. But given that his first dream had been just two nights ago and the siblings had them much longer, while averaging out the time most people lasted with Sin, he felt they needed the pills more than he did.

A loud bang caused the pair to jump in their seats. Turning around, the door to the classroom had been flung wide open. In the archway stood the tall, skinny, red headed Joseph, captain of the Air Rifle Team. Dried blood marked the spot of the bandage around his head where Clay had smacked the broom into him just the week before. Slung over his shoulder was his brown air rifle and in his right hand was an aluminium baseball bat. There was no doubt he was there for a fight.

Joseph said through gritted teeth, "Where's Clay?"

The other students sat stone-still in their seats, eyeing the senior with wide, fearful looks, afraid to move in case it agitated him.

Tim got to his feet and turned his back to Stella. At the same time, Stella stood from her seat as well. He waved his right hand behind him, signalling for her to hide behind his back. She did so, holding tightly onto his shirt and leaning into him like a pillar.

Under a hushed whisper, she said to Tim, "Why doesn't anyone ask about the girl these days?"

Tim smirked. *Like brother like sister.* Calm in the face of danger, witty against foes, not a single damn given to the tension of a situation.

"I ask again," Joseph growled. He raised his bat and slammed it against the nearest empty table. The other students jumped in their seats. The sound was deafening in the small room, a crack forming in the plastic desk. He looked Tim squarely in the eyes, shouting, "Where is Clay Barber?"

Keeping his calm, Tim placed his hands on the desk in front of him. "Don't know. Maybe you should leave a message after the beep."

A maniacal anger flashed across Joseph's face. His brows contracted, lips frowned, and a glistening of madness could be seen in his eyes. "That disgusting faggot gave me that stupid nightmare disease."

Joseph caught sight of Stella's small form behind Tim. "You're the sister aren't you?"

Stepping out from Tim's shadow while still holding onto his shirt, she defiantly replied, "Sorry, but I don't date meatheads like you."

"Stupid bitch!" The senior moved towards them, raising the bat over his shoulder. "You're gonna tell me where your brother is or I'm gonna fucking kill you!"

Joseph was halfway across the classroom. Tim slid his hands under the table he leaned against. His classmates started to scatter for the exit. Joseph was three-quarters away from the pair. Stella let go of Tim's shirt. Joseph raised the bat above his head.

Tim shouted, "Now!" He pulled his arms up, flipping and throwing the table into Joseph. Stella bolted for the back door, sliding in between tables and chairs as their classmates started shouting and screaming as they ran.

Joseph stumbled back, cursing under his breath as blood flowed from a brand new head wound the table caused. He regained his footing and swung his bat at Tim's head. Tim ducked, the weapon scraping the nape of his neck. Tim grabbed the legs of the nearest chair, stepped forward, and rammed his shoulders into Joseph, dragging the chair across the floor.

Joseph lost his balance again, tripping backwards and slamming back first into the white-board. he slumped to a kneel and Tim brought the chair crashing down against his spine and forcing the senior to drop face flat on the floor.

Stella shouted from the door, "Tim!" He turned to face her as she gestured to him. "Let's go!"

Tim turned back to his captain, who miraculously, was still trying to push himself back on his feet.

Not letting the opportunity slip by him, Tim ran for where Stella stood. Grabbing her hand, he pulled her out of the classroom just as the glass panel of a notice board opposite them shattered with a crack.

They ran through the hallway, their footsteps loud as drums in the empty, dimly lit corridor. A few students peeked out from their respective classrooms and Mrs. Harway, with her frilly grey hair shouted, "No running in the halls!"

A loud clang echoed against the steel lockers as another one of Joseph's pellets shot at them. They reached the bathrooms that faced each other and Tim pushed Stella towards the male one, which she entered without question. He jumped into the female one and closed the door behind him, leaning into it with his shoulders and an ear to the wood.

A gasp of surprise drew his attention. He glanced from the corner of his eyes and could make out the figure of two girls near the basin. He let out an angled grin, "Hey ladies." He returned to focus on the noise outside, despite the voices of objections from the two females.

Save for the whispers of his schoolmates in the bathroom with him, everything else protruded a deafening silence and Tim wondered if Joseph might have left, or passed out from the hit from the chair in the end. A loud bang from the corridor proved him wrong and hushed the girls in the bathroom.

"Get out here, Timmy-boy! I'm not through with you yet!" Joseph hammered again at the door of the male bathroom, as Tim had hoped he would, drawing attention away from himself.

Slowly, he opened his bathroom door and with as small an opening as possible, shimmied his way back into the hallway. He watched as Joseph raised his bat and smashed against the male bathroom door a third time, digging a visible splintered dent into the wood. Tim closed his door slowly and noiselessly.

Tim shallowed his breathing and approached Joseph on tiptoe. Joseph slammed his bat into the door a forth time as Tim crossed the middle point of the hallway. Joseph raised the bat again. This time, Tim reached out, grabbed the tip of the bat firmly with both hands and yanked it away, sending the weapon clattering across the tile floor.

Not giving his enemy time to rest, Tim jumped onto the senior's back and pulled, using his weight to counterbalance until his feet could touch the ground again, angling Joseph's spine in an unnatural arc.

Joseph managed to reach out with his lanky arms and wrapped his hands around Tim's head, intending to break Tim's neck should they fall. They stared, eye to eye, neither budging from their awkward hold.

"Stella!" Tim shouted.

The girl, on cue, stepped out of the bathroom, a mop in hand, with a strangely fitting grace and flow in her steps. With a golf club grip, she stepped forward and swung the cleaning equipment at Joseph's testicles.

Tim could see the fight leave Joseph's bloodshot eyes when the hit connected. He released his grip on Tim and fell backwards. Though just to be sure, Tim extended his knee to the back of Joseph's head and slammed into it. The senior's body limped. His legs, losing their grip, slipped forward and he fell to the floor out cold.

Stella poked their opponent with the mop before calmly declaring, "He's not getting up for a while."

Panting slightly, Tim stood to height, taking in the fresh smell of victory, which oddly, scented of blueberry detergent. After assessing the scene, he unclipped Joseph's air rifle and slung it over his own shoulder.

"What's happening here?" Mrs. Harway, with her frilly hair, shouted from further down the hall.

Tim and Stella exchanged a quick glance and he said, "We should run."

"Yes, we should," she replied.

CHAPTER THIRTEEN

Call Connected

"Sometimes you need to get hit in the head to know you're in a fight."
- *Michael Jordan*

10:58 A.M.
11 days earlier

Aside from Tim and Stella, the city bus had only two other passengers. The usual dank smell of hastily eaten fast food and sweat that were so synonymous with public transport were non-existent that day. There were no spilt drinks on the floor, no teenagers blasting their headphones with metal music or the usual chatter of businessmen and women on their phones. Any less noise would mean the bus had probably stalled. The pair sat at the last row, looking out the window onto the scarcely populated city streets.

Stella held back her strawberry blonde hair as she leaned her face against the window to look outside. "What in the world is going on?" she said as she scanned the streets.

"I'm not sure," Tim replied. "But if I have to make a guess, I'm thinking most of the people just contracted Sin."

"This is really weird."

"Tell me about it." It was made more so by the fact that just two days ago he had seen thousands of people holding the protest at the park. As the bus neared their stop, he stood from his seat. "Let's go."

The bus pulled up a few blocks away from the library, allowing them to alight. As it drove off, they could hear the echo of its engine chugging down the empty road. Given how scarce with life the footpaths were, Tim was sure the bus could have driven on the pedestrian walkway and not hit a single soul.

He met Stella's glance. Her otherwise soft face was scrunched up with worry. They nodded to each other, wordlessly agreeing on the oddity of the situation before heading towards the library, each of their steps audible within the dying city.

Stella spoke up, "I don't think Sin alone can do this. Remove this many people from the streets."

"I agree. Let's see what Clay has for us first before we get too fantastical with our imaginations."

"It's like the calm before the storm here."

"You're getting that feeling too?"

"Like the world's gonna end?"

"I was just going to say that bad things might happen."

"Like millions of people dying?"

"As long as it's not billions."

"Maybe billions," she added, as if to spite him.

He wasn't sure if she meant it as a joke or a serious thought that she just happened to speak her mind of. "Maybe billions," he found himself repeating as they walked up the steps to Ridge Valley Central Library.

The automated doors slid open soundlessly, the burst of cool air relaxing their bodies. Stella let out an audible sigh of comfort. Howard Galloway looked up from his usual desk in the library, jumping onto his feet upon seeing the pair.

"Aha! I had a feeling you two would be coming," he greeted enthusiastically. "Though I must admit, I was sceptical of that idea. Seeing the mythical Timothy Kleve two days in a row? 'Banish the thought!' I said," he waved his hands wildly as he approached.

"What am I? A fucking unicorn?"

Stella smiled gently, greeting the man with an outstretched hand. "Always a pleasure, Mr. Galloway."

"Pleasure's all mine, Stella Barber." He took her hands in both of his, raised them up and lightly kissed the back of hers. "And you, Tim, my boy, I hope my assistance yesterday was sufficient in your endeavour?"

"It was, Mr. Galloway. Thanks," Tim replied.

Stella turned to Tim, "You were here yesterday?"

Tim replied, "Yeah, I thought I told you?"

"You just said you were in the city. What were you doing here?"

"This boy," Howard cuts in, putting one arm over Tim's shoulders, "Came in here after years, not even to say 'hi'! Got my old legs running about for all sorts of articles and books, researching Sin. No consideration to a man my age, I tell you."

69

Annoyed, Tim wiggled out of the light grip. "Isn't it your job to help people in the library?"

Stella interjected before Howard could reply. To Tim, she asked, "You came here researching Sin?"

"Yeah," Tim replied. "I haven't been reading the news much these past few months, so I had a lot of catching up to do if I wanted to help."

A small smile formed from her lips as she mouthed something akin to a 'thanks'.

"That reminds me," Howard said, clapping his hands together as he did so. "Clay came in here looking for the same things you were, so I just passed him all the notes you left behind yesterday. He should still be upstairs."

The two thanked the old librarian and climbed the stairs to the second floor. That level was designed in such a way that the centre contained the bulk of the books in roundel shelves. Surrounding them were sets of white, plastic round tables and chairs in a neat circle. In the furthest corner nearest to the window sat Clay Barber, with his albino hair glowing with sunlight, at a table filled with small mountains of books and a mess of newspapers and magazines. He typed away at his laptop, occasionally looking over to his tablet before returning to the computer.

As the pair approached, they could smell the scent of the open books, the waft of leftover coffee from the plastic cups on the table. Clay had been there since school started in the early morning, and had obviously made himself comfortable. He had unbuckled the belt of his brown cargo shorts, and his oversized grey shirt had more than a couple of coffee stains on them.

Looking up from his laptop, Clay greeted his sister and Tim with a three fingered salute. "Hey kids. Aren't you suppose to be in school?"

Tim replied, "Had to leave early. Your favourite senior decided to pay us a visit."

Clay pondered for a few seconds before replying, "Jacob?"

"No, the other one."

"Ryo?"

"No," Stella said, rolling her eyes. "The other, other one."

Her brother took a deep breath, as if to clear his head. "Dwain?"

Tim took a seat beside his best friend. "No. It's the one you thwacked with a mop."

"Oh...Joseph. Yeah..." Clay replied, folding his arms and nodding in a joking attempt to look serious. "If I remember everyone I pissed off in school, I'd be a savant."

Stella sat opposite Tim, moving her chair closer to her brother. "If everyone you've ever pissed off remembered you, you'd be dead."

Clay replied in agreement, "That is true."

"So," Tim said. "What have you got?"

"Not much," Clay said, stretching his back and arms. "There's not really anything that we don't already know and you've covered almost all the statistics side of things in your research yesterday. Seriously though kid, you did all that in one day?" he looked to Tim.

"Yeah...why?" Tim replied.

"Just, it's amazing. I wouldn't even know where or what to begin searching with." Clay turned back to the table of notes. "Have you seen the streets though? Fucking ghost town shit out there."

"Yeah," Stella replied. "What's up with that?"

"There were cop cars and military trucks all over the place this morning moving people off the streets. Some were even arrested." Clay turned his computer around so they could see a website he had pulled up that featured a wallpaper that proclaimed it was undergoing maintenance. "All the major news websites are running pages like these now. And independent sites like blogs and social media sites are being shut down left and right."

Tim was speechless. He took over the laptops' track pad and opened up the other tabs Clay had on the browser. Each of them showed the same thing, just as Clay said.

Clay continued, "The last blog I read shut down about an hour ago. Forums are starting to go offline as well. There's a good chance the internet might just get cut off at this rate. Doesn't take a genius to know there's been a cover-up."

"What about the dark web?"

"A handful of them are still pinging. But the updates have slowed. Not much new information there, though. And It seems there's an effort to close it off as well."

Tim leaned back into his seat, scratching his chin in contemplation. "There's not much we can do about this. If the government is involved to the point where they are willing to shut down so many websites, the only thing left for us is to go with the flow. But we can still focus on the smaller things. What have you got on Sin itself? Anything new?"

"Like I've said, you covered most of that already," Clay replied, turning the computer back to him. "The only other thing new I could come up with was this forum post where a guy says he's been dreaming his memories. I've never heard of that before."

Stella chimed in, "Dreaming his memories? Like a flashback?"

71

"Something like that. According to him, it's more like the world the dream created was based on his memories. It makes sense though, if these nightmares are happening in our heads and – dude, what are you looking at?" Clay tilted his head to Tim.

"Shush!" Tim silenced Clay as he stared off into space, his eyes widened as his mind concentrated intensely on a train of thought. He thought back to the night before in the diner with the old lady that tried to feed him to death, and of what the girl in white said.

I don't know, it's not my memories.

He had made the deduction that the barn was a possible alternate universe, but the diner was based off his memories for a place as he remembered it. But something felt off and Tim shifted uncomfortably in his seat as he tried to figure out what it was.

He mouthed the phrase his mother used to say, "The worth of a person was less what they're willing to live for and more what they'd die for."

Stella leaned over the table so she could look Tim in the eye. "Are you...having a stroke?"

Ignoring her jest, Tim asked the siblings, "Saturday's strike, the newspaper said it was over unfair wages. What do you know about that?"

Clay started, "Well, the official reason was a wages strike. But there's some words floating around the online chat rooms that it was actually to protest hiding the truth of the statistics of the Vashmir Pandemic. We won't get confirmation about it until tomorrow, when the news fire gets the chance to spread. But even then, with websites shutting down, we might not get any info at all."

Tim has stopped listening at the mention of the Vashmir Pandemic. "The worth of a person was less what they're willing to live for and more what they'd die for," he repeated. "My mother said that. My mother said that. My mother said – I wasn't in the diner!" Like a lock clicking into place, Tim snapped to his feet, his chair falling backwards as he did so.

"Tim?" he could hear Stella's worried voice like a whisper in a tunnel.

He replied, more to himself than the siblings, "It was my dad's memories. If it was my memory, I would be in the diner with my dad. And the waitress...was mom. And I – it was my dad's memory. I was in my dad's memory!"

For the second time that day, Tim found himself running. Sprinting towards the stairs of the library, bolting down the steps. He pulled his phone out and speed-dialled his father. The line did not go through. He bolted past Howard on the first floor and out the door of the building, dialling his home phone in the process.

The phone rang once, twice, three times. On the twelfth ring, the call ended. "Fuck!" He cursed out loud as he cut across the road, dashing through office buildings towards the bus stop on the opposite end of the area, hoping to reach there before the bus did.

CHAPTER FOURTEEN

Deep Dive

"Truth is everybody is going to hurt you: you just gotta find the ones worth suffering for."
- Unknown

01:55 P.M.
11 days earlier

With the elevator under maintenance, he took the four stories of stairs three steps at a time, his legs stretching further than he had ever thought was possible. Panting, shirt soaked with sweat, Tim pulled out his set of house keys and jammed it into the lock without any fumbling, pushing the door hard enough that the wooden frame gave a small crack across the centre as it hits the wall behind it.

"Dad?" Tim yelled out into their small apartment to no reply.

He crossed the threshold and into the living room where the door to his father's room was half open. Throwing the air rifle onto the couch, he approached the room. He stepped up to the door, pushing it open fully and realised it was the first time he had seen his father's room in over two years.

Tim had expected to find beer cans and bottles to litter the place as it had when he last stepped inside. Instead, the room was neat, with the small desk and chair properly pushed in. A pile of clothes and pants were folded neatly on a bedside table. The one thing that seemed out of place of the neatness was the blanket on the floor. Crumpled in a heap, it seemed to have been kicked off the bed. His father, who was lying on the mattress in the same white shirt and boxers from earlier in the morning, was apparently fast asleep.

But Tim could tell something was wrong as he approached his father.

"Dad?" he called out. Silence. The man did not even twitch in his sleep, though the slow rising and falling of his chest assured Tim that he was alive. "Dad?"

Tim placed an arm on the sleeping man's shoulder and gently shook it. "Hey, dad. Wake up." With no response, he shook harder. "Dad!" The man did not stir. Tim quickly checked for a pulse and found it easily. Though the situation was weird, it did not appear to be life threatening.

However, Tim still felt a chill flowing down his spine, his guts churning uncomfortably as if telling him to think and act fast as something terrible was happening right under his nose.

"Okay, kid," he called himself by Clay's nickname for him. "Gotta keep calm and figure this out."

His father was asleep with no way of waking up. His theory that his father had Sin was being reinforced by the minute but he had never heard of people with Sin unable to be awoken from the outside before, adding a new layer of weirdness to an already strange situation. Or at least, nobody has ever tried. He watched his father's sleeping figure and noticed just how weary the older man seemed. Despite the muscular physique of the construction worker, there was a sense of age wrinkled into the skin. Years of weariness etched into the eyes.

"Sorry old man..." Tim said under his breath. "I haven't been the easiest kid to deal with."

He turned around and headed to his room and into his bathroom. Flipping open the medicine cabinet hidden behind his small basin mirror, he looked at the dozens of bottles of pills that he had not touched in over a year, picking one with a yellow tape around the cap. The number '2' was written in black marker on the top. He poured out four pills and left the bathroom.

In his room, Tim sat on his bed, the four pills in hand. Two of them would usually help him get to sleep but he felt his body was in too much of an adrenaline rush for it to be effective. Five and above would put him unconscious. Four sounded like a safe number in his head. Maybe. Probably.

He was able to invade his father's memories the night before. Assuming he could do so again, they might be able to meet in the dream world.

"No point in dwelling," he finally said to himself.

He downed the pills without water.

Tim woke up coughing violently, facing the sky. His lungs suddenly

75

burned with pain as if he had just swallowed acid. Struggling for air as liquid filled his throat, he turned to his sides and vomited a concoction of bile, blood, phlegm, and chunks of unidentified meat. He rolled away from his own pool of regurgitation and onto his back again. Still coughing, though less violently, he was able to breathe again.

A familiar dainty voice rang in his ears. "Now that's just disgusting."

Tim tilted his head to the left and saw the girl in the white dress sitting alone on a park bench. He focused on her for a second before examining his surroundings. They were in an empty field of dirt, devoid of any other life. Not even a single blade of grass grew in any direction that he could see. The sun was setting across the horizon to his right, a glow of blood red and orange stretching across the cloudless sky. He attempted to raise his right hand to wipe at his face, only to awkwardly wave his bandaged stump around instead. The pain of his amputated limb had subsided considerably and the discomfort was barely a tinge of what it was the night before.

He sat up forcefully, his stomach muscles straining as he did so. Calming his breathing, he grunted in an attempt to clear his throat of the burning sensation. When he realised it was not going away any time soon, he looked to the girl and asked, croaking, "Who are you?"

"Now that's not very polite, asking a girl for her name without giving yours," she replied with a playful tone.

Her grey eyes were piercing, as if they read every line of his being, right down to the fabric of his soul. Unable to maintain eye contact, Tim looked away to his surroundings again, surveying the empty plain that stretched as far as he could see.

"Tsk," the girl sounded, annoyed at his silent treatment. "If you really must know, I'm The Sister."

"The what?" He turned back.

"The Sister. That's my name."

"Your name is *The* Sister? Really?"

"Well, not really, really," she shrugged with the reply. "None of us remember our names so it's more of a title to call by."

"Wait a second. Us?" Tim replied as he got to his feet.

"Yeah. You've met them, don't you remember? The old granny from last night? That's The Grandmother. Not my actual grandmother, mind you," she added the last line hastily. She sifted to the side of the bench and tapped the empty seat on her left with a sly smile. "Come on. I won't bite."

Though he was hesitant, Tim nonetheless took the seat offered. "Okay," he said, leaning into his knees as he sat down, crunching his stomach to quell the pain. "I'm guessing that small boy in the barn and that business lady are part of your 'Family' as well?"

"Bingo!" she replied, slapping him playfully on his back. Though a light tap, he felt as if his skin had been in contact with ice where he was hit. Sister continued, "Those two are Son and Mother."

He recalled what Clay said about his 'hunter'. "And the one with the bat?"

"You know a lot more than I'd thought," she replied with a grin. "That's The Brother."

He looked to his stump of an arm and thought of the man-creature, that cut it off. "And that person in the straw hat, that Sawman, does he have a name?"

Her voice softened to a near whisper and he thought he sensed a quiver of fear in her tone. "The Father. That's The Father..." her voice trailed off and she did not elaborate further. Tim wanted to continue questioning her, but her silence stopped him.

He felt a sense of concern for her, though he wasn't sure why, having never met her before the whole ordeal. All he knew was that he felt asking her more might dig into her and hurt her, and he cared enough not to do that for some reason. The girl called Sister had powers that baffled him, and could probably hurt or kill him like The Grandmother and The Father could. But he felt she was not an enemy.

Suddenly, a cold sensation ran up his right shoulder and he tensed up in shock before realising it was Sister leaning against what remained of his arm. The fabric of her dress was maddeningly thin, and he could feel her cold, pale skin even through it. Though her entire body was leaned into him, it felt as though she weighed no more than a feather.

"Um..." Tim tried to regain his focus to speak but he could not help but be entranced by the beautiful girl who stared sadly into the empty red horizon. "Hey..."

"You have to stop him," she said in a gentle tone. Her voice like a melody. Her eyelids slowly closing as if falling asleep. Her body glowing a soft light paler than her skin. "You're the only one who can."

The light erupted into a blinding flash, forcing Tim to look away and close his eyes. By the time the light subsided and he was able to readjust his vision, the girl was gone, leaving not a single trace of her on the seat. Somehow, he had expected that to happen and was not the least bit surprised by her sudden disappearance this time.

Zoot. Zoon. Zoot. Zoon.

The sound of the saw, cutting through bone, echoing in his head. He expected that too.

Zoot. Zoon. Zoot. Zoon.

Tim looked forward where it was once an endless dirt plain that led eternally into a blood red horizon.

Zoot. Zoon.

A metal warehouse had appeared where nothing once was, right below the edge of the setting sun, glowing a menacing red.

Zoot. Zoon.

His father was in there. His guts were telling him so.

Zoot.

In there.

Zoon.

With the Sawman.

CHAPTER FIFTEEN

The Father

"Life is pleasant. Death is peaceful. It's the transition that is troublesome."
- *Isaac Asimov*

Screeching, the rusted hinges of the metal warehouse door closed shut behind Tim. Though the thin dust fog restricted his vision, it was not enough to even dim the sight of the shipping containers in front of him. To his left and right, the rows and columns of the containers stretched to the walls of the far ends of the building. Vertically, the containers were stacked up in piles of four, some five, few a little more. Faded red, blue, grey, and rusty brown decorated the walls of the metal boxes. The yellowish glow of incandescent lamps hung overhead, lighting the warehouse like tiny suns. A stench of rusted metal hung in the air.

Josh's voice echoed through the warehouse. "Take this!" A loud crash followed, ending in a thunderous rain of metal clanking off concrete. From the sound of it, whatever fell had to be large, metallic and heavy.

"Dad?" Tim called out. He began running towards the source of the commotion, circling round the containers that blocked him. He ran through the maze-like aisles, his footsteps echoing along the concrete floor. The dust wasn't thick enough to affect his breathing, but he coughed at every turn of the corner, tasting the metallic pang of rust on his tongue with each huff of air.

After what seemed to be miles of running within the labyrinth, he took a left turn and had to abruptly skid to a halt as he reached a change in scenery, kicking up dusts at his sudden change in momentum. Surrounded by the walls of containers, he stood in a large soccer field-sized scrap yard. Small mounts of metal and parts scattered around the place, with pipes, wood planks and rebars sticking out. A pile of a dozen or so large steel

79

tubes were heaped haphazardly in a corner, an out of place forklift sat at their side.

Unable to see the driver seat, Tim warily approached the forklift. Each step forward brought up a cloud of dust. He wanted to call out to his father again, but every fibre of his being screamed at him to keep silent. A metal pipe stuck out from a scrap pile next to him. It felt light as Tim picked it up, even though his left hand was not his dominant one. Thinking to himself, he hoped it was steel and not some weak aluminium crap.

He held his breath as he circled out of the blind spot of the vehicle, slowly stepping closer to it as he did so. With the pipe raised and only a short jump forward to swinging length, he leaped sideways into view of the driver seat, ready to swing at...nothing.

Letting out a sigh of relief, Tim lowered his weapon and stepped up to the empty forklift. Now up close, he could see that it had ploughed through the scrap yard, having left a tyre trail behind it.

As he approached the tracks to investigate further, a clang from behind got him to spin around. He raised his pipe and pointed it blindly at the source of the noise, only to see one of the steel tubes had rolled off its pile.

"Just a tube," he whispered to himself. But try as he might, his body would not allow him to lower his weapon. He watched as his hand trembled, his body tensing up with either fear or anticipation, he wasn't sure. The aching pain in what's left of his right arm prickling at him, a nagging reminder of danger to come.

The steel pile seemed to shake with his hand.

Another pipe fell off.

And a third.

His instincts shouted, *Duck!*

Tim dove to the side and behind the forklift, just as the pile of steel pipes exploded outwards. The Sawman, on his feet, slashed through the metal like paper. Shrapnel of steel cut through the air, slicing and sparking off the edges of the forklift as Tim rolled up into a crouching position to avoid the projectiles. The larger pieces flew over the vehicle and burst across and all around him, loudly slamming into containers and scrap piles. The impact lifted up a gale of dust, forcing the teenager to bury his face in his arms to avoid being blinded.

Zoot. Zoon. Zoot. Zoon.

His heart skipped a beat as the sound thumped through his mind. The storm of dust died down and he swung around, blindly whipping the pipe at where he felt fear oozing. Like paper, his aluminium pipe was sliced in half by The Father's saw.

Tim stumbled and fell onto his back, cursing, "Fucking aluminium!"

The creature took a step towards Tim as he tried to back away but his stumped arm made ground retreat difficult. Desperate, Tim kicked at its shin, an action he immediately regretted for it felt like kicking concrete.

"Son of a–!" he recoiled his feet, ankle in pain. The Sawman raised up his weapon, ready to slash down at Tim's fleshy body with the same strength as it did the steel tubes and the fucking aluminium pipe.

"Get away from my son!" Josh charged in from the flank. A longer – this time definitely steel – pipe swung at the head of the Sawman. Tim expected the attack to fail, that both him and his father would get brutally murdered at the hands of the concrete super-monster.

The Sawman let out an inhumane howl of pain after the hit.   It stumbled back, holding its 'face' with its free hand, swinging its saw blindly with rage.

"How did you do that?" Tim asked, mouth wide in shock. "I kicked him and nothing happened."

His father pulled him up. "Does it matter? We gotta go!"

Josh was wearing his sleeping clothes. A set of white singlet and shorts, brown and muddied. His skin dirtied. His golden hair a pale white. His arms had cuts and bruises that ran down their entirety.

Following his father, Tim ran towards the nearest opening in the wall of containers.

"What happened to you arm?" the older man asked.

Tim replied, "Long story, tell you later." They neared the exit.

Then, Tim's gut clenched in fear as instincts grabbed him. He reached out with his hand and pulled his father back just as one of the large steel tubes flew over their heads, slamming into the container pile. The tube pierced the metal containers cleanly on one side and the stack of red containers above it tilted and slid before crashing noisily, sealing them from their exit.

"Shit," Josh cursed as the dust died down. The nearest exit was where Tim had came from, right behind where the Sawman stood. A third exit was inconveniently placed at the far end. "Okay, here's the plan. I'm gonna run towards that exit on the other side and draw the thing's attention. And you'll get out from the one on the right."

"Are you high? You're gonna get killed!" Tim replied, though never taking his eyes off the Sawman who was slowly walking towards them.

Zoot. Zoon. Zoot. Zoon.

"Listen, we just have to survive until we wake up. We split up and we'll have a better chance that one of us survives."

"That's a fucking stupid plan!"

81

The Sawman was closing in. Josh readied himself.

"Best I've got now."

Though reluctant, Tim positioned himself to run. However, he grabbed hold of his father's hand before they started. Looking the older man in the eye, Tim tried to get the words 'I love you' out from his lips, but only managed a feeble, "We're cool."

His dad smiled. The first smile Tim had seen on him in a long time. "I love you, too."

Tim let go of his hand and the older man ran, scooping up stones and small objects from the ground as he did so, throwing it in the direction of the Sawman.

"Come on, you piece of shit!" he yelled. The Sawman turned its attention to him as a piece of rock bounced off its straw hat. The older man continued his barrage.

Once the creature started to move towards his father, Tim bolted from his spot. The Sawman seemed to walk-float, but the speed was just that of a jogging man. Tim felt it was impossible for it to catch up with his father. Confident of his analysis, Tim turned his attention back to his exit, dodging scrap piles as fast as they appeared in his field of vision. A quarter to the exit and nothing happened. Halfway and a smile broke across his face. Three quarters and passed the forklift and he knew he was going to make it. The exit was within arms reach.

A scream rang through the warehouse; a gurgled, pain-filled, primal scream, followed by an ear piercing silence that etched the last note of the cry in his ears. He stopped in his tracks.

Tim panted hard, heart beating fast. His mind went through dozens of scenarios as to what could cause such a painful yell before slowly and shakily, he turned back to look in the direction of the Sawman.

It stood over his father's body, which was slumped down against a container. His father's shirt was drenched blood red and Tim could not see any signs of movement, not even the rising of his chest.

"Dad?" Tim mumbled. He took two wobbling steps towards his father. "Dad!" He broke into a sprint.

He swiped a steel bar that protruded from the ground, roaring in righteous anger. The Father, the monster man with the straw hat turned to face its next challenger. It strolled towards him, strides long and confident.

Tim crossed the field. A quarter. Halfway. Three quarters. Within reach. He brought his weapon up across his face and behind his right shoulder. The Sawman swung its saw at him and he swung back at the weapon. Steel clashed again steel, the Sawman drawing back its weapon arm, knocked back by the force of the swing. The Sawman sliced down again. Tim swiped his weapon upwards.

"Go–" he knocked the saw out of his opponent's hand. The steel bar raised over his head and he sent it striking down. "–to–" The Sawman stumbled once more and Tim pulled his weapon back behind him. "–hell!"

Tim leaped forward, thrusting the steel weapon at The Sawman's 'face'. The bar went through the hat and he felt it impact whatever that served as a skull underneath it. As if he had just punctured a bag of rice, sand exploded out the back of the monster's head and the body instantly crumbled into dust, leaving a heap of particles on the floor as the clothes of the creature flopped down onto it. The straw hat hanging from the steel bar that pierced it.

Panting hard, his heart pounding against his chest like a cop on the door, Tim slowly lowered his weapon. The hat slid off the bar and floated to the floor. The weapon clanged against the ground when he dropped it shortly after, ringing across the empty warehouse and likely, the universe in which they resided. Then he turned to his father. Adrenaline clouded his head, dazed from the rush of the fight and speechless by the blood he saw in front of him.

Wavering, Tim eyed the injuries more intently the closer he got. A large cut traced down from Josh's right shoulder to his stomach. His blood drenched ribs were visible, his right shoulder limply hanging from its tendons, having already been detached from the bone that held it to the torso. Blood had pooled around the body all the way passed the legs. Dark red and shining under the incandescent yellow lights above, a glowing pond of black.

Tim knelt down beside his father, dipping his pants into the blood, staring blankly into the opened wound. He couldn't fix that. Didn't know how. Don't think it possible. Voice coarse, he croaked, "Dad?"

Josh's eyes slowly fluttered open with a small glint of life. Each breath he took pierced what remained of his lungs but he was in too much pain to feel it properly. With what strength he could muster, he looked up to see his son's face. Scared. Confused. Pained. Alive. And hidden in all of that: determination.

He raised his one good hand up and cupped it around Tim's face. "Look at you," he smiled. The light left his eyes. His hands slumped down beside him, thumping into the pool of his own blood, a growing pond of black.

CHAPTER SIXTEEN

I, Police

"He who fights with monsters should look to it that he himself does not become a monster. And if you gaze long into an abyss, the abyss also gazes into you."
- Friedrich Nietzsche

00:28 A.M.
10 days earlier

By the time he woke, Tim's bed was soaked with cold sweat. Sleeping at an odd angle, his neck hurt and his back froze from the drenched mattress. His room was dark and the outside of his window was shadowed enough that he could not even see the white linings of the brick wall opposite. He breathed deeply, erratically, desperately trying to regain the rhythm of his breathing. His ears rang, hands shook, his eyes strained in pain as he tried to regain his sight in the darkness.

In the shadow of his room, he finally managed to hone in on the chirping of crickets outside as the focus on his surroundings slowly returned. His watch on his desk faced him, and he could make out the faint outline of the time. He had slept the day away.

Like a brick, the thought hit him. "Dad," he hissed under his breath.

He shot out of his bed, only to have his legs buckle under him as he attempted to stand, forcing him to lean against the wall in discomfort as the grogginess from the medication he took earlier continued to affect him.

Shaking and holding onto the walls for support, Tim made his way out of his small room. He turned the corner that is his living room, leaning against the old CRT Television, sliding over it lazily, his vision crossing as he stepped up to the door of his father's room. He shook his head in a futile attempt to clear the grogginess but only achieved a split second of clarity

84

before being inebriated again. Resigning to his intoxication, he pushed himself through the doorway.

An odour of rust washed up against his nose the moment he stepped in, and for a moment, he saw flashes of the warehouse barrelling past his sights. Tim massaged his eyes in an attempt to rub the images away. The scent of rust overbearing.

No. Not rust.

Blood. He made the connection and slowly waved his hands to wipe away his vision.

He had watched films where characters who are faced with death for the first time react in disgust, often vomiting or passing out, usually comically. He felt neither of those things as he stared at his father's lifeless body. The older man looked to be at peace in death, the last look he gave Tim in the dream world etched into his face, eyes closed, a soft smile. He would have been mistaken for just being asleep and having a happy dream were it not for his blood drenched shirt and the pool of red forming around him on the mattress.

"Dad..." Tim stepped towards the body, the drowsiness having almost instantaneously faded out of him. He was careful not to step in the small puddle of blood that had formed on the floor. He stared at the man with the golden hair. Drunkard. Construction worker. Father. "We were supposed to go see mom."

01:32 A.M.
10 days earlier

It wasn't sure how the boy named Timothy Kleve managed to call for help, given the circumstances. But by the time Detective Julianne Smith arrived on the scene with her partner, Detective Oliver Hardy, the coroner had already stepped out of the apartment, lab kit in hand. An officer stood beside Tim as the boy sat in the corridor outside the apartment, head buried in his arms.

The coroner approached the two partners. "The scene's all yours detectives. I've got another place to get to. Call in for the van when you're done," he said, yawning as he ended.

"Whoa," Oliver Hardy said in a gruff tone, raising a tanned, rugged arm to stop the coroner from leaving. The bald detective, with his hazel eyes and rough round face stared down the older man. "That's it? Julie and I just got here. Don't you guys usually stay till the investigation's over?"

Though only in his late twenties, Oliver's well toned body and bulky,

85

muscular arms gave him a size advantage over most men. A thick, dark brown trench coat, grey shirt, black pants and a pair of muddied boots gave him an overwhelming umbrageous aura. Intimidating, often straightforward, most people would think twice of challenging him and his classic hard-boiled police sway; the coroner included.

"Let him go, Ollie," Julie said, putting a gentle arm on Oliver's to lower it. The coroner took the gesture, slipped past the two detectives, and went on his way, giving her a nod of thanks as he did so. She explained, "They're as swamped as we are with the death rates spiking."

Tim took the commotion as a cue to look up. His eyes met Julie's and a sudden sense of forebode took over both of them. The female detective looked nothing like her partner, wearing a more modern black suit and pants, white inner shirt and onyx shined shoes. She was young enough that Tim found her attractive. Her flame-orange hair, tied neatly in a ponytail, matched the consuming personality that he felt behind her intense blue stare.

Tim told the officer watching him, "I need to make a phone call." He stood up. Slipping his phone out of his pocket, Tim went over to the far corner of the corridor to make his call in private.

"Weird kid." Oliver watched as the teen walked away before asking his partner, "What do you think of him?"

"Don't know yet," she replied, the moonlight shining her hair like a pool of blood. "Let's take a look at the crime scene before we make any decisions."

The detectives entered the small apartment and a stench of blood hung thinly in the air. Even in the now-lit home, the place looked dank and murky, but it was visibly clean and relatively neat, nothing out of the ordinary in the detectives' eyes.

Instinctively, Oliver raised his hands to cover his nose. Even after half a decade dealing with homicide cases, he still could not bear the initial odour of death. "That smell is strong. What time did they say this was called in?"

"Don't be weak. It's been barely an hour since the body was found. The body shouldn't even be smelling yet," Julie replied nonchalantly. "Now, which room did they say was the father's?"

Oliver pointed to the closer of two doors. "That one."

"Good. You go check it out." She headed for Tim's room instead.

"But the body's not in yours!" Oliver called out from behind but was ignored. He gave a sigh of resignation and with a hand over his nose, entered the foetid room. His grievous complains continued to pour through the house.

86

In Tim's room, Julie went over to the sweat-stained mattress. The bed sheets were crumpled and the single pillow had been pushed up against the corner of the wall. She was surprised how small the room was. She could touch the desk, bed, bathroom door, and entrance, all by standing in a single spot.

She glanced at the dimly lit brick wall outside the window. "Not much of a view," she whispered to herself.

Turning on the spot, she easily opened the door to the small bathroom. Like the bedroom, it was surprisingly small and was easy to take in. Nothing was out of the ordinary save for a half opened medicine cabinet. About a dozen bottles of pills were in there, some she recognised and a few she had not seen before. From what she saw, she had a rough idea of what they were for.

A voice came from outside the room. "Uh, detective?"

She stepped out and met the coroner. He handed her a file.

"What's this?" she asked, opening it to glance through.

"It's my investigation notes. I forgot to hand them to you." He gave a half-hearted salute and walked out of the apartment, leaving her to the report.

Oliver came out of the other room, no longer covering his nose. A look of disgust had settled across his face. "That's a straight up murder right there. We should call the van and get a bag."

Julie, after being fixated on the report, closed the files. "Call the precinct to get a room ready while you're at it."

She made her way out the apartment, leaving a confused Oliver to follow. Outside, the temperature had dropped and a cold wind blew in from the sea. Tim had finished his call when the two detectives walked towards him and he eyed them suspiciously.

"What are we doing?" Oliver asked his partner in a whisper.

She did not reply. Taking commanding strides over to the boy, she could see the uncertainty in his eyes as they approached, the look of hesitation on his face. Stopping just short of arms reach from each other, Julie sized   him up.

Average size, average looking, average kid. Though she felt an overwhelming personality behind his eyes.

"Timothy Kleve?" she asked, knowing the answer.

Tim replied, "Last I checked." He steeled himself to face her stare.

A roguish grin formed on her beautiful face. Her hair colour suddenly reminded him of blood. "You're under arrest for the murder of Joshua Kleve."

CHAPTER SEVENTEEN

Interrogate

"The nearer emotional life approaches to hysteria, to continual outward show, the less genuine it becomes. Feeling becomes equated with vehemence of expression, so that insincerity becomes permanent."
- *Theodore Dalrymple,   A Neglected Genius*

03:58 A.M.
10 days earlier

It wasn't like the olden noir films where a single light bulb dangled from the ceiling of a dark room. Modern interrogation rooms, like the one Tim had been stuffed into, were no more extraordinary than an office cubicle. Bright white fluorescent lights did nothing to help the already dull white room, shining as if heaven's judgement had surrounded him. Shoved into the corner was a single chair in which he sat, next to a table aligned to the wall. Since no evidence had been brought to him, he was technically not in custody and was thus not handcuffed.

The two detectives stood before him on the other side of the table, a folder of documents in each of their hands, the usual one-way mirror beside them, and a blatant camera above the door probably recorded their every words and movements.

Looking the female detective dead in the eyes, Tim asked, "Can I get my phone call now?"

She replied, "Only after you've told us why and how you killed your father."

"And what makes you think I'd do something like that?" He leaned against the corner of the room, letting out a sigh of comfort as he did so. He knew the reason the table was placed in the corner was to make him feel trapped. He made no attempt to hide that the trick to strain him into a

88

confession was not working.

"For one thing," Detective Hardy said, "You claim a man in a straw hat chased you in your dreams and killed your father."

Smith continued, "And we found antidepressants in your room. Almost half a dozen bottles of them." From her folder, she took out pictures of the familiar medicine cabinet and laid them across the table. "So here's what happened. You forgot to take your meds, had a little episode. Maybe hallucinated a little. Cut up your dad, got rid of the weapon, and in your delusion, called the cops on some make believe monster."

Tim replied to only half her accusation, "Sin isn't fiction. It's real and medically recognised."

Julie Smith leaned over the table, bearing her entire person to overshadow Tim. "Not by the judicial system. And definitely not by me." He wondered how a beautiful woman could have such an ugly attitude before remembering his own personality was no better.

"So," Tim continued, pretending to not have heard her. "Where's my lawyer?"

"You're not getting one."

"Well that's not fair," he replied with a playful tone. "In that case, I guess I'll just keep my mouth shut."

Smith stepped back but Hardy slid in from the side, a stern expression on his face. "You're under heavy shit here. Your father's dead and you're the most likely suspect in his murder. You think this is a joke?"

The smile slipped from Tim's face, almost instantaneously. "Joke?" he stood up from his seat. The two detectives instinctively backed away, their hands reaching for the firearms hidden behind their backs. Not a single creak of hesitation rested in Tim's eyes as he delivered his lines. "My father is dead. The people I care about are being targeted by an illness with no cure and I might be next. So no, this isn't a joke."

"So there are other people you're targeting?" Smith asked.

"That's what you got out of that?" Tim replied, outraged.

"Fine, let's talk about the drugs. What are they for?" she changed the subject quickly in an attempt to confuse him.

He took a breath to calm himself before settling back in his seat. Despite his initially collected demeanour, he felt he had fallen into some form of trap by raising his voice.

You're just a kid, his dad had once told him during one of their arguing sessions. *No matter how smart you are, how talented you'll be, you can't beat experience.*

"Listen up, boy," Hardy said. "It's best if you just tell the truth now. There's nothing to gain from being an ass."

Tim contemplated silently as the detectives stared him down. Despite the pressure that exuded from the two adults, he held their gaze.

"Fine," he replied. "I had major depression when my mom died. I took those medications to help make it through back then. I stopped taking them after I stabilised and kept them around just in case. Happy?"

Smith pulled up a devious smile. "So you are off your medication and things got bad..."

"That's not it–" Tim tried to correct her.

The female detective was relentless. "And since your father was the cause of your mother's death..."

He got to his feet, furious. "Stop accusing me of–"

Hardy tried to cut in, "Julie, ease up."

But the pleas fell on death ears as she finished, "You got into an argument and killed him!"

Tim found himself vaulting over the table, the plastic chair flying back from under him by the force of his jump forward. He swung his legs wide, kicking across the air as the two detectives attempted to jump back to avoid the attack. Tim was sure he had at least hit Smith, for droplets of blood as red as her hair trickled to the floor.

On the other side of the table, he found his footing quickly before attempting to rush in and tackle the female detective. However, instead of the soft impact of shoulder blade to stomach that he was expecting, he found himself twirling into the table, crying in pain as his face slammed violently into the wooden furniture from Hardy's punch.

He tried to stand again but was forced down against the tabletop by the vice-tight, smooth-skinned grip of Detective Smith. The cold slap of metal followed by the sharp tightening sensation on his wrists signalled his handcuffing and the end of his outburst. He could taste the blood from the molar that cracked on impact from the punch, a stinging pain through the nerves, the pouch of blood pooling in his mouth.

Smith violently grabbed Tim's collar, pulled him to a stand and barked, "Now! You're under arrest, you fucking kid!" She spat over his shoulder and the phlegm of blood that landed on the table concluded he had at least managed to injure her.

04:45 A.M.
10 days earlier

Most of their fellow officers at the precinct didn't particularly have a love for doughnuts, but with the neighbourhood doughnut shop being the only nearby restaurant open twenty-four hours a day, they were a common sight in the break room after midnight. The room was fashioned with a floral theme since the previous police chief had a hobby for gardening. Red and white flower tiles lined the floor. The tables and chairs, though made of plastic, were laminated with wooden designs.

Julie sat in one of the chairs. Finally taking a sip from her coffee, she stuck her tongue out in disgust; the cold having neutered the flavour and her bleeding gums soured the taste. The bruise Tim gave her cheek did not help either.

"All I'm saying is," Oliver continued, "You should have gone easy on the kid. What if you're wrong? You'll just accuse an innocent boy of murdering his father. What if this Sin thing is real?"

"It's not fucking real," she replied, crossing her arms in disdain. "It's just mass hysteria and people are using it to commit crimes."

"There's no proof that–"

"Exactly!" she cut in, not allowing him to finish. "There's no proof of its existence. Everything from the heart attacks to Somnidin can be explained by mass hallucination, nothing more."

Oliver raised his cup of Joe and pointed out, "That's a pretty far fetched theory you've got there partner."

"More far fetched than murdering dream monsters?"

"Touché." He leaned back in his seat, accepting the rebuttal, taking a sip of his coffee. "But we still can't get him for murder. All we've got is some flimsy logic and your gut hunch."

"Our gut hunch," she corrected.

"Your gut hunch," he insisted. "I still don't think he did it. And I don't think throwing him in the holding cell will get us anywhere either."

"At least he's not *going* anywhere. No family to bail him out, not a dime to his name. He'll stay here till we can find the time to settle him."

"It's almost as if you've got a personal vendetta against this kid."

"This kid is a murderer, using the lamest of all excuses," she attempted again to force her point, her flaming locks flailing as she discussed the issue passionately. "The whole city is going wonky from this bloody pandemic thing. We've got enough on our hands without having to deal with another budding psychopath."

"Julie, you've always been the smarter one. I hope to God you're right on this," Oliver replied, wearily leaning his face into his perched hand. "I don't want to be that guy that traumatises a kid into *becoming* a psychopath."

91

CHAPTER EIGHTEEN

Endless Blue Sky

"The meeting of two personalities is like the contact of two chemical substances: if there is any reaction, both are transformed."
- Carl Gustav Jung

04:38 A.M.
10 days earlier

"I thought there'd be more people here," Tim spoke out to the corridor outside his holding cell. The white light of his cell sent soft shadows of the bars into what would otherwise be a dimly lit pathway.

"The 'normal' cells are upstairs," Pearlman replied in his monotonous voice. "We're in the ones for special people."

Tim's cell, as he guessed of all the others, had walls that were tiled white, with questionable brown stains on each of the ceramic pieces. A single mat on a concrete ledge in the wall served as a bed with a stainless steel sink and toilet combination in the corner. The entrance was blocked by grey painted bars, allowing him and Pearlman, the man in the cell beside him to communicate.

Pacing up to the bars, Tim slipped his hands through them and rested his elbows on the horizontal piece. Leaning in, he could see another pair of hands protruding from the cell to his left, though the angle at which they stood prevented them from seeing one another's faces.

Casually, Tim asked, "So what did you do to get here?"

"Oh, you know," Pearlman gestured a 'whatever' with his hands. "Apparently the cops think I'm some high profile case that needs to get locked up solo till trial. You?"

"Hit a cop," he replied calmly.

"Wow," though the tone did not convey surprise. "And how did you

92

end up in punching range?"

Hesitant, but also reluctant to block out what was possibly his only source of conversation there, Tim replied, "Got accused of killing my dad."

"Sorry for your loss." Instead of sounding sympathetic, Pearlman sounded impressed instead. "But did you do it?"

"No," Tim replied flatly. "Fucking no."

"Okay then," Tim watched as Pearlman withdrew his hands from the bar. "Best get some sleep. It'll be a long day ahead for you."

Tim looked to the mat that he was expected to sleep on. The lights in the cell could not be turned off from the inside. With everything else that had happened, he was sure he would not sleep a wink. Sitting down on the lumpy concrete ledge, he leaned clumsily against the walls and immediately dozed off.

Tim's eyes creaked opened to the light of a clear blue sky, a flock of birds cutting through the air above him in formation. He looked down his body to find himself once again wearing his black shirt and cargo combo. His 'dream attire'. His right arm was still missing, the same bloodstained bandaged.stump in its place.

Sister walked up to him, her small form towered from where he lay. "You awake yet?" she asked in her sing-song voice. The silhouette of her petite figure casted through her white dress by the sunlight behind her. A smile spread across her face.

"No," he replied, slightly annoyed. She looked overtly cheerful to him. "I'm asleep."

With a groan, he pushed himself to sit up, his back aching as he did so. They were on a plateau of sorts; the grassy, flowered land stretched for about half a mile before ending abruptly, with nothing visible beyond save for the endless blue sky. With another heave, Tim got to his feet and stretched his back. He looked at Sister only to turn away when their eyes met. He started walking.

She followed after him despite his attempt to walk faster to get away from her. Her steps seemed to glide noiselessly across the ground and she caught up with his pace with seemingly no effort on her part. "And where do you think you're going?"

"To jump off a ledge," he replied coldly.

"Wait, are you serious?"

"Yes."

She sped up her pace so she could move in front of him. Though seemingly walking backwards, he was sure she was gliding.

"What makes you want to do something crazy like that?" she asked in her usual cheerful tone.

"That's how you wake up, right?" he replied, looking at the ground behind her instead of directly at her. "You die from 'natural' causes and you wake up. As long as I don't get killed by one of you Family members, I get to live."

"That's a crazy speculation you've got going there," she reacted in genuine amazement, slowing down her steps till they were walking side by side.

"That's what I do. It's the only thing I'm good for," he said grimly. "When I 'died' at the diner from that car, I woke up. But when my father died by The Father's hands, he died for real. It's what I do. I speculate. It's the only thing I can do."

"Are you okay?"

"Fine," he replied, his tone glacial. He could see the edge of the plateau now. "Just fine," he extended his strides.

"Are you trying to avoid me?" she asked.

Without hesitation, he replied, "Yes."

"Why?"

Tim stopped in his tracks, turned to face Sister, and shouted, "Because you left my father to die. You could have helped!"

"And do what?" she calmly replied. "My powers don't work on any of the others and it's not my job to save people."

"You don't save people?" Tim scoffed. "Then that night in the barn. Why did you save me? Why are you helping me?"

"Because I killed you!" she screamed back. "That night at the barn, I didn't save you. I killed you. Right after The Father cut off your arm, I drove a spike straight into your heart and you survived. That's why I'm helping you. The only person who even has a chance of stopping The Father right now is you, the only person who has ever survived."

Tim, shocked by the outburst of the first time she had raised her voice past her normal delicate tone, stood stunned. "You killed me?"

"Yes," she replied unhesitatingly.

"Why?"

Looking down at her bare feet, she said, "It's our job. We're grim reapers." Looking back up and staring Tim in the eye, she would find neither anger, confusion, nor fear, but a questioning gaze. "Remember how I told you the dreamscapes are parts of alternate universes?"

"Yeah..."

She circled around him, her white dress dragging against the grass and the dirt, but never staining, its length extending and diminishing randomly. "That's where your consciousness goes after you die. Other worlds. Our job is to separate your consciousness from your physical body and send it on to the next world. We used to be living humans, like you. We died and made a deal with some creature from another dimension. In return for a hundred and thirty nine years of servitude, we get a second chance at life on Earth again."

She changed direction and headed for the edge of the plateau. This time, Tim followed in her steps, listening intensely.

"It wasn't always like it is now. We didn't go around killing indiscriminately. We take the life from people at the edge of death. That is, until The Father went insane. He corrupted most of us with the promise of power. To feed on human consciousness to get stronger. Enough power to tear our way back into reality and be kings and queens."

"Even you?" Tim asked. A part of him knew the answer.

"Yeah," she replied softly, barely audible over the wind. "Even me. For a while. Then I came back to my senses, a short while back. But the rest were too overcome by power to talk out of it."

Something Sister said struck the curiosity in Tim. "Why one-three-nine years? What's so significant about that time?" Tim asked.

She explained, "Time doesn't flow at the same rate in every world. An hour in your world could be a second here. Maybe even a day. I'm guessing a hundred and thirty nine years is equivalent to some odd number of time for whoever gave us these positions. That's my theory anyway."

Before they knew it, they were at the edge of the plateau. As expected, looking down, he saw nothing but a thick layer of cloud.

Tim continued, "You haven't told me why me yet."

"There were four of us at the barn that night. Me, The Father, The Son, and The Mother," she paused.

After waiting for her to continue, which seemed to not be coming, he pushed on. "So?"

Sister turned to him, and he saw a look of grimness that he felt unfitting of her bright and crease-less face. She replied, "We've never had more than one of us on one target before. It's not suppose to be possible."

And he realised the implication. Having more than one hunter meant being able to piece together more information than any other living person could. It meant that Sister could communicate with him while he actively fought the other members of The Family, instead of being cut off and being unable to do anything. If he was only faced with The Father, Tim would never have gotten these bits of information from Sister. If it was just

The Sister, he won't be able to use the information against the Sawman, since they would never meet.

She turned away from him and peered down the vertical drop. "Are you still going to jump?" she asked.

"I have to test out my theory."

"It'll definitely work. You guessed right."

Tim forced out a laugh, "It's not that I don't trust you but, well, actually, I don't trust you." He turned back to her and caught her stare. "Not entirely. Besides, nothing left to lose. My father's dead. Best friends are next. If I fail at whatever heroic thing you expect me to do, I'm not going to have much left to live for anyway."

He stepped closer to the ledge, but upon looking down, his body froze, as bodies do when faced with death defying actions and logic.

Sister sounded concerned as she asked, "What's wrong?"

"Nothing. Enjoying the scenery."

Abruptly, he felt her press herself against his back. The sudden movement almost made his footing slip, his body jerking slightly in reaction. Sister placed her hands on the blades of his shoulders, and said, with her voice echoing, "I am sorry about your father."

A sudden feeling of sexual attraction surged through his body and he felt the urge to spin around to embrace the girl fully. Preferably naked. He had felt that sensation before and knew that whatever power the girl had was what forced the sharp spike in his lust. He had never acted on it for he had always felt a certain sense of fear in his chest when she used her powers that way. Originally, he was unable to identify that terror, but knew now that it was bloodlust. *Her bloodlust.*

She continued, her voice increasingly sexual, "But you are wrong about one thing."

He swallowed hard before replying, "And what's that?"

"That night at the barn, I didn't feel any connection with you. Someone must have gotten to you first," she started saying. He remembered meeting The Son before her. "I'm feeling the connection now. Which means I've marked you. You're mine. So if I were to push you instead of you jumping off yourself..."

"I'll die for real."

Sister pushed softly against his back. Not much strength was used but it was enough to cause him to tip forward. Snapping out of his trance, Tim bent his legs, looked up to the endless blue sky and jumped from the edge into the abyss below.

96

CHAPTER NINETEEN

Deuteragonists

"A question that sometimes drives me hazy: am I or are the others crazy?"
- *Albert Einstein: a documentary biography, Carl Seelig*

09:30 A.M.
10 days earlier

Tim woke to the clang of metal.

Detective Oliver Hardy stood at the grill bars, a plastic box in his hand. "You awake, kid?" he asked, his words kinder than his rough voice should allow.

"Yeah," Tim replied, stretching his back to relieve the soreness. He checked his watch and found it to be 9:31 in the morning and was surprised he had managed such a long sleep. "What's up?" He found the rugged male detective to be friendlier than his beautiful female counterpart, which, when based on stereotypical thinking, boggled his mind.

"Brought you breakfast." Oliver held up the plastic box.

Warily, but too hungry and tired to refuse the gesture, Tim approached the bar. The detective held the box through the grills and Tim took it without any problem. Opening the plastic lid, the inside contained just one miserable looking plain doughnut and an apple juice box.

"Wow," Tim said. "Looks tastier than oatmeal."

Oliver shrugged his shoulders, replying, "Jail food. Can't ask for much."

From the cell beside them, Pearlman voiced, "Here here!" in agreement. Oliver ignored him.

Tim took a bite out of the doughnut. It was nothing terrible.

97

"So what's this? You're the good cop, she's the bad cop?" Tim asked, referring to Detective Smith. "I'd prefer it the other way around. She's easier on the eyes."

"I get that a lot," the man replied. "But no, this isn't like that. I just don't think it's right to lock up a kid when the evidence is so flimsy."

Pearlman cut in again, "What about me?"

"You're going to rot," Oliver replied without hesitation.

Tim put the half eaten doughnut back in the box. The juice box was missing its straw so he dug open the aluminium covering with his nails and drank straight from the hole. The artificially sweetened apple juice washed down the chunky bread delightfully.

Oliver continued, "I'm going to see if I can arrange for your phone call."

"No need," Tim replied confidently. "I'll be out on bail before nightfall."

11:40 A.M.
10 days earlier

The basement of the library was where older records and books were kept. Hundreds of thousands of records arranged neatly in metal filing cabinets and stored in boxes on old warehouse shelves made of steel beams and cardboard. Contrary to the futuristic main library, the 100 meters long basement was dusty, and the aisles were lined with dim hanging incandescent bulbs that only lent a yellowish gloom. The walls were simply bricked, lazily painted with an uninteresting grey, not even white.

"Is it really okay to just leave him there?" Stella asked, looking up from the laptop monitor she worked from, connected to the Internet from one of the rare Ethernet ports, sitting on one of the rarer tables and chairs in the basement. In a leaf green top and brown pleated skirt, she was the only sight of nature in the noir tinted room, her strawberry blonde hair glowing a faint gold in the light.

Clay replied, "He probably wanted some time to think." He continued digging through the metal filing cabinet, occasionally puling out one of the laminated newspaper clippings, only to shove them back into their container. Sweeping off the layer of dust that had piled on his urban grey camouflaged shirt and mud brown cargo shorts, scratching his feet through the gaps in his sandals, he continued, "We should do as he says and go bail him out later."

Unconvinced, Stella continued, "If what he says is true, and his dad really did just die from Sin, shouldn't we be there to comfort him or something?"

Closing the file cabinet, he turned to his sister, "You know Tim. He gets emotional sometimes. But that voice mail he left us last night sounded as if nothing had happened."

"And that's good?" She cocked an eyebrow in question.

He took another deep breath. "I don't know. If – and I say if – I'm not wrong, he's trying to focus himself to help us with this Sin thing. I mean, if I were in his shoes, I wouldn't want my friends to end up dead as well. He'd probably want to keep the crying until everything's over."

"I guess..." she replied, equally uncertain. "I wonder what he's doing now?"

Clay pulled up a seat beside her. "Probably sleeping. I'd knock out too if I went through all that in one night."

"Maybe he dropped the soap," Stella said casually, turning the direction of the conversation like a bus about to crash.

"Uh...I don't think he's been in there long enough to need a bath."

Ignoring her brother, she continued, "Maybe he's jerking off."

"I'm not comfortable talking about my best friend's masturbation habits with my sister."

"Adopted sister," she corrected him.

"Still not comfortable."

"We can talk about your masturbation habits if you'd like?"

"Wait, you're doing that thing you always do with Tim aren't you?" Clay accused. "Where you guys talk about weird and creepy stuff and you try to top him all the time."

"Yeah...it's the little things that keeps me happy," Stella admitted with a smile before returning to her laptop screen. "And I've found something, if you're interested."

Clay dragged his chair closer. "What have you got?"

A photograph was open on her screen. It depicted a modest bedroom, ordinary save for the blood stains that splattered the walls and bed. The rest of the room was relatively neat, with the exception of the pillows strewn across the floor. "One of the guys on the forum worked the Vashmir case and when I told him what we're trying to do, he said he'd try to sneak some stuff for us."

"Isn't this illegal?" Clay asked, worried more about his sister getting caught rather than the notion of legality.

"Your face is illegal."

"Ouch." Clay brushed off the insult and asked, "What's so special about the picture?"

"This," Stella pointed to the desk barely visible in the corner. On it, there was a book with the blurred but readable words 'Journal' on it. "We haven't found much from our research. I'm guessing the officials wants to keep tabs on the information, for whatever reason. But if Vashmir Commons kept a journal..."

"He'd probably wrote his experiences down in it. Good going!" he praised, to which Stella blushed slightly. "Do we have an address?"

"Yeah," she showed an email sent to her by the forum user, which included the photo attachment and the Commons' address along with some helpless case files. "It's about half a day drive from here though."

"We'll probably be there for a day or two. And another day to drive to-and-fro. That's three days gone," Clay calculated. "Wait, more importantly, is the journal even at the house?"

"Yeah. The guy said that most of the personal belongings have been returned to the family by now. But they left the house a few months ago for a vacation and never came back."

"Good," Clay clapped his hands together, satisfied at their progress. "Now we just gotta wait for Tim."

"Yeah, he'd throw a fit if he knew we left without him."

04:11 P.M.
10 days earlier

"Heads," Tim said, hands stretched out from between the bars.

From the corner of his eyes he saw his jail-mate, Pearlman, open the palm of his hand to reveal the cardboard cut-out of a coin with a crudely drawn triangle on it.

Pearlman replied, "Nope, tails."

"How do you do that?" Tim asked after losing for the tenth time in a row.

"The trick's in the palm man," Pearlman replied with a proud tone. "Used to do magic tricks as a kid."

"How did you end up here then?"

"Oh you know, magic tricks turned to pickpocketing, then drug dealing. Etcetera etcetera. Here I am."

"Ever thought of going the straight and narrow?"

Pearlman sneered, "And how's that working out for you?"

Tim looked around his jail cell before replying sarcastically, "Not bad actually."

They both laughed at the joke and partially at their predicament. Their laughter was cut short as Detective Julianne Smith, followed by her partner, Oliver Hardy, came walking into view. Tim backed away from the cell's entrance.

The female detective snarled a little as she said, "Glad to know you're fitting in with the scum of the Earth."

With a sardonic tone, Tim replied, "'Hi' to you too, detective. But if you don't mind we'd like to get back to our brotherly bonding session right now." He heard Pearlman puff out a small laugh.

"I would love to keep you here forever," she replied.

Oliver cut in, "But you've been bailed out, Mr. Kleve." The male detective gave a look of surprise as if to convey, *just like you said.* He reached around his partner and with key in hand, unlocked Tim's cell door.

"Well, it was nice talking with you Pearlman," Tim said as he stepped out of the cell.

Pearlman replied, "Pleasure's all mine."

Tim still could not see his jail-mate's face from the angle. The stairs up were to his right at the end of the corridor, with a officer in blue standing guard at the entrance to it. Tim turned left to try to get a glimpse of his new acquaintance. However, Detective Smith forcefully grabbed him by the elbow.

"Let's not drag this disgusting charade out any longer," she barked.

"Fine," Tim replied, jerking his arm away from her grip. He headed for the stairs.

Oliver approached him before he could walk too far away. "The officer will take you upstairs to process your release."

"Got it, thanks," Tim replied, devoid of the hostility he held for Julianne, before leaving the detectives behind.

As he headed towards the escort, the female detective jabbed one last cliché at him, "Don't go far."

CHAPTER TWENTY

Days to the End of the World

"This is the way the world ends. Not with a bang but a whimper."
- Thomas Stearns Eliot, The Hollow Men

05:31 P.M.
10 days earlier

Gordon Barber was a black man that drove an SUV. The vehicle was black and slick, a large 8-seater for a small family. He once said it was for work, that having a large, shiny, black car was empowering and subconsciously drew in respect. Tim always felt that the man's constantly styled ghastly white hair and sharp maroon eyes were terrifying enough as they were to command the respect of any and all demonic legions. His crisp white shirt and steamed ironed pants were the splitting image of the modern businessman's version of a devil's advocate. For a long time, before knowing the kind soul underneath the otherwise straight-laced exterior, Tim had doubted the man's integrity.

"So," Gordon said to Tim as he drove passed a red light. The road was as empty as the previous days, if not, even more so. With little to no pedestrians and vehicles on the road, the way out of the city to the suburbs was as close to a ghost town as it could have gotten. There was nothing on the radio but static so they turned it off. "Are you okay, boy?"

It had been a while since Tim saw his best friends' father and had almost forgotten the latter's habit, similar to his son, of calling him by a child's title. "I'm fine, Mister Barber," he replied from the passenger seat. "Just a little shook up."

Gordon glanced over at him with a look of worry in his eyes. "Are you sure? After what happened to your father?"

The image of his father's body, unmoving, slumbering peacefully for eternity on his bed with a gash of blood on his shoulder flashed through Tim's mind. He closed his eyes to let the vision pass. "Yeah," Tim finally replied, reopening his eyes. "I guess things just haven't sunk in yet. With all the police interrogations and stuff, I'm still feeling a little on guard."

"This really is too much," Gordon hissed angrily. "Those detectives, arresting you like that! Don't you worry, boy. If anything happens, we'll get you a lawyer and everything!"

"You don't have to do that, Mr. Barber," Tim said. "I'm sure the state will provide a lawyer for me."

"Nonsense!" the man waved off the notion with one hand, keeping the other on the steering wheel. He spoke with a stern, energetic, but caring voice. "You're like family to Clay. A brother to my son is family to me. And don't worry about your father. Once they release the body, we'll pay for whatever funeral you want for him."

No matter how strong a person is, they would tear up at such an offer, Tim included. He drew a deep breath that rustled through his nose, clearing his watering eyes. "Thanks, Mister Barber."

The car turned down the streets that would lead to the exit out of the city. A peaceful but eerie silence fell over the vehicle as they passed through the once bustling market district. Only half a dozen of the popular roadside stores were still open for business, and a countable amount of customers dragged their feet through the streets.

Gordon, unable to bear the quiet any longer, broke it with, "It's like the end of the world here. And there's no news about anything either."

"What do you mean 'no news'?" Tim asked, his curiosity captured immediately.

They sped out of the market district at the first available exit. "The newspaper didn't arrive this morning, and none of the news sites online were updated either."

"What about blogs? Alternate news sites?"

"Most of them got shut down. It was kind of expected really. I was the only person at work yesterday. Even my boss was getting ready to leave and never come back," Gordon explained, staring intently at the road, as if in some kind of trance. "Can you imagine that, boy? All the knowledge and media we've mastered and garnered over the centuries, gone overnight."

"I wonder what happened?" Tim mused to himself. "Maybe they'll be back up tomorrow?"

"Don't count on it, boy," Gordon replied. "Best we can hope for is things not getting violent at this rate. This Sin thing is really taking an ugly turn."

He remembered the female detective, Julianne Smith, and how her partner, Oliver Hardy told him she thought Sin was just a case of mass hysteria. "Do you believe Sin is real?" Tim asked the older man.

"You'd have to be borderline retarded to think it's fake by this point," Gordon replied almost instantly. "Look around us. The only people out looks like they've had the life sucked out of them. I'm just glad it hasn't happened to us," the older man finished, unaware that both his children and Tim himself had Sin.

"I wonder what would make someone believe all this is fake?"

"Most people can't handle changes, especially bad ones," Gordon started off again without hesitation, as if the man had been waiting for questions like those his whole life. "When things go haywire, we rely on what we know, things that work and are effective. Be it religion or science or a lifestyle. We lean back and find our pillar of confidence, even if doing so might doom us all."

"Are we doomed?" Tim asked.

"Well, boy, truth be told, I think we were doomed to die the moment the A-bomb dropped."

06:21 P.M.
10 days earlier

Their SUV pulled up the driveway of the beach-side house. Almost as soon as the tires screeched up the pavement, the front door of the house opened, with Clay and Stella, followed by their mother – Matilda Barber with her white cotton candy hair – came trampling across the lawn and towards the vehicle. Gordon turned off the engine, marking the safe time for Tim to open the door, which he did so and jumped out of the car to a tight hug from Stella.

Stella was the first to speak. "Sorry about your father, Tim." She let go of him after.

Gordon circled the car and placed a reassuring hand on Tim's right shoulder. "You can stay with us as long as you like," he said, before heading to his wife and into the house.

From his left, Clay placed another strong grip on his shoulder, and once the door to the house closed behind his parents, he said, "We're not staying here tonight, by the way."

Tim looked quizzically at him. "What do you mean?"

Stella explained, "We have Vashmir Common's address. We think he might have kept a journal that could help us."

"And where is it?"

"About half a day drive up north," Stella replied.

"And how are we going to get there?" Tim asked again.

Clay replied, "We'll take my dad's car."

"We're gonna steal your dad's car?"

"We're borrowing, kid," Clay folded his arms, acting offended. "There's a difference."

Tim was surprised at the suggestion. He had known the Barber siblings ever since they were in preschool. Though the pair had a penchant for getting into trouble, they had never done anything illegal in the proximity of their parents.

Tim sighed and said, "I don't think this is the reason your father taught you how to drive though."

Stella brought up the point, "Well, you can drive, right?" she asked Tim.

"Yeah...but I don't have a license yet."

Clay added on, "Neither do I. What's your point?"

"Okay, I just got out of jail." Tim gestured with his hands the shape of a square to represent his cell. He then moved them to the side as a symbol of him moving out of it. "I don't reeeaa-lly want to go back in. The detective there's kind of a bitch."

"Look around you, kid," Clay replied, waving to the empty streets behind him. "There isn't exactly anyone left on the road to catch us. We're going. If you don't want to come with us, fine. But me and Stella are still going."

Tim sighed and concluded, "You're that serious about this?"

His best friend looked grimly back, "We're kind of running out of time, if you haven't noticed."

Defeated, he replied, "Alright, fine. I'll go with you."

Tim looked across the siblings to their house on the beach and thought of Matilda and Gordon Barber, the two adults who decided to take him in without questions and how he was about to betray their trust. "But promise me that once we get back, you guys tell your parents everything."

Clay, slightly taken aback by his behaviour asked, "When did you become such a stickler?"

Without hesitating, Tim replied, "Since my father died."

Stella started to tear up. "Tim..."

"If anything happens to us, they deserve to know. If these really are

105

going to be the last few days till the end of the world, we'll face it together. All of us. With no regrets and no questions between us left unanswered."

Clay's head bobbed back and forth in an unconscious nod. "Okay kid, we'll tell them. It's a promise." He placed both hands on Tim's shoulders and looked his friend dead in the eyes. "We leave at midnight."

CHAPTER TWENTY-ONE

The Road

"I'd rather laugh with the sinners than cry with the saints. The sinners are much more fun."
- Billy Joel

12:01 A.M.
9 days earlier

"Remember to block my parents' numbers before we leave," Clay reminded as he threw the bags of spare clothes into the back of his father's SUV. He had changed into a pair of blue shorts and a white shirt, wearing sandals for comfort for the long journey ahead. He closed the compartment door gently. "We don't want them calling us in some bad situation."

Tim complied, navigating the buttons on his old flip phone to activate the block function as he opened the passenger side door. Clay was designated to drive the first half of the way and Tim the second. The latter was also dressed for comfort, wearing a dark grey, loose fitting pair of pants and one of his many hooded shirts, this one brown.

Stella popped out from the door that connected the garage to the kitchen, locking the same door behind her. "I've left the letters on the kitchen counter." She had her strawberry blonde hair held back by a headband, wearing a cloudy blue dress and white slippers. "If we're going to leave, we gotta do it fast. Remember, dad's a light sleeper."

"I got it, I got it," Clay replied, annoyed as he circled to the drivers side and entered. His sister jumped into the back seat. "Okay, ready?"

Stella nodded to Clay from the rear-view mirror and Tim replied with a quick, "Yup."

Clay, with the remote for the garage door in hand, replied, "Let's do this!" he hit the button and the door rose clunkily, shaking and clattering as it did so. Reaching behind the wheel, he turned on the ignition, the engine churning awake.

Stella rushed, "Come on, come on!"

"The door's not high enough yet," Clay replied, as he readied to leave by shifting the gear into reverse.

The door to the kitchen started to shake and they could hear Gordon Barber's muffled shout from the other side.

Once the shutter was two-thirds the way up, Tim shouted, "Go!"

Clay reversed out of the garage just as the door to the kitchen burst open, Gordon standing there dumbfounded as he locked eyes with his son in the car. The vehicle roof scrapped under the garage door by mere centimetres, the car grinding out onto the pavement and onto the road.

Stella watched as her adopted mother ran out of the front door of the house, her hair bouncing as she moved, intending to chase the car on foot.

"Get us out of here!" she egged her brother on.

Clay turned the steering wheel tightly, shifted the gears, and floored the gas. The car careened in a small crescent before finding a path on the open suburban road before it. After a slight drift, Clay swivelled the steering wheel back and burst through the streets in a roar of speed.

Stella looked back towards their parents, her mother hopelessly chasing them until they turned out from the avenue. "I feel bad."

Once they were out of the radius of their neighbourhood, Clay slowed down his driving, making their way out of the suburbs and turning onto the long, straight highway that stretched to the horizons and out of Ridge Valley.

Finally given breath, Clay told Tim, "You should catch some sleep. I'll wake you up when it's your turn to drive."

"I'm fine," Tim replied, waving away the suggestion. "I've slept enough for the day."

Surprised, Tim let out a, "Huh," staring around the empty dreamscape he was thrown into. "Maybe I haven't slept enough."

He was on an empty road that stretched endlessly in all directions. Tall prairie grass surrounded him on both sides with mountains lining the horizon. The sun was not visible but still managed to bathe the fields in bright red. He no longer felt any discomfort in his stump of a right elbow. Though quite certain his injuries had healed – given the time difference he previously learnt about the dream world and the real world – he played it safe and kept the blood stained bandages on.

"Where the fuck am I now?" he asked, hoping to hear the white dressed Sister replying to him.

Cart turned on its heels...

Tim spun around to the sound of the words, sung by a young child's voice too pitched to be a boy but too rough to be a girl. About ten meters down the road, a large fire, which had not been there before, burned brightly by the roadside, an unidentifiable black heap in its centre.

Filled with blood and horror.

Taking wearied steps, Tim approached the inferno. The fire coiled and rose, dancing like snakes under charm. For a second, he could have sworn he saw a face within the flames.

Up. Down. Through the filth...

As he neared it enough to feel the heat, he could hear a harp playing softly in his head to the tune of the rhyme being sung.

Shoot the man turned monster!

Whatever was beneath the flames exploded, the force of the blast threw Tim on his back. He looked up and the fire seemed to part like a seam. From within the blaze, the Sawman stepped out, his straw hat untouched by the fire, not a scorch on his clothes.

"Shit!" Tim cursed, scrambling frantically to his feet, painfully supporting himself on what was left of his right elbow to stand faster.

But before he could fully get off the ground, the Sawman closed the gap between them and slashed at him with its weapon, barely missing Tim as he tumbled backwards, a poor attempt at dodging. Again, he fell, but without the strength to lift himself up a second time, he laid on his back, eyes closed, and waited for death. Only, the searing pain he was expecting from getting slashed by the saw never came.

His eyes opened, only to be instantly blinded by the bright light of the blue sky, a stark contrast to his previous dull red environment. Swinging wildly as he attempted to get back to his feet, eyes tearing as he frantically tried to regain his sight, he somehow managed to stand, stumbling around in a circle before his vision finally settled.

Taking in his new, brighter surroundings, he found himself on the roof of his school. It was a five-story building, with a view of the surrounding suburbs and the city's skyline in the distance. Ventilation turbines littered the cracked, grey concrete tiled floor at intervals. A similarly depressing grey box-like structure marked the roof access stairwell.

"I'm surprised to see you here," Tim turned to Sister, her white dress flowing at length behind as she calmly walked towards him, a sly smile on her innocent looking face. "Usually I'm the one who finds you. You must really miss me."

"What the hell, Sister?" he shot through her advances, physically closing in on the girl. He was still agitated from his encounter with the Sawman and attempted to slow his breathing, his heart a beating mess. "I just saw The Father!"

"What's so surprising about that?" Sister replied, seductively coiling her slender arms around his neck. "You are dreaming after all."

A third female voice, sing-song in tone, but nowhere near as melodic as Sister's, called out, "Tim?"

"Not now!" He raised his one hand to signal to the figure that he was busy. He told Sister, "It can't be him! No way!"

"Why?" Sister asked, leaning closer until he could clearly see the freckles on her face.

"Cause I killed him," he replied, lowering his voice to almost a hiss. "Stabbed a pipe right through his face and he turned to dust, right in front of my eyes."

"That's not possible," she pulled herself slightly back in genuine shock. "None of us can die here. We're gods of death for a reason."

The third voice asked again, "What happened to your arm?"

Tim shushed her with a "Later!" He returned his attention to Sister. "Then what's going on? You say he can't die but I'm pretty damn sure I murder-faced him at the warehouse."

The third person yelled, "Timothy Kleve! You will answer me right now!"

"What is it, Stell?" he shouted back, turning around to face his friend.

She stood with her arms crossed, wearing the red tunic, white tights and black slippers combo she wore to class almost two weeks ago. However, her hair, kept in a bun that day, had been untied and let to flow freely behind her.

He had not told the Barber siblings about him having Sin yet, and as the realisation of his appearance there dawned on him. He mouthed, "Oh shit," realising Sister's arms were still wrapped around him, he hastily swiped them away. "It's not what you think!" He could hear Sister snickering at his predicament.

In all the years Tim had known her, Stella had rarely looked as annoyed as she did then. "What's going on?" she asked sternly.

But just as he was about to answer, he heard the twang of the harp.

Tick. Tock. Goes the clock...

He asked the two girls, "Do you guys hear that?"

Jack is led to slaughter.

Sister replied, "Hear what?"

Tick. Tock. Goes the clock...

Stella too, said, "I don't hear anything," confirming his theory that

110

only he could hear the hymns.

Six days till the rapture!

A new sound intruded mid note. Perhaps the most terrifying sound he will never experience again in his life if he makes it through the entire ordeal. He would have nightmares about it till the day he dies.

Zoot. Zun. Zoot. Zun.

The group turned to the roof access door. Even though the sound was something in their heads, it seemed to have a direction.

"Okay," Stella said, her tone suddenly shaking. "I heard that one."

Zoot. Zun. Zoot. Zun.

"Sister?" Tim asked, remembering what she told him before about how the only way to get killed by a Family member is if that person had been marked by one of them beforehand, and how only one mark can exist on a prey at any one time. "Have you marked Stella?"

"No," she replied. "Didn't think I needed to." He also recalled how usually only one hunter is able to interact with one prey.

"Can you mark her now?" a loud bang echoed out of the door of the roof access as the Sawman hammered against it. He could visibly see the door vibrating even from the distance he stood from. "Like, right now, now?"

After a short second of silence from Sister, she replied, her tone as he had never heard it before, "I can't. The Father must have marked her."

Zoot. Zun. Zoot. Zun.

With a loud bang, the door tore from its hinges, exploding outward as if TNT had been placed behind it, flying through the air, over the roofs' edge and crashing to the ground floor below.

"Stella!" Tim shouted, extending his hand behind him. She grabbed it without hesitation and he instructed, "This way!" before pulling her in the opposite direction of the Sawman.

Practically flying across the rooftop, he crossed the short distance between where they stood and the edge in a sprint.

Stella asked, "Where are we going?"

They reached the edge of the roof. Even though they were looking down the deadly five stories drop, Tim did not feel his legs turning into jelly as it did previously when he stared down the plateau. Turning back, they watched as the Sawman step out of the doorway and onto the rooftop with the same feared confidence in its steps. Sister stood in the middle of the roof, watching the two groups.

Having never seen the man in the straw hat before, Stella asked, "What is that?

"Sorry about this," Tim put his hand on her stomach and before she could react, pushed her off the roof.

Her screams on the way down pierced him in the heart like daggers, but the sudden cut-off of her voice when she hit the ground was the bullet that stopped it. He had just murdered one of his best friends. Even though it was to save her life, the idea that he did it without hesitation still bit him harder than a shark.

Directing his attention to Sister, he pointed sternly at her and shouted, "We're still not done talking!"

The Father crossed the rooftop with the same lack of resistance to the laws of physics as Sister did before. With one last breath, Tim, without taking his eyes off his hunter, took a step back off the roof and plummeted to his death.

CHAPTER TWENTY-TWO

Secrets

"Three may keep a secret, if two of them are dead."
- Benjamin Franklin

08:11 A.M.
9 days earlier

The Pixie Diner was the sole establishment for food and gas for the last 200 miles to the town in which Vashmir Commons lived and died. As seen in most road trip movies, the roadside diner had the full 80's ensemble in its design. From black and white chequered tiles floor to the red leather upholsteries of the seats. The bar was lined with chrome plated metal, the counter-top marbled, and a jukebox was settled neatly in the corner playing pop music from the previous decade.

With the pandemic spreading, the diner had just two other patrons at the barstools while Tim and Stella sat in a corner booth. Clay struck up a conversation with the sole waitress at the bar, who also doubled as the cook that day, as she was the only one working.

Tim's mind was distracted by the intense staring contest that had erupted between him and Stella, the two of them not having said a word to each other since waking up from their sleep. Not wanting Clay to overhear their predicament, there had been a wordless, mutual agreement on temporary silence.

Tim was the one who broke the long silence with the first accusation, "You haven't been taking your medication!"

Not willing to be put in the hot seat, Stella, replied, "Well, you have Sin!"

"I don't think my issue is as pressing as yours right now."

"I'm fine. Nothing has happened all this time."

113

"What if you get killed?"

"By who? Sister?" She was genuinely surprised by the thought. "She's not going to hurt me."

Even though Tim did not fully trust the dream entity, Sister had yet to lead him astray. "Just be careful. We don't know what her game is."

"Right. Well, for now at least, I'm pretty safe," Stella reluctantly agreed. She seems to have realised that despite their relationship, Sister and her were still in a way, strangers. "But your hunter is openly after you."

"I can take care of myself."

"That's what my brother said at first," she punctuated with a look of worry. "Look at him now. Can't go a night without taking that damn Somnidin."

Tim replied, "Well, compared to your brother, I have a couple more options," referencing his ability to jump into other peoples' dreams, and his experience killing The Father once. Though the latter event was something Stella had yet to find out.

"I don't know how you do that." She rested her head on her hands, looking at him quizzically. "I've never heard of anyone jumping dreams before."

"Me neither," he admitted. "I only found out about it yesterday."

"And how long have you had Sin?"

"Four days, maybe." They fell into a short quiet as they contemplated what else to ask of each other.

Stella's tone shifted grimly as a question popped into her head. She asked, "Were you there?"

It didn't take his keen sense of deduction to know what she was referring to. "Yeah. Looked him in the eye till the last second," he recounted the death of his father.

Stella took his right hand and cupped it in both of hers. Her small hands just barely encasing his fist. "I know you're not the type but...you can cry, you know?"

"I'll do that once all this is over."

Sighing, resigned to the stoicism of Tim's emotional state, her only card left of a helping hand was to offer him her share of Somnidin.

He replied, "Thanks. I'll get some from you when I need it."

"Don't take too much though. It's addictive."

"So I've heard." He stared out the window and at the empty highway, recollecting how throughout the drive, there had not been any significant traffic. The bell above the door chimed out as the two other patrons left the diner. "Which reminds me, we have to set some rules."

"For what?"

"The only thing I know right now about this 'dream jumping' is that it only happens when I'm physically close to another sleeping person with Sin," he explained his observation. "And since we don't want Clay to find out–"

"We?"

"Yeah! If Clay finds out about this, he's going to lose focus. He's just gonna worry about me as well and, knowing him, he might just go all hero on us and do something stupid like..." He held out two fingers to air-quote. "Self-sacrifice."

"You have a point there." She recalled the incident with the drug dealer, Adam.

"Right, so that means when he's sleeping, I have to stay awake. So I can only sleep with you."

Stella raised her eyebrows and pulled a playful grin, replying, "Sexy."

Immediately realising his mistake, he waved his hands in vehement denial, "No! Not like that! I mean, I should only sleep while you're asleep, or at least, when Clay's awake. And one of us should take Somnidin so we don't both get in trouble with me jumping dreams. Don't want a repeat of me bringing that Sawman to you."

"That's too bad. Guess I'm just not good enough for you," she smiled playfully.

Sarcastically, he laughed, having gotten used to her playful advances. "You're pretty, but not my type."

Clay returned to the table with a tray of food in hand. Three identical breakfast sets of sausages, scrambled eggs, bacon strips, and cups of coffee. "You guys won't believe what I've found," he exclaimed as he passed the food around before taking a seat beside his sister. "Alright, the waitress says Vashmir's town has been blocked off. No one has gone in or out in the last twenty four hours."

Shocked at the new information, Tim exclaimed, "What happened?"

Clay explained, "A riot apparently. People going crazy, looting pharmacies for Somnidin, raiding police stations, all that junk. The rioters barricaded most of the main roads and the cops are struggling to contain the rest."

Stella asked, "Why haven't we heard about this?"

"The media's been down since yesterday," Tim theorised, based on his talk with Gordon Barber the previous day. "If cities like ours just went down, I guess it's safe to say that small towns probably got taken off the grid even earlier."

The girl gracefully sliced through the sausage on her plate, "Guess we can't get to the Common's place then." She took the slice of meat, brought it delicately up to her palette, and ate it with a closed mouth, chewing softly.

Her brother on the other hand, clanked through his meal, the metal utensils clinking the ceramic loudly. After swallowing the eggs he had practically shovelled into his gullet, he continued, "Not true. Turns out, their place is on the edge of the town. We could go off road, circle round the perimeter and sneak in."

Nodding with approval as he chewed off a strip of bacon, Tim replied, "That could work. Sneaking around angry mobs, armed policemen, violent looters, and crazy Somnidin junkies; to look for the home of a dead man murdered by vicious dream entity. Sounds fun."

012:22 P.M.
9 days earlier

Clay snoozed quietly in the back seat, his body laying across all three of the seat cushions. Having happily passed over the driving detail to Tim, he took two pills from his diminishing supply of Somnidin and promptly fell asleep. On the passenger side, Stella also decided to take a short nap, her seat tilted backwards at a gentle incline for comfort.

For Tim, the past hour had been spent staring at an increasingly bleak highway. Initially, there were a few cars passing every other ten minutes or so. But as they got closer to the town, the numbers dwindled till him not having seen another soul for hours. He had been unable to turn on the car radio and was left with listening to the rumble of the engine. With farmlands on both sides for as far as he could see, and dark clouds that hung in the distance, his sense of forebode only intensified.

"There's no rain either," he muttered to himself, staring at the clouds. "Creepy. I don't like this."

Stirring from her sleep, Stella replied, "Neither do I."

Tim took a quick look to his side to find her seemingly fresh and fully awake, having none of the symptoms of having just gotten out of her sleep, the elegant teen simply readjusted her reclined chair upright and sat with her hands cupped neatly in her lap, scanning the outside world. The car started up a long, gentle hill.

"How was your nap?" Tim asked, feeling slightly more energetic now that he had a companion to talk to again after the long drive.

"Didn't run into my brother," she stated, though not the reply he was

116

expecting. "So the dream jumping thing is uniquely you I'm guessing. But then again, he has Somnidin."

"Did you talk with Sister?"

"I did. She told me about all the things you did, and how you killed that Father creature once?"

Taking a quick look in the rear view mirror to make sure Clay was still asleep, Tim replied, "I did. Or at least, I thought I did."

"That might be a key to how to beat this thing, what you did."

As they lolled over the edge of the hill, Tim slowed the car to a halt. "One problem at a time," he said, staring in shock and awe at the scenery before him.

"One problem at a time," Stella repeated, equally stunned.

Black smoke continued to rise from half of the buildings of the town of Roagnark, with cars burning in the streets. A makeshift barricade had been formed a couple of miles down the main road, blocking the entrance with scorched abandoned cars. Blue and red lights of emergency vehicles flashed across the canvas of buildings of the two mile long town, occasionally flickering out, followed by flashes of flame.

Under her breath, Stella whispered, "Ocean of fire."

Dreams of fire,

"What?" Tim asked, unsure if he heard her right, nor of the meaning behind her words. He turned back to look at Clay, asleep from the drugs.

Salves of healing.

"The town," she explained, "It's like the ocean has been set aflame."

"Are one thy?" he mumbled the lyrics. "Are one thy?

CHAPTER TWENTY-THREE

Borderline Dangerous

"Dreams so often become nightmares. Family can so easily become foes. And people are always more stupid than you give them credit for."
- Mike A. Lancaster, 0.4

01:20 P.M.
9 days earlier

A mile west off the main road and a football field away from the nearest building, the group left the black SUV behind a large rock formation, barely hidden from the line of sight of the town. Tim wished that they had stopped by an auto shop on the way and painted the exterior to a lighter colour for camouflage. He shared the idea with the group.

Unloading their backpacks from the trunk, Clay sounded out, "Don't be stupid. The nearest auto shop is in the town."

They each had a set of flashlights, two water bottles, and matching hand-held radios. After assessing the situation in town, they also decided it'd be best if they each had a weapon with them. Clay returned Tim's air rifle while Stella equipped herself with the one they disarmed from Joseph two days before. Though the weapons were non-lethal at range, they served as a steadfast distraction and their wooden stocks could be used in close encounters. After some contemplation, Clay settled for a lug wrench they found in the car's toolbox.

After having cold lunch from food they bought at the diner, they changed into clothes more fitting for the situation than a long drive. Clay put on a fresh grey shirt and a cargo shorts whose pockets he stuffed with multi-tools from the garage, a lock-blade knife from his father, and a spare battery for his phone.

When asked why he decided to turn himself into Doraemon, Clay

118

replied, "I like to be prepared," while putting on a pair of waterproof hiking shoes.

Tim kept his hooded shirt but switched to cargo pants instead. However, he did not stuff his pockets with what he considered to be useless trinkets. He got kicked out of the car by Stella after putting on a pair of canvas shoes, followed shortly by Clay. They were directed behind the rock formation while she changed into a green top, blue jeans, and brown leather boots.

When they returned from their exile, Tim asked, "Do you really need to dress so stylishly?"

She sarcastically replied, "Be glad I didn't do my make-up, okay?"

Once ready, the group set out across the plains. Though it was relatively early in the afternoon, the smog from the small fires that had spread across the town had blocked out a good amount of sunlight, making the journey comparatively cooler than it otherwise would have been. They walked diagonally westward towards the outer perimeter of Roagnark.

Stella chimed in as their vehicle disappeared from their view, "I hope we don't run into any coyotes."

Tim explained, "It's still lights out. The animals shouldn't be that active yet."

He never admitted that he had worried about the coyotes.

2:30 P.M.
9 days earlier

Greeneries began sprouting into view as they neared the suburbs of the town. The riots were apparently concentrated in the town square and main roads, with the residential districts relatively unscathed. Clay took the lead of their motley crew of three and whenever he sighted any looters or potential threats, signalled for Tim and Stella to stop and waited for whatever situation that happened to pass.

"We don't get involved," Clay kept reminding the two. "We're here for the diary."

The trio progressed through the town slowly, clearing the distance of two blocks of buildings in slightly over half an hour. Looters escaping the town centre stampeded through the streets with their stolen goods. Stella held mapped out they had twelve more blocks to go through before reaching the Commons' household.

As Clay leaned out slightly from the corner wall they hid behind, Stella asked, "Maybe we should just cut through the back alleys. Looks

119

like most of the rioters are on the main road anyway."

"Good idea," her brother replied, watching a group of looters smashing through the display window of an electronics store. "If we continued at this rate, we would get to Vashmir's place by sundown."

They circled back and around the apartment buildings, dodging into an alleyway that led straight through for half a dozen blocks.

Clay instructed Tim, "Watch our backs, kid."

The latter complied, carefully walking backwards as he kept an eye on the alley entrance. Shrieks of terror and sadistic screams bounced off the parallel buildings by their sides, echoing an eerie sound of nature. Compared to the barren alley, the town around them seemed to almost be at war with itself. Sirens continuously blared and whenever it seemed they had faded into the distance, a new set of sirens began their audio reign.

Then, a woman's gut wrenching scream sliced through the alley. It wasn't like the ones from the town square. The source for this one was right down their paths from one of the buildings before them.

Clay whispered out, "Shit."

The back door of an apartment building to their left burst opened and a man in a denim jacket with a black hood, bloodstained white shirt and torn jeans bolted out of it. He turned towards the trios' direction and started to run, but immediately noticed them and, nearly falling over as he did so, made a 180 degree turn for the other direction.

From the door the man came from, a woman dressed in teal shorts and a green top jumped out after him, blood flowing down a wound in her short red hair. She ran barefooted across the pavement, cutting off the man with her arms opened wide, attempting to block him despite their size difference.

"Please!" she shouted in a begging tone, "My son needs those meds!"

Tim scanned the hooded man and noticed the pill bottle he held in his left hand. "Somnidin," Tim whispered under his breath, just loud enough for Clay and Stella to hear.

The man tried to walk past the woman, but she desperately reached out and clung onto his arms with both hands. He punched her in the cheek with his free hand, sending the woman crumpling to the ground in a groan of pain.

Tim took a step forward only to be stopped by Clay's outstretched arm. "Don't get involved," the white-haired teen repeated.

Now freed, the man began walking away, only to be held back again as the woman reached out feebly, just barely managing to grab hold onto the hem edge of his jeans.

Weak from the powerful strike, she only managed a groan.

"Please...my son..."

From his belt, the man pulled out a pistol which Tim recognised immediately as a Glock 22 from countless movies and television shows. "Clay..." he begged his friend to act.

"We don't get involved," Clay replied coldly. He passed Tim his bottle of Somnidin from his pocket and, contrary to what he said, the former started walking towards the conflict. "We don't get involved."

The man raised the pistol towards the downed woman's head and growled, "Let go, bitch. It's every man for himself now."

From behind Tim, Stella shouted, "Hey!" she raised her air rifle to the man. "You want this?" Holding the light gun in one hand, she took out her bottle of Somnidin from her back pocket and waved it at the man.

Realising what the siblings were trying to do, Tim aimed down the sights of his rifle at the man, shaking his pill bottle as he did so, attracting the guys attention. "I've got some too!" he exclaimed.

The hooded man turned to the three teenagers, gun still pointed at the woman. When he first saw the guns, a look of panic stretched across his face. But the moment he took notice of the drugs, his eyes widened and a toothy smile glued itself to his lips.

Breathing heavily, the man said in a low, croaking voice, "Give them to me...now...now!"

Tim started circling the man clockwise while Stella did the same in the opposite direction. He replied, "Give the lady her pills back first."

The man redirected his gun to Tim. Unlike the air rifle, the pistol was real and Tim instinctively knew the man was not bluffing about its fire-power.

"Hey!" Stella called out, and the man turned his aim at her instead. She continued to circle him in a counter-clockwise direction. Giving him a playful smile, she shook her pill bottle again. "You want this? Drop you gun."

"I'm not stupid!" the man replied. "Why don't you drop your toys and I don't shoot your pretty face, girl?"

Tim, having crossed the 9 o'clock mark on his circling, replied, "You're not stupid, you say?"

The man turned, his crazed state of mind forgetting there was a second person behind him.

"That's not what I see."

"Shut up!" He turned frantically between Tim and Stella, the two now walking towards each other, having both passed by the man from where they started. "Stop moving you little shits!" He swiped his gun frantically between the two.

121

Stella smugly replied, "What are you going to do about it?"

He cocked the gun and settled on her as the target. From behind him, Clay brought the iron lug wrench down hard on the man's nape, the impact sending the gunman flying forward and off his feet before crashing face down on the ground.

"Woohoo!" Stella raised her hands in glee, her rifle over her head. "Teamwork!"

Clay squatted down beside the now unconscious man. Checking his wrist, he found a pulse that brought a breath of relief from him. After disarming the man and storing the gun in his back right pocket, covered by his over-sized shirt, he retrieved the bottle of Somnidin and helped the woman to her feet.

He asked her, "How's your head, ma'am?"

"It's just a scratch," she replied, attempting to wipe away her tears only to smear the blood from her forehead across her cheeks. "Thank you."

"Good," Clay looked down at the bottle of drugs in his hand.

The woman reached out to take the pills back from him but he backed away, bringing the bottle up to his chest protectively. In a nervous mumble, he said, "No..."

When he noticed, Tim rushed up to his best friend. "Clay!"

Clay turned to Tim and Stella, who stood by with looks of worry etched into their otherwise fearless personalities. "Kid..." With shaking hands, he quickly passed the bottle back to the woman and turned away from her. "Lock your doors. Don't come out until this is over."

Controlling the sudden shudders that had taken over his body, Clay walked to his friend and sister. A soft whisper of a second thanks came from behind him as he listened to the apartment building door close with a rusty creak.

Stella walked up to her brother and placed a caring hand over his cheeks. "You okay?"

He cupped a hand over hers and leaned into the warmth of his beloved sister. "Yeah." They hugged.

Tim slung his rifle over his back as Clay unwillingly reminded him of the grim reality of the situation before them. "The world's gone crazy."

The trio turned down the alley and watched a new stream of smoke rise from the town centre, snaking it's way into the sky to join the already dark clouds above.

Tim continued, "And we're just a bunch of kids. Are we really going to be able to stop this?"

Stella replied, "We're doing this because no one else has stepped up to the plate."

"Plus," Clay added, "We're trying to save our own skin. But whatever the reason, we're going to do it."

"We're nuts," Tim finished.

Clay let out a puff of derision. "Good. We'll fit right in."

CHAPTER TWENTY-FOUR

Don't Look Back

"It is sometimes an appropriate response to reality to go insane."
- Philip K. Dick, VALIS

4:34 P.M.
9 days earlier

At the centre of the intersection of Vashmir Common's street, a pile of body burned. With no one left to bury them, the deceased were cremated in bulk. Even from where they stood, Tim could smell the stench of the burning bodies.

Stella turned away. "Let's uh...let's move on."

The rest agreed and the trio continued down to the their destination.

Vashmir Commons' townhouse was lodged between a sex shop and a biker bar. For Tim, it didn't matter if the shops came before or after the house, being equally disturbing a location to live in either way. Someone had decided it was appropriate to either build those shops around the house, or build a house around the shops.

Stella noted, "Doesn't look like anyone's home."

Most of the blinds of the building were drawn shut, and those not were boarded up by wooden planks. Unlike the other buildings surrounding the trio, the Commons' two story black-bricked Victorian was the sole structure left untouched by looters or rioters. A group of wandering bandits simply circled around the building, staring with amazement at the three teenagers that stood before it. Eyes gazed out of the apartment buildings opposite the street, fearfully watching their every move.

Clay scanned the people, meeting their gazes, only to have them break eye contact or duck away into the darkness of their homes. "That's not creepy at all," he noted sarcastically.

124

From his bag, Tim pulled out a flashlight and the others followed suit. "Let's get this over with."

He climbed the steps and opened the door to his side, letting Clay and Stella in first. Tim turned back and analysed the streets, seeing something in the eyes of the watchers aside from fear.

"Reverence," Tim mumbled his observation. Turning his back on the watchers, he closed the door behind them.

In the main hallway, darkness swallowed most of the corners. The light that gleamed through the blinds barely made it past their rooms to even reach them.

"The power's out," Clay deduced as he flicked the light switch a few times before they turned on their flashlight.

The trio ran their beams over the hallway, their lights reflecting hazily on the plastic sheets that covered the leftover furniture.

Tim asked Stella, "I thought you said Vashmir had a family?"

"He did," she replied. "But they left for vacation quite a while ago. Never bothered to return. Maybe they've moved?"

"Too many memories in a home like this, I guess," Clay continued, "And from the looks of the people outside, nobody's likely to disturb us."

Tim replied, "Good. There will be no one stopping us from ransacking the place. Let's split up. You and Clay search around here. I'll go upstairs and see what I can find."

As Tim stepped onto the steps of the stairs, Clay spoke, "Remember to look for the diary, kid. That's what we came for."

Tim gave a thumbs up as Clay headed into the living room and Stella left to explore the rest of the first floor. Tim watched their lights fade as the siblings dispersed to their own investigations before turning back up the stairs.

Dried and lacking maintenance for unknown months, the wooden boards creaked and bent with every step. The darkness was disorienting. He fully expected that when he looked back up, the Sawman would be staring back at him from the landing, having crossed the boundaries of realities and dreams in its hunt for him.

When he reached the second floor and do so however, he saw nothing but a wall with an oil painting of a farm in the countryside. "Get a grip," he criticised himself.

The second floor corridor was bland and straight. Without any windows, it stretched into the void until he brought his light up. Equally plain with lighting as it was without, the two doors on the left stood out in the empty path like a baseball player on a soccer field. Stepping fully into the shadow, he headed for the closest door to him.

125

Surprisingly, the old oak door opened noiselessly and without resistance. Peering in, the room was somewhat lit by the light that seeped through the curtains. Though the room was large, only a single bed frame – devoid of its mattress – was kept in it. It wasn't hard to conclude there was nothing there from sight alone so he closed the door behind him and headed for the second one further down. Once there, he faced the closed entrance, a gut feeling telling him that this was Vashmir Commons' room.

Then his flashlight went out and threw Tim into complete darkness. Panicking, he leapt forward to find the knob, only to smash his nose into the wall instead. Losing his balance, he was about to tumble over when his outstretched hand found the metal grip. Using it, he pulled himself up to regain his balance, only to crash face first onto the floor of the room as his grasp slipped and the door opened inward.

"Ow," he groaned as he lifted himself off the ground.

"Kid?" he heard Clay shout. "You okay?"

"Yeah," Tim replied, watching the blood from his nose drip onto the blue carpeted floor. "Just tripped over myself, that's all."

Getting to his feet, he scanned the room while rubbing his bleeding nose with his shirt, knowing full well it would stain. His nose did not feel fractured or broken, but the bruising pain still lingered enough to make his eyes water.

The first thing he noticed was that the windows had been boarded up, but not enough to prevent rays of light from shining through, floating in the air on the reflection of dusts, platforms of light in suspension. Aside from that, the room was the same as the one from the picture Stella had showed him. Dried blood still stained the walls and the yellow-green striped bed sheets. Even the pillows were left untouched on the floor and he wished he had the luck to have fallen on them instead. The room was a stark contrast to the otherwise emptied-out house, and an even stranger scene when the blood was factored in.

A small desk was installed into the wall closest to the window, which was where the diary was placed in the photo. The sole difference between the picture from months ago and the present was the cardboard box on the desk then. Though the hair on his hands stood and Tim felt his heart was beating fast enough to punch a hole through his ribs, he managed to gather enough strength after a deep breath to approach the table.

In large red lettering, 'EVIDENCE' was stamped on the side of the box. A piece of paper detailing the contents and identity of the owner, in this case, Vashmir Commons, was pasted on the lid. A 'Diary' was listed as one of the things kept in the box.

Sure enough, when he opened the lid, the leather bound diary was at the top of the pile. He took out the book and set it aside on the table and rummaged through the remaining items in the box. A stained shirt, a toothbrush, and a pen missing its cap. Nothing of interest.

Returning his attention to the diary, he unfettered the strap that held the book closed and flipped randomly to one of the middle pages. Vashmir wrote of his day at work and a few other thoughts about his life. Again, nothing out of the ordinary. Running his fingers through the edge of the book, he found the last few entries of the man and glanced through from there instead.

They keep coming. Every night. I can't take it. Everyone's telling me I'm just having bad dreams but I know they are real. When I wake up, I feel the pain from all the falls I took while running. My friends keep telling me to see a doctor. They don't know I already am. It's not helping. I'm not crazy! It's been three days since I've last slept. I don't think I can keep it up much longer. So tired. But they're coming.

It seemed obvious to Tim that the man was suffering from Sin, but he reminded himself that at that time, it was not a recognised phenomenon and understood why Vashmir would have been taken for being insane. He flipped the pages, glancing at lines after lines of similar experiences from night to night. Then an entry popped up, shorter than the previous half dozen.

I met a guy in the dreams. He said he can get me out. Give me power to fight back. All I have to do is agree to his conditions.

The record abruptly ended, and the pages after that contained no other entries. Tim turned through the remaining pages of the diary and after over a dozen empty pages, he found one sentence scrawled hastily, all in uppercase letters, in red ink across two full pages near the end of the book.

THE END IS HERE!

Tim turned to the next page and was bombarded by scrawls of red ink and dabs of blood, all repeating the same message.

The world will end in 139 days and we will ascend. The world will end in 139 days and we will ascend. The world will end in 139 days. In 139 days. 139 days. The world will end. We will ascend. 139 days. In 139 days. 139. 139. 139 139 139 139 139 139

The number continued to repeat itself, covering the rest of the pages before Vashmir, having found no other room on the two pages to continue, started filling in the gaps between the lines with the number.

"What the fuck?" Tim let out, closing the book in fear. He had never thought pure text would be able to spook him out as much as the diary had.

He stored the diary in his backpack and almost immediately, the bag felt heavier, as if the weight of the diary consisted of the physical manifestation of Vashmir's experience with Sin. The teen turned back to leave the room, again expecting some sort of spectral form of the late Vashmir to appear before him, ready to murder him for going through it's belonging, but no such entity existed.

Exiting into the corridor, he left the door to Vashmir's room open to allow some light to guide him. He headed back past the empty room with the soundless door, ignored the farm painting on the wall, and went down the dry stairs with the eerie creaks. A wave of relief washed over him as he heard the voices of Clay and Stella coming from the living room. He entered after them.

The pair stood in the middle of an otherwise normal looking living room, save for the obvious empty space on the television table. All the remaining furnitures had been wrapped in plastic. A fireplace resided in the corner, though Tim was sure he had not seen any chimney from the outside.

Tim asked the pair, "You guys find anything?"

They turned to him and Clay held up a large, soot covered book. "Photo album. Seems like the Commons tried to burn it but fucked up, since the fireplace isn't even real."

Stella added, "But most of it is covered in soot or damaged. Lot's of the pictures will take some cleaning to get anything out of them. Did you get the diary?"

Tim thumbed to the bag on his back as a sign of affirmation. She then shone her flashlight light over his face, temporarily blinding him. "Hey," he called out in discomfort.

"What happened to your nose, kid?"

"You're bleeding."

"Fell," Tim replied. "Can we just get out of here? This place gives me the creeps."

Stella took the light off him, granting him vision again. Clay noted, "I've never seen you scared before."

"Yeah, well, you haven't seen what's in the damn diary. Come on, let's get back to the car before sundown."

Stella corrected, "S.U.V."

CHAPTER TWENTY-FIVE

The Man with the Remote Control

"We revel in the laxness of the path we take."
- Charles Baudelaire

Tim thought the scene in front of him was straight out of a classic horror movie. The television in the dark room showed a repeating loop of a Tom and Jerry's cartoon where the mouse joined a space program. It would have been a relatively normal dreamscape had he not been standing behind a single red leather recliner that faced the television, away from him. An on-screen explosion lit the surroundings in a bright flash akin to lightning, revealing the outline of hundreds of skeletons and decomposing bodies surrounding the chair.

Run. Tim thought to himself.

The image of the moat of corpses stayed vivid in his mind, even as the reduced glow from the television diminished his sight. The bodies' positions suggested they died scrambling away from the chair, creating an odd doughnut of corpses where the middle was bare.

But running's hard.

His body still could not move. It felt tired, about to fall asleep. He wondered what would happen if he fell asleep in the dream world. Maybe he would wake up. Maybe he would die.

Maybe I'll turn into a frog.

Despite his inability to command his body, his legs began walking towards the recliner on its own. Desperately fighting the urge to sleep, he staggered leftwards in his failing attempt to regain control of his feet. He looked back up to the recliner and saw the left facing portrait of a pot-bellied man in white sleeveless shirt and boxer shorts, intensely watching the show, not once laughing at the gimmicks of the cat and mouse nor paying any heed to his existence. Right leg first, he took a step up onto the

129

pile, bones crunching beneath his feet.

"Tim!" Sister shouted from behind him.

He felt her cold hand gripped his right shoulder and with a heavy yank, she spun him around to face her. White-eyed with worry, Sister placed both of her hands on his arms to prevent him from toppling over from weariness. He felt the sudden urge to walk back towards the man in the recliner.

"Give it a moment," she said, tightening her grip as his body made a lazy attempt to turn around. "You'll get control back soon."

Voice slurring, he asked, "Who...is...that?"

"The Uncle. Don't worry, he's not under The Father," she explained.

A wave of energy washed over him without warning, as if he had just been woken up by an alarm clock and downed an entire can of energy drink at the same time. His knees buckled as his sleeping body unsuccessfully tried to catch up to his mind.

He fell forward, but was caught in an embrace by the petite girl. "I got you," she said with heaving breaths from his weight. Clumsily, he managed to jelly-leg his way back to standing. "I got you."

"Thanks," he replied. They pulled themselves apart. Breathing deeply, Tim continued, "But...holy crap! What the hell was that?"

She took a hold of his hand and led him away from The Uncle. The further the pair was from him, the brighter their surroundings became, until he could make out the outline of the corridor they walked in and the door placed at the end.

She explained, "The Uncle can literally tire you to death. It'll get to the point where you won't even have the energy to open your eyes."

"And what did you mean by him not being under The Father?" he skipped forward and asked, absorbing information as fast as his brain allowed.

"He's not a hunter. His victims goes to him. The Father has no need for someone that doesn't openly kill. Your luck must be terrible if you managed to fall into his world."

The couple reached the end of the hallway. Without hesitation, she flung the door opened, blinding him with the light from the outside. He felt the tug on his arm as she dragged him out into the Sun.

Even before his vision adjusted, he could already hear the sound of the waves beating against the shore and felt the breeze of the sea on his skin. Standing on a wooden pier with the Sun half set into the ocean on the horizon, he breathed in the fresh air of the parallel world. Bathed orange by the sunset, the world looked as if filtered summer itself.

He jumped as the door behind him slammed shut and he turned to see a wooden fishing hut built into the side of the pier. It was nowhere near large enough to accommodate the room they had exited from but Tim had long since stopped questioning the physics of the dream world.

"Is he okay?" he heard Stella's voice. He turned back as Sister let go of his hand. Despite her grip being ice cold to the touch, he felt his heart sink as she released him.

Sister approached Stella as she jogged down the pier, still wearing the same red tunic and white tights from their previous in-dream meeting.

"He's fine. Poor boy's a little groggy that's all," she replied condescendingly, though her tone was playful.

Rubbing his eyes to regain some form of concentration, he remembered what he had asked of Stella before falling asleep in the car on their way back. "Did you tell her about what happened?"

"Yeah. The diary, the photo album, the birthmark on your butt. Everything."

"Why did you tell her about my birthmark?"

"I just thought it'd be funny," she grinned.

Tim stood stunned as the cogs of his mind worked to place a missing puzzle piece. "How did you know about my birthmark?"

Stella replied with cheeky smile. "Not telling." The girls laughed.

Feeling a headache coming along, he diverted the topic back onto a serious track. "So, Sister, is there anything you can tell us about Vashmir that could help?"

She shook her head, "Nothing comes to mind. I think this is another dead end for you."

Thinking her reply as strange, he folded his arms in thought and said while contemplating, "That can't be right..."

Sister whispered to Stella, "He's so hot when he's all serious."

Ignoring them, Tim continued, "In Vashmir's diary, he specifically mentioned being chased by The Family. That means he wasn't being targeted by just one of you."

Stella caught on and pointed out, "So he's like you?"

Sister replied, "How can that be? I don't remember anyone before Tim who had multiple encounters."

"It's likely he just got lucky and ended with only one hunter each time. Or maybe you've only ever met him by yourself," Tim theorised. "It's like with The Uncle. Back then, you guys didn't hunt openly. You don't jump for the people who are still alive. Maybe that's why you didn't find him all the time, cause you were focused on your respective preys."

The goddess of death nodded, "Okay, that makes sense." Tim felt a grim chill at her not denying they were her 'preys'.

But Tim had another theory in mind that was even more worrisome, but did not have a single shred of evidence to point to it; that someone else was working behind the scenes, even further away into fantasy than the dream world.

Stella added, "There's one thing I'm not getting. Vashmir wrote that he made a 'deal'. What's this deal?" She looked to Sister for answers.

She replied, "I don't know. The only one of us who makes deals is The Mother."

Tim remembered the woman with the fire-red hair from the barn, who stood dry despite being out in the rain. "The woman in the business clothes."

"That's her," Sister acknowledged. "She gives you what you want in exchange for your soul."

Having read her fair share of horror books about demons and deals with the devils, Stella scoffed at the premise of The Mother's powers. "That's really cliché don't you think? Who in the world in this time and age still falls for that sort of trick?"

"Enough to keep her busy," Sister replied.

"So we go look for The Mother and interrogate her," Tim suggested. Though he knew that it was an act that was easier said than done. Weary of their odd and grim situation, Tim sighed, "Interrogating a supernatural being. This is some fucking dream."

Suddenly, he felt as if he had been injected by a dose of anaesthesia and fell to his knees. He looked up to see the two girls continuing their conversation as if nothing was happening to him.

He asked, "What's going on?"

Stella replied, "You're waking up." Having experienced more of the phenomenon herself, she was not only stoic about the situation, but also sounded confused at his lack of knowledge.

"Normally for once. Without dying that is," Sister added. She bent over seductively, showing cleavage through her soft white dress, leaning her face in to his, close enough for him to smell her cherry scented breath. His vision started to cross and fatigue overtook his physical body. She kissed him on the nose, devilishly whispering, "Sleep tight."

The sunbathed ocean was engulfed by darkness.

12:54 A.M.
8 days earlier

Tim woke up in the passenger seat of the S.U.V with Clay at the wheel. The in-built digital clock flashed from 12:54 to 12:55 and the darkness that surrounded them on the highway confirmed the time as past midnight. As before, no cars crossed, trailed, or led them. Surrounded by the smog of night, even the stars seemed to have disappeared within the clouds. Only their headlights were left to shine a path ahead on the dark and empty road.

Rubbing his eyes awake as he adjusted to the change in scenery, he realised it was the first time since he had gotten Sin that he had the chance to wake up normally. He sat watching the seconds blink on the digital clock, wondering if it would be his first and last 'normal' awakening from the nightmares.

He asked Clay, "Why didn't you wake me up?" His shift to drive had started almost an hour ago.

"I couldn't sleep so I thought I'd drive it off. Too much shit in my head."

"Like what?"

"All the normal shit in my head."

Tim turned to the back to see Stella still peacefully asleep across the seats. One of Clay's oversized jackets covered her body. Her brother must have stopped mid-drive to get it from the trunk.

Clay continued, "You were pretty amazing back there. Against that thug."

"Can't say I was terrified though." Tim turned back to watch the road, remembering how oddly composed he had felt during the event. "But you were the one who stepped up first."

"I don't know how you can be so calm. I was scared shit-less, kid. Especially when the dude pointed his gun at me." Clay fixed his attention to the road even as he spoke. The reflection of light from the front highlighted the dark rings around his eyes. "Didn't even know if you or Stella noticed how bat-shit crazy the man was, or even what to do with that."

"We're not stupid you know."

"I know. But it just feels like we've been trusting our luck to survive so far. The deal with Adam and Joseph and all that. It's like we got out by the scrape of our hair. I trusted you guys to deal, you know. What if the next scrape comes too close to our heads?"

"Don't worry, we'll continue scraping."

"What if we stop lucking out? What if we miscommunicate even once the next time shit goes down?"

"We've been friends for years, man." Tim turned worriedly to his best friend. "I've got your back."

133

From behind them, Stella murmured, "Me too," as she began to stir.

Without replying, Clay decelerated despite the empty road. Curious of his action, Tim looked out his window and saw that they were passing the diner from earlier. However, the buildings, from the eatery to the motel, were unlit. Not a single bulb of light. The red tail lights of a white pickup glowed in the darkness like the eyes of the devil itself.

Slowing down to a crawl, Clay turned the car sharply right, shining its headlights over the scene. They watched as Joseph dragged the limp body of the waitress from the morning out of the diner door, piling it onto a small mountain of corpses.

Stella, now fully awake, let out an unfamiliar voice of shock, "What. The. Fuck."

Joseph turned towards the source of the light, and for a moment, squinted in their direction while trying to make out the figure behind the hood.

Tim shook Clay's arm fiercely. "Drive."

Joseph's eyes widened in surprise before a sadistic, manic grin ripped opened his lips, the shine of their headlights reflecting against his teeth and the blood stains on his face.

Tim repeated, "Drive! DRIVE!"

Clay floored the gas and their S.U.V. screeched and jetted away from the diner. Stella peeked out the rear window and watched as the headlights to Joseph's pickup flashed on.

She warned, "He's coming."

CHAPTER TWENTY-SIX

The Stadium

"We passed from laughter to terror which, like love and hate, are close relatives."
- *Lise Deharme*

02:45 A.M.
8 days earlier

Having grown up watching countless action movies with his father, Tim had high expectations for his first car chase. Sadly, reality was much, much more boring. Having driven for over 7 hours without stopping, Clay Barber's initial adrenaline of driving away from Joseph had all but waned and was on the verge of keeling over at the wheel from fatigue. He yawned every other minute and nodded off once for a brief second, nearly swerving off the empty highway. Without any other cars around and the added incentive of a homicidal maniac chasing them, they had been driving at full speed for nearly 2 hours, with Ridge Valley shining just over the horizon.

Joseph's pick-up's top speed was apparently, brimming with coincidence, clocked in just a notch under their SUV.

Clay took a quick glance at his rear view mirror and sure enough, Joseph's pick-up was still trailing behind them, though the slower vehicle was now only a small headlight in the distance.

"This isn't going to work," Clay said.

"What are you talking about," Tim replied, checking his air rifle for the twelfth time in the past two hours. "We can barely see him now and we're almost back into the city."

Stella chimed in, "And I've managed to call the cops. They said they would get a unit out so we should meet somewhere between here and the

135

city."

"That's not what I meant," Clay said sheepishly, swaying left and right as he desperately fought to keep himself awake. "We're running out of gas."

"What?" Tim leaned over and confirmed via the gauge. The needle was already on 'E'. "How's that possible?"

Clay replied, slightly annoyed, "How the hell are we suppose to refuel when we've been chased for two hours?"

From the back, Stella passed the loaded pistol they took from the looter in Roagnark to Clay. Her brother then slotted it into a cup holder by his gear-shift. "You think he's tired?" the girl asked. "Joseph that is."

Tim laughed at her ability to joke under such situations. "Why don't we stop and ask him?" He turned back to look at her but saw something that made his heart beat twice instead. "Where's the pick-up?"

"What?" Clay glanced back up to his rear-view mirror and to his fenders'. The light from the pick-up had disappeared and the only thing following them was darkness. "Do you think he ran out of gas?"

Tim replied, "I highly doubt that," noting to himself that if Joseph had stopped at the diner for long, he would have refuelled.

"I have to slow down or we're going to lose the lights," Clay said.

"No!" Tim cut in suddenly, an idea forming in his mind. "I think I know what Joseph in doing. Cut the lights, cut everything. And stop on the opposite side of the road."

"But we'll be sitting ducks!"

"I know," he replied solemnly, acknowledging the disadvantage. "Stella, get the flashlights out but don't turn them on yet."

"Got them already," the girl replied, somehow having seen into the future.

Though not fully convinced, or even know what his friend was doing, Clay let loose of the accelerator and kept one hand on the keys in the ignition. "Turning off in three...two...one."

Clay turned off the engine and they were engulfed in shadows. Without street lamps or headlights, and the stars and moon covered by clouds, the light from the city was their only source of illumination, barely showing the outline of each of their faces. Their breathing was prominent without the hum of the engine and air-conditioner as the car slowed to a stop.

"What's your plan, kid?" Clay asked, taking off his seatbelt to face the others.

"If my hunch is right, Joseph turned off his lights to sneak up on us.

He won't be expecting us to do the same," Tim explained.

Stella chimed, "So we just wait and hope for him to drive by us?"

"That's the plan."

"That's a terrible plan! It's all luck based. How often do your plans fail?"

"It's a rare occurrence," Tim admitted, "One in ten? Plus or minus a few. I'm quite lucky."

"Wait," Clay shushed him with a hand on his shoulder. "Do you guys hear that?"

In the shroud of night and deep silence, the trio raised their ears to the air. The soft hum of an engine approached them and Stella turned back to watch the rear. However, she could see nothing behind them, despite the angle of the city's lights giving them an edge in sight.

"Nothing," she informed.

Clay asked, "Where's it coming from?"

Tim read somewhere once that a human had more senses than the traditional five. Amongst them were a sense of time, a sense of heat, and for the occasion, a sense of direction. He looked out his passenger side window and could only make out half the outline of the pick-up barrelling towards them from the field. But it was enough.

"Shit," was all the reaction time he had before the truck rammed into them.

He felt himself fly through the air on impact and tumble through space. Tim catapulted through the air and slid over the smooth, waxed floor of an empty stadium corridor, slowing down enough to make his contact with the wall just a light tap. In a panic, he attempted to get to his feet but instead flopped back on his chest as his decapitated arm found no hand to hold below it.

With his nose against the floor and a vision of the empty hallway, he calmed himself down enough to wish the lack of a right hand meant he was back in his dreams and that he had not actually lost it in real life. Slowly, he managed himself back onto his feet and sure enough, his right arm remained in the makeshift bandage Sister had made for him.

"Okay. I'm probably unconscious right now," he theorised of his situation in the real world. Looking down both paths of the corridor, he found himself alone again in the dream world. "At least I'm not dead."

It's our jobs, he remembered Sister saying once. *We're grim reapers.*

He wondered if his physical body might have actually died and this was his final sleep. A part of him wished that if it was his time to die, that Sister would be the one to send him on his way. One last chance to see her again.

"Stella!" he shouted out, only to listen to his voice echo down the hall. "STELL!"

Zoot. Zun. Zoot. Zun.

He physically jumped at the sound of the saw. Settling, he cursed the lack of time to compose himself or to decide where to run. Right. Left. Only two ways to escape.

Zoot. Zun. Zoot. Zun.

"Come on. Come on, sonofabitch!" he egged, more to psych himself up than to antagonise the monster. "Where are you?"

From down his left, a familiar voice reverberated to him. "Come on you asshole!" Clay shouted. "Fuck this shit! Fuck you!"

With his choice made for him, Tim bolted down the corridor towards the sound of his friend, glimpsing the elongated shadow of the man in the straw hat from the other path and was alleviated of the fear of running into The Father.

His footsteps slammed like gongs against the concrete floor, ringing through the corridor as he ran. He followed the winding road and swore to curse everything if he was running in some dream loop, only to be proved false as the light from the exit tunnel shone brightly around one of the turns.

Blasting out from the hallway, he jetted up a flight of stairs and shot out onto the first level of the stands of the baseball stadium, right behind third base. The flood lights lit the field in an otherwise starry night. On the pitcher's mound, Clay stood in dark blue shorts and a white shirt which had been muddied brown. Obviously unprepared for his dive into Sin, he had no footwear on, his feet soaked in the mud of the field. He had a wooden baseball bat in his hand, ready to swing. Nervously, he turned on the spot, scanning the empty field.

Tim yelled, "Clay!" He vaulted over the rail of the stands, falling two story onto the soft mud, his shoes digging in as he landed.

"What the fuck are you doing here, kid?" Clay asked, shocked at the appearance of another person in his dreams.

"We've got to get out of here, now!" Tim said, ignoring the question. He started to jog towards his friend.

"No! Don't come any closer!" Clay stopped him, raising his bat as if it were a gun capable of firing stop signs.

As he said that, a teenage boy in a black-white striped baseball uniform appeared on third base in a rupture of sand and dust, bringing Tim to a halt. It stood between Tim and Clay, facing the former, his cap covering his eyes and the tip of his aluminium baseball bat set in the sand.

Tim raised his hand in peace and attempted to parley. "Okay, you're The Brother right? You can talk. I know you can. You're not like The Father I'm sure. Whatever he's offering you, it's not worth it!"

He blinked and Brother seemingly teleported towards him, a trail of risen dust behind it. Shocked by the sudden movement, Tim fell backwards onto the ground. The Brother raised its bat menacingly, ready to bring down the metal weapon on him. From behind, Clay swung his wooden bat at The Brother's head and the creature disappeared in a burst of dust just before the weapon collided.

Clay pulled his friend to his feet. "Okay, I have a lot of questions for you, kid."

The Brother reappeared with a whirl of dust and wind on the pitcher's mount and began its advance on them again, dragging its bat behind it. The pair stood their ground, Clay with his bat raised and Tim looking left and right for an escape route.

Zoot. Zun. Zoot. Zun.

The sound of the saw rang out loudly in Tim's mind, worrying him enough to turn his attention away from one homicidal dream creature to another. The door to the dugout burst off its hinges, flying out onto the muddied field. From the darkness of the corridor behind it, the Sawman stepped out, walking as calmly and slowly as it always had, which was what terrified Tim the most. The confidence in its invulnerability.

"What was that?" Clay asked, a rare tone of anxiety in his voice.

Back-to-back, Tim replied, "Nothing. Just prepare to run and keep your eyes on The Brother."

"Brother? What brother?"

"That fucking baseball kid!" Tim yelled frustratingly. He continued to look for an escape but the only way out of the field – which was the door to the dugout – was guarded by the Sawman.

The Sawman stepped onto the grounds and the two felt their hearts trying to burst out of their chest from the sudden fear that swallowed them. Tim's mind went into overdrive, trying to figure out if The Father had been able to mark him as his victim before The Brother did. He was sure that since Clay had been marked by The Brother, the Sawman could kill his friend with no life and death consequences. Almost sure.

Then, as if remembering a homework he had forgotten to do, Tim realised something was amiss and urged, "We need to wake up. We need to wake up now."

"Why?"

"Cause Stella's not here." Solving the puzzle that was his train of thoughts, Tim finished, "And neither is Joseph."

02:53 A.M.
8 days earlier

Lying on her neck on the ceiling of the car, Stella stayed as still as she could, trying to stop the drum bursting ringing that had built up in her ears. Warm blood flowed out of her mouth and around her nose, making it all the way to her strawberry blonde hair. Held upside down by her seatbelt, she watched dizzily as the gas tank from their car, which had detached itself in the impact and ensuing tumble, burned softly in the dark outside her window. The right half of the back-seats of the SUV had been crushed by the collision, compacting just passed the middle, almost reaching her side of the car by mere inches. The passenger's seat had been twisted outwards, but she could still see Tim's chest rising and falling with each breath. Reaching around the driver's headrest, she felt for her brother's neck but found his wrist instead, but still breathed a sigh of relief when a pulse was detected.

She knew that from her position, she would be unable to do anything for them. Unable to turn her head in the awkward pose, she held her weight up with her left hand while searching for the release button for her seatbelt. She traced the strap and found the mechanism, but fumbled with the button for a moment before pressing it. Her body crumbled over the unsupported side and she winced as she twisted into an uncomfortable position.

Cart turned on its heels...

Regaining her composure, she manoeuvred onto all fours despite the tight space thanks to her small size and began checking her body for injuries. Shoulders, elbows, hands, ribs, hips, knees, ankles. Everything seemed fine save for a lost right premolar and a cut on her left temple, which explained the blood. She wiped the red off her face with the sleeves of her shirt, staining the green to brown.

Clay's body lay entirely face down on the ceiling of the car. Having unbuckled shortly before the crash, her brother was entirely out of his seat, leaning unnaturally with his right leg stuck out of the broken windscreen and his left below Tim's dangling head. The latter was still buckled in, his legs held in position against the side of his seat by the crushed door, though not in a noticeable vice hard enough to break them. Just a gentle pin. Both of them bled from more parts of their bodies, having taken more of the impact, but otherwise looked physically fine.

Filled with blood and horror.

"Brother..." She shook his arms gently, with too little strength left to raise her voice and worried she might accidentally further any injuries if she shook too hard. "Wake up..."

She turned to Tim and did the same. Neither replied. Then, the fire from the near-empty gas tank flickered and she heard the closing of a car door. She could see the wheels of the pick-up from the right side of the car, as well as Joseph's feet heading towards them.

"Joseph..." she reminded herself of their adversary.

Miraculously, the pistol still hung from the cup holder it was last placed in. A silver lining in the cloud, since if the gun had been kept anywhere else, it would have likely been flung out of reach. Taking the firearm, she held it at her side, finger resting lightly on the trigger.

She grabbed one of the flashlights on the ceiling and climbed out of her window, hiding behind the overturned vehicle.

Up. Down. Through the filth...

The gas from the tank ran out and the fire flickered to an ember.

Back in the dark.

The ringing stopped.

Shoot the man turned monster.

Safety off.

CHAPTER TWENTY-SEVEN

Phobophobia

*"That Ghosts have just as good a right in every way, to fear the light,
as Men to fear the dark."*
- Lewis Carroll, Phantasmagoria

02:56 A.M.
8 days earlier

Stella pulled the gun up to her chest, the weight of the weapon heavier than its size. With the sky covered by clouds, not even the light of the stars and moon could be seen. Her sight extended merely to a hand's reach away. In the deep darkness of nowhere, she relied on her hearing, listening carefully to the crunching footsteps of her approaching enemy.

She did not know if Joseph was armed or if he had the means to see her. Keeping her back hunched, she stepped to the rear end of the overturned S.U.V, where the impact had mangled the car enough that whoever was on the other side would be unable to see her feet through the windows below. She needed to flank him, knowing full well she might end up taking his life. As the thought of killing went through her mind, the loaded pistol felt even heavier than before and she drooped it back down to her side.

Stopping at the corner that separated 'her side' and Joseph, she crouched low, listening for the heavy padding feet of Joseph. For a while, she could hear it nearing, steadily growing louder. And then, nothing. Silence fell upon her and the only sound left was her slow and steadied breathing. Her mind raced with what could have muted him. She imagined him bending over to peer into the car, pistol in hand, ready to shoot her brother and best friend.

Her hands steadied instantly, and with a loud pump of her heart that

142

she was sure the world could hear, she spun around the corner of the car, gun in one hand and turned on her flashlight with the other. With a squeeze, she let one round fly at the first thing that moved and the bullet ricocheted off the ground with a puff of dust.

Nothing.

The movement was a trick of her eyes, a shadow glimpsed from her peripherals. But the figure that moved to her left was no illusion. She dived forward as Joseph raised his hunting rifle, squeezing off with a louder bang than her own gun.

Even before she hit the ground, her shin flared as if scorched by fire. Her flashlight flew out of her hands and landed farther than she could reach, the light pointing right on her, as if a spotlight on a stage and she was the show. She rolled on the ground onto her back and aimed her pistol up just as Joseph walked into view. Firing three times, she missed the first two shots, the recoil too much for her arm to aim. Her third sparked off against the barrel of Joseph's rifle, causing him to drop the firearm from the force of the impact. It did not dissuade him however, and the crazed man moved quickly over her.

In her panic to back away, she fired two random shots, one that flew overhead to nowhere and yonder while the second grazed him by the cheek. Still undeterred, Joseph swiped for the gun.

Knowing she would be overpowered, Stella threw the pistol away but he merely jumped on her and wrapped his hands around her small neck.

"Pass me your bat," Tim said to Clay, the two friends standing back-to-back against their adversaries.

The Sawman and The Brother continued their saunter, closing in on the pair with each step. Though Tim had seen them move at high speed before, they seemed to almost relish in building up tension and fear between themselves and their prey.

Clay handed the weapon over, "I hope you have a plan, kid."

"When I say 'run', you make a beeline for the other dugout."

"What are you going to do?"

Ignoring the question, Tim yelled, "Run!"

Clay hesitated, but with a slight push from Tim, he began doing as he was told and sprinted towards the dugout exit on the other side of the field. Tim raised the bat, did a 180 degree turn and charged towards The Brother.

Despite being closer, The Brother kept its attention on Clay, which reaffirmed Tim's suspicion that Tim was marked by The Father instead.

143

Without any fear of immediate death, he intercepted The Brother's path, swinging the bat with all his might at The Brother.

The bat swooshed through the air at mach speed, but inexplicably stopped right before impact. The Brother stopped walking and turned towards Tim as the latter tried to push the bat through the invisible force field that prevented him from hitting it.

The Brother raised its bat and Tim drew back his. The two swung, their bats clanging on impact, but his wooden one broke at the handle. The Brother, bat and all, disappeared in another whirl of dust. Tim took the chance as the monster recuperated and dropped the broken handle and chased after Clay into the dugout. His friend held the exit door open and he ran through it at full speed, looking back for just one final glimpse of the Sawman who was already walking past first base before Clay closed the door behind them.

They started jogging through the long corridor, putting some distance between them and their hunters. Clay exclaimed, "I have a lot of questions for you, kid!"

"Can't this wait until we've survived this?"

"Fine!" Clay snapped back. "But you better have a plan."

They turned a corner and through a gate that led to the loading bay. The shutter's to the bay, however, were closed and they saw no way to raise them. Caught in a dead end, the pair each grabbed one of the tools lying around as a weapon, Tim a crowbar and Clay a wrench. The two stood in the middle of the bay, facing the way they came, ready for a fight.

"Alright, kid. You seem to know more about this place than I do. How do we get out of here?" Clay asked.

"You have to trust me on this."

"Spit it out."

"You have to get killed by The Father. The man with the saw. And I get killed by your baseball kid."

Clay grabbed Tim by the shoulder and spun him round to face him. "What the fuck kind of plan is that?"

"It's how we're getting out of this. There's too much to explain right now. You just have to trust me."

"You do know we'll *die* if we get killed here right?" Clay emphasised.

"Look, I'm ninety-eight percent sure we'll survive this if we do this!"

"Just ninety-eight percent?" Clay denied the plan with his trademark sarcasm.

"We've gone on much, *much* less in the past!"

"That's because we weren't putting our lives on the line!" he shouted

144

back.

Tim stared at Clay as if seeing his friend for the first time. "What are you talking about, man? We were always risking something. Sometimes even our lives." He took a step closer, looking straight into Clay's eyes. "You're scared. You're really scared."

"Tim. I don't mind dying. But this place, it messes with your head."

"And you're scared because of that?" Clay did not reply, prompting Tim to continue. "What happened to you? Your sister is out there. Probably kicking Joseph's ass, because sure, why won't she? But you need to suck it up right now and help her!"

Zoot. Zun. Zoot. Zun.

The sound of the saw.

Clang.

The metal bat, tapping against the ground.

Clang.

The two turned to the entrance, facing both The Brother and The Father.

Tim asked Clay, "So what's it going to be...kid?"

03:01 A.M.
8 days earlier

Unable to breathe, Stella felt the world around her dim. She scratched at Joseph's face, her nails digging deep enough to draw blood. But as if drawing energy from each drop of blood lost, he continued his assault, the hold on her throat getting stronger every second. She tried to wiggle free but he had her pinned under his heavier weight. The pistol laid just out of reach to her right and she wondered if throwing it away had helped her survival or doomed her to die.

Suddenly, a metal pellet smacked right into Joseph's face, the impact distracting enough that she managed to raise her knees to his crotch. The low blow caused him to squirm in pain, only to for Joseph to be immediately tackled by Clay flying in from the side. The two males rolled off Stella and into parts unlit by the torchlight. She turned to see Tim reloading his rifle, though still trapped upside down within the car, unable to free himself.

Clay managed to break off from Joseph's grasp, kicking away and jumping back to his feet to put some distance between them.

"What the fuck's wrong with you, dude?" Clay screamed.

Joseph crawled away from Clay and went scrambling for his hunting

145

rifle. Clay saw the movement and tried to intercept, but lost when Joseph grabbed the butt of the gun and swung it at his face. The rifle barrel smacked across Clay's mouth and he though he might have lost a tooth as he backed off in pain.

Joseph pointed his gun at him. Clay froze on the spot, staring defiantly back, clutching his broken right elbow with his left hand, his arms bleeding from multiple cuts.

Joseph said maniacally, saliva spewing with each word. "You gave me Sin! So once I kill you, it's gonna go away!"

"What kind of fucked up logic is that?" Clay yelled back. "How did you even find us?"

"The woman with the red hair. She told me where you were. And here you are!" His eyes gleamed with insanity.

"What woman?" Clay shouted.

"From the dreams. Don't you see? She can save me! She can give me anything I want! And right now, I want to kill you!"

With rifle raised and an inability to be reasoned with, Joseph readied himself to shoot. He pulled the bolt, the empty bullet casing jumping out as a new round clicked into place.

The shot rang through the night.

At first he wobbled on his feet, the bullet having cleanly went through his skull. When the muscle memory of his body was no longer able to support his weight, Joseph fell backwards, his lifeless eyes staring up at the night sky.

Clay breathed erratically, heart still pumping. He turned to the sound of Stella's whimper, the girl leaning against the crashed car with pistol in hand. He ran to his sister the moment he saw a tear roll down her cheek.

Taking the gun out of her hands and ignoring the pain in his arms, he hugged her tightly and she hugged back. "It's okay baby-sis." He pulled her closer and tighter, until the only place she could sob into was his shoulder. "It's over."

CHAPTER TWENTY-EIGHT

Meet the Man

"One should not as a rule reveal one's secrets, since one does not know if and when one may need them again."
- Paul Joseph Goebbels, Churchill's Lie Factory

08:36 A.M.
8 days earlier

Less then 48 hours as a free man and Timothy Kleve found himself back in the basement cell of Ridge Valley Police Department.

"Wow," his neighbouring cellmate, Pearlman, greeted with amazement. "You going for a record or something, boy?"

"I just thought I'd stopped by and visit."

"Did you bring cake?"

From the corridor, they heard two distinct set of footsteps; the loud clanking of Detective Julianne Smith's flats and the soft thump of Detective Oliver Hardy's boots. The pair still wore their familiar suit and trench coat duo, making Tim theorise the two either had yet to change since they last met, or that ensemble was the only style in their wardrobe. He leaned towards the latter.

Condescending, and with a strong frosting of expectancy, Julianne said, "Can't say I'm surprised to see you again." She opened the file folder she had in her hands, flipping through the report. "Joseph Camein Price, killed in self defence. Alleged four civilians murdered by Price at the motel."

"Pfft!" Tim choked back a laughter, "His middle name is Camein?"

Not helping the strict detective's mood, she fiercely countered, "You can still joke after committing first degree murder!?"

"It was self defence, you said so yourself!"

147

"The hell I'd believe that bullshit!" she screamed, shocking Tim enough that he took a step away from the bars. Even Oliver looked taken aback by his partner's sudden outburst. "First your father and now this? You expect me to believe that you had nothing to do with any of this? Np! You are going to rot in jail young man. Rot. In. Jail!" she stuck her face into the bars of the cell, shouting through it.

Pearlman whistled, impressed.

That was when Tim saw the glint in the female detective's eyes, instantly recognising the spirit behind her force. He stepped forward, leaning just close enough to Julianne to analyse her face. Dark rings circled her fire-red eyes, fatigue heavier than those of Oliver or any other law enforcement agents he had seen before. Heavy breathing. Teeth gritted with enough intensity to crack diamonds.

He accused, "You have Sin."

She reached across the threshold, her slender arms slipping through the bars and grabbing his neck with ease. Her sharp fingernails dug into the skin of his throat. "There's no such thing as Sin!" she growled.

Her grip was tight and painful, but was not debilitating. As Tim struggled to pull away from his attacker, he found solace in an unexpected ally. He met the shocked stare of Oliver Hardy and knew the man agreed that the female detective had indeed gone mad.

Laying a gentle hand on his partner's shoulder, Oliver said, "Easy Julie. Maybe you should rest."

She snapped him a fierce stare, releasing her grip on Tim's throat in the process. "This whole city has gone nuts from this Sin bullshit. Everyone thinking it's fine to do whatever they want simply because of some mass hysteria!" She turned away from Tim. "And who has to clean this shit up? Us! The cops and detectives, running around like the city's bitches to scoop up their shit!" She stormed out of Tim's view, leaving her bewildered partner with the two prisoners.

Pearlman said, "That lady has issues."

Oliver turned to Tim, "Don't worry. I've got a good feeling you're innocent in all this."

"Thanks," Tim replied, settling down on his concrete bed. "But your feeling ain't gonna do a lick of help without any proof, and you know that. 'Sides, we really did kill Joseph...Camein Price."

"The city's gone insane. Everyone's dying left and right. There's no doubt now that Sin is real. Some of us are just having a hard time dealing with that truth." He looked away towards where Julianne walked off to. "You've been to Roagnark. You know how mad society has gotten there in the chaos. We officers are just running around trying to prevent the same

148

thing from happening here."

"How bad is it?" Tim asked.

"We had another riot yesterday. It was bad. Casualties." He looked pleadingly at Tim, "My cop instinct's telling me you're a part of what's happening. It's telling me you can stop it."

"That's some instinct."

"Am I wrong?"

Tim held his gaze. "No."

Nodding in affirmation, Oliver continued, "Your friends are at the hospital getting treated. Once they're done, I'll try to see if there's some way for me to get you all out."

Pearlman chimed, "What about me?"

Ignoring the convict, the detective continued, "Julianne has Sin. She hates that idea more than anything and won't admit it. I can't even pretend to understand what it's like, but the stress from it is really ripping her mind apart." He sighed again, a look of worry across his face. "But I don't have as much pride as her, so I don't mind asking for help when I need it. I hope you can end this whole thing before she dies."

Tim recognised the look in the man's eyes. It was the same look of desperation that Clay gave earlier in the dream world as they fought for their lives. The same plea that Clay made to protect his sister.

"I'll try."

"There is no try," the detective said solemnly. "If you fail here, I don't think even society will be able to survive. If you've really been in Roagnark for the past twenty-four hours, you don't know the half of what happened in the city."

10:13 A.M.
8 days earlier

"Are the cuffs really necessary?" Clay asked from his seat in the hospital's corridor. Chained to the handles of the chair by his left wrist and watched by a female officer in uniform, he shifted uncomfortably as an itch formed in his splinted and slung right arm. "It's not like I'm gonna run away while my sister's here."

The officer continued to ignore him as she had done the whole night. She stood attentively with both hands on her belt as if she was a cardboard cutout.

Undaunted, Clay continued, "Maybe you could just let me walk around a bit? Get some nuggets from the cafeteria?" Though he masked it well with his tomfoolery, his twitchy behaviour gave away his worry for his sister's condition. "I could drop in and see how my sister's doing. Say 'Hi,' maybe get her something to drink? Would you like something to drink? Orange Whip?"

"Your sister is fine," the officer spoke for the first time, though without looking his way. "The bullets missed her arteries and only scraped her bone. Don't worry."

"Right," he took a deep breath, trying to calm himself. "She's strong. No worries there. Of course not. Why would I?"

Five seconds into the ensuing silence, his nervousness began to show again as he tapped his feet impatiently. He could hear the officer letting out a sigh of resignation at quieting him down. The clock on the wall behind them ticked the seconds away. A minute. Ten. Half an hour of silence passed.

A voice from down the hall called out, "Officer!" The two turned to see a young man waving from down the corridor. "We need your help over here!"

She looked down at her charge and Clay exchanged a glance of suspicion with her. They both knew that the situation was odd, considering their location.

"Don't do it," Clay warned.

However the officer's sense of duty must have overwhelmed her other senses, like that of logic. "On my way, sir!" she raised her voice back to the man. She made her way towards him as the person disappeared back round the corner.

Clay pulled at his cuffs, desperation setting in the moment the officer vanished behind the turn. The moment he heard the succeeding scuffle from down the hall, he yanked hard, loud, and violently at his chains. But with one arm immobilised, his movements were limited. He searched around him and found the shine of a safety pin lodged between the cushions four seats from him.

He lifted his slung arm over and around his head, freeing it. Through gritted teeth, spitting saliva of pain, straightened his broken elbow to reach for the small piece of metal. He lay across the chairs and snapped the pin between his middle and index fingers, only to feel the cold steel of a guns' barrel pushed into the back of his head.

A gruff male voice, definitely not that of the detective, growled, "My boss wants to see you."

12:22 P.M.
8 days earlier

Tim sat on his concrete bed, ears picked intensely at the sounds that came from the floors above. A series of gunshots rang through to his chamber, echoing against the walls of his cell. Blood curdling screams and about ten seconds of non-stop gunfire followed after, preceded by a skin raising silence that seemed louder than the screams before.

From the cell next to his, Pearlman calmly said, "About time."

It took Tim quicker than he could blink to deduce what the man had meant. A minute later, the sound of rushed footsteps slapped against the floor and down into their underground   corridor. The teen got to his feet just as a uniformed officer and a tall, muscular, and heavily tattooed man shot passed his cell door and towards Pearlman. Both men carried variants of sub-machine guns with them.

"Time to go, boss," Tim heard Tattoo croak.

"You'll keep your promise?" the officer asked.

"Of course," Pearlman replied to the jingle of keys. The sound of the convict's rusty cell door squeaked opened. "I'll get you your Somnidin. How many of you are there?"

The officer replied, "About twenty more."

"Good," Pearlman said. "If you kill fifteen of them once we get out, I'll double your reward."

Tim could only stand and watch as the two prison breakers ran back towards the stairs to clear the path out of the station. As relaxed as if he was heading for a banquet, Pearlman walked in front of Tim's cell door and turned to him.

"It's been nice talking to you, Timmy-boy." Despite being forced to wear the tacky white pants and shirt that long duration inmates at the station had to, the man managed to maintain a neat and presentable look. The sleeves of his clothes were rolled up to tighten the otherwise baggy shirt and his pants tapered neatly. He slicked his onyx hair back and Tim immediately recognised him from the newspaper report just four days earlier. "But I've got a schedule to keep with a certain meddling kid."

Adam Pearlman was a drug dealer. But with his stash of Somnidin in a world full of people in need of them, was now a crime lord with a store of the biggest commodity. Complete with his own prison break for a portfolio, the man Clay helped put in jail for less than a week walked out of Tim's line of sight and into the sound of gunshots.

CHAPTER TWENTY-NINE

Say When

"Why do they call it rush hour when nothing moves?"
- Robin Williams

02:26 P.M.
8 days earlier

Having pulled out one of the metal pipes from his toilet, Tim used it as a lever in a desperate attempt to yank apart his cell bars. Grunting from the force, the last two hours of work gave a bare result of two centimetres of widening.

He stopped his effort to escape, stepping back to the centre of his cell to access his situation. "This isn't working," Tim huffed, before analysing the room again.

The cell was still as bare as it had been, save for the toilet which had been forcefully kicked and pried from its loose attachment to the wall. The water that continued to leak from the exposed piping ran off into a drain in the corner.

For the dozenth time that day, he swung the pipe against the metal grills, letting out a clang loud enough to continue ringing in his ears even after the original sound subsided.

"Anyone out there?" he shouted into the empty corridor. As before, the only reply he got was silence.

For the first time in a long, long while, Tim had ran out of ideas. Dejected, he sat back down on his concrete bed. His mind continued to race with thoughts of power drills and TNT.

I've got a schedule to keep with a certain meddling kid.

Though he knew patience was the only thing that could possibly get him out, Adam Pearlman's last words to him kept him itching to move. He had no doubt the 'meddling kid' was Clay, and without any contact with the outside world since the breakout, he had no idea what the situation was like, leaving him in a constant state of agitation.

"Timothy!" the crackling, energetic voice of the librarian, Howard Galloway echoed into the hallway. "Are you in here, my boy?"

"Mister Galloway?" Tim called back, surprised. "I'm down in the basement! Holding cells!"

In a tone of shock, the older man yelled back, "W-who said that?"

"It's me, Mister Galloway. Tim."

"Oh right! I was looking for you."

"I know. I can hear you."

"Right! Sorry. Forgot about that. Got excited."

"Excited by what?"

Tim's call was followed by a period of silence. He could faintly hear the footsteps of the librarian, the audio a deafening loudness after the hour of solitude.

Suddenly, Howard excitedly said, "There's a lot of dead bodies up here."

Tim's heart skipped a beat when he heard those words, the eccentric tone worried him. "You okay there?"

"Just fine," Howard replied. This time, Tim knew the voice came from his hallway, as the sound was clear and did not echo as it did before. "Where are the keys?"

"They should be in the cell to my left," Tim went to the bars and stuck his hands through them, waving for Howard's attention.

"Ah!" I see you. "Those are your hands right?"

"Whose else would they be?"

"I don't know." Howard walked into Tim's line of sight and the teen stepped back in surprise and awe. "Maybe some bad guy who wants to take advantage of an old man?"

But Tim could not focus on his words, for Howard had seemingly grown younger. Though the man had always been chided for looking youthful, Tim had no doubt the librarian was actually younger then. His hair, once soot black, now had a glossy shade of brown attached to it. The mess remained, though with a lusher and slicker flow for each strand. The scars that once adorned his skin had faded considerably, and the rare wrinkles had all but disappeared.

"Ah!" Howard exclaimed and walked off to the left. "The key." He returned with the ring of keys to unlock the cell door.

Though the door swung opened to his freedom, Tim stood in his cell, still dumbstruck by Howard's de-ageing. "What happened to you?"

"What do you mean?" Howard stared down at his body, expecting to find perhaps a giant spider that had latched on to him, or his body bleeding and disfigured. "There's nothing on me. Oh no. Did a bird poop on my head?"

Taking his steps out of the cell, Tim continued to stare intently at the man, analysing the almost foreign features. "You look...younger."

"Oh...right! About that, well, now's not the time to explain." From his pocket, the librarian took out a white envelope and handed it to Tim. "I think you have a best friend to save."

"How did you—"

"Stella called. Said her brother disappeared from the hospital."

"And she called you instead of her parents or the cops? Why?"

Howard grinned. "Think about it."

The logic quickly came to him. "Parents and cops will get flustered and ask questions, delaying time. She wants me out and acting as soon as possible."

"Smart boy."

"I still have questions for you though."

"It'll all be answered in due time," Howard replied.

"Why can't you just tell me now?" Tim exclaimed. "This isn't a movie where you need to go, 'No time to explain!'"

"Yes, well, we do have time. But not enough to talk you through my situation and help Clay. For now, you have to just trust me and go save your friend." Howard opened his arms wide, telling Tim to look at the situation around them. "I already gave you a deus ex machina. I suggest you take your blessings now and go." He nodded towards the staircase out.

Tim turned to the direction pointed, "Can't you explain on our way?" He turned back, but Howard had disappeared from where he stood. Stunned, Tim could only express, "What the fuck?"

He scanned his surroundings, taking a quick look into Adam's cell to make sure he had not missed anything. Indeed, the librarian was no longer in the vicinity, as if he had never existed. Tim looked down to the envelope, the only evidence left that the man had been there with him. On it, scribbled in barely legible cursive, was 'For Clay'. As he started walking towards the stairwell, he carefully tore the envelope open. Within it was a neatly folded piece of paper and two newspaper clippings. He unfolded the paper, showing a printed photograph of an unfamiliar school's baseball team. Deeming the newspaper clippings too troublesome to read at the time, Tim slotted the photo back into the envelope and slid them into his back pocket.

The lights above flickered as he neared the stairs. Ascending, the sudden stench of blood, thick as mist, hung in the air. He noted the two bullet holes in the wall on the first landing. After turning the corner, he jumped back from the sight of a policeman, awkwardly lying on the top step of the stairs, blood dripping below him.

There's a lot of dead bodies up here.

Howard's words echoed in his mind and he wondered just how many more. His question was almost immediately answered when he stepped onto the landing of the main holding cell. The entire hallway was bathed red, liquid oozing out from the two dozen cells. A couple of officers slumped against the metal grills, unmoving.

Something gripped at his stomach, the stench of blood strong enough that he wanted to puke. Swallowing the taste of vomit back in, Tim pushed through the massacre. He ascended the stairs once more to the main floor.

Even through the lobby of the police station, he could see from the corner of his eyes the bodies that littered the room. And then he saw a pile too massive to ignore. Fifteen bodies of both men and women, two in police uniforms and the rest in casual civilian clothing, all with sub-machine guns slung around their shoulders, piled right beside the entrance.

If you kill fifteen of them once we get out, I'll double your reward.

Adam Pearlman, with his drugs and control, ordered the killing of fifteen of his own. Just so he could distribute less of his precious Somnidin. A sudden sense of rage welled up inside Tim and he could feel his hands balling into fists.

He walked up to the pile of bodies, the queasiness vanishing completely in his unexpected righteous fury. From the body nearest to him, Tim searched the pockets to find a phone. However, it was password protected. Not wanting to waste time cracking it, he reached to the next nearest corpse and looted one without the restriction.

Scrolling through the messages, he read through the ones filed under that of an anonymous contact. Within were messages presumably sent from one of Adam's men, detailing a meeting location for which to go to after the prison break, likely to collect the Somnidin reward. Without the time to check the legitimacy of the information, or find other leads, the teen took a revolver from an officer, along with the belt and holster. He put the equipment on and hid the firearm under his shirt. He unloaded another officer's revolver for spare ammunition, storing it in the bottom right pocket of his cargo pants.

Geared up and with a destination, he exited via the main entrance, leaving the bloodbath behind. Out in the fresh air at last, he vomited onto the sidewalk.

CHAPTER THIRTY

Crawl, Run, Fall

"Conform and be dull."
- James Frank Dobie, The Voice of the Coyote

04:31 P.M.
8 days earlier

"Do you know the kind of world we live in right now?" Adam asked, circling Clay.

The teen was bound by his hands and legs to a steel chair, bolted to the floor. Breathing heavily, with blood flowing from the corner of his lips and fresh bruises added to the ones he already had. He stared at his knees in silence, drained of energy from the events of the past few days and the pain of the abuse that the drug dealer had put him through.

Adam wiped the dust off the sleeves of his suit and continued, "A world where sleep is a commodity and Somnidin the currency." He leaned into the armrest of the chair, bringing his face close to Clay. "Look around you, boy. I am the richest of us all."

Surrounding them were crates and boxes, stacked to the brim of the small storage room, with only the centre kept bare to hold Clay in place. The dank lighting composed of a single fluorescent lamp that hung above his head. The swinging lamp was enough to make the scene look like a 90s torture cum interrogation chamber.

Adam continued, "I like your style. Smart, quick witted. I could use someone like you. So, last offer." He held a pill bottle of Somnidin to Clay's face. "Join me. And I'll give you all the Somnidin you'll ever need. Reject me, and I'll torture you for the fun," he finished with a smile.

Clay looked up, face-to-face with the criminal. But his stare was on the bottle, a wanting glare that sought the solace of a night's rest. "I..."

157

"Come on. You're a smart boy. Logical even." Adam shook the bottle, rattling the teen in the heart and mind. "Take it."

With sparse breath, Clay replied, "I...I would...I would rather fuck a cactus." He spat at the man's face.

Adam wiped the spit off with his sleeves. Letting out a small chuckle, "Too bad. I like you, kid. You're funny. You're like me. You probably learnt to run before you could walk. That makes you different. Some sort of misplaced pride in your nonconformity." He half-turned to walk away but stepped back and backhanded Clay, hard. "But your pride will be the death of you."

The door to the storage room opened and one of Adam's henchman walked through. Clay recognised him as the tattooed Mexican from their previous meeting.

Adam asked Tattoo, "What are you doing here?"

"Getting the payment for the guys, boss."

"Right. The cop killers," Adam replied calmly. "Take one box to them. And here's a little bonus." He tossed Clay's pill bottle to him.

Tattoo raised the bottle in thanks, pocketed it, and picked up a box of the drug nearest to him. "Thanks boss."

Adam asked, "What's happening at the police station?"

"They just got their first responders. The entire city's civil force is out chasing all these death by Sin cases. No one's available to even clean up the bodies."

"Good. That means we can do whatever we want. See you later," Adam said. The tattooed man nodded and left with the drugs. Adam turned back to Clay. Holding up his prisoner's face by a vice grip on his jaw. He growled, "Now, let's see how long you can stay awake before the nightmare gets you."

06:57 P.M.
8 days earlier

Westlay Street was deserted, with overturned vehicles blocking the road. Some embers glowed within some of the charred cars, a remnant of the destruction that happened the day before. Tim looked up and down the road from his seat in the sole café that remained opened. Broken bottles, baseball bats, crowbars, and other makeshift melee weapons lay on the tar road, bathed red by the setting sun like the aftermath of a blood-soaked battlefield. A lone street sweeper on the other side of the road repeatedly brushed garbage off the pavement. A waitress stepped out of the café, a tray in hand. She sets the tray down on the table next to Tim and from it, removed the cup of coffee, placing it softly on the table.

"Here you go," she said happily. "First customer of the day."

Tim passed her extra in cash. "First customer?" He looked around and noticed that every single chair around him were still pushed into their tables. "Not a single person came in the whole day?"

"Nope." The waitress tucked the tray under her arm. Her name tag read 'Lily'. "Just you. Not surprising, after what happened last night."

"I'm guessing riot?" Tim assessed the overturned cars.

"Yeah. Stretched out the whole block. I think the whole city knows by now," she said in surprised by Tim's lack of knowledge. "Where were you the past day?"

Blankly, Tim replied, "Out of town."

His attention was caught by an old black car that had driven up across the street, parking right across the café. Tattoo exited the vehicle, circling around to the back. From the trunk, he carried out a cardboard box. With a beep audible within the dead quiet city, he locked the car and proceeded down the street with his delivery.

"Got to go," Tim got up from his seat and meandered out of the café, only turning back once to shoot the waitress two thumbs up. "Coffee's on me."

He jogged across the littered road just as Tattoo turned into an alley. With the sun past the edge of the buildings, a sudden shadow fell over the streets, only to be instantly illuminated by spots of white as the street lamps turned on.

At the car, he looked through the driver side window, hoping to find a GPS that could lead him to the car's last travelled location. The dashboard was empty, and Tim comforted himself by reasoning GPS might not even be working with the world's media in the disarray that it was in.

He went around to the trunk, looking to the café to make sure the waitress had gone back inside. The street sweeper had turned the corner onto Aston Avenue, leaving Tim the last man on the road. He picked up a nearby crowbar, dried blood stuck to the edge of the tool.

Shoving the crowbar into the gap between the trunk, he hoped the lock was weak or worn out. Given the state of the car – dents, rust and all – it was a reasonable request. He was proved right when without much effort, the trunk popped open. It was empty, which bode well for his plan as it meant the tattooed man would have no reason to look back in. Tim climbed in with his new crowbar, closing the trunk just enough so that the lock only engaged lightly.

In complete darkness, he waited, occasionally lighting up his watch to check the time. The trunk smelled of something between rusted metal and mud.

A minute passed. Then two. Ten. Twenty. Half an hour flew by and Tim wondered if he had made a mistake, and that perhaps the henchman had intended to leave the car here to get rid of some sort of evidence, and instead was hoofing it to wherever Adam was holding out. The trunk was getting warmer by the minute. A slight thirst took him and he wished he had drank that cup of coffee.

Then, the car shook as a door opened and the man he assumed was the Mexican got in. A slam indicated the shutting of the door. Soon after, the engine revved. Tim held onto the sides of the trunk with his hands and feet as the car sped off.

08:33 P.M.
8 days earlier

Tim fought boredom and the urge to sleep. Partially because he worried of the deadly consequences that might befall him in the dream world, but also as a precaution to the deadly consequences that might befall him in the real world. The hour long drive had beyond tired him.

He felt the car turn and drive over a hump, as if leaving the main road behind. A while later, the vehicle slowed down to a stop before reversing into what he assumed was a parking space. The engine turned off and the opening and closing of the driver door followed. They had reached wherever they were.

Tim gave ten minutes to waiting and listening, making sure that there was absolutely no one audibly near him before crowbarring the trunk open again. He climbed out, careful to avoid his left leg which had gone numb during the ride. Gently, he closed the trunk, all the while nursing the blood back into his leg with tiny shakes. He took a quick scan of the area.

He was in the middle of a storage lot, with rows of storage lockers extending left and right, cutting off at the fenced boundary. Now in enemy territory, he drew his revolver and holstered the crowbar onto one of his belt loops. He did a quick check to make sure his gun was loaded, before feeling the cold brunt of a metal pipe slamming into the back of his neck. His legs buckled from the pain and his vision blurred, his body falling to the ground.

"What should we do with him?" Tim heard a man say. His body, paralysed by the hit to the tip of his spine, refused to move. The only thing he saw was the ground before him.

Adam's voice replied, "Throw him in with that Clay kid. We'll deal with them both later."

As the world around him dimmed, he watched from his view of the concrete lot as a well shined leather shoe stepped into his sights.

"Timmy-boy," he heard Adam say. "You shouldn't have come."

One of the shoes raised into the air before swinging against his face.

CHAPTER THIRTY-ONE

The Corridor

"Character consists of what you do on the third and fourth tries."
- James Albert Michener, Chesapeake

Galaxies littered the night sky. Like an entire bathtub of milk that had been flushed down hundreds of small drains. Larger than stars and brighter than the moon, the sight was one of the most breathtaking displays of the dream world that Tim had seen yet. It was the entire universe, shrunk down to the size of the canvas that stretched out before him, an endless domain of wonder. He sat up, the dew of the damp grass sticking to his clothes. To his sides and back, about two meters apart, five story tall walls blocked his way, with the only clear path being forward. But even that ended with a fork a short way down.

Careful to watch his right stump, Tim got to his feet, scanning the area for anything out of the ordinary. At least, as out of the ordinary as the situation could get. The only thing he noticed was that the grass was artificial. Plastic. But the dirt beneath it was real.

"Alright. Fake grass." He reached his hand out and touched the wall. "Real concrete."

The walls were smooth, almost as if scrapped flat by a passing sandstorm. With no visible footholds or even a blemish, they were impossible to scale. With no other option left to him, Tim started towards the fork in the road, the fake grass crunching under his feet.

At the junction, which split diagonally, the right let to another fork, while the left curved slowly, the road disappearing after some distance.

"This is a maze," Tim thought aloud.

Clang

Like The Father's saw, the sound of the metal bat only echoed within his mind, but Tim had no doubts who or where it came from. He turned to

162

look down the curved left path, and sure enough, The Brother walked out from behind the walls. Without a second thought, Tim bolted down the right road, turning left at the next junction. On and on the path went, with more forks and turns as he went on. A right turn. A left. Up a flight of stairs and under an archway. Another left. And a third. He did not slow down, did not dare to. Trapped in the endless corridor, he had no other choice but to run and make up some distance between him and his hunter. A sudden sharp right and a flash of white.

Like a scene right out of a high school romance drama, Tim collided with the girl in the white dress. He swore he could hear romantic music playing within his mind for a second. But unlike a show, Sister wasn't knocked off her feet, and the pair did not find themselves delightfully coiled up on the floor. Despite her tiny stature, she withstood the full brunt of Tim's weight and momentum, not even staggering an inch, while Tim awkwardly found himself in a half embrace.

"Tim!" Sister exclaimed excitedly, ignoring the whole fact that she had just phased through the laws of physics. "Finally found you. So...how's it going?" she asked playfully. She wrapped her arms around his neck, leaning her body seductively into his, her face drawing exceedingly closer to him.

He felt her aura wash over him as he fought the sudden lustful desires and thoughts that crossed his mind. "Cut that out. I'm being chased by The Brother!"

"Oh...that is worrisome," she replied, though not with any of the sense of urgency as her words would have implied. However, the seductive atmosphere disappeared and Tim could concentrate again. Sister moved her arms down to his waist. "And disappointing. I missed you."

Admittedly, he wasn't uncomfortable with her intimacy. Even without her aura, he was quite attracted to the beautiful, spectral girl. "What are you doing?" he asked.

She only replied with a devilish smile. "Hold on tight."

Taking a step back from him, he had just a second to wonder what she meant before the white cloth tied around his waist pulled him up and off his feet.

"Whoa!" He was dragged up and against the wall by the makeshift rope. At three stories up, he looked down to see Sister waving and laughing at his shock.

Slowly, he was lifted to the top of the wall. He turned and positioned himself to climb onto the platform. Once the edge crossed his view however, he found himself facing a dumbfounded Clay, panting heavily and sweating as if he had just walked out of a pool.

163

Surprised, Clay let out, "Kid?" before offering his best friend a hand. Tim took it without hesitation and was pulled onto the landing. "What are you doing here?"

Panting himself, Tim replied, "Aren't you guys tired of asking that?" He looked back and down into the maze, but Sister and her magic cloth had vanished. He glanced around their level and saw that the maze extended endlessly into the galaxy filled horizon. "It's a pretty repetitive question, isn't it?"

"No. Cause I haven't had my answer yet."

"Do we really have the time for that now?"

Sarcastically, he replied, "Well, my body has been beaten unconscious by a psychopathic drug dealer and I'm being chased by a homicidal dream monster. So yeah, we got time."

A memory jogged from the recess of Tim's mind. "Wait, there's something I have to tell you. It's about The Brother." He remembered the envelope given to him by the librarian, Howard Galloway.

"The baseball kid?"

"Yes. The thing you asked from Howard, he got it. The Brother's a kid from our world. You were right. They exist in our world as well, somehow." Tim could see Clay wanting to speak so he raised a finger to hush the later. "Let me finish. He used to be from some baseball team out west. Committed suicide twelve years ago, after his team lost in some national's finals. The dude's name was Harrison Smith."

Ecstatic, Clay exclaimed, "Fantastic!"A period of silence followed, though he wore a smile on his face. The grin broke when he said, "So what now?"

"What?"

"So what do I do with the information?" Clay asked with a blank face.

"I don't know! You're the one who went looking for it. I thought you had a plan?"

"Not really. I was just sort of going with it. There isn't really any other leads to follow, you know."

A faint *clang* echoed into their minds.

Shivers ran down their spines when they heard the sound. Thinking fast, Tim recited the rules of the dream world to his friend, "Okay, if we kill ourselves, we'll be able to wake up."

"Are you crazy?" Clay said in a panicked tone, "How sure are you?"

"Did it twice. Kinda confident about it." He looked over his shoulder and down the five stories wall. However, what used to be hard ground and fake grass was replaced by sand, which cut the drop to a mere five meters, nothing more than a cushioned fall. "Okay, that's not going to happen."

"The sand wasn't there before."

"Must be The Brother."

"What if I strangled you?" Clay asked nonchalantly.

Surprised, Tim replied, "What? Why would you do that?"

"You said the last time if we don't get killed by the thing hunting us, we'd survive. And we did. So if I killed you, you would wake up?"

"Yeah," Tim confirmed, but a thought of worry crossed him. "But if you do that, you'll get killed by The Brother."

Clang.

The sound got closer. As if they had headphones on, the audio was both something they could hear and sense in their minds at the same time.

Clay explained, "My body's tied up in the real world. There's nothing I can do even if I wake up."

"No. No! No! I should be killing you!" Tim raised his voice in protest, unwilling to let his friend make the sacrifice. "I have more chance of surviving here! I know more about this place than you do. I can fight!"

Matching his tone, Clay rebutted, "What about Adam? I'm tied up in a chair, kid. I'm as dead out there as I am here."

"I'm not gonna let you do this," Tim rejected the plan, turning away from his friend. A small whirlwind of dust caught his attention, signalling the arrival of The Brother.

"You don't have choice," he heard Clay mumbled from behind.

He didn't even have time to react as his friend's bony arms wrapped around his neck in a sleeper hold.

"Clay!" Tim gasped, struggling as his airway was wrenched tighter. He kicked wildly, body instinctively expending energy in a desperate attempt to break free. He tried to pull apart Clay's grip, but the smaller hand was buried beneath his chin, disabling him from getting a grip.

Despite the scratches drawing blood and a few strong kicks to the shin, Clay held his stance, not once letting lose his hold. "I'm sorry," he whispered, "I'm so sorry." Tim's frantic struggle slowed to a few jerks and weak attempts to wrench free, before finally, his body slowly slumped from lack of oxygen, though still barely clinging on to consciousness.

A whirl of sand formed on the platform opposite Clay, and the body of The Brother materialised from within.

"Just you and me," Clay said, a calm having settled over him after saving his friend. A fiery look flashed in his eyes as he felt a final confrontation approaching. "Let's do this."

Like the after image left on a screen, Tim's consciousness and body slowly faded, until even the physical weight of it disappeared, leaving Clay hugging the air.

CHAPTER THIRTY-TWO

Turn and Face the Mirror

"Only the dead have seen the end of war."
- George Santayana, Soliloquies in England

12:02 A.M.
7 days earlier

Hanging onto the thread of consciousness, Tim breathed in deeply, hoping the influx of oxygen would give his brain the kick it needed to restart. Instead, all it gave him was a sharp headache that caused him to wince. In pitch darkness, he was blinded. Attempting to feel his way around only forced the rope that tied his arms behind him to burn his wrist from the friction. He stopped moving once the discomfort set in. With his hands and back, he felt for the shape of what held him down. A metal angle iron at the hands and T-section joints along his spine shaped the outline of a metal shelf, with his arms tied at the frame of the structure.

Breathing a sigh of relief at the stupidity of whoever chained him, Tim tucked his legs to his body, keeping both feet flat against the ground. Digging his left shoulder into the metal bracket of the lowest shelf, he winced as the sharp edge sunk into his skin. With a heave, he began rising to his feet, using his body as a lever to lift the shelf off its legs.

"Argh..." he groaned through gritted teeth as the metal bit into his shoulder. "Come on. Come on!"

The shelf was heavier than he had initially thought. Even though he only needed to lift it an inch off the ground to slip his tied hands underneath and out, the weight of the furniture made the task backbreaking work. He felt the shelf starting to angle. Quickly, he shimmied his arms down the stand, pulling against it in an attempt to find the edge. He found it.

With a steadied body and a growl that was between the sound of being constipated and a chain smoker's cough, he yanked hard, and his hands flicked free of the leg. The weight of the shelf crammed down on his shoulder and he was forced back onto his ass, the shelf thumping to the ground with a loud clank.

Bindings loosened, he quickly slipped out of the rope, immediately reaching over to message his left shoulder. He could feel the indent in his skin from where the metal bracket held its place.

From outside the storage room, he could hear a man say, "What was that?"

"Shit," Tim cursed out.

He quickly got to his feet and felt around for something he could use as a weapon. The long, cold body of a metal pipe found its way into his hand. At first touch, it had a length of about half a meter, enough to use as a bat. With a quick sweep with the weapon over the shelves, he sent everything on them crashing to the floor.

"Hey boss, I heard some noise in the store. I'm gonna go check it out." Tim heard from the man outside, followed by the jingling of keys.

"Right," Pearlman's distorted voice replied over a radio. "Let me know what you find."

Hastily, Tim scrambled to find the shelf leg he was tied to and sat back down with his hands behind his back, as if he was bound. The metal pipe hid in the corner gap of the angled iron legs.

The door unlocked with a click and swung open, brightening the room with the dim light outside. Tim bent his head over so no one could see his eyes and pretended to be asleep. With a click, the lights turned on. Looking up to his peripherals, Tim saw Clay's unconscious body tied to a chair in the middle of the room.

A short burst of static emerged from the radio as it connected. "Hey boss. Just a bunch of boxes that fell over."

Pearlman radioed back, "Copy that. Clean it up and get back to the truck. We'll leave in half an hour."

Without replying, the henchman crossed the aisle of shelves past Tim. The teen turned his head slightly to see the mess he had made. Boxes of packages of Somnidin lay scattered on the floor. The tattooed man knelt down at the pile, putting them back into their boxes.

Slowly, with as much stealth as he could muster, Tim freed himself from his false binding, careful to grab his weapon without any noise as he did so.

"Shit!" Tattoo cursed, shocking Tim to freeze mid rise. "Package's damaged," the man muttered to himself, before pocketing the faulty medication; a self given bonus.

Tim silently got to his feet just as the man stood up with a box of the medication. He turned, Tim raised the pipe. With a swing, Tim brought the weapon across the man's face, the thug dropping the box as he stumbled back from the strike.

Continuing his assault, Tim jumped over the box while the man pulled out a pistol from the back of his belt. He swung the pipe back, knocking the gun out of the man's hand before the latter had the chance to even get his finger on the trigger, the firearm clattering into a corner. Maniacal with energy, Tim dropped another hit square on the man's forehead. However, his adversary did not fall, despite the blood that flowed profusely down his face. Another swing. Tattoo avoided with a step back. Rearing up, the man charged at Tim with his broad shoulder spearing him in the gut.

Tim held his ground, striking the spine of the man again with his weapon, but stumbled back after the thug pushed against him. Tripping over the box that dropped behind him, Tim fell backwards onto the floor. The henchman flung himself onto Tim, reeled his hand back, and, with pistons for muscles, punched Tim square on the nose.

He tasted the blood that seeped into his mouth, his nose creaking as it dislocated. But Tim knew that to worry about one injury now would only cost him his life. He pulled his weapon arm across his face, blocking another painful strike with his forearm. He countered with a backhanded pipe across the man's temple. Howling in pain, the henchman was flung to the side by the force of the attack, and he rolled onto his back.

Tables turned, Tim jumped on the man. With a burst of adrenaline and maddened survival instincts, he bashed the pipe repeatedly into the man's skull. Blood that was not his own splattered across Tim's face. The man kicked and struggled, but his entire body, arms included, were pinned under the boy, his strength sapped by his injuries.

Then, the kicking stopped. Tim's assault continued. His breathing heavy and erratic, but in tune with each strike. He continued to pummel the dead man's head.

12:32 A.M.
7 days earlier

Stella sat in the corridor of the hospital in a wheelchair, having already changed out of her hospital robes into a clean set of green pleated skirt and a brown sweater. Her left leg, from the knee down, was wrapped in a cast. The painkillers having long since taken effect made the pain in her leg just

169

a bearable ache. Her strawberry blonde hair stood out like a cheery beacon in the otherwise gloomy hallway, though her feelings were as far from the happy hair colour as they could possibly be. Her parents, Matilda and Gordon, stepped out of the room opposite her.

The white haired housewife knelt down beside her, "The doctor said we can bring you home."

Intuitively, Stella replied, "They don't have enough staff left to take care of me here. Right?"

Her father sighed, "You and your brother. Too smart for your own good sometimes."

She smiled weakly back. "Have they found him?" referring to Clay.

Matilda held her daughter's hand reassuringly. "The detectives are looking for him right now."

Knowing there was nothing she could do in her injured state, Stella woefully nodded, a rare frown on her face.

Gordon continued, "Your mother and I are going upstairs to fill out your discharge forms. We'll be right back for you, okay?"

Stella nodded with a forced smile, enough to alleviate some worries from her parents. The two adults walked off, with her father ruffling her hair affectionately before doing so. She hated it when he did that.

Just when the two turned a corner into the elevator lobby, Stella's phone rang. She took it out from one of the inbuilt pockets of the wheelchair. It was an unknown number. Not feeling in the mood to entertain any telemarketers, she hung up. Before she even got the chance to close her phone, the same caller rang again.

Slightly annoyed but now curious, she answered the call with a stern, "Hello?" On the other end came a series of heavy breathing. When no reply came to her, she asked, "Who's this?"

After a short pause, Tim replied, "It's me, Stell. I found Clay."

"Oh my..." she almost stood up in her excitement, but remembered her injury in time. "Where are you two? Is he okay? Are you okay?"

"The answers to your questions are, 'I don't know', 'I'm not sure', and 'yes, sort of.'" Another short pause as Tim scrambled around on the other end. "We're in a storage locker. Those small ones, like room sized. It's an hour and a half away from Westlay Street. That's all I have for you. You have to make it work."

She replied earnestly, "I'll make it work." She noted mentally there were only three storage lots throughout the city.

"Good. I need to go. Got to see if I can get your brother out."

Before he had the chance to hang up, she nervously asked, "How is he?"

170

He replied with half a dozen seconds of silence. "He's alive."

"For now?"

Another period of quiet. "You'll see him again. I promise." He cancelled the call, leaving Stella to sit dumbfounded and alone in the corridor.

She took a deep breath to calm down, gathering back her focus. She scrolled through her contact list in her phone and dialled. It rang once. Twice. A third time.

Halfway through the forth ring, the other side greeted her with a, "Hello?"

"Detective Hardy," Stella said. "This is Stella Barber. I know where my brother is."

"Great!" the detective replied.

But before he could continue, she cut in, "But there's one favour I need to ask of you."

"Why are you doing this?" Clay asked The Brother. "You and that Father character?"

Still at the top of the maze that was slowly being filled with sand, he found himself in a standoff with the creature from another world.

"Tim said you could talk, so talk!"

The Brother merely stood opposite him. Neither of them moving from their position. Deciding to take a chance though, Clay took a step back, and The Brother followed with a step forward.

"What? You copying me now?" Clay decided to take a step forward. But instead of backing off, The Brother took another step closer instead, as if purposefully toying with him. "Okay, guess not."

From the corner of his eyes, he could see the sand of the corridors having filled to merely a meter off from the edge. The source was a mystery, perhaps only known by the hunters of the dream world.

"Why are you doing this?" Clay asked again. Frustrated by the lack of progress, he yelled, "Answer me!"

They continued their standoff in silence, and Clay was starting to wonder if The Brother could even think, let alone talk. Suddenly, *Power.* The crackling voice echoed within Clay's mind.

"What?" he replied, shocked.

I. Need. Power.

"Why? Why do you need power?"

To. Be. Strong. To. Win.

Clay processed the message in his mind. After a second of thinking, he let out an unwilling chuckle. "Hah..." he started, but could not hold back as he burst out in a fit of laughter.

What. Is. So. Funny?

"It's a power trip! That's retarded! What are we? In a movie or something?" Clay said in energetic mania. "So you lost your little baseball game in the real world and died. Now you want power! You're just another classic, B-rated, movie monster. And you don't even have a good backstory."

The Brother took a step forward, raising its bat at being antagonised.

Unfazed by the threat, Clay continued, "Don't you get it, kid? You're dead! There's nothing left to win." He took a step forward towards his adversary. The Brother however, did not react. The sand had reached their level. "Time to stop dreaming, Brother! No. Do you prefer your real name? Harrison Smith?"

In a literal blink of his eyes, the entire dream world vanished before him and was replaced by the dimly lit storage locker he was held in. However, his bindings had been removed, liberating him from the chair. The body of the dead tattooed henchman lay on the floor to his right, face pummelled beyond recognition.

"The fuck?"

Clang.

Clay swore his heart stopped. The sound that was not supposed to exist outside his nightmare rang out clear within his head.

Clang.

Panicking, he jumped to his feet. He turned around, eyes widening in shock at the creature before him. Backing up against the garage door, his entire body trembled as he pointed out, "You–you're not suppose to be here."

He wasn't dreaming anymore.

But The Brother stood before him like a nightmare.

CHAPTER THIRTY-THREE

The Brother

"The ultimate test of man's conscience may be his willingness to sacrifice something today for future generations whose words of thanks will not be heard."
- Gaylord Anton Nelson

12:51 A.M.
7 days earlier

32 rounds. Either the henchman did not know how to count, or he ran out of bullets. Whatever the case, Tim felt the extended 33 rounds magazine of the pistol made the gun slightly back heavy and was uncomfortable with its grip. He sighed in recognition that the 'gangster gun' was his best option of a weapon at that point and tucked in into his belt.

Clay had been untied. But with both their injuries, it was impossible for Tim to move him and himself without suffering from pain and further damage to their bodies, even though Tim had managed to painfully relocate his nose. He had no choice but to hold the fort, awaiting Stella and her backup. He looked at his watch. Twenty minutes had passed since he called her. Fifty since the now dead and bloodied henchman had his last contact with Adam Pearlman.

As if on queue with his thoughts, Pearlman's voice rang out from Tattoo's radio. "Hey moron, what's taking you so long?"

Tim thought fast, reaching over to the radio on the corpse's belt, careful not to look at the pulp that was now the thug's face in worry that he might vomit.

With his best imitation of the man's thick accent, Tim radioed back, "Still packing things, boss."

173

It seemed Pearlman bought it, for he radioed back, "Damn it. We've got to get to the docks in thirty minutes. I'm coming over to help."

"No!" Tim panicked, his voice croaking slightly. He cleared his throat, "I'll be done in five minutes."

The beat of his own heart and each breath he took was as clear to him as the ticking of the hands on the thug's Rolex. He could see his window of success closing. Adam had probably figured out his plans and was making preparations to return and take him down, having seen through his dreadful attempt at voice acting.

His worry was eased when Adam finally replied, "Fine," and Tim let out a breath of relief. "By the way, your accent is terrible. See you in ten, Timmy-boy."

False hope was the most cruel thing in Tim's view. And it seemed Adam Pearlman was someone who was willing to play the card for a psychological advantage. Determined not to fall into the throes of the man's game, Tim started to plan. He could try to move Clay out of the storage room, but felt they would not get far. The room was too small to be a good place to set up a defence. If Adam was desperate enough and willing to sacrifice some of his stash of Somnidin, a simple Molotov would be enough to turn them to ashes. Though he was betting that the drug dealer would not resort to such means so as to preserve his goods, Tim did not want to take that chance. The confined space also meant the likelihood of any gunfire exchanged could hit the immobile Clay.

Stepping out of the now unlocked door, he clicked his tongue in disappointment as he found themselves in the centre storage locker of a row of fifteen. With no clear hiding space left or right of him, he was stuck with the option of barricading the door. That was also not a good option, as Adam would likely have the keys to open the larger garage door, which would be impossible to block.

With the addition of moonlight, he turned to face the shelf-filled room. His mother taught him that sometimes, to move fast, he had to go slow. He breathed calmly, scanning the place for something he could use. Behind him, the open road had no hiding place. The inside of the room however, was too cramped. He kept floating back between those two locations and plans. Then, from the corner of his eyes, something glinted. And he grinned.

01:01 A.M.
7 days earlier

Adam strolled down the aisle of storage lockers calmly and with the confident gait of a king. He caught sight of a black cat running by the opposite end. He smiled at the display. Never having understood the reasoning of people of old for believing that a black cat signified misfortune, he instead found the creature slick, clean, and a pleasant view for the eyes. As much so as the suit that he wore and favoured. It was a symbol of wealth to him. The ability to afford a colour that was a blend of everything.

As he passed storage locker 5, he pulled out his 38. Magnum from the holster under his blazer, feeling the heavy weight of the firearm in his hand. He liked the gun for its sheer power, and was as confident in its explosive strength as he was in his ability to wield it.

He was also confident that Tim would stay in the vicinity. Either in the storage locker itself, or around the far corner. That was the problem with good guys. They had something else to protect. Adam called those things 'burdens'.

He reached the door, trying the knob. Not to his surprise, it was locked. "Come on, Timmy!" he called out to the occupant inside, banging the door. From his pocket, he retrieved the remote control that would open the garage door. "Don't make me come in there!"

In a prone position, Tim lined his sights, his left wrist resting over his right, holding down the entirety of his arm against the coming recoil. With a shorter barrel, the key to accuracy, as was taught in his air rifle club, was a steady arm. But he wasn't shooting a pellet anymore. He could feel the awkward weight of the extended magazine and the heavy implications that came when Adam drew his gun. The idea that he was about to attempt to take someone's life crossed him. And he fired.

Adam's right shoulder jerked as the bullet grazed just over the top. Tim fired two more rounds from his perch on the opposing flat roof, both shots ricocheting off the concrete floor.

The drug dealer turned and spotted him above. Adam fired hastily, the larger, more powerful magnum round blasting a chunk off the concrete roof.

Tim put up the stepladder he used to climb up in front of him, using it as a poor makeshift shield between him and Adam, knowing full well the thin metal would do nothing to stop the bullet. But he hoped it would do enough to disconcert the man's aim. And it worked.

His opponent's next two shots missed him entirely, allowing him the time to recover. He got onto his knees and unloaded half his magazine onto Adam in a hopeful barrage, forcing the man to run towards the building Tim stood on, and running out of Tim's sight beneath him.

Not willing to give the man any room to recuperate, Tim jumped to his feet and fired over the edge. He heard the distinct sound of bullets striking concrete. Looking over, Adam had disappeared. Instead, the man had ran off towards the left, attempting to escape the disadvantage in elevation by creating distance.

Tim gave chase.

Adam fired over his shoulder, the bullet grazing the edge of the roof. Tim shot another five wild rounds at his opponent, the bullets spraying all over the place, except on their mark. He was no action movie hero, and once again cursed films for portraying gunfights as easy, with guarantee kills every shot.

From the horizon of the storage lockers, streaks of red and blue light flashed against the buildings opposite. At the same time, half a dozen lights turned on from the apartments around them, eager shadows popping to the windows to catch a glimpse of the action. The sirens of the police vehicles wailed into the night. Backup had arrived.

Suddenly, the garage door behind them exploded from its hinges, blasting out and slamming like a crashing car into the locker facing it.

From the smoke, Clay stumbled out, holding his broken arm to his chest, his free hand gripping the same bloodied steel pipe Tim used earlier to murder the henchman.

Clay saw Adam first, a glint of mania in his eyes as he eyed the drug dealer's gun. Clay began running towards Adam, shouting, "Shoot him! SHOOT HIM, DAMN IT!"

From Adam's escape route, a muscle car braked sharply at the junction, blocking the exit. From the passenger's side, the red haired detective, Julianne Smith, jumped out.

"Stay in the car!" she shouted to the back seat.

From the driver side, Oliver Hardy stood from the seemingly undersized door, his muscular figure overshadowing all the combatants that had gathered like a juggernaut amongst gladiators. He stepped towards the convict with his gun raised. "Adam Pearlman! You are under arrest!"

His partner did the same. However, she pointed her firearm up at Tim instead. "You too, boy!" The female detective was on the verge of running over, eyes gleaming with mad excitement. "Put down your gun or we'll shoot!"

But the two former prisoners weren't listening. For trailing Clay was a cloud of dust, slowly twisting and turning like a small twister. Denser and denser it got until it started to form the rough silhouette of a person. Lines of sand coiled around the mini-twister, moulding the finer details. Then, colours set into the grains, and the form of The Brother appeared before them, baseball bat and all.

The detectives, especially Oliver, stared in wide-eyed disbelief at the phenomenon. The pair rushed forward and changed their targets to the forming creature. Adam however, was the only adult that kept his poker face throughout the dust show.

Clang.

Instinctively upon hearing the sound, Tim turned his gun to The Brother and started firing. Clay jumped to the ground as Adam and the detectives did the same, unloading their rounds into the general direction of the creature. Bits of The Brother's skin chipped away with each impact, but quickly turned to sand instead, as if the dust was an armour that it wore. And the bullets were nothing but pellets that scrapped the coating.

"Clay!" Stella called out in worry, climbing out of the car with her crutches under her arms.

"Get back in the car!" Oliver demanded.

"Not until you get my brother here!"

Tim was the first to stop firing. Not because he ran out of bullets, but because he realised they were doing absolutely no damage to the dream entity. Adam followed, taking the opportunity to reload his gun. Even Oliver stopped. The Brother continued its slow, confident walk towards the group, but started to speed up the closer he got to Clay.

Still, Julianne continued shooting, pulling her trigger constantly in a blind frenzy. Even after her gun had ran out of bullets, she continued to fire blankly, the trigger clacking against the barrel with no effect.

"That thing shouldn't be here!" she yelled, her voice shaking with fear.

Taking the panic as an opportunity, Adam ran past the two flustered detectives. With a strong backhand, he smashed the butt of his gun into the head of the distracted Julianne and the female detective crumpled to the floor like paper. With gun loaded, he headed straight for Stella.

"Clay!" the girl screamed as the dealer grabbed her by the throat, bringing her in front of him as a human shield. Her crutches dropped to the ground and she desperately stood on one leg to maintain balance.

"Shit," Oliver cursed, turning his attention to the hostage situation. "Let her go, asshole!"

Adam replied, licking his lips, "Give me your keys!"

"You're not exactly the big problem here!" Oliver replied.

"And we just shot that thing to hell!" Adam screamed back. "It's still coming, and I know when to make a retreat. Now give me your keys!"

177

Tim jumped off from his rooftop perch, landing painfully on his already tired and injured legs. He ran over to help his best friend to his feet. "Come on!" he heaved through gritted teeth, the muscles of his body starting to give way. "Stella needs you!"

Like magic words, Clay found the strength to stand. Gripping the steel pipe tighter than before, he turned to analyse the hostage situation. "Can you make the shot, kid?"

Tim turned to look at the confrontation between Adam and Oliver, then to the approaching Brother, before replying sternly, "I need time."

"I'll do you one better," Clay said with brimming confidence. From his pocket, he retrieved two bottles of Somnidin, passing them to Tim. Without looking at his friend, he said, "Don't need them anymore." He walked off to face The Brother.

Tim trusted Clay. And that trust was a two-way street. He turned to face Adam, their distance far enough apart that the older man did not even have Tim in his immediate vicinity of attention. Tim notched his gun arm over his free forearm, using it as a stabiliser. He took his aim, lining the sights to encompass Adam's head within the two iron pieces, then raised the gun just a millimetre higher.

Clay approached The Brother. Pipe in his hand, he said, "Let's do this, Harrison Smith."

He raised the pipe just as The Brother raised its bat. The two metals clashed as Clay swung to block the attack. He swung back up, the pipe smacking The Brother across the jaw. But instead of the burst of dust and sand that was expected, a trickle of blood drew from its lips. Clay took a step back. The Brother, taking the opportunity, struck his bat right onto Clay's head. Clay's knees nearly gave way as he heard the cracking of his skull.

From behind them, Stella screamed, "Clay!"

The gun still felt awkward in Tim's hand. Back heavy. Then he realised the reason. Ejecting the crude extended magazine, he re-aimed his shot, a single bullet in the chamber. The pistol felt balanced.

Another blow from the bat onto Clay's injured right shoulder. Gritting through the pain, he wrapped his broken arm around the metal weapon and yanked as hard as he could, pulling the weapon out of The Brother's hands and sent it clanking over the ground. Clay was sure he had dislocated his shoulder. And the blood that profusely bled from his arm told him he might have broken it beyond recovery. But the adrenaline pumped ferociously through him, numbing him from all pain and thought.

Tim pulled the trigger.

Clay swung his pipe.

178

The bullet bounced off the top of Adam's magnum, sending the weapon flying. Ricocheting off the firearm, the round changed its course straight through the criminal's eyes.

Knocking The Brother off its feet, Clay slid his hand up the length of the pipe, soaking his palm in the blood of the henchman until he held the weapon in reverse. With a primal yell, he sent the weapon piercing down into The Brother's face. The creature exploded into a cloud of dust, the force of the burst knocked Clay off his feet and sent him flying a few meters back, landing with a loud crunch on the concrete ground where he continued to lay, unmoving.

Adam, with his brains punctured and no longer in control of his body, released Stella from his grip. She hopped and staggered over towards Oliver, but passed the detective entirely, sweeping away the man's offered hand, and headed straight for her brother. She tripped, fell face flat on the ground, sobbing at her helplessness. Oliver picked her up in his arms as one would a basket of kittens, carrying her over to Clay as Adam's deceased body fell to his knees, gravity dragging it to lean against the car door, its temporary resting place.

Tim turned to his friend, lying unconscious on the floor, the surrounding ground covered in a layer of dust and blood. Oliver set Stella down beside him and the girl gently cupped her brother's face in her hands.

From behind, Julianne reared, groaning as she slowly regained consciousness. Tim looked to the kind giant, Detective Hardy, who told him, "Run. Get out of here."

Tim looked to Stella, who through tears, and despite needing comfort and a shoulder, nodded to Tim. "Go."

Though they had won the battle, Tim felt they had lost the war. With a heavy heart, he turned away from the group and ran.

CHAPTER THIRTY-FOUR
Breathe

"War is hell."
- William Tecumseh Sherman

10:21 A.M.
7 days earlier

Detective Julianne Smith, with a bandage wrapped around her forehead, entered the ward with her partner, Oliver Hardy. She strode with purpose towards Stella, a daunting gaze in her eyes despite the atmosphere. Stella ignored the new presence from her seat beside her brother's bedside, the ECG beeping away the seconds. Wrapped in bandages from head to toe, his broken arm in a cast that dangled from a sling strung to the ceiling, Clay breathed with the aid of a tube down his throat, his chest rising and falling to the chug of the ventilator.

She knew what the detectives were there to ask, and her answer would remain the same.

"Where's Timothy Kleve?" Smith asked.

"I told you," Stella replied. "I don't know."

"Do you really expect me to believe that?"

Oliver cut in, "Julie, I don't think she knows anything."

"These kids are somehow part of it with that baseball boy. I just know it," she replied to her partner before turning her attention back to Stella, "People have died because of them."

Without looking, Stella replied confidently, "Tim will save them."

Julianne leaned into the chair, trapping Stella within her long, slender arms, like an insect in a web. "Do you think this is a game? Your friend is a murderer. The world is going to hell because of this stupid mass hysteria. There's been a massacre at the police station, and our information and

180

media has just been wiped from the face of the Earth. What do you think a bunch of kids like you can do?" She stepped back, arms crossed. "It may seem peaceful now, but that's only because everyone's too scared and confused to do anything. You've been to Roagnark. You saw the riots. It's only a matter of time before Ridge Valley explodes as well."

"And what do you hope to accomplish by catching Tim? Will that stop the inevitable? Will imprisoning the one person who stands a chance at stopping this help us in any way?" Stella grabbed one of her crutches from against the wall and got to her feet, standing toe-to-toe with the detective. She was ready to pounce. She was pissed.

"My brother is unconscious and you have my parents under house arrest. And for some reason, you're hell bent on capturing the single person you deem as a 'kid' that you say have no ability to affect what's happening." She pushed closer with her crutch, now face-to-face, eye-to-eye. She could smell the sweat on the female detective and the stench of... "Fear. That's why you're doing this. You're afraid because you don't know what's happening. And you want someone to blame. So you grab hold of the first thing you see that's a threat to your belief and you bite it like a dog."

Stella saw the slap coming a mile away. Stepping back ever so slightly, the unintended scratch from the detective's nails drew three lines of red across Stella's left cheek. But even as blood rolled down from the wound, her stare did not waver.

Fiercely, the girl continued, "You think we wanted this? To fight for our lives? This was the hand we were dealt. We're dealing with it. You can blame others all you want, but running around in circles won't change anything." She expected another slap, but none came. Instead, Julianne stared at her audacity with wide-eyed disbelief. "You're not getting anything out of me. You're going to turn around and walk out that door and continue to cower in your fear."

The detective opened her mouth as if to speak, but only muted air came out. Without another word, she turned and left the ward, slamming the door on her way.

Oliver just stood where he was, having been ignored by both parties the entire time. Finally, he spoke, "The three of you..." He looked to Stella, then to her brother. "You're all something, I'll give you that."

Calming down from her out of character outburst, and feeling the strain from standing, Stella settled back in her chair. With eloquence and a tone of finesse that was not present in her dealing with Smith, she replied to Oliver, "Thanks detective. I'll take those words as compliments."

He stepped forward to her, retrieving a folded note from his pocket.

"He asked me to give this to you." He handed the paper over and headed for the door. Looking over to Clay and back to her, he said, "I'm sorry. About everything."

Stella stared at the door long after the echoes of the click had faded from her mind. The ECG beeping keeping her company, along with the aided breathing of her brother.

She unfolded the note. Written in Tim's scribble of a handwriting was a request.

Sleep before 12
Ask Sister to find me

The sun set over the horizon of the sea, waves slapping gently against the sandy shore. A lighthouse continued to spin its light along the cliffs to the north, the building towering over all natural structures in sight. Sitting on the fallen trunk of a coconut tree, the moment was the first period of grace that Tim had in the last three days, with a sight soothing enough to warrant a resort built in its presence. He wished the world would stay that way for even an hour longer. But the two approaching girls from along the shore signalled the end of his relaxation and marked the start of yet another frantic run. He got to his feet.

Sister closed in to him in her typical seductive manner, sliding her arm against his. "Well, aren't you all high and mighty, calling me here."

"I needed to make sure The Father doesn't mark me, that's all."

"Aw..." She danced away and around him. "And here I thought you just wanted to see me."

A little. But he wore his best poker face. Turning to Stella, he asked "How is he? Clay?"

"He's on life support right now," she explained grimly, looking down at the grains of sand beneath her feet, as if a solution to all her problem lay between the cracks. "The doctors managed to close his wounds but...he's hurt bad, Tim. He hasn't woken up yet, and he's not breathing naturally either."

Tim nodded back, expression doleful. Even the usually cheerful Sister looked solemnly from the side, her antics cast away for the moment.

Tim continued, "I see." But his tone betrayed his expectant of the situation.

Stella further explained, "And the detective, the female one. She seems hell bent on capturing you."

"She's deluded. Afraid." He turned towards a wooden pier on the far south of the shoreline where two shadowy figures sat and fished from the edge. "Can't blame her. But I can't let her catch me now. For some reason, I can cross dreams. It's something I can use to solve this whole thing."

"Where are you now?" Stella asked. "In the real world I mean. Don't you have to be in some close proximity to jump dreams?"

He held out a 'V' with his fingers. "Two floors down from you. In one of the empty doctor's offices. Stealing fentanyl."

"What's that?"

"Knockout drugs, basically. I figured that if we're gonna have a chance at beating this thing, I'm going to need to be able to sleep as-and-when I can as well," Tim explained.

Sister cut in, "But if you sleep, you'll get hunted by everyone here. The Father, Brother, Mother, everyone! I'm not going to be able to reach you first all the time."

"I know," he smiled at her reassuringly, happy to know that despite her initial apathetic actions, the girl in white did actually care for his life. "But I have a theory. And I think, it's going to be the most important theory ever, of all time. Which is why, Sister, you need to tell me this. Clay beat The Brother in the real world. Like how I did The Father here. But I need to know, can you tell if The Brother's dead? Dead and can't stand again?"

"If you're asking if I have some sort of telepathic connection with the others, then no. I can't tell if they're standing right behind me without seeing them," Sister said. Twirling the end of her hair on her finger like a spool of silk. She continued explaining, "But I don't think he's dead. None of us have died in the time I've been here. And from what I know, we're as good as immortals. We're connected to the dreamscape. As long as we are in thing place, the only way we can 'die' is if we finish our term of service to whatever entity put us here. And even then, we only know one of us has left if we see a replacement."

Having expected the answer, Tim replied, "That's fine. It's what we're here to find out." Hw turned to Stella. He placed his one hand on her shoulder and, with a crestfallen gaze, said, "We're here to meet someone. And I need you to be strong."

Stella's lips trembled when the meaning of the words sunk in. "W-why?" she asked, her voice breaking slightly, her eyes glimmered with surfacing tears.

He swallowed hard and forced the words out. "Cause we're here for Clay."

Looking back to the pier, the two fishermen had disappeared. In their place, a single figure stood at the end, admiring the blood-red sun. His hair gleaming white in the setting light.

CHAPTER THIRTY-FIVE

Thanks, And

"It is a far, far better thing that I do, than I have ever done; it is a far, far better rest that I go to than I have ever known."
- Charles Dickens

Ripples broke the smooth water surface as the pebble skipped three times along it. At the end of its journey, the stone plopped into the sea, the final ripple wider than any before. From within his hand, Clay materialised a second pebble, once again sending it skipping across the water. Tim, Stella and Sister approached him on the pier. The wispy girl in white looked on in amazement; Stella with concern; Tim with sombreness.

Tim said, "You look like you're enjoying yourself."

Clay closed his palm and reopened them, and another pebble appeared. "Not much to do here," he sighed without facing them. He still wore his grey shirt and cargo pants from the day before, complete with bloodstains and dirt patches from his fight with The Brother and encounter with Adam.

"That's a neat trick," Tim noted the magically appearing stones. "How'd you do that?"

"No idea," he replied, twirling his fingers. "One day, just...poof. Guess it's true what they say about being able to manipulate your own dream. But I can only do simple things though. Rocks. Sticks. Stuff like that."

"Brother..." Stella began, but Tim paused her with a raise of his hand.

"Days. You said a few days."

"Yeah, I did. Just like you, kid, to notice things like that," Clay sighed in resignation, finally turning to the group. "I've been here for three days. Jumping from one dreamscape to another, being chased by The Father. Sometimes there's a break between the running, like right now. But they're starting to get fewer and farther between."

"Impossible. It's only been a few hours in the real world!" Stella stepped forward and hugged her brother, her eyes glistening with held-back tears. "You're coming back. We're going to bring you back."

He returned the hug but slowly pulled apart. He looked over her shoulder to Sister and asked, "You're Sister, aren't you? I sort of figured some things out in the past few days. Time doesn't go straight here." He paused as he tried to get the impossible words out. "I'm stuck here, aren't I?"

The girl in white nodded back, "I'm sorry."

Clay nodded dejectedly. A part of him had held hope, though the realist inside him knew chances were slim to none.

Stella grabbed her brother by the hand, "No! We're bringing you back. I won't let you stay here." She turned to Tim pleadingly, "Think of something. Have...have some clever deduction or come up with a plan! Like you always do!"

However, Tim could only look to his feet in shame. His reply equal in emotion as the atmosphere, if not more. "There's nothing I can do."

She charged at him, pouncing on him by the shoulders, sinking her nails into his skin. "THEN WHAT ARE YOU HERE FOR?" she yelled while shaking Tim in desperation, her composure finally broken.

Tim didn't dare to look her in the eyes, instead, he stared off towards Sister at the side, who looked on sadly, though not with pity.

Clay said, "He's here for what I know." Their eyes met. And Clay smiled at his best friend, showing his understanding of the situation and forgiveness. "He needs to know what I did to The Brother."

Sister asked, "Is The Brother dead?"

A small smile formed at the corner of his lips as he replied, "Yeah. Haven't seen him once since I came here. That's pretty much the silver lining. He's dead. But The Father somehow seems to be...taking on his victims." He turned to Tim, "It's the name. Their real names. I think the name brings them to our world. Makes them real. It's this place, I think. The realm between worlds. As long they are here, they can't die."

Realising her situation, Sister exclaimed, "That's why we can't remember our names and part of our pasts. It's like a...like an anchor. To keep us in the dream world." Still with questions, she asked Clay, "But how did you kill him then?"

"Emotions," Tim replied in his stead. "That's how your powers work, right? You overwhelm our emotions. My father's rage with fear. Clay's confidence with anxiety. And my clarity with your..."

"Lust," Sister said, not denying the deduction. "Yeah. But I never thought it would–"

"It would actually work the other way around?" Tim cut in, feeling the

185

fire of his deductive reasoning being lit. "I know. That's cause until this whole Sin business, and me, everyone's been isolated or otherwise..." He glanced over in Clay's direction as a nod to the latter's current condition. "Incapacitated. It's a struggle over emotions. It may be corny but, the one with the strongest willpower wins."

Stella, dumbfounded by the casualness of the conversation, demanded, "What about Clay?" Clay stepped towards his sister, who continued to protest, "We have to get him out! We have to–"

She was suppressed by Clay's gentle hug. He kissed her forehead tenderly. "I'm not going Stella. I know my real body's beaten to shit, so I'm not waking up any time soon." He stroked her golden hair as the girl broke out in tears, dropping to their knees and crying into his chest. "Like you said, it's only been a few hours for you, yet three days for me. And I can't run from The Father forever. The only reason I survived this long was cause I needed to tell Tim what I knew. I'm out of juice now, and I don't see a way out for me this time."

"No..." her muffled cries stung the air.

"I'm sorry, Stell." He held her close, comforting her in his embrace. A blanket of dark fog rolled up the horizon, slowly cutting away the light like a rising curtain in the sky. Looking to Tim, he said to his best friend, "We're running out of time. Kid, keep her safe."

Tim knew it was a promise that was easier said than done. But it was one he intended to keep. Their eyes crossed intently, as if all of Clay's pride and confidence were to be passed on through their gaze. "I promise."

Clay smiled back, "Good! If you break that promise, I'll personally come to kill you, kid." He helped Stella to her feet as the girl tried to control her sobbing, to little success. Reading Clay's intention, Tim helped separate the siblings, taking Stella in his arms. To his sister, Clay asked, "Tell mom and dad, 'Thanks for everything'. And I love them. And I love you. All of you."

Speaking through sobs and choking tears, she managed a pained, "I love you too." The horizon fog had crossed a quarter of the sky, covering half the water in darkness.

CLay turned his attention to Sister. "Sorry, I know this is the first time we've met but, could you do me a favour?" He smiled cheekily. "I think a smart and pretty girl like you already know what it is though."

"Yeah," Sister replied. She floated over, her dress extending to the ground as she did, covering her feet in the process. "I'll make it painless."

"Thanks." He turned back to his friend and sister who were both slowly vanishing before his eyes, the fog darkened the ocean and crossed over them, covering them in shadows. He smiled at them, and right before they awoke from the dream, Tim could have sworn that the smile was that of a man who had found peace, who had lived a life with pride and no regrets, despite his short time alive. "And goodbye."

Sister kissed Clay, and the light of the world extinguished before them.

5:02 A.M.
6 days earlier

Even though he was awake, Tim could only stare blankly at the ceiling. Shrouded by darkness, he lay on the examination bed of the empty doctors' office. His body ached and every fibre of muscle screamed for him to stay still and go back to sleep. He could barely make out the shadowy figure sitting behind the desk, watching him lie motionless on the bed. He knew who it was and felt no fear. However, hesitation overwhelmed him from acting, and he continued to maintain his position.

The desk clock ticked away the seconds, and he counted the minutes that passed.

In silence, the two of them stayed in the room until Stella finally said, "He's gone." Her tone void of emotion. "Clay's dead. Cardiac arrest." He could hear her gulping saliva to find the words to continue. "What do we do now?"

He wondered what was the point. What had they accomplished in the week that lead up to that moment in time? His dad was gone. Clay was gone. Everything they had retrieved from Vashmir Commons' house had been taken as evidence by the police. He had killed Tattoo and Adam Pearlman, and Stella killed Joseph Price. They had blood on their hands with nothing to show for their efforts.

Himself, Stella, Oliver Hardy, and Sister. They were the last remaining players in his dwindling circle of allies. Julianne Smith had become a wall between them and the Vashmir evidence. The Father continued to hound his heels in dreams.

Steeling himself, Tim explained, "We get the diary and photo album back from the police. See if there's a clue there to The Father's real name." He listened to Stella's steady breathing and the rhythmic beat of his own heart. "And then we kill him. End this thing, once and for all. Make it worth while."

CHAPTER THIRTY-SIX

Riot

"Unthinking respect for authority is the greatest enemy of truth."
- Albert Einstein, Letter to Jost Winteler

8:12 A.M.
6 days earlier

"This way!" Oliver Hardy yelled back to his partner as they sprinted through the corridors of the hospital, his coat fluttering in the move. The sound of the crowd got louder with each step.

Julie ran behind him, "How many?" she asked, refreshed from a change of clothes to comfortable blue jeans and a red shirt. Her gun was tucked underneath her leather jacket.

"Fifty?" he panted back. "Maybe more."

The pair stepped around the last corner, shooting out into the hospital lobby. A horde of citizens were gathered, desperately trying to push their way through the half a dozen uniformed officers and two security guards standing at the entrance to the pharmacy. Nurses stood fearfully opposite the counter, backing up as far as they could to the walls.

"We want Somnidin!" shouted one of the males at the front of the mob.

"We told you," one of the nurses replied, "There's none left!"

"You're lying!"

A woman climbed onto a chair, capturing the attention of her fellows. "I say we go in there and find it!"

The crowd roared in unanimous agreement and resumed their push with added ferocity. One man slipped past the line of officers, managing to climb halfway over the counter before being violently pulled back by one of the police, tumbling back into the crowd.

188

Oliver asked, "What do we do, Julie?"

She pulled out her gun from her shoulder holster and fired into the ceiling. Bits and chips blasted off the wooden board, showering her in a rain of white particles. The entire lobby stilled to a hush. The mob turned to face the source of the gunshot in fear.

"What the hell?" Oliver exclaimed, jumping away in surprise.

She ignored him. Her voice booming in the now silent room, she shouted, "You are all going to calm the fuck down! Or I will have all of you arrested!"

The peace broke when an old man stepped forward, "Do your worst, cop! There's no medicine left, so we'll die anyway!" The crowd chanted in agreement.

She pointed her gun at the crowd and the whole mob backed away in united terror, the fear of dying etched into the whites of their eyes.

Julie said, "Come back at night and we will get you a new batch of Somnidin."

Oliver whispered to her, "I hope you're not saying what I think you're saying. Those drugs are evidence in a homicide!"

"If we don't give them Pearlman's stash, we're going to have a riot on our hands," she murmured back. "The lab just needs one crate anyway. We can give the rest away."

"Yeah but–"

"There's no station right now. We're all spread too thin. We have to control the situation, whatever the means." She turned back to the crowd without waiting for Oliver to reply. "Everyone, I assure you, we will have a new batch of medicine tonight. Please go wait at home until then."

Murmurs erupted within the crowd as discussions ensued. 'Lies' were one of the words that managed to float to the detectives. Despite the apparent distrust, the mob slowly dispersed, glaring menacingly back at the pair as they did. The two security guards came up to the detectives.

The taller one, with a beard that seemed almost apart from his face, commented, "Thanks detectives. I don't know what would have happened if you weren't here."

But Julie was critical. "How did you two let such a large group get past you?"

Nervously, the shorter guard replied, "We were called upstairs. One of our medical stores and equipment room was broken into. Looks like theft."

Oliver asked, "What was stolen?"

"A few syringes and a couple of bottles of fentanyl."

"Knock out drugs? Aren't you supposed to have those under locks and keys?"

189

The tall one replied, "We're kind of short handed here. What with the Vashmir Pandemic and all that. The anaesthetist on duty was called for an emergency surgery."

"Right," Oliver replied, nodding understandingly. "Anything else?"

"They also took two walkie-talkies," the tall guard added. "Good ones. Long range. No interferences. We use them for power outages and emergencies."

Julie sighed, "I think I know who took them."

11:39 A.M.
6 days earlier

"Tim," Stella's voice croaked through the two-way radio. "Can you hear me?"

Walking down the empty streets, Tim took the walkie-talkie out of his pocket and radioed back, "You're suppose to say 'over', over." He snickered.

"I refuse to stoop to your level of childishness."

"Now you're just being a downer. Are you at the library?"

"Yeah," Stella's tired heaves could be heard, even over the static. The city's public transportation had shut down, forcing the pair to travel everywhere by foot. Stella's injured leg was no doubt giving her a problem. "You're right though, Mister Galloway's gone."

"I had a feeling that would happen." He did not know who or what the librarian was then, especially after the old man's vanishing act at the station. But he felt Howard was there to help, and he needed all the aid he could get. "Did he leave anything behind? Like maybe a note or something?"

A short pause later, Stella replied, "Doesn't seem like it. Want me to come find you?"

"No, you stay there." He knew Stella would suggest meeting up. But he was worried of her condition. Not just her injury, but also her emotional health after losing her brother. She had insisted on continuing to aid him despite his disapproval, but he intended to keep her as far away from the physical dangers as possible. "Take a look around, see if there's anything he may have hidden."

"Alright," she replied, rather disappointed but seemingly understanding of his decision. "Are you at the station yet?"

"Not yet. I'll radio in again once I'm there. We can't communicate after

190

that or I might get caught. We still don't know what that place is like since Adam ran through it." He gave a pause, but did not let go of his transmitter. "Listen, Stell, about Clay. You sure you don't want to talk about it?"

She insisted, "Look, I don't care what he said. I'm going to help you."

"I know that. I know that. But that's not what I meant." He released his call to allow her to reply. But when none came, he continued, "Do you want to talk about it?"

"Yeah. I want to talk about it," she said. The receiver continued to run, preventing him from replying. He could hear light sobs coming from the other end. "But not now. Not yet. I'm not ready yet."

Tim nodded, though he was unsure what for as there was no one around to witness his actions. "Okay. We'll talk when you're ready."

"Thanks."

He walked the last two streets to the police station in silence. His mind fell onto Clay and his own father, and he could not escape the idea that the two of them had sacrificed themselves to give him a chance. But before he could delve further into his self-loathing, he turned the last corner onto the street that housed the police station and halted in his track.

Cars were parked haphazardly on the road. Ambulances and coroner vans were stationed at the perimeter. Bodies, covered in white sheets, stained with blood, were slowly being carried out of the station to the weeping tears of families and friends who had gathered at the foot of the building in waiting. Waiting to identify the bodies. Even from as far as he stood, he could hear the cries of sadness, the wails that echoed throughout the world.

Tim thought of Adam, and the realisation that a single man with a stock of Somnidin managed to do this gave him a conclusion. The world was changing. It might have already changed and was forever so.

He raised his radio. "Stella. I'm at the station."

"Alright," she replied. "How are things there?"

"Fine," he lied, as a woman fell to her knees in front of the latest stretcher carried out. "I don't know how we're going to do it, but we are going to stop this."

"Of course we are."

He headed towards the alley that led to the back of the station. With the attention focused on the front, he found no resistance. Scanning the building, his only way of entering was an open window on the second floor.

He pondered to himself, "Okay, now what?" Looking deeper into the alley, he saw a dumpster and a used bed frame leaning against the wall.

"Pile of trash. Just my speed."

Pushing the container and lining it under the window, he stacked the bed in front of it. Backing up against the opposing wall, he created some distance between him and his platforms.

With a deep breath for composure, and a thought to Clay and his dad to protect him, he dashed towards his makeshift launcher at full speed, bolting up the bed and onto the dumpster, he kicked against the wall as he flung himself up towards the ledge of the open window, both hands outstretched. He managed to grab hold of the edge and pulled himself up and over into the empty office.

CHAPTER THIRTY-SEVEN
Rat and Trap

"The reason I talk to myself is because I'm the only one whose answers I accept."
- George Carlin

12:22 A.M.
6 days earlier

'Vice' emblazoned the frosted glass window of the ajar door of the office. Two columns of three desks lined the side of the room, facing a whiteboard which was scribbled with details of crimes that Adam Pearlman had been linked with, the deceased man's name appearing multiple times across the board as if written during a schizoids' madness.

But what bothered Tim the most was the shattered glass that showed the hallway outside and the bullet holes in the walls behind him. Pools of dried blood marked the ground, with one of the desks on the further end smeared red with it. The bodies of the officers were nowhere to be seen, which lead him to believe that the second floor had been cleared of the dead. He remembered smelling and almost puking at the stench of death just days ago, and was surprised at how well he was already handling the current situation.

A lone revolver sat on the desk closest to the door. He walked by it on his way out and contemplated taking it. Another idea came to him instead and he ransacked the drawers to find a shining brass police badge and a box of spare ammunition. He pocketed the bullets, holstered the gun in his belt, and clipped the metal badge to his left pocket, where it could be seen even with his shirt untucked and hiding the firearm. It was a flimsy disguise at best, as anyone who looked closer would realise the farce and that he was in fact, just a teenager. But he only needed it to get him as far

193

as the evidence room. Any windows from then on would suffice as an escape.

He stepped out of Vice and into the empty hallway. Blood splattered the wall opposite the office, a single bullet lodged into the wall behind the red. He walked by it, focusing on the road before him, afraid that if he stopped to look back, he would be overwhelmed by the knowledge of the death that had happened.

He made it to the stairs without any other disruption and could hear, even from the top of the steps, the crying of family over the ones lost. He thought of his father, and willed himself away from being mystified by the tears.

Taking a deep breath, Tim took the steps down. The wailing got louder as he proceeded. He turned the corner at the first landing and saw the spotlessly clean floor of the station lobby. Despite it, the image of the bloodbath days before still overlaid his vision, and he could clearly picture the positions of the blood and bodies.

Without knowing it, he had reached the bottom of the landing. A uniformed officer approached him, snapping him out of his trance.

"What are you doing here?" The man looked down and saw Tim's badge and added, "Detective?"

Off the tip of his tongue, Tim replied, "Phelps. Detective Phelps from Vice."

"Ah, checking up on the Pearlman case I assume?"

"Yes. That's right. Just went up to look through some files."

The officer looked Tim up and down, raising a brow of suspicion. "Forgive me but...you look a little young to be a detective."

Quickly changing the subject, Tim said, "Sad what happened here."

"What?"

"You know, the shooting?"

"Oh," the officer replied as if he had just been slapped awake. He turned to look at the scene. "Terrible. We lost a lot of good people. I mean, my partner's in the hospital right now. One of the two survivors. It's just...bullshit, you know?"

"Yeah..." Tim replied. Though he did not want to be rude, he knew the longer he stood there, the higher was the chance of him being caught. "Listen, I need to get to the evidence locker."

"Right." The officer turned back. He looked over Tim's shoulder and towards the stairs down, indirectly pointing the way. "I'll leave you to it, detective."

Tim bid farewell and the officer returned to comfort the grieving families. A group of coroners carried out bodies from the opposite end of the station, up from the stairs that led to the holding cells. Tim sighed at the sight and descended to the basement.

At the end of the stairs down, he was greeted by a sign and faced with a short hallway. To his right was the gun range and equipment room. To his left was a single door at the end of a corridor that led to the evidence room. He was glad to see that the lock of the door had been blasted apart. Metal pellets on the ground indicated a shotgun was used.

He opened the door and was immediately greeted by the stench of rotting corpses. The room had stacks of cardboard boxes arranged onto metal grated shelves. Each with two dozen boxes covered up most of the space in the cramped room. To the left of the entrance was a small room where the body of a woman, white eyed, lay slumped against the wall from a shot to the head, working the cage in silence. In between the aisles were two lab technicians in bloodied coats that lay sprawled and unmoving in pools of their own blood. The door of the room had been closed for a while, and the odour only rotting flesh could provide had coagulated in the air, enough to make him dizzy with vile just from standing.

Not wanting to waste any more time than needed, Tim reached through the steel bars of the counter and grabbed the blood splattered logbook from the desk. He flipped through the pages, finding his name under the case code #139-HM. Aisle 13. Shelf 6. Box number 21.

He manoeuvred his way to the aisle. Down the shelves. Over a body. And to the empty spot that once housed box 21.

"What the hell?" Tim voiced out, feeling the air in front of him to make sure it was not some sort of dreamscape illusion.

From the end of the aisle came, "Looking for this?"

Tim turned to see the brown coated Detective Oliver Hardy standing with both diary and charred photo album in hand. Both pieces of evidence kept clean within clear plastic bags.

"Detective," Tim voiced his surprised. "How did you know I was here?"

"Boy, I may not look like it, but I did earn my badge," the man said, throwing the bag of books to Tim who caught them without problems. "After we heard the hospital got robbed of two walkie-talkies, I sort of figured that you'd make your way here for your stuff. Figured you would try to sneak in. Didn't think you'd succeed though," he explained, looking at the stolen badge at Tim's pocket.

"Yeah, sorry about this," Tim noted the badge himself. He looked around the place warily for signs of a trap. "Where's the other detective? The hot one."

"She's at the hospital. A little too in over her head trying to catch you to think clearly," Hardy said as he scratched his nose. Even his experience on the force had not prepared him fully for the smell of the room, apparently. "Obsessed, Julie. Her logic got twisted till she thinks you're behind all of this."

"Am I?"

"I don't know," he replied in earnest. "But I do know you are involved. And that means you at least have the power to do something about it."

"You're involved too, detective."

"Yeah," he scratched his head, contemplating his position. "Not enough to do much for my partner."

"And I am?" Tim replied, still not completely trusting the detective. "I'm a kid. You two said so yourselves."

"Maybe that's what we need right now. A mind that's not tied up by jobs, family, money, or duty. Someone whose sole goal is to stop this thing. Who can dedicate all their time and resource to it."

"Like me?"

Oliver rubbed the shine of his badge. "I am a cop after all. There's are a few things I can't do. Like, steal a car, breaking and entering, stealing drugs, murder..."

"You're making me out to sound like a lunatic."

"Your words, not mine," Oliver said. Tim sighed. Oliver continued, "You should go."

The teen nodded in stoic agreement and turned to leave with his prize, but stopped in his track to ask, "This is probably going to be the last time we meet under such amicable situations so let me ask you this. What if you're wrong? What if I fail?"

"Then we'll have to hope that there are other people out there trying as well. And if there isn't, then, given what's happening, it might be the end of the world."

The grim news passed onto Tim like a car just fell on him. "So I'm the only thing that's standing between us and the apocalypse?" he chuckled at the thought. How outlandish the idea was that he, an ordinary teenager would be charged with the safety of mankind. "I'm just trying to save my friends here, not the world."

"How's that working out for you?"

Tim thought back to Clay and his last promise to protect Stella. "Still working on it."

"I've been on the force for a long time now. I've seen many people die," Oliver started, looking up and down the shelves of evidence, then through to the corpse behind the aisle they stood, reminiscing on lives long lost. "If there's one thing that I've learned, is that sacrifice can only happen when the people left behind decide to do something about the deaths."

"What are you saying? That I'm not doing something to avenge Clay?"

"If that's what you're thinking, than you got the idea of sacrifice wrong. Clay gave up his life to give you a chance. Use his death. Step on his body if you must. Because your friend's dead."

"I hope you have a point detective," Tim said through gritted teeth. "Cause you're starting to piss me off a little."

Oliver gave out a muffled chuckled, as if his hardened features were actually preventing his facial muscles from moving. "He's giving you a fighting chance. You have to use him. Don't push his memory aside to mourn later. Look at what he did now, and what he left behind. His spirit or whatever."

Tim looked towards the detective, unspeaking. Absorbing the words into his hardened emotions.

"From what I know, Clay only cared about one thing. Saving his sister. That's what he left for you. His wish. Save his sister, and you'll also save us all."

CHAPTER THIRTY-EIGHT

Catch

"Man cries, his tears dry up and run out. So he becomes a devil, reduced to a monster."
- *Kōta Hirano*

02:22 P.M.
6 days earlier

Leaving behind the wailing and crying, Tim darted through the alley opposite the police station. He came up beside a trashcan and stopped to ponder if he should discard the police badge he had stolen. He found no logical reason to keep it threw it away.

He fished out his two way radio and turned it on. "Stella, are you there?" But for the few long seconds, only static replied. "Stella?" he called out again, this time slightly worried.

"Yes!" Stella finally answered, though sounding surprised with a sheepish groan. "I'm here. You got them?"

"I got them," he replied. "Are you okay though? You sound tired."

"Yeah, I was just taking a nap."

"A nap?" he asked in concern. When they last met, Clay had said that The Father was jumping dreams and was going after The Brother's victims. He wondered if it could have the ability to go even further. "Are you alright?"

"Yeah. I was with Sister. Catching her up on stuff here."

"No Father? No problems?"

"Yup, just like the last few dozen times I've slept," she said, sounding slightly annoyed. "Can we get back to business?"

"Right. Do you know of a place we can meet? Maybe your place or something?"

198

"If you wanted to get romantic with me, you could have just asked."

"Really?"

"No," She replied flatly. "And my house is out of the question. Detective Smith managed to get an officer to stand watch there."

He clicked his tongue in frustration. "But aren't they having some manpower issue right now?"

"Well, she found a way."

"Great. What now? I don't think the library is a good place to stay. Too public."

"Wait," Stella said, followed by a moment of silent thinking. Tim could practically see the cogs in her brains turning and churning out an answer. "I got just the place."

08:12 p.m

6 days earlier

She was not sure, but Detective Julliane Smith thought there were even more people in the hospital than the amount of the mob from earlier in the day. But unlike earlier, the group of civilians queued up neatly in a line in front of the medication counter as an officer with a megaphone called out instructions.

"Everyone, please form up in an orderly line," the officer said as more people began coming in through the door. "To collect your medication, provide any form of identification at the counter and you will be given one bottle of Somnidin. Be reminded that only one bottle is allowed per person."

"Detective." A male nurse came up to Jullie as she kept her eye on the crowd. "Thanks again for doing this. I have no idea how we would have handled the morning if you weren't there."

"No need," Jullie replied. "I'm just doing my job. By the way, have you seen my partner?"

"The big beefy guy? I haven't seen him since he left in the afternoon," the nurse replied. "Have you tried calling?"

"Yes, but it seems the there's no signal." She patted the man on the shoulder, "Thanks for the help anyway." She walked away towards the line of people.

She watched as one by one, the once near desperate and angered mob peacefully surrendered to conformity to cure their supposed ailments. She thought of her own condition, and wondered if it would reached a point where she would also want the help of the fictional medication.

A woman who looked to be in her late forties, with rough brown hair and bags under her eyes that seemed to have sunk down to her bones, approached the detective.

"Detective," she said, pill bottle in hand. "Thank you for this. You've saved all our lives."

Jullie smiled back, "Think nothing of it. Besides, I don't think this pandemic business is all that real."

"Really?" the woman replied in surprise. "You must be one of the lucky ones."

"I'm sure there's a logical explanation to all this. And once the culprit is caught, I'm sure this thing will end."

"Culprit?" the woman replied in confusion.

From the line, a man stepped out and asked, "You're saying someone did this to us?" His voice travelled far down the queue and chatter erupted amongst them.

Realising her mistake in accidentally revealing case information, Julliane tried to assure the crowd, "We are currently investigating some of these supposed Sin killings and, though we can't be sure yet, we do have a suspect," suddenly, the rasp of the crowd toned to an ear shattering silence. She had somehow gathered everyone's attention. "We um...the police force are currently on hand with this and are in midst of arresting the suspect, so there's no need for you to worry."

A man from the crowd yelled, "Who is the suspect?"

Another asked, "Is there anything we can do?"

Jullie continued to try to rest the crowd, but felt that any attempts were futile from then on. "We are appreciative of this community effort but the police will be able to handle this."

The woman in front of her ask, "But there must be something we can do?"

"Yeah," a man said. "I don't want to sit back and wait to die like this!"

A light flipped within Jullie's mind. "Actually..." she began with a grin.

12:13 A.M.
5 days earlier

Though the blood had been cleaned and the body removed, Tim could not get the image of his father's dead body out of his mind. Back in his own home, he stood at the doorway to his father's room, looking in on the still surprisingly neat space, picturing his father's corpse, a cut down his torso, lying unmoving on the bed.

Sighing, he closed the door behind him and returned to the small living room table, where he and Stella had been combing through information from the library and Vashmir Commons' journal for the better part of the day. Stella had stepped out to call her parents from a pay phone as all cell phones were down and only landlines were left working. The apartment would be the last place anyone would look, as it was small, had no resources, and was the scene of an earlier crime, making it the least logical place to hide.

He sat back down, looking at his table of messy research which had so far, yielded no results. "Nothing," he huffed, picking up Vashmir's journal dejectedly, before unceremoniously dropping it back. He looked towards his father's room and muttered, "Sorry dad."

No matter how many times he combed through it, the journal contained nothing more than Vashmir's account of his weeks with Sin, degrading into undecipherable madness towards the last pages. He had even tried shading the hard cover backing for some hopeful indents from a perhaps missing page to no avail.

The burned photo album remained as it was, with only a few pictures still visible through the char and age, all of which depicted farms and barns and other photographs from Vashmir's youth. Though the two had attempted to restore some of the photos, it was turning out to be a painstakingly slow process, having already ruined two photographs out of their seven attempts.

Two vials of fentanyl and a couple of capped syringes lay on the corner of the table, making the scene looked slightly akin to that of a drug den. Clay's bottle of Somnidin, which was given to Stella, was placed beside the rest of the pharmaceuticals.

As he contemplated taking a pill and returning to his room for a nap, the front door opened and Stella came in on her crutches.

"Hey Stell," he greeted her. "How did it go with you parents?"

Gently, she set her crutches against the wall and slowly lowered herself to sit beside him. "They are...quite pissed. They want me to come home."

"I think you should," he replied in earnest. "I don't want you to get hurt with me or anything."

"Don't be stupid," she reprimanded. "Besides, I'm not helping you. I'm making sure my brother's efforts to stop this wasn't a waste. Also, there's this..." From her back pocket, she pulled out a folded piece of paper and passed it to him.

201

Tim unveiled it to reveal the picture of him the police took during his first arrest. And in bold words below it was;

WANTED
Timothy Kleve
Suspected bio-terrorist of Vashmir Pandemic
Citizen's arrest allowed

Shocked, Tim stared at the wanted posters with eyes wide. "What is this?"

"I think that female detective has managed to pin this on you."

"There's no evidence or...anything! She has a hunch, and a bad one!" he exclaimed. "They can't do this!"

"Tim," Stella started sympathetically. "She's afraid, and desperate. Everyone is. And I think you just became their blame."

CHAPTER THIRTY-NINE

The Wish

"There is the great lesson of 'Beauty and the Beast', that a thing must be loved before it is lovable."
- G.K. Chesterton, The Ethics of Elfland

Uncountable grains of sand flowed down the side of the cliff like a waterfall of dust, falling neatly into a swirling basin below. Surrounded by a thriving forest with cawing crows and growls of animals, Timothy stood by the bay of the sand basin, entranced as he watched the grains spiral towards the centre, vanishing into an invisible drain below.

"How is that happening?" he asked Sister.

The girl in the white dress replied, "How is what happening?" From her seat on a fallen log behind him, her white dress rested in an impossibly long spiral around her.

"The sand. How does it keep going like that?"

"Aren't you a curious one?" She got to her feet and walked to his side, staring down the same phenomenon as he did. "Truth is, I don't know how it works. I don't really know how much of anything here works. They just sort of happen, as if they were always there."

"Then what about you?" he asked, turning to her. "How do you work?"

"What do you mean?" she asked, baffled.

"Your powers. Your abilities. How you get me all...um..."

"Sexually aroused?"

He could feel his cheeks heating up at the statement, but did not deny it. "Yeah. How do you do that?"

She smiled playfully, putting her arms around him and getting physically closer. He wasn't capable of stopping his heart from beating faster. "I knew you thought I was pretty." She kissed him on the cheek.

Embarrassed, he asked, annoyed, "Are you going to tell me or not?"

"Well, it's not that hard to understand." She danced away from him, spinning on her feet in glee. "I just multiply your arousal for me."

"Multiply? So...if a person has no attraction to you-"

"Which you do," she interrupted.

Defensively, Tim corrected, "Which I don't!" He shot her an irritated stare only for her to laugh giddily back. "As I was saying, if a person doesn't have attraction to you, at all..."

"Then the power would not work! Which means you like me!"

He just stared back wide-eyed, his deduction having backfired on him. Surrendering to the better wit of his opponent, he took a seat on the sandy shore. Sister followed, taking her place beside him all whilst grinning from ear to ear.

As he watched the whirlpool of sand spiral into the earth, he calmly asked, "What if, hypothetically of course, I had feelings for you. How would that work?"

"Well," Sister replied, with a tone more solemn than what he would expect from her personality. "If it happens, I would ask you to put your hypothetical feelings aside. Since we are separated by dimensions and life and all that."

"But hypothetically, would you return those feelings?"

Sister remained quiet to that question. He remained unwavering, keeping his eyes forward despite an overwhelming wish to turn to her to see her reaction. But a part of him felt that his life would be endangered for viewing her at a vulnerable moment.

Then, Sister replied, "I will...tell you, hypothetically...yes. But...I can't leave here."

Without thinking, he replied, "I can save you."

"Hah!" she let out, "I don't need you to save me. I can take care of myself."

"I know that," he turned to face her, their eyes crossing in earnest. "But I can still save you."

"Look, Tim, you are amazing," she replied with a gentle smile, one that nearly melted him. "But there's only so much that even you can do. And you have to save Stella. She comes first."

"I'll save both of you," he replied seriously. "I can do it."

She chuckled. "You're surprisingly optimistic today."

"Yes," he said softly, remembering the last sleep he had. The final image of Clay on the pier and his final request for Tim and the resulting promise. He then thought of his father, and how he was once again sleeping beside his father's room, though the man was no longer and will never again be there. "I guess I'm just sick of losing by now."

They sat together in silence, a short moment of peace for Tim that was needed as much as every single others that came before. The brief relief had become both bliss and torture for him, as he not only had the time to rest, but also to think of everything that led up to that point.

"If," Sister began with the hypothetical, "I could have a wish, I would like to go with you."

"Then–"

"But," Sister cut in. "You have to focus on saving Stella first. Right now, you have more than enough on your plate." She paused and took his one good hand, wrapping her fingers around it gently. "And you have to, most importantly, save yourself. I am a monster Tim. I am one of them. And I have killed...a lot of people. And I do not deserve you saving me."

"But you saved me. That counts for something in my book."

She sighed sadly, getting to her feet. "I wonder if your feelings are because of my powers. After all, we barely know each other." She turned to him with a forlorn smile. "I bet even you can't figure out where one line ends and the other begin. Even with your power of deduction."

"It's real, I'm sure of it," he replied without hesitation. "Whether you believe it or not, you are funny, and kind, and full of life. Especially for a girl who claims to be dead." He stood up purposefully. "What I feel for you, be it romantic or not, is good. I am absolutely sure of that."

"Are you?" Her smile slipped, just slightly in thoughts of disappointment. "I can feel it in me that soon, I will have to do something that you won't like. And when that time comes, I hope you can forgive me."

9:22 A.M.
5 days earlier

He woke to the chirping of a jackhammer going off outside. Tim stirred groggily on the couch, having given up his bed for Stella to sleep. However, he found the girl steadily working at the table, surrounded by store bought chemicals, carefully cleaning off her fifth photograph from Vashmir's album.

"Morning," she greeted without looking his way.

"Hey. Morning." He rubbed his eyes in a futile but very human and natural attempt to gain clarity. "I didn't see you in my dreams last night."

He paused, realising his mistake too late.

"Aw," she replied sarcastically. "I love you too, Timmy boy. Wanna make out now that you're awake?"

"Shut up..." He got up, finally gaining some lucidity. "You know what I meant."

"I know," she said playfully. "Sister said she wanted to talk to you privately when she got the chance, so I took some Somnidin."

"Wait, you sure about that? They are addictive, remember?"

"It's just one pill, dad." She smiled slyly. "I'm fine. So, what did you and Sister talk about?"

He was suddenly struck by anger for the fact that humans are unable to see their own faces, for he felt his was red again and wanted to tell it to cut it out. "Nothing!" He stood defensively, rushing to his bathroom to wash his face. "Just, you know, stuff about...you know...stuff."

"Mmm hmm." He could hear her even from his room. Though it was no surprise considering how small the apartment was. "Well, what are you going to do today? Sticking around to clean these photos?"

"I don't think so." Tim walked out with a towel around his shoulders, his messy hair seemingly neater despite being slightly wet, a contradiction for the ages. "There's something I want to check out. And we need more leads than these photos. Right now, they're quite a long shot."

"Good. Cause if you said you were staying, I would have said it was a waste of your time," Stella replied, finally taking her focus off the restoration work. "But be careful, you are wanted now. There will be people out specifically looking for you."

"I'm not too worried about that," he replied, returning to his room, throwing the towel unceremoniously on his bed. Grabbing a fresh change of clothes, a white shirt and black cargo pants, he even managed to uncover a clean pair of socks hiding under his bed. He started getting changed. "We haven't seen anyone on the streets lately, I doubt that's about to change."

"Still, watch out."

"You should listen to yourself, Miss Gunshot Wound. You're not exactly in a good position either."

"Don't worry, honey. I can take care of myself."

I can take care of myself. Sister said that to him earlier. And he wondered if there was even a need to be overly worried about the two girls in his life. Both were fierce in their own rights, and had aided him a lot more than anything he had done for them.

He put on the holster and checked the revolver he kept from the police station, making sure it was still loaded. He found his rarely used black hooded jacket and slipped into it, completing his ensemble of looking like the world's tiniest and least imposing grim reaper, the weapon hidden beneath his jacket. He headed for the door.

"I'll be back soon," he turned back to say, slipping into his one good pair of shoes.

"Sure. You'll be back before I know it."

CHAPTER FORTY

The Ever Young

"The more I learn about the universe, the less convinced I am that there's any sort of benevolent force that has anything to do with it, at all."
- Neil deGrasse Tyson

3:12 P.M.
5 days earlier

Tim darted and slipped out from the alley, his hood up, the trek to the city library having taken a quarter of his day away. He kept his head low as another group of people on the opposite side of the street crossed him. A fowl stench had continued to waft from the drains as it had the whole day. He could have considered it the stench of fear if it was not physically scratching at his throat.

"Stupid detective..." he cursed under his breath, nearing the steps of the library. The pressure of the manhunt the latter placed on him was heavily impacting his ability to move around and investigate.

He walked up to the glass door, which on normal occasions, would automatically slide open. However, that day, it stayed shut. His translucent reflection staring back at him.

"Come on, Galloway," he muttered, pressing his face against the glass to peer inside. "I know you're in there."

"Actually, I'm out here."

Tim jumped in surprise as the voice came from behind, turning on his feet and nearly tumbling back into the door.

Just like the time in the prison cell, the man that stood in front of him seemed significantly younger. Howard Galloway looked to be in his early twenties, as if the previous years of his life had just vanished. Wearing a grey trench coat and white inner shirt with fitting blue jeans, he was all but

208

unrecognisable, save for the slight similarity in facial bone structure.

"Mister...Galloway?" Tim greeted questioningly.

"Yes? Yes! That's right, that's me!" the librarian replied, initially confused. "Howard Galloway, librarian!" He struck a dramatic victory pose, as invigorated as his seeming age.

"I'm starting to think you're not just a librarian."

"Very good, Tim, my boy! What else are you getting with that amazing deduction skill of yours?"

"Nothing really, cause I have no idea what you could be. You are literally getting younger by the day and you just popped up behind me," he said, sure that no one had followed him.

"Bah! Now that's just boring."

"Listen, Mister Galloway?" he asked, unsure if the new youth the man had found meant their age was now closer and if the suffix would stick. But the older man seemed not to mind. "I need information on something."

"Oh?" Galloway replied, though his tone gave away that he already somehow knew what Tim wanted to ask. "And what would that be?"

"I'm looking for a girl. Fifteen, maybe eighteen years old tops."

"That's a very vague description you have there but can't say I've seen many teens round here lately," he replied playfully. "Have you tried dating websites?"

"In case you haven't noticed, the internet is pretty much down for the count. And she's not from around here. She's dead. Probably for a while now."

"And how am I suppose to find a dead girl?" Howard replied sarcastically.

"I was hoping you'd, I don't know, look through the library archives or something. Her death had something to do with a white dress. Maybe she was buried with it. Maybe it was some sort of medical gown. I don't know, but I thought that would be a good place to start."

"Geez, I'd love to help, but the library's closed."

Tim cocked a brow at the man, who met his stare with a sly smile. "But you're the librarian. Can't you just, you know, open it?"

"I could. But I won't."

"Why not?" Tim replied in frustration. He could feel his facial muscles tensing up as anger started to build. The older man's games were starting to annoy him. "And who the hell are you really? Why are you younger? And what's with all this appearing out of nowhere business? And–" A thought came to him that stunned him for a split moment. Intensely, he asked, "Are you the one causing all this?"

209

With a voice that neared disappointment, Howard replied, "Close, kid. But not close enough. I will admit that I know quite a bit about what's happening here, but I am not the one behind it. That knowledge is a mystery, even to me."

"But you can help me?"

"I can't. It's part of the rule."

Tim sighed dejectedly, closing his eyes in a quick mediation between his temper and his control. Seething, he replied, "Fuck you, old man. Can you please stop being so fucking cryptic about this? Clay is dead and Stella's next. I really don't have the mood for all this deduction crap."

"Sorry my boy. But I can't help you this time. You'll have to solve this puzzle yourself."

Tim threw his hand up in frustration, "What the hell is up with all of you people? You, Oliver, Sister. Everyone thinks I'm some hero that's going to somehow figure all this crap out."

"But you are. You just don't know it yet."

"So what am I suppose to do now? You won't let me in. Do I have to break the door with a brick?"

"Please don't do that again." The man waved off the notion flamboyantly. "Look, I will tell you one thing. I'm not the one who can help you with this. But you do have another ally here that can."

"Who? Stella?" Tim replied hesitantly. "I don't know. She just lost her brother and I don't think what I'm looking for is exactly at the top of her list. Can't you just do a search of the archives here?"

"Sure. Just give me a second." He stopped moving, rolling his eyes around upwards in thought and replied stoutly, "Nope. Nothing."

"Don't be a dick."

"Look, there really isn't anything you're looking for in there. Go to Stella, and just ask her to help. She will be able to find it. I guarantee."

"How do you know that?" Tim turned away from the man to point to the still closed glass doors of the library. "I mean, just open it up and let's take a look at—" he turned back, but as abruptly as he appeared, Howard Galloway was then nowhere to be seen.

7:34 P.M.
5 days earlier

Stella focused entirely on the photograph she was cleaning. The process was therapeutic, gently cleaning off the soot of the pictures in the tray of cold water gave her a strange clarity and distraction from what had otherwise been days of hectic losses. The old Discman she found among Joshua's belongings repeated the tracks of a classical mix, fighting back the stale smell of the apartment with Beethoven's 5th.

"You know, Clay," she said to her lonesome. "You never gave me a chance to say goodbye."

Despite having skipped both lunch and dinner, she did not feel any hunger, just a continued numbness throughout her body, as if she had been anaesthetised from physical discomfort.

"If you think about it, it's really my fault. If I didn't get shot by Joseph and forced the detectives to take me with them, you wouldn't have to make that sacrifice. You wouldn't have to save me." Her hands began to shake, beads of tears splashed into the tray of water in front of her. She sobbed, "I miss you so much..."

She felt her body start to ache, her stomach clench tightly as she full on wept after the long afternoon of solitude. Her nose ran and her eyes held firmly shut in a futile attempt to hold back the tears.

"It hurts...it hurts," she whimpered. "I'm sorry, Clay! I'm so sorry!"

Burying her face into her hands, she screamed, Beethoven drowning out her sorrow.

CHAPTER FORTY-ONE

The Portal

"The way to learn whether a person is trustworthy is to trust him.."
- Ernest Hemingway, Papa Hemingway: A Personal Memoir

9:52 P.M.
5 days earlier

If there was ever one thing Tim wasn't sure of, it was his hesitation of opening the door back to his home that day. He stood outside in the shadow of the night, the hallway lights having burnt out, with a light drizzle of rain building up behind him. His hand was on the door handle but he could not find a good enough reason to put force behind it to open. It was stark scene reminiscence of his final night with his father.

"Stella," he muttered under his breath, rehearsing his speech. "I need you to help me find out what Sister's name is."

Out loud, nothing sounded wrong with the request. It was research work on a person who had long since been dead. But his dreaded instinct clawed at him uncomfortably, keeping him on the edge as he inexplicably felt something terrible would happen if he made the request.

"Come on..." he egged himself. "Just ask her. She'll make a few calls, dig up some articles. She probably won't even meet another person while doing this. Completely safe."

Yet inexplicably, he couldn't convince himself of those words.

He had half a mind to turn back but the door swung open without his effort, the handle ripped away from his grip. The feeling of déjà vu was strong. On the opposite of the archway, Stella stood on her crutches in a pair of Tim's old light blue pyjamas.

He greeted her with, "You found my old clothes?"

"Yeah. Can't keep wearing the same thing for days now, can I?" she

212

replied. "Why are you standing out there like an idiot?" She looked down to his still outstretched hand, still grasping at air. He quickly pulled it back. "You high?"

"What? No!"

"You on drugs?"

"Isn't that the same thing?"

"Are you hiding something?"

"No..." he replied truthfully. "Just a little hesitant..." He dragged and paused.

"About...asking me out?"

"What?" he exclaimed, "No! No! I'm not asking you out. Why would I at a time like this?"

"But you've considered it?"

"No!"

"Then stop beating around the bush and ask me whatever."

"Fine. Look, I need you to help me to find out Sister's real name."

"What?" she replied, surprised. "That's it?"

Unsure of himself, Tim let out, "I...guess so."

"Sure, I can do that. I mean, I have been trying since day one. I've came close to it but with everything that's been happening, I've put the search on hold. I can start it up again though," she told him her situation, not one bit of hesitation with agreeing to the request. "Why would you balk at asking me that?"

"I don't know. I just have this terrible feeling in my stomach that kept telling me not to."

She looked down at her body, checking for any sudden defects, as if a third arm would start growing out of her belly. "I look fine to me."

"Yeah...I don't know what I was worried about," he replied, though still unable to untie the knot in his guts. "Should we...I don't know, head in?"

In the distance, a shriek dragged into the night, the sound seemingly having been carried from beyond the neighbourhood they were in. Unlike the daily howls of drunken bar-goers or gang members, this one chilled them, drawing their attention. And in the split seconds after, reverberating murmurs began to rise around them. Murmurs that seemed to reach out from all directions.

Tim could only let out a brief, "What the hell?"

Waves of screams and shouts pierced through the air.

Stella stepped out of the apartment as Tim leaned over the railings to look down at the streets. Dozens of people rushed out of the buildings, running frenziedly down the road, gathering at the junction. The crowd stood there in between green lights, staring at the city. Some pointed, others gasped. One fell to his knees and cried.

To Stella, Tim said, "Something's happening."

Sharply, she replied, "No shit."

Ignoring her snide, he simply said, "Let's go." He bolted for the stairs.

"Hey!" she shouted. Her rarely raised voice enough to stop even his curiosity. He turned and she gestured to her cast covered leg. "Slow down."

"Can't," he told her before squatting down with his back to her. Tapping his shoulder, he signalled, "Get on."

"You've got to be kidding me."

When she realised he wasn't, Stella gave a sigh and dropped her crutches at the door, hopping to him on one leg. Awkwardly climbing onto his back, she buckled in as he, with a heave, got to his feet. Once stable, he made a mad dash for the stairs, pushing his momentum forward so as to make the climb with the extra human weight on his back possible. Two floors later, he ascended the last flight to the rooftop with heaves and pants.

He jibbed, "You need...to lose weight." He earned a slap across his head.

"I'm letting you feel my thighs, so shut up and climb."

And he could not argue with her reasoning. He was holding on quite tightly, mostly because he was out of breath and was afraid any loosened grip would send his friend tumbling down the steps behind them.

With one last leg and push, he kicked open the door to the rooftop and stepped out under the open sky, the towering stretch of skyscrapers of the city laid out before him. Though panting and sweating, his breath still managed to get taken away.

"What..." he was speechless at the sight. Slowly, he knelt down to let Stella dismount beside the entrance to the roof.

She leaned against the wall, a look of surprise etched across her face, her jaws hanging loosely. "...the hell?"

Even from where they stood, they could smell the noxious fumes of smoke and could see the black smog that continued to climb from the city streets. Flames flickered orange against the buildings' sides as bushels of fire spreads across the city. However, it was not the sight of the riot that broke out or the broken screams and shouts that seemed to echo on forever that entranced them.

A swirling mass of purple gas hung above Hotel Alexandria, the third tallest building of the city. It looked almost as if someone had ripped a hole in the sky, and the atmosphere swirled around it like water down a drain. Blue crystals, the size of two entire levels of the building, encrusted the tip of the hotel like spikes on a mace, while thin, purple, rolling mists floated down the sides of the building.

"We need to get to the dream world," Tim said, though unable to take his eyes off the phenomenon. "We need to go, now."

He finally managed to tear himself away from the spectacle. Returning to Stella, he let her climb onto his back again. With a much more manageable slope down and renewed energy from the mysterious event, he took the flights of stairs two at a time.

Stella asked, "What was that thing?"

"No idea," he replied between breaths. "But...I'm sure...The Father...has something...to do with it!"

Reaching his landing, he took a sharp left into the corridor, smoothly picking up Stella's crutches from the ground as he dodged back into his open home.

Letting Stella off at the couch, he went into his bathroom in strides and pulled opened the medicine cabinet with such energy that the hinges creaked from the torque. From within, he took out a pair of syringes and the bottle of fentanyl and returned to the living room.

Sticking the needle through the rubber cap of the bottle, he asked Stella, "How much should I use?"

"What? You took it without checking?"

"I did!" he replied, drawing the liquid out of the bottle. Pulling the syringe out, he checked it for air bubbles, pushing back out some of the drugs to get rid of them as he had seen in movies. "But I'm still not a doctor." He toyed with the needle in his hand, contemplating the injection. He wondered if it would be better to let himself fall asleep naturally instead, but felt his blood was pumping too much to calm himself down soon enough without wasting too much time.

Stella said, "I think I should go instead. You just stay awake and on the lookout."

"What? Why?" he questioned, a little more dramatically than he would have liked, waving his hand around. "I thought we were both going?"

"Tim, you don't have your arm in the dream world, and I don't have my leg here. Whatever situation is happening, I think we're going to need to be at our best, don't you?"

He was reluctant, the clench of his instincts from before had yet to subside and he was not comfortable with her taking the risk. Any risk. Yet, he could not find a hole in her argument.

Stella continued, "If something happens here and I can't wake up, you

215

can carry me off. I'd even let you touch all of me." Her tone was her usual playful self, but Tim felt it carried more weight behind it and could not find it in him to rebut. "And I sure as hell can't carry you."

Conceding the argument, Tim handed the syringe to her. "Fine. But if anything happens–"

"There is absolutely nothing I can do to warn you," she cut him off, saving him from the embarrassment of having to think of a solution to a problem with no answer. "We're just going to have to wing it from here."

"Your brother and I say 'wing it'. I'm not so sure I like it when you say it."

"Tim," she stopped him from continuing, unhesitatingly injecting the drug into her forearm. "Stop dragging. We have a magic purple sky hole to deal with."

CHAPTER FORTY-TWO

A Hard Place

"The search for a scapegoat is the easiest of all hunting expeditions."
- Dwight D. Eisenhower

02:12 A.M.
4 days earlier

The stack of clean pictures had grown. About a novel thick, most of them were photographs of landscapes. Barns, farmlands and a river populated a majority of the images, with the occasional cropping of an elderly male farmer and his wife, a chair bound woman that was often pictured in a rocking chair on a porch. Tim was beginning to lose hope that the photo album would be able to provide them with any sort of clue as to what was happening with Sin and that it might have simply been one of Vashmir's personal belongings that he threw into the fire in a fit of madness. Tim was not even sure what he expected to find, but the lack of leads meant it was either that or to sit and wait to die.

Stella breathed softly in his room. Having kept a peaceful sleep despite the noises of the world outside. He had taken a peek out to find the streets filled with cars attempting to leave the city. Since their apartment was nearer to the edge of the metropolis, he could watch the slowly growing waves of refugees getting into the gridlock, more people than he had seen in the past two weeks combined.

Honks blared through the whole city and into the night. Behind him, the city centre continued to turn with screams and shouts, the cycle of which had become a strange rhythm that echoed as a gentle heartbeat to his ears.

Once again, Tim stepped out of the apartment and stared over the parapet. On the ground, most of the cars had moved forward, with a new

217

batch in their places. However, Tim could see a few that had stopped their advances. The driver seats emptied. A sparse group of people weaved between the cars as they proceeded forward on foot.

Then, the flitting flash of flashlights cast long shadows across the street. Catching his eyes, he leaned slightly over to look down to the walkway below.

A group of about a dozen people stood in a circle at the entrance to his apartment building. He watched them discuss noisily, though the five stories distance meant their voices were still muffled enough that he could not make out what they were saying. It was during the prolonged conversation that he saw it. Each of the men and women were armed with a variety of garden appliances. From hoes to shovels and sickles and pitchforks.

To himself, Tim noted, "That's a mob." With that, one of the woman in the group looked up at him. Their eyes crossed and she pointed him out to the others. "Oh. That's *my* mob."

The group broke off, with two staying on the ground level while the rest disappeared into the building. Tim took the movement as a sign to retreat back into his apartment, locking the door behind him.

"Shit. Shit. Shit. Shit. Shit," he cursed as he fumbled into the apartment. He hurried back into his room where Stella slept. Shaking the girl by the shoulder, he begged, "Wake up. Come on, wake up!" She continued to stay unconscious without even a flicker of her eyelids.

"Okay. Okay. Okay. Think fast." He ran back into the living room and grabbed all the photographs and album off the coffee table and brought it to his father's room. Junking the evidence under the bed, he went back out and shifted the furniture aside, making way for the couch to be pushed to the door.

With heaves and huffs, he moved the small furniture into the narrow entrance. Sweating and panting, he rammed the sofa against the frame of the door and added to the weight by lifting the shoe cabinet onto the barricade. All this just in time as the furious knocks from the mob came from the outside.

"Open up, Timothy Kleve!" a man shouted. "We don't want anyone getting hurt!"

Tim shouted back as he re-entered his room, "Says the people armed with gardening supplies!" As gently as possible, he lifted Stella off the bed. "What are you trying to do if not hurt me? Give me a fucking trim?" He actually felt his hair was getting quite long and could in fact, do with a visit to a barber.

"Look." A woman's voice this time. "If you're not coming out, we're coming in!"

He carried Stella into Joshua's room. Watching her leg, he placed her down on the floor beside the bed. "Don't believe those stupid posters, you idiots!" Heaving, he pushed Stella under the bed. Luckily, her full body pyjamas meant she simply slid across the floor without resistance. "Sorry," he whispered to her. He pulled the blanket of the bed over to cover the gap.

From outside, he could hear the woman say, "Ralph, do the thing."

"No, Ralph!" he shouted back. Getting to his feet, he did a quick scan to make sure Stella was completely hidden underneath. "Don't do the thing!" His pleas were ignored as the sound of a body ramming against wood banged through the household.

Tim bolted back out into the living room. It was impossible for him to escape while carrying Stella, but at the very least, even if he was caught, she would be safe. However, he had no intention of giving in. Grabbing his revolver, he managed a plan as he put on the holster.

"I've got a gun!" he yelled back, trying to buy some time.

And almost instantaneously, a man called, "He's lying!"

"Fucking idiots," he whispered under his breath. He held his gun out to the ceiling and fired a warning shot, flecks of paint falling onto him. The women outside screamed and he could hear Ralph the Battering Ram flailing and falling back in fear, crashing into everyone around him. In the confusion, he loaded a new round into the fired chamber, grabbed his jacket, and headed into his room.

About an arms reach away from his window was the unceremoniously bland brick wall of his neighbouring apartment, a sight which he had hated for years yet found inexplicably lovable at that moment. He climbed over and onto his desk. Once balanced, he pulled his jacket over his hands. Holding onto the inside wall of his room with a foot on the window sill, he reached his left hand out and arched into the brick wall opposite, finding some grip for his fingers. He did the same with his left leg, managing a foothold in one of the larger crevices. Slowly, he eased his entire body out of the room, where he hung between the building gaps like a mutated starfish.

As the ramming of the door returned, he looked down the five stories difference between him and the ground and huffed out, "Dumbest. Idea. Ever."

With that self-cursing, he manoeuvred himself back and away from his windows. Grunting as his muscles strained with his weight. He pushed his limbs to lock himself in place between the two walls. Knowing full well that loosening too much would mean him pin-balling to the ground below.

Slowly, he loosened the grip his feet had, adjusting until he felt them just about to slide away from the walls. "Okay. Okay. Okay," he tried pumping himself.

The door to his apartment broke open with a crash signalling his time for an all or nothing. He locked his legs' muscles and released his fingers from the crevice and began his slide down the walls at a speed much faster than he had thought he would. Past the forth floor, past the third, he plummeted downward, desperately trying to control his descent with his hands. Protected by the jacket sleeves, he pushed his arms against the wall and he slowed slightly, though not without a grunt of pain. Once past the second floor though, he released all his limbs and free-fell the last four meters to the ground, breaking his fall with a roll.

His hands were scratched and bleeding. Yet, he had no time to rest. He needed to draw attention away from his house and in turn, from Stella. He needed to get the attention of the mob, which was not hard, as he grunted out loud, "FUCK!" while squeezing his aching hands in pain, the sleeves of his jacket having been ripped to shreds.

"What was that?" he heard the female ground floor watch voiced out.

"It came from there!" another man exclaimed.

Tim got to his feet and began limp-jogging towards the back alley. He heard a woman behind him go, "He's down here!" shouting loud enough for her conspirators upstairs to get wind of. "He's getting away!"

He looked back to see the pair chasing him struggle to fit through the small pathway with their larger builds. Easing himself through the last leg, Tim tucked out into the back alley. Looking left and right for cars that did not exist, he made sure he was not followed from elsewhere before running towards a garbage pile to his left.

Without worrying further, he sauntered over and into the midst of the black garbage bags. Pulling up his hood and zipping up his jacket, he squatted into the trash, camouflaging himself amongst the shadow of the alley, the darkness of the night, and the black of the bags. He had to raise his jacket up and over his nose to cover not just his face, but the nauseating stench of being in a pile of waste. His two pursuers stepped out of the pathway and into his view.

"Where did he go?" the man asked, his eyes scanning right over the corner of darkness that Tim was in. His heart skipped a beat when his eyes lingered at him, but soon turned away. Tim held back his sigh of relief as the man commanded, "You go that way, I'll head down here. He couldn't have gotten far." He pointed to the two opposing directions before splitting up with his partner.

Once the pair was out of earshot, he quietly climbed out of the garbage

220

pile and stepped out into a thankful breath of fresh air. Wasting no time, he bolted down the alleyway opposite him, away from his two pursuers and before the main mob could join back up.

His home was no longer safe. He needed somewhere else to hide.

CHAPTER FORTY-THREE

The Graveyard

"How often have I lain beneath rain on a strange roof, thinking of home."
- William Faulkner, As I Lay Dying

12:12 P.M.
4 days earlier

The grass that surrounded the gravestones had thickened to a comfortable fluff from the lack of maintenance over the past week.

Under a lengthily grown oak tree and beside a row of simple stone graves, Timothy Kleve sat back into the trunk of the plant, nursing his aching feet from the long, meandering walk to that spot. The roots of the trees had long since grown into the path of much of the nearby graves, the ground protruding uncomfortably in some spots.

From behind him, the crunching of leaves drew his attention and he turned around to find Stella, on her crutches and still wearing his pyjamas, limping towards him over the jagged earth.

"I thought I would find you here," she said. "You left me under the bed!"

Surprised by her appearance, he asked, "How did you get here so fast? I just got here like an hour ago."

"Parents picked me up," she replied, grunting as she settled down beside him. "They're waiting outside to take us home. Told them to let me talk to you first."

"I guess they're not very happy with what we're doing?"

"We're going to have talks later. Or more precisely, they are going to talk and I'm going to listen and nod."

"Isn't your place under watch right now?"

222

"They had to pull the police out. I guess the force is really dwindled now with what's going on in the city."

"A big giant purple hole in the sky spewing god knows whatever kind of gas? Yeah, I think that will scare some people," Tim stated sarcastically. Remembering that Stella had gone to sleep earlier to speak with Sister, he asked, "What did Sister say by the way?"

She sighed, stretching her injured leg out and massaging her good thigh. "She said the walls between the dream world and ours are breaking down."

"What? Is that even possible?"

"Apparently." She leaned back against the tree. "All the souls The Father has killed, he has kept them. Sister told you what they were supposed to do with them, right?"

"Yeah. Grim reapers. Take our consciousness and send them to a new world," he repeated the information.

"But Father kept all of them and they've been piling up in the dream world. That weight has ripped a hole between there and here," she explained. "He's like a fat guy sitting on a cardboard box right now."

Grimly, with a frustrated sigh, Tim said, "And we are the box. Fuck..." he cursed with a hiss. Closing his eyes and leaning his head against the tree, he resisted the fatigue that he felt trying to drag him into sleep. "We killed one guy. And we're not even sure how we did it. Not to mention everyone in the city right now is after my hide, and there's also a hole to another universe tearing into our skies." He sighed again, almost resigning his fate to the situation. "I don't see how we're going to get out of this."

He felt her place a hand on his shoulder, comforting him. "You'll find a way. Come on. Let's head back, clean those photos, and figure out Sister's name."

Tim dropped his arms to his side. Opening his eyes, he tried taking a breath to clear his mind but found his nose slightly blocked to do so. Light shone through the canopy of the trees, like stars dancing through the leaves.

He replied, "You go ahead. I'll catch up in a while. I want to clear my head here." He felt as if his brain had absorbed too much information to process and would explode any second. "Your house isn't that far. I can walk."

She nodded understandingly. "Just be careful, okay?" She got up and prepared to leave.

"Stella." He stopped her. "How did you know I was here?"

She giggled lightly. "I was thinking of the last time you thought you

223

felt safe. You felt at home. And thought that if I was you, this would be the only place I'd go to."

Tim chuckled. Though it was not so much an answer from deduction as it was an instinctual wild guess, she was spot on.

Softly, Stella asked, "Did you talk to her about this?"

Staring at the gravestone before him, the name 'Miranda Kleve' etched into it, he blankly replied, "Yeah. I did."

She did not continue her questioning. Without looking to her, Tim could hear Stella slowly crunching the grass beneath her feet and crutches as she walked away. Her footsteps quickly faded and he could faintly hear the start of an engine in the distance as the Barbers drove off.

"You know, mom?" he said out loud, reminiscing of the fading memories of her. "Right before dad died, we said we would finally visit you together. But he's gone now. And so is Clay. And I have to help save Stella, and everyone's out to get me." He pulled his knees up and buried his face in it as hot tears soaked into his pants. "You always knew what to do. And right now, I don't know what to do. And I miss you. And I don't know what to do."

Tim blinked blankly at the sudden change in environment. He sat in a comfortable, ergonomic, plastic office chair in front of a sleek, lacquered, mahogany office desk. To his right was a long glass wall that viewed out above the clouds to a scene of the sky that stretched on forever. It was the only view in the otherwise empty, white-walled office, illuminated by dull, white fluorescent lamps in the ceiling while the arid smell of paper and sound of photocopiers floated through the air.

He huffed to himself, "I'm really getting sick of this bullshit."

A smooth, female voice replied, "Is that a statement or a fact?"

Tim jumped in his seat, the chair rolling backwards as he did so. Turning forward, he was stunned to see a figure before him that he was sure wasn't there before.

A woman with long flaming red hair, sharp chin, tightly folded middle-aged skin that was almost motherly in nature, and a piercing cat-like golden gaze that seemed to stab him with each passing second, sat in a newly materialised seat opposite him, behind the desk. Crisp black blazer and ironed inner white shirt, her knee-skirted legs long and crossed, the being known as The Mother poised herself with a composure equivalent of a queen.

"You are The Mother," Tim muttered out.

"Correct. That is a fact," she replied. She reached out her slender arm

224

and waved it over the desk. A paper contract, like the one she presented to him in the barn, appeared where her hands left off. "And you are Timothy Kleve. Is that a fact?"

He did not know the reason for the question, but felt that if he did not play by her rules, he would be in tremendous danger. "That is a fact," he replied, a chill running down his spine as he said so. The same kind of shiver one gets when they just stepped away from the edge of a cliff.

"Very good," she smiled. Though it was a welcoming grin, he could feel the animosity beneath emanating at him. "Now, sign this paper and you will get anything and everything that you want."

Anything? Could she bring back dad? Clay? Mom?

But another question popped into his mind, and for the first time in a long while, he was glad of his curiosity overpowering his other senses. His insatiable appetite for answers kicking in. "Is that a statement?"

"What?" Suddenly, her glare shot at him and he felt her power physically tugging at his heart. He knew then that his wants for the revival of his loved ones was caused by her power. A power to pull out a person's desires.

Resisting the temptation, he asked again, "Is that a statement?" He was glad that he was faced with a more mental-centric foe than a physical one like The Father or The Brother.

"No," she said, uncrossing her legs and sitting back into her seat, a look of seriousness across her face. "That is a fact."

"Prove it."

"Sign the contract."

"Prove it first."

"How?"

Putting on the best poker face he could, Tim internally smiled as he realised he had somehow managed to pull The Mother into his playing field. It was a chance to find more information. But he also needed to plan an escape while he did so. He needed to buy as much time as possible then.

Annoyed at Tim taking his time with answering, The Mother growled, her voice croaking like a tiger, "How do I prove that fact?"

"If you can give me anything, than you should know everything." He swallowed hard, licking his dry lips to ready himself for a linguistic barrage. "If you can answer all my questions, I will sign your contract."

"A test?" Interest piqued, The Mother crossed her hands together and leaned back in her seat. "And what questions do you have in mind?"

"First question," he said. "How do you stop The Father?"

CHAPTER FORTY-FOUR

The Mother

"He who is not satisfied with a little, is satisfied with nothing."
- Epicurus

The Mother looked almost on the verge of laughter, with a lipsticked grin that stretched across her face like the painted smile of a clown.

"Stop The Father?" she replied, a faint chuckle behind the words. "The Father cannot be stopped. The Father is going to tear into your world and there's nothing you can do but watch it happen."

Tim twiddled his thumb at his side, feeling the clamminess of his palm as he carefully waded through the verbal battle. He looked at the piece of paper provided, the sentences reading as gibberish to him. Even though he could make out the letters as that of the alphabets, he could not form them into words for his mind, as if he had sudden dyslexia, or his brain had sprung a leak. "If that's the case, then I'm not signing your contract. You obviously cannot provide everything, so there's no guarantee you can provide me anything."

"There are other ways to make you sign."

"But don't you think it would be easier to just talk me into it?"

"Dead men don't usually ask many questions."

"I'm not dead yet."

She screamed, "You're about to be!" Her voice echoed sharply through the room, piercing his ears with its sudden shrillness. Her anger however, quickly subsided and she stated, "You can close the portal after it has been opened. If you have the right ingredients."

"And what would those ingredients be?" he pushed carefully, not wanting to step too far into The Mother's comfort zone. He needed to make sure she was answering her question, but at her own will so she would feel in control and he could continue the conversation instead of

226

moving on to some form of torture. "Of course, you can choose not to answer, but that will just make me doubt you more."

She scanned him, eyes lolling up and down his body, measuring his stature. "You're small in size, but that's just to mask your cunning. You'd make a great businessman."

As casual as talking with a friend, Tim replied, "I was thinking more along the line of detective or police officer."

"What's the difference?" she asked without batting an eye. Leaning further back into her seat, she answered, "To close the portal, you'll need someone who's able to manipulate this."

Putting a finger into the air, she drew a line horizontally across his vision. Her fingers elegantly slashed through the air, leaving a trail of blue mist in their wake. Her eyes wandered across the floating tracks with a lustful glint, licking her cherry lips in anticipation.

Without waiting, Tim asked, "What's that?" The Mother immediately jumped forward in her seat and hissed back, her eyes flushed bright red, with anger or annoyance he was unsure.

The creature took a deep breath, the luminescence in her eyes slowly dissipated as the cloud before her vanished back into the air. With a calming inhale, she sat back into her chair for the third time.

She continued, "Prana. Mana. Mist. Aether. Seither. Dark Matter. Many names for it across many worlds. And every universe has a certain amount of it, which is how we are all connected here." She waved her arms around her, gesturing towards the universe they resided in. "Dream-world. Peninsula. Fourth dimension. Whatever you call it, the source of the matter that you see before originates here, leaking into all the multiverses. The weave that ties realities. So long as you exist here, you are made entirely of it."

"How do I control it?"

"You can't. Your time doesn't have the technology, nor has your species evolved to the point as to be able to manipulate it."

"If that's the case, you can't help me. And it just proves that you are not all powerful."

She leaned forward and with one slender arm, slipped the paper contract further towards him. "I can give you the power to manipulate the Mist. All you need to do is sign."

"But that's not enough any more."

"And why not?" He could see wrinkles crunch her forehead, her hair grew impossibly more crimson than it was a second ago. Her iris seemed to slit themselves, almost cat-like as her annoyance with his dragging grew. "What more do you need?"

Keeping his best stoic face, he replied, "There's nothing more I need from you."

She growled, "I can tell you how to kill The Father."

"I already know how to kill him," he lied. "Besides, why would you tell me?"

"Because I know you can't succeed. And that once you see the futility of your effort, you will be begging for my power." He watched as her eyes darted around in thought. Almost as if different visual stimulus could give her clarity. Before long, with less of a growl than earlier, she continued, "You already know you need his real name to bring him back to your world. You also know that to counteract his powers, you need to surpass his control over your emotions."

His heart beat with anticipation, but he kept his excitement hidden with cool indifference. "And?"

"But he won't be able to die permanently. Someone must be willing to take his place. Otherwise, our...boss would just put him back to serve out the rest of his...contract. If you kill him in your world, it would take a much longer time because of the disconnect between dimensions, but Father would eventually return."

"So..." His mind began piecing together the new information. "Someone has to die and replace The Father after he is killed in the real world?"

"Exactly," she replied with the same faux smile. "Someone willing to suffer through a hundred fifth dimensional years in his place. Someone like you." Again, she inched the contract ever closer.

Lost in thought however, he did not notice the gesture, nor that he had muttered, "So I can't save Sister either."

"No, you can't," The Mother replied, to his initial surprise. "Not without someone taking her place." He thought of a reply but was cut off. "But your friend already knew that."

He felt the wind knocked out of him as if a car had decided to use him as a road. "What...did you say?"

Realising she had hit a spot, The Mother's grin grew wider. "The girl with the pretty blonde hair. She was like you, asking all these questions."

"Not possible," he denied outright. "She's not your target. And she can't jump dreams."

"We don't choose our targets. Our targets chooses us. Depending on their personalities. The closer they are to our requirements, the easier it is for us to bridge the gaps between our minds, and yours. A short lapse in judgement, maybe a traumatic event for one moment, that's all it takes."

For the first time, she stood from her seat and circled around her chair. Leaning into the spine of it, she said, "Sign the contract." Finally, a pen materialised on the desk, signifying the end of their discussion.

Tim stood to his feet, fist balled as a sense of urgency overwhelmed him. "I know how your power works. It's so cliché, Miss Businesswoman." He circled his own seat, increasing the gap between him and his opponent. "Father kills with physical harm, Sister with a kiss. The Grandmother with food. You, for some reason, do it with a contract. I sign it with the promise of having anything I want, but you never specify where or how I will get it. That's what you did with Joseph, right? You told him that you could give him the power to find us. And he did. But he died from doing that. Classic movie premises really."

He looked down at the contract and the words started to make sense. The first word he saw being 'death'. Gripping the spine of his chair tightly, flexing his muscles, Tim readied himself.

"Clever boy," she hissed. "But you're not getting away. I will have your soul."

Her nails grew to the length of daggers. And with them, she swiped viscously at him. With all his strength, he pulled the chair up as a shield, the claws slashing into the cushion of the backrest, the force of the attack pushed him a step back.

Crossing his legs, he pivoted on the spot, spinning the chair with all the strength he could muster, the muscles in his entire left arm straining from the weight. Despite that, and with a desperate heave, he managed to fling the chair towards the window, falling over his own feet just as The Mother slashed overhead with another attack, leaving her mark in the wall behind.

The chair crashed through the glass pane, and fell off into the abyss below the building.

Tim scrambled to his feet, desperately charging towards the opening he had made. Behind him, The Mother let out an inhumane screech, his eardrums nearly popping from the pitch. He could not tell if the scream was getting louder or if she was closing in on him. He made no effort to turn back to satisfy that curiosity.

At the edge of the floor, between the window pane and a plummet to his death, he jumped without hesitation into the open sky, the claw-nails just scratching away an inch of his pants leg before he began his drop down the impossibly tall building.

Through the cloud and out into the lower atmosphere, he saw that the office building was the sole structure within a large, barren dessert. Seconds counted down the drawn-out fall, long enough for him to reflect on The Mother's words, including Stella's knowledge about the conditions to kill the dream creatures. On top of that, she had continued to search for Sister's real name despite that knowledge, and had not told him of the conditions. Which could only mean one thing.

Stella intends to take Sister's place.

He smashed face first into the sand below.

CHAPTER FORTY-FIVE

The Sister

"Even if we forget the faces of our friends, we will never forget the bonds that were carved into our souls."
- Jun Maeda, Angel Beats!

Lightning flashed and thunder roared ceaselessly, setting space ablaze with white fire. Dark clouds littered the sky, shadowing the world from the light of the sun. Despite the raging weather, the open-rooftop basketball court remained dry, the constant drumming of nature a muffled burp.

One. Two. One. Two. To a slow tempo, Stella circled her steps, dancing to the melody that only she could hear. One. Two. One. Two. Her eyes closed, bathing in the rhythmic thump of rain outside the muted bubble of the rooftop. One. Two. One. Two.

The ground of the old orphanage was as she remembered. Right down to each and every curve within the concrete, the friction in her steps. Though the building had long ago been demolished, the dream version was as real as it had been decades ago. Even the smell of badly cooked chicken that wafted from the kitchen below had a scent of nostalgia behind the burn.

"What are you doing?" Sister asked from one of the benches.

"Dancing," Stella replied matter-of-factly.

"I can see that. But why?"

"I dance when I'm sad." She stopped, opening her eyes to a slowly clearing sky. Beams of light shot through gaps in the clouds like spotlights on a stage. "It's what I always did, even as a kid. I've just not have much reasons to be sad lately."

Stella walked towards the dream entity and sat down beside her. Over the past few weeks, she had come to think of Sister as her friend. Perhaps, outside of Tim and Clay, her best friend.

231

Sister asked, "And why are you sad? Tim bullied you or something?"

"I have this memory. Of when I was very young." Stella ignored the original question. "I can remember this girl who picked me up from my crib whenever I was crying. She'd hum this tune and dance this dance. But I can't for the love of me, remember her face." A smile crossed her face as it does whenever she recalled the memory, for reasons she never knew. "I wanted to be like her. I remembered being very sad back then, but whenever I saw her, I was happy. So I grew up with her in my mind. Kind. Gentle. But so lithe and wispy."

"Who was she?" Sister asked. Stella could tell Sister was interested. Sister had been interested the past six times she told her that story.

"I did something," Stella said, lowering her head in shame. I wanted something. And I wanted it bad enough that I made a deal that I probably shouldn't have.

A look of worry etched Sister's face. "What are you talking about? Stella, you're not making any sense."

"I made a deal with The Mother." She could hear her friend's gasp. Before Sister could cut in, she continued, "I wanted to save you. But I couldn't figure out how. I wanted it so badly, The Mother managed to find me and told me how I could get you out of the dream world."

"Why would you do that?" Sister took Stella's hands in hers.

Cold as they always were, Stella somehow found warmth within them. Stella stated, "Because I found out who you are in the real world."

Stunned, Sister replied, "Who...am I?"

"I've told you your name before and brought you back to our world. But you kept forgetting it and you'd just fade back to the dream world after awhile." The rain had stopped completely. And on cue, the clouds parted. But the sky turned dark almost instantly as night overtook, stars blinking in and out of existence rapidly as if the birth of the universe was being fast forwarded through the heavens above. Stella turned to Sister. "You are my sister. The girl who danced."

A confused look marked Sister's face. Her eyes wide in shock as she tried to come to terms with the news. "I'm your sister? I'm not adopted like you and Clay, am I?"

"No, no. You're my blood sister. I was born, Stella Sparrow. You are a Sparrow. My sister."

"How did you find that out?"

"The girl in my memory, I remembered she wore a white dress." Stella pinched a piece of Sister's dress between her slender fingers. "Just like yours. I didn't think much of it at first, but when Tim asked me to find out

232

your real name, I thought I'd dig further. And here we are."

Sister looked on worryingly, questions seemingly running through her mind. But it wasn't long before she settled on the most troubling question of all. "Why are you sad?"

Stella smiled back gently, touched that her sister was still capable of asking the one question that would reach her heart. "I'm going to become The Sister. I want to take your place."

"No!" Sister shot up from her seat, her fists clenched with worried rage. "You'd have to die to do that!"

Stella got to her feet and with a caring hand, place it gently on Sister's cheek, gently stroking the familiar contours. *Just like mine.* She noted the familiar facial features, further validating her research. "You know, the report of our family said that you were raped by our father. But you managed to save me by sacrificing yourself." She pulled Sister in and hugged her tight. "You already gave up your life for me. Please let me do the same. I couldn't save my brother. So at least let me save you."

"Stella..." Sister whimpered. "Don't..."

They pulled apart, and with her usual, playful, carefree smile, Stella said, "I'm not here to say hello. I'm here to say goodbye. I love you, sister. And I sure am gonna miss you."

CHAPTER FORTY-SIX

The Snap

"What's right is what's left when you do everything else wrong."
- Robin Williams

8:13 P.M.
4 days earlier

The street that housed the Barber's home was strangely quiet compared to the rest of the city. The lights of each house from the end of the road to where Tim stood remained dark, as if abandoned. Even the street lamps were off. But shadows darting from windows to windows had him questioning whether or not he was truly alone under the sky that night. The Barber house, like all the others, was drenched in darkness, save for a single room on the second floor which window glowed softly in the night. Stella's room.

"Stella!" Tim called out from the lawn. "I know you're home! Answer me!"

He waited for a reply, but the only sound that called back was the barking of the neighbour's dog and the screeching of tires in the distance, wailing like a banshee. The dog went quiet. Tim walked up to the house and knocked on the door.

Trying the handle, he found it locked. "Mister, Missus Barber! It's me! Tim! Open up!" He pressed the electronic doorbell, the electronic tune of *Que Sera Sera* rang through the house. "It's Stella, I think she's in trouble! Please! Let me in!" The silence continued to answer. "Shit. Shit! Where's everyone?" he cursed to himself.

Desperate, he banged even harder on the door to which only the echoes of his effort replied. Sighing in resignation, he stepped back out onto the lawn to distance himself and survey his options.

The garage door remained closed and likely empty. Whatever happened in the past six hours, the Barbers, at least the parents, were no longer home. He contemplated circling around to the patio behind, but the fenced up stretch of road would require him to circle the entire district to reach it. The second floor window was too high up for him to climb as well. He studied the garage door again. It was one of the older models, a analogue operated plate that blocked off the entire entrance. Not a possible access.

He knew the Barbers had kept a spare key outside the house, but never found out exactly where it was hidden. Scanning the landscape, there was nothing visible to hide under. No flower pots, nor a welcome mat. Aside from the bricks that made up the structure, there was nothing else exposed.

Then it hit him. "Doorbell." He smacked his forehead to make it literal.

Jogging back to the front porch, he carefully removed the outer casing of the device. He missed sight of it in the dark and the key dropped clanging to his feet. He picked up the key, tried the door, and it clicked open.

Tim called out, "Hello?" just to make sure he was indeed by himself. As expected, there was no reply from within. He stepped inside and headed for the stairs.

"Tim?" the familiar female voice called out from the second floor.

It was, however, not the one that he had hoped, or expected to hear. "Sister?" he asked back.

In a frenzy, he dashed up the stairs, turned the full 180 at the first landing, and bolted the last flight three steps at a time.

The second floor remained dark, save for the faint light beaming out from the gap of Stella's corner room. Rushing over, he flung the door wide open with enough force that it slammed into the wall behind it.

It was a relatively large room, with a long, white painted desk facing the window. On the table, the mess of the photo album and cleaning supplies were laid out across it. The sole light in the room was from the reading light left on. In front of him, in the darkness, stood the girl in the white dress. Both her hands clutching her chest, scrunching up the neck of her dress in her palms.

Through tear filled eyes, she said to him, "I'm sorry, Tim. She asked me to do it. And it was too late. I had to."

He reached for the light switch, "What are you—" He flipped the switch and the room immediately burst with white light. The phantom girl disappeared from his sight as if he had blinked her away.

Behind where she stood, laying on the bed in the same clothes she wore in the afternoon, her cast leg dangling from the side of the bed, Stella lay unmoving.

"No..." he let out softly, fear and dread spreading over him, a man drowning on dry land. "No. No. No! NO!" He rushed to her bedside, furiously shaking the unmoving body. "Wake up, Stella! WAKE UP! You can't do this to me! You can't do this too!" Hot tears streamed down his face as he frantically scanned the room.

On the nightstand was a bottle of sleep medication, emptied and uncapped. Suddenly, Stella looked as fragile as Clay in his final confrontation with The Brother. The siblings, pillars of support for Tim all his life now needed him the most, and he had no idea what to do. He had a promise to keep to the brother, and the life of the sister to save.

Hopelessly, he started CPR on her. Pushing frantically into her chest with huffs, and kissing breaths of life in desperate attempts at revival.

"Come on! Come on!" He stopped, moved, and wrapped his arms under her shoulders and hurriedly picked her up. Wrapping his arms around her stomach, he squeezed her as hard as he could. "Come on! Just puke it out!"

He cried as he did so, the act of carrying her body while crying knocked the wind out of him, growing increasingly tired as the seconds ticked past. He spent a full five minutes desperately trying to revive her, until his legs could no longer support their weight as he slowly lowered her to the ground, dropping to his knees dejectedly, sobbing uncontrollably as he did so, his tears soaking everything from his shirt to her back.

"S-Stella! Stella!" he cried while hugging her tightly. He felt something within him break, a pressure welled up in his chest as his heart got torn asunder. "Ah...ah...argh...AAAAAAAAAAAAARGH!"

He found himself running, bolting out through the front door of the house and out on the streets. Blacking out, he sprinted through a deserted forest and off a cliff. Regaining consciousness, he was still running, halfway down the streets and away from the Barbers' and from Stella. Half crying, half panting, he passed out again, waking in the vast ocean as he frantically tried to keep himself afloat, with his cognition breaking apart at the seams. Liquid started to fill his lungs as he kicked his legs desperately, only to find himself lying face first in the middle of a road, choking on air as if water had filled his lungs. Crawling to his feet, stumbling forward, he blacked out. Stumbling around a floating platform in the sky. Fell off. Woke up.

Limped over and hugging a street lamp. Pain welled up in his head as he felt the overwhelming rush of sadness engulf him, his mind feeling as if it were trying to claw itself out of his skull. He pulled his head back and without hesitation, slammed it into the lamppost.

CHAPTER FORTY-SEVEN

Hymns

"The ultimate test of man's conscience may be his willingness to sacrifice something today for future generations whose words of thanks will not be heard."
- Gaylord Nelson

The stars will rise, in the western skies.
Sitting on the sandy shores of the empty beach, Tim sang the song alone, carrying the voice across the sea, which waves were muted by the mystical workings of the dream world.
The Watcher deems, the peace will last.
Sister strolled to him from a ways down, her long dress dragging snakes in the sand, her trademark smile, often sly, was nowhere to be seen. Replaced by a solemn sadness.
The gathered stars, living after death.
And one last tale, one last battle fought.
"Our future's done..." he ended monotonously. Sister stood beside him, unwavering. Not even fluttering in the breeze. Tim continued, "I've finally figure it out."
"Figured what out?"
"The singing. From the first night, I've heard this singing."
"What does the singing do?" she asked.
But he remained silent, watching the soundless wave crash at his feet, dirtied water washing his legs, soaking his shoes.
Ignoring her question, he said, "I figured out that I can close the portal. It's possible I may be the only person alive who can do it. Maybe it's because I've smashed my head in. Or maybe I just don't have anything left to fight for. No more worries. Never felt this clear headed in years." He stood up, taking in a deep breath of the ocean air, which he was thankful

existed, unlike the sound around him. Turning to Sister, he said, "I'm going to kiss you."

Before she could reply, he leaned in. She stumbled back to avoid him, somehow tripping over herself, her entire calm demeanour vanished as she fell flat on her back. She screamed at him, "You can't do that! You'll die!"

"I know," he stoically replied. He took a step forward, the scene disturbingly similar to that of a girl about to be raped.

Regaining her senses, Sister pushed herself off and floated far away from Tim, before gently hovering to her feet. White cloth ropes extended from the end of her dress, shooting towards Tim and wrapping themselves around his arms and legs, binding him in place.

She asked, "Why are you doing this?"

Instead of fighting against his captor, he dropped to his knees in defeat, arms limp by his sides. Tears streamed down his face like water from a fall. They gushed without stopping, mucus dripping unceremoniously out of his nose. All the movies he watched that showed heroes crying beautifully with a single drop of tear were wrong. He cursed the movies. They were always wrong.

"Everyone's gone!" he cried. "My father. My best friends. Everyone's dead!"

"Tim..." She wanted to approach him, but was afraid he was still too unstable to control himself.

"You killed her! YOU KILLED STELLA!"

He wondered if as a dream entity, she was able of tears. Turns out, with the water that ran down her eyes, she was. "I had to. If I didn't take her, she would be trapped here. She would never move on."

Tim fell to the ground, arms and legs still bound. "I know...I know..." He sobbed. "That's the worst part. I know."

She ran to him, kneeling behind him, cradling his head in her arms. She held him tight, making sure he could not bring his head up to her lips before fully embracing his back.

Continuing through tears, "There's no one left to save," Tim sobbed. "There's no one left to fight for."

"Tim. This is not the time to give up. The world is about to end, and you said you're probably the only person who can close the portal. You can't give up now."

"I couldn't save the people closest to me. Now you're expecting me to save the world? I can't just close the portal. I have to kill The Father as well, or it'll just happen again. I can't do all that! I'm just a stupid kid." He gently pushed himself away from her.

Sister faced him.

239

Tim continued, "I can't save anyone."

"You have to try." She placed her hands reassuringly on his shoulders, rubbing them gently in comfort like a mother would a child. "The people you loved, loved you as much as you loved them. You're not the only one willing to die for the other. They gave up their lives to get you here. Your dad. Clay. Stella."

"There's no one left to save. There's no one left," he repeated the mantra, eyes looking blankly down at the grains of sand beneath him. He looked up, staring into Sister's misty grey eyes. His stare widened and his pupils dilated as his brain strained itself with the connection. "There's no one left to save!" He leapt to his feet, hands on his head, ruffling through his hair madly as all the thoughts flowed in.

"Tim?" Sister asked, worried. "Are you okay?"

Again, he ignored her, and she was getting slightly annoyed by it. He exclaimed, "You were there! You were in Stella's room!" he said excitedly. "You were right. They would sacrifice themselves for me. My friends. My dad. They did just that. But Stella, she had time to prepare. She wouldn't do it unless she knew I could handle it! Don't you see? Hah!" A maniacal smile spread across his face.

"I don't say this often but you are seriously scaring me right now."

He pulled her up to standing and hugged her joyously, all while the last remnants of his tears and mucus dripped and dangled. "Wait!" He pushed her apart again. "What did you say Father is doing with the souls of the people killed?"

"He's...trapping them in the dream world to tear open the fabric of reality..." she stopped as Tim burst out laughing.

He exclaimed, "Oh! This is fantastic! Do you know what this means?"

"That...you've finally lost it?"

"No," he pulled her close until his nose was scrapping hers. Looking her in the eyes to make sure she understood how serious he was, he said, "It means I can save everyone. Happy endings for all!"

Zoot. Zun. Zoot. Zun.

Grinning, Tim stated, "He's here," before asking Sister, "You've marked me?"

"Yes," she replied. "You're safe. What are you thinking?"

"I'm thinking, after what I'm about to say, he's gonna want to kill me." He spun on his heel, turning around to face the newly materialised Father. Still grinning, still manic, he stepped towards the creature without fear.

"Hello. My name's Timothy Kleve. I'll be your demise soon. Are you my daddy? Of course not. Not yet anyway. Soon though, hah!"

240

The creature growled, raised its rusted saw with its blade to Tim's throat, an act of hostile threat unbecoming of a mindless beast. But of course, Tim already knew none of the hunters were actually 'mindless'.

"You don't scare me anymore. Because in this exact order, I'm going to save my best friend. Then, I'm going to close the portal, save the world. I'm going to save her," he pointed to Sister behind him. "After that, I'm going to kill you."

The Father roared, though Tim could not see its lips move underneath the straw hat.

"I'm going to save my father. And last but not least, I'm going to save my best friend's sister. Well, maybe not that exact order, but I am going to do all of that!"

The Father pulled its weapon back and swung it at Timothy's neck. Sister gasped, but the saw, though as sharp as it ever was, merely pierced and stopped just half an inch into the skin. Though bleeding, though enduring the pain through gritted teeth, Tim managed to spit his last retort at The Father.

"You are going to lose."

The creature pulled the weapon, slicing off his neck.

11:56 P.M.
3 days earlier

He wasn't sure if the pain in his neck was due to having smashed his head against a steel post or the after effects of being decapitated. He knew though, that the blood flowing down his face and into his lips were his own. His watch beeped as it passed the midnight line, and through veils of red, he saw he had been unconscious for over 24 hours. Tim wondered how his body, still slumped against the lamppost, was left untouched for such a long time, until he realised that people probably had more problems on their hands with a hole in the sky than a kid passed out on the streets.

His head throbbed, and wished the constant ringing would stop, until he realised the sound was that of a vehicle's alarm wailing into the night.

Slowly, he climbed to his feet, using the bloodied pole as a support to stand. He smelled of blood and sweat, and a small swarm of flies vacated his forehead as he stood. He hoped they had not infected his wounds. He was still in the suburbs but almost half a mile away from where the Barbers' house was. He must have ran all the way to that one random street corner, which would explain why his entire body, not just his skull, was burning with aches and pain.

Steeling himself, he wiped off what he could of the blood on his face with the sleeves of his shirt. A glint reflected from the light in his eyes as he said to himself, "Let's end this."

CHAPTER FORTY-EIGHT

Goodbye

"Your friend is that man who knows all about you, and still likes you."
- Elbert Hubbard, The Note Book of Elbert Hubbard

1:36 A.M.
2 days earlier

Though it was past midnight, every single light in the Barber's house was on, full brightness. Tim stood on their doorstep, finger on the door bell. On the way over, he had prepared a speech. Apologetic, sympathetic, and true. But just before ringing in, everything he had wanted to say floated out of his mind.

The door swung opened. Under the archway stood Gordon and Matilda Barber. Husband and wife. Father and mother of Stella and Clay. He still wore his working suit, which, given the occasion, was a ghastly mirror of a mourning outfit. She wore one of her many flowery dress, white to the bone, her marshmallow fluffed hair drooped to one side. Both of their eyes were red from crying, and their cheeks shone from residual tears.

Tim looked up at the two adults, heart beating as fast as guilt could coat him. "Mis-Mister and Missus Barber..." he mumbled, turning his stare down to their feet. "About Stella. And Clay. I'm sorry. I should have protected them. I should have done more. I should–"

Matilda pulled him in, taking his entire body in her arms in a sombre embrace. It was then Tim was reminded of his age, that he was still no more than a kid, despite his personality. She cried, and he cried too. Gordon placed a soothing hand on his shoulders.

"Timmy," the woman said soothingly, her voice a croaking hum. He was reminded of his mother, and how she would hum tunes to get him to

243

sleep when he was younger. "You're family."

His legs gave way and he sank to his knees, sobbing into her dress. "I-I need to keep going. I-I'm almost done."

"We know," she admitted as she rubbed his back. "Stella told us everything. Anything you need. Just say it."

He nodded fiercely. He shut his eyes tightly in a poor attempt at holding back the tears, but they continued to flood through.

2:26 A.M.
2 days earlier

"Here you go," Gordon said, opening the door to Stella's room. The two paused at the doorway while Stella's body lay peacefully on the bed. They had dressed her in one of her white dresses, had cleaned her, combed her, and made her as presentable as they could. It wasn't hard. Stella was beautiful in life. Even in death, she had a wispy, nebulous glow.

They had set the thermostat to the lowest temperature, keeping the room at a frosty cold, enough to bring Tim a slight shiver.

Gordon tore his eyes away from his daughter, wiping away a tear that had gathered. "What are you looking for, boy?"

Tim looked away, entering the room and focusing on the desk with all the things they were working on before her suicide. "She would have left me something. Something I could use. She'd probably have left me everything I needed." He scanned the desk, over the charred photo album and diary. "Something small." He opened the diary, revealing a sealed envelope with his name on it.

He recalled how after his mother died, he had written a note similar to this. How Stella and Clay comforted him through the days that came after the funeral. How he tore it into pieces in the year that followed. He had never once thought that he would be on the receiving end of one of their letters.

To Gordon, Tim asked, "Did she write one for you too?"

"Of course," he stated. "She told us everything that happened in them. Said she loved us. Told us to be happy. Told us not to worry cause she'll take care of Clay for us," his voice broke towards the end.

Tim nodded. He breathed in deeply, gathering strength, "What are you planning to do with her body?" he asked. "If there's a funeral, I'd like to be there."

"Of course you'll be there," Gordon replied. "We're going to drive down to the morgue, first thing in the morning. We'll collect Clay and bring him home," he stopped and licked his dry lips. The words seemingly lost to him as he tried to finish his answer. "We'll wait a day of two. See if all the craziness dies down. Then we'll give them a proper burial."

"And if it doesn't die down?"

The man paused. Tim could hear him taking breath after breath, trying to speak, but always stopping right before the words would come. "We might have to improvise something." Tears rolled down his cheeks again, and the stern looking, monstrously large man Tim had known for years suddenly shrunk in front of him. "Whatever happens, we'll see them off properly."

Tim held up the envelope in his hand, staring at his name. "Sorry sir, but do you mind if I read this alone?"

Gordon looked to his daughter, nodded understandingly, and closed the door behind him. Tim listened to the man's footstep echo away and the sobbing restarting as he continued to mourn.

Pulling up a chair beside the bed, he sat beside his friend. Carefully, he tore opened the envelope. In it was a photograph wrapped in a bag. He held the picture in the light, depicting a younger Vashmir Commons standing in front of a lumber rack, straw-hat on his head, suspenders on his body, saw in hand.

Also in the envelope was a folded paper and a printed image of an old newspaper article. Setting the article aside, he noticed a strand of hair had settled against Stella's eyelid. Gently, with his finger, he shifted it back to place. Unfolding her note, careful not to damage it, her beautiful cursive words, occasionally muddled by dried spots of tears, littered the page.

My endearing Timothy,

I know you are hurting. You are probably blaming yourself for what happened. Please don't. I chose to do this. I missed my brother and loved him too much. Besides, it would never have worked out between us. After all, I had a huge crush on my brother. Incestuous, scandalous, I know. I think you did too. You never judged though, and for that, I am eternally grateful.

I do hope this letter finds you, and the contents of the envelope. It's all I can give you at this time. I know you made a promise to Clay that you would protect me. Sorry I broke that promise. Let me make it up to you. Let me save you and Sister. And please don't blame Sister. It's not her fault I'm gone. She went through so much, and yet still helped us. We should return that favour at least.

Do you remember the first time we met as kids? You and Clay saved me from a bunch of guys that were picking on me because of my braces.

And the two of you got beaten up for it. My heroes. You told me I should just paint my braces white, and I told you to shave yourself bald. You said to give your hair a try, and I said I'd rather date a kettle. I'm going to miss that, wherever I'm going. The back and forth between us.

I hope I can find my brother.

"He'll probably find you first."

Maybe he'll find me.

"That's what I said!"

One day though, I hope we'll find you again.

"The three of us."

Together again.

Take care of my parents for me. Take care of Sister. Know that you are loved from beyond. Your father loves you. Your mother loves you. Clay loves you. And I love you. Live happily, Timothy Kleve.

Goodbye,

-Stella Barber

He had to hold the note away from his body, for fear that his tears would ruin the last words his friend wrote. Setting the paper and envelope on the bed, Tim took Stella's cold hand in his, crying into it as if he were praying to a god.

"I'll find you," he cried. "I'll find all of you. I promise."

CHAPTER FORTY-NINE

The World Between

"A dream you dream alone is only a dream. A dream you dream together is reality."
- Yoko Ono, All We Are Saying

7:16 A.M.
2 days earlier

Matilda Barber set the cup of hot chocolate down on the coffee table. Before Tim was the photograph of Vashmir Commons, the notes from Stella, and the revolver he took from the police station. He stared at the exhibition, his mind blank from fatigue, exhausted from the long week. He had mourned Stella, washed up, showered, ate, and changed into one of Clay's slightly oversized white shirts and brown cargo pants.

"Are you sure about this?" Gordon Barber asked from behind him.

The morning sun was rising over the water, its light shining through the glass patio doors, bathing the room in a soothing orange.

Slowly, Tim picked up the gun and checked the cylinder. The chambers were all still loaded. "I have to stop this. I think I'm the only one who can."

Matilda said, "I don't understand."

"Me neither," Tim replied truthfully, reclining into the couch.

She asked, "Tired?"

"Yeah. I think I'll take a nap."

Gordon asked, "You want some of those medicines? Somnidin?"

"No," he replied curtly. "Those things are almost as bad as the dreams."

He could feel the tension in his shoulders giving way. His eyelids refused to stay open. He could hear Matilda and Gordon saying something

247

to him, but his beaten brain refused to make sense of the words. The sun felt warm on his skin, and all the aches in his body evaporated as he was numbed by slumber.

Fluorescent lights lit the corridor in hospital white, the floor carpeted in white fur. As far as his eyes could see, the passageway led on forever before and behind him. Countless doors lined the walls on his left and right. Some echoed screams of pain and others whispered hushed laughter.

"Don't worry," Sister said, appearing beside him. He wasn't shocked though, having grown accustomed to her sudden appearances. "This place isn't that dangerous once you get used to it."

"Where are we?" he asked, staring around.

"Corridor of some sort. This is a shady corner of the dream world. Nobody ever comes here."

"What about you?"

"I was looking for you. Specifically. I just followed your scent here."

He stared at her oddly, "Are you a bloodhound now?"

She laughed daintily, and he smiled.

Then, a thought crossed his mind and he asked seriously, "Can The Father track me?"

"Yes. But he has to do it consciously. And it's easier when your personality suits his powers better. And I don't think he's hunting you right now. He's busy with that whole, 'ripping a hole into your universe' thing," she explained, taking a seat on the floor, leaning against the wall. "It's all very complicated."

"I know," he replied, pacing up and down the corridor, trying to drown out the disturbing noises with his own footsteps. "I have a question though. If he's trying to get into our world from here, there must be, like, a gateway or something, right? A place where he's pushing through?"

"Of course. I'm guessing you want to see it?"

"Yes," he replied without hesitation.

She jumped to her feet excitedly, clapping in joyous anticipation like a child about to go on an adventure. "Alright, follow me," she opened the door closest to them, where laughter was emitting.

But instead of a room, or a person, or anything resembling a place where sound could come from, they were faced with a literal wall of black. It did not reflect nor shimmer. No glow emitted nor any sign of movement was shown. Just black.

Without missing a beat, Sister stepped into the wall, disappearing into it as easily as a one would jump into water. Even then, the aftermath broke Tim's expectation. No ripples followed her, and the wall remained as seemingly solid as it did before.

Gathering a breath for courage, he placed one foot through. The air did not feel any different on the other side. Though he tried not to close his eyes as his leg passed through, by the time his face was close enough to touch it, he blinked, and he opened his eyes to a space impossibly emptier than the last.

He wanted to call the place a room, but there were no walls. He wanted to describe it as an outdoor plain, but there was a ceiling above. He wanted to call what he stood on 'ground', but his legs were soaked shin deep in clear water. The ceiling was also impossibly made from the same liquid. Colourless and clear, yet he was unable to see his own two feet nor a reflection. Below the liquid, below where his feet should be standing on, was an empty white that stretched infinitely in all directions.

Tim exclaimed, "What the hell is that?" He pointed towards a white, whirling tube that spiralled up from the ground to the 'ceiling', hundreds of feet top to bottom. Though miles away, the whirlwind still looked imposingly huge, stretching across his vision.

Sister explained, "We're in The World Between. One of them at least." She stepped towards the whirlwind. Despite how ferocious the phenomenon looked, there was not even a breeze from it. "This is one of the places where the space between two universes are at their thinnest."

"I thought you said the dream worlds were of different universes?" Tim asked, confused.

"Sort of. They are like after-images. A world a little bit forward and back in time, out of synch with the present. You're sort of there, and not." She bent over, scooping up a handful of the liquid below. The liquid stayed connected like slime, never completely breaking apart. "What you're standing on is pure energy. It's what we manipulate to give us our powers. When the universes are apart, these are mixed together, creating the dream world. But when they are close enough, they stabilise, and we get a place like this."

Tim looked to the top of the whirlwind. "You're saying that the ceiling is another universe?"

"Yeah. And the ground is yours. Specifically, the bottom of that whirlwind is Ridge Valley."

Tim was left speechless. He had questions, but did not know what those were. He was both confused and clear-headed at the same time, and that conflicting feeling was making his head spin.

He then thought out loud, "Wait, so that whirlwind is the portal thing

249

in Ridge Valley? Does that mean it's a gateway to another universe?"

She nodded hesitantly, an unsure look on her face. "Sort of. I'm not sure how to say this, but that thing hasn't fully connected to your universe yet. That whirlwind is like a drain. It's sucking energy in from the other universe."

The blue Mist, he thought. "There's this blue gas that's been spewing out from the portal."

"That could be it. But it's not completely connected to your world yet. That's what The Father is doing. He's withholding all the souls, the energy of the people killed so that they'll try to return to your universe. It's like he's holding a super magnet against a balloon." She walked back to him, a worried look in her eyes. "You said you have a way to close the portal. How?"

"I'm...not sure," he said. "I'm still trying to get the hang of it."

"Of what?" She was flustered, confused. He thought that she looked cute like that. "That thing is made of pure energy. You can't just cut it off. Believe me, I've tried. The only way is to close it is to cut off the end. The portal in your world. Even then, you have to be able to manipulate energy to do so, otherwise, it's just a solid thing. You can't even really touch it. It'll be as hard as concrete."

Reassuringly, Tim tried to stop her, "Sister."

"What?" she yelled, though not meaning to. Realising how tense she was getting, she calmed herself down and tried again. "What?"

"My feet are in the water."

"What?"

"My feet. They're in the water."

She looked down, and sure enough, Tim was submerged in the liquid just as she was.

Her eyes widened, surprise etched across her face. "That's not possible. It should be like stone to you. You shouldn't be able to even break the surface!" She grabbed his shoulder tightly. "How are you doing this?"

"The singing. I've been hearing these hymns since I started coming here. And I could also travel between dreams. You said it wasn't normal, so I did some deduction. I figured it must be me, reacting to something in the dream world." He looked around him, the pure energy that flowed beneath him swirled around his legs. "Now that I know about this energy thing, it makes sense. I can manipulate energy here. Which means I can also close the portal from the other end."

She looked distressed. More so than he had ever seen her. "No. You can't do that. We don't know what will happen if you close the portal from the real world. You could really die."

"I know."

"No. No! You...you have what Stella left you?" she asked frantically. "You have my real name! You can just call me to your world, and I'll close it from there! I'm already dead, so it's okay."

Tim took her in his arms, her small body settled into his chest. For the first time, he felt like her equal. She was not helping him with her knowledge, nor overwhelming him with her powers. She was as worried, unsure, and capable as he was.

Gently, he said, "I need you here."

"Why?" she asked, stunned.

"I'm going to the portal. Then, I'm going to drag The Father out and kill him so he can't do this again." He wondered when it was that he started saying 'kill' with such ease. "When he dies, I need you to find my father. He's one of the souls that are trapped. And I need you to tell him to take over The Father's duty so that monster can never revive again."

Softly, regretfully, she muttered, "And then you'll close the portal?"

His steady breathing was all that they could hear. "Yes," he replied, unbent.

Slowly, she pulled away from him. With a calm but sad smile across her face, she said, "Once the portal closes, all these things that you've been doing, you might not be able to do them again. The only reason we can even talk now is because of the portal. Time between our worlds synchronising. But once that closes..."

"I know," he spoke for her. "I'll stop remembering my dreams. Everything will go back to normal."

"So this will be the last time we get to talk."

"Probably," he replied, staring down to his feet, not in shame, but disappointment. "Until the day I die at least."

She bit her lower lip nervously, her eyes not daring to meet his. "I guess I should say everything I want to say then."

Sister extended a piece of cloth from her dress, gently wrapping it around Tim's head until it covered his mouth. His eyes bolted wide in confusion. However, the cloth had muted him, and he could only look at Sister in disarray as the later smiled lovingly.

Without any of her seductive poses or powers, nor any of her fond bodily contacts, she professed, "I love you, Timothy Kleve."

She leaned in to kiss his lips over the cloth.

10:39 P.M.
24 hours earlier

The sun had long since risen and set. The Barbers had laid one of Clay's old blanket over him as he slept. He breathed heavily, and though his body felt refreshed, his mind still felt like it was breaking down from the time he spent in the dream world. He needed to put an end to the ordeal before he mentally crumbled.

10:39 blinked on the television set-top box, signalling the end of his 15 hour long sleep. He looked to the right where Matilda lay sleeping on Gordon's shoulder, both snoring gently away.

Tim got to his feet, taking the blanket and returning their care by gently laying it across the couple.

From the coffee table, he picked up the revolver, but left Stella's note and photograph. He could feel it. The last chapter was coming. And he finally had a plan to finish it.

CHAPTER FIFTY
The Streets Below

"The way to learn whether a person is trustworthy is to trust him."
-Ernest Hemingway, Papa Hemingway

5:59 P.M.
5 hours earlier

Three blocks away from them, Hotel Alexandria stood with a hole into another universe above its roof. The otherworldly blue crystals, as large as an entire level, hung from the edges of the roof like freezer frost. The building, a millennium age glass structure, looked fragile with its windowed exterior design.

"Did you know I was in a war a few hundred years ago? Or was it a hundred years later? I always get those mixed up."

"Was it anything like this?" Tim asked monotonously.

Howard Galloway replied, "Pretty close actually. Just a lot more people though."

The pair of them stood on the roof of the apartment building. Tim had walked to the city from the Barber's house, leaving the couple behind for their safety. He had chosen that location to rest his weary legs when somehow, amid all the chaos, the librarian managed to find him. Behind them, the sun was slowly setting between the gap of the horizon and black clouds.

Below them, in a sea of fire, cars burned and barrels were lit with flames. Mixed in an ocean of mass, rioters and looters pillaged and rampaged through the streets. Rescue vehicles were overturned while a group of teenagers repeatedly smashed a fire hydrant with baseball bats and crowbars.

Tim noted, "It's senseless."

253

"War always is. What are you going to do now?"

"I need to get to Hotel Alexandria. That's where the portal is."

Standing on one of the overturned cars, Detective Julianne Smith stood with a megaphone in one hand and a pistol in the other. Her flaming red hair stood out even in the burning streets. With ferocity he had not seen in her before, she shouted out orders to those who followed her.

Find Timothy Kleve.

Kill the boy.

All the Somnidin you want.

Save the world.

The librarian said, "She's gone mad." Tim merely nodded in agreement. The man asked, "Are you going to stop her?"

Tim stepped away from the edge of the roof, hand resting gently on the butt of his revolver. He headed for the door. "Not my call."

Tim turned and nodded a farewell, before leaving the man behind on the rooftop. Taking the stairs down the apartment building two at a time, he arrived on the ground floor within a dozen breaths of air. Staring up at the glowing exit sign that marked the back door of the apartment, he drew his revolver. The gun felt heavier than it had ever been.

He remembered the image of the bullet going through Adam Pearlman's forehead. How Clay took a bat to The Brother. How Stella shot Joseph Camein Price. How His dad had saved him from The Father.

"Chin up, kid," he said to himself as he headed for the door. "It's going to be fine."

6:10 P.M.

4 hours earlier

Megaphones were amazing inventions. Whoever wielded them would feel empowered, full of control. But it wasn't the megaphone that gave Julie her confidence, it was the stash of Somnidin she had hidden in a secure warehouse, where the only one with the password and key was her.

"Find the boy!" she yelled into the machine. "You find him and kill him and this nightmare will all be over!"

Even through the crowd, Oliver stood out like a sore thumb. Pushing through the masses, he headed towards his partner, screaming, "What are you doing? This isn't like you, Julie! Snap out of it!"

Ignoring her partner, her eyes, sharp and trained from years on the force, spotted the maroon headed teen popping out of the apartment building. Tim stood outside the door, making sure the coast was clear.

However, their eyes met, and he knew that he could only run.

She grinned. "Gotcha."

Tim bolted across the street, pushing through the crowd, gun hanging by his side.

Dropping her megaphone and at the top of her voice, Julie shouted, "THERE HE IS!" She raised her pistol and fired at Tim.

Oliver shouted, "JULIE!"

The bullet ricochet off a car door as Tim ducked to avoid the shrapnel. The boy darted into the crowd, keeping low as he moved through the walls of human shield.

"Damn that kid," she cursed. A group of her followers charged in the general direction she had fired at. She jumped off the car, chasing after him.

Oliver cursed, "Fuck!" He followed after her, shouting, "Stop it! This isn't you!"

She swung her gun back and fired at his feet, bringing him to a halt. "If you follow me, I'll put one between your eyes!" She turned back to her target and fired another round just as Tim darted into a corner alley. Blood burst from his shoulder, splattering against the brick wall right before he disappeared from her sight.

"Shit..."

Tim held his shoulder, panting in both pain and exhaustion as the hurt from the gunshot wound sunk in. His vision blurred as Hotel Alexandria's large neon sign came into view. The skyscraper, with the whirling portal overhead, was just two streets over, looking menacingly similar to a super villain's lair in a cheesy 1990s superhero movie.

He could feel his own blood soaking into his hand. Instinctively, he wiped the beads of sweat from his forehead, only to have the blood smear into his hair. From behind, another gunshot rang through the alley and he knew the detective had caught up to him even before the bullet plunked off the wall beside him. The adrenaline kept him awake, and he dashed back into another crowd, toppling over the television set a man had stolen from one of the stores.

Pushing through to another alley, he almost stopped to catch his breath again, only to turn back to see the redhead flowing through the people like a knife through water. She was, at that moment, almost as terrifying as any hunter he had in the nightmares.

"Crazy bitch," he huffed under his breath. He sped through the last alley, knocking over trash cans as he passed.

But the alleyway was long and had a clear line of sight between him and Julie. The detective raised her gun in a jog, firing wildly at him as he zigzagged to dodge the hail of bullets. She emptied her magazine, slowed further to reload, giving Tim enough time to turn a corner at the end of the alley, crossing the final street that stood between him and the hotel.

The entrance of the hotel had a driveway curving into it. But what used to be a magnificent set of double oak doors had a black, smoking limousine embedded through it.

Sucking up the pain in his injured arm, Tim climbed on top of the vehicle, a lot slower than he had hoped to do. He slipped on the windscreen and screamed in pain as he slammed shoulder first onto the roof of the car. His entire body almost gave in to the pain, his vision blurred further as the border of consciousness greeted him.

"Stop right there!" Julie commanded from behind.

That shout both saved him from passing out and scared the living hell out of him. Slowly, he got to his feet and stood on the roof of the car. Even slower, he turned to face the female detective whose gun was aimed at him. But also, to the back of Oliver Hardy, who stood between his partner and the teenager, his own gun raised at the former.

Julie barked, "Get out of the way, Ollie!" Her red eyes reflecting her anger. Her once beautiful face scrunched in a crazed rage.

"You–" Oliver started through gritted teeth and panting breaths, "You are a detective."

"I won't say it again," she insisted, taking a menacing step forward, better positioning herself to make her intentions clear. "Get out of my way."

Her partner took a breath and steadied himself. "You're not the only one with a gun here. If you try to hurt him, I will shoot you."

"You won't shoot me," she called his bluff, taking aim at Tim.

Tim got ready to jump away, but Oliver made good on his word and fired a round at her feet. Stunned by his action, she momentarily snapped out of whatever mad trance she had been engulfed in.

Oliver reasoned, "You are one of the best detectives I've ever met. One of the most logical, fierce, and loyal people I've ever met. If you can give me one shred of proof that this kid is behind all of this, then I will turn around and shoot him myself. But until then, he is an innocent civilian and I will not let you lay a finger on him." He turned to Tim and nodded for the teen to go ahead.

Tim mouthed back his thanks, asking the detective to, "Evacuate as many as you can. Get as far away from the city as possible." He climbed off the car and into the hotel.

Still shocked by her partner's actions, Julie did not give chase.

Oliver returned her his attention. "You are my partner, and my best friend. I will not let you waste an entire life of right for this one wrong. Even if it means I have to take you down."

From behind her, through the crowd, her followers pushed through, clumsier and slower than their leader, but approaching all the same, a mass of frightened individuals ready to tear apart a single life to save their own.

"What's it going to be? Are we partners?" Oliver asked before raising his gun sight to line with her head. "Or enemies?"

Her gun still half raised, she stared at her partner in confused deliberation. "Ollie..." her hands shook as she muttered his name. Her fears seemingly subsided, her thoughts no longer fixated on her impending demise by Sin, she lowered her gun. Sighing in relief, Oliver did the same.

From behind, a woman leading the mob ran up to her. "Detective! Where is the boy?"

Still numbed, the words somehow managed to force their way out of Julie's mouth. "He went that way," she lied and redirected them down the street, knowing that talking them off would take too long. "Make sure no one gets hurt."

The mob gave a loud shout, a poor attempt at a war cry, only to sound like the whistle of a punctured heater. As they left, Oliver walked up to her, covering her shivering body with his coat.

She said to him, "I hope you're right, Ollie." She turned to look up at the towering building. "If you are wrong..."

"I'll buy you a cup of coffee."

"Okay," she agreed. "Coffee sounds good right now."

CHAPTER FIFTY-ONE

Hello, Brother

"Do you know how cruel your God can be, David. How fantastically cruel? ...Sometimes he makes us live."
-Stephen King, Desperation

10:19 P.M.
20 minutes earlier

Unlike most hotels, The Alexandria doubled as an office building for the first 49 stories, before the last 30 became the hotel. Usually, this would not have posed a problem as there were 6 elevators available, two for staff, three for guests, and one for goods. But the power to the city grid was unstable and the elevator could not be made to work, no matter how hard Tim pressed the buttons or kicked furiously at the doors. With another group of looters closing in, he had no choice but to staunch his wound with a makeshift tourniquet and head up on foot.

He let out his last breath on the 60th flight of stairs with a curse. Though the hotel rooms started 10 floors ago, the 60th were home to the junior suites, which, according to the log books kept at reception, were the minimum suite size required for the mini bar to be stocked with vodka.

"Fucking...sixty...stories!" Even with multiple breaks between floors, he was almost sure he would pass out from exhaustion before bleeding to death, and recognised the miracle that he didn't do either one. "Three...fucking...hours!" he heaved, pushing open the fire doors and stepping into the hallway, which he was beyond grateful was still somewhat air-conditioned. Pigs would blush if they could see him sweat.

Most of the lights in the corridor remained operational, but some blinked in-and-out of the shadows. The maintenance light blinking on the LED screen served as a constant reminder that the elevators were still not operational.

Keeping pressure on his wound, he reached into his pocket and pulled out the master key he made at reception and headed for the closest room. He swiped the card once but it did not read. The second try failed as well. That was when he realised his blood was smeared across the magnetic strip and he frantically wiped them away with his shirt. On the third try, the door lit green, and he stumbled into the room. Despite the modern exterior, the inside of the suite was classically decorated. Veiled mostly in darkness, with only a flickering incandescent red lamp on the nightstand illuminating the place, the furniture, themed on mahogany and heartwood, had their shadows dancing across the walls in bursts. The curtains were drawn closed but the light of the fires outside blipped through the cloth. He thought the room looked like hell.

Though sure he wasn't followed, Tim wanted to make his safety a guarantee. After locking and latching the room, with what strength he could muster, he pushed the cabinet to the door. The fact that it was empty made the job easier.

He was still amazed how he had managed to stay conscious, or how it was possible that he had not yet bled out. He wondered if it had anything to do with his newfound ability to manipulate energy and his proximity to the portal. Either way, he knew that if he did not treat or at least bandaged his wound better, he could still end up in trouble impossibly worse than what he was already in.

From the bathroom, he yanked the hand towel from its holder, then headed to the mini-fridge and received the first good news that day: a bottle of vodka, strangely priced a dollar cheaper than a bottle of water beside it, sat cooled within. He downed the water in seconds.

"Finally," he huffed with a smile as he threw the empty bottle away and grabbed the vodka to compliment his towel.

With his makeshift first-aid kit, he headed for the dresser.

He sat in the dresser chair, feeling the pain in his shoulder that marked him as living. With each deep breath, he felt the sting of the wound in his left shoulder. The bullet wound was a clean through and through, but the pain was only felt in the front as his back had gone numb. He winced when he tore away his bloodied shirt sleeve and let out a seething gasp of pain. With his free hand, he took the vodka and leaned back against the recliner he sat in. He could feel the spine of the chair drenched warm, probably with his blood more than sweat.

"Okay," he said to himself, taking deep breaths once more. He saw his reflection in the dresser mirror. Though his eyes had a black ring of fatigue around them, his skin was bleached white. His maroon hair was darkened

259

by blood, oily and unkempt. His green eyes were as distant as great grass plains. Given the situation, he felt that the mirror was doing him a favour, making him out as clean as he was.

"Okay," he said again, trying to squeeze out the remnants of hesitation in him. He hovered the bottle of vodka over his injured shoulder. "Okay."

He overturned the bottle and its contents poured over his wound. Through gritted teeth, he let out a scream, foaming and drooling. The bottle fell out of his hand before it was even half emptied, spilling over the carpet floor. Quickly, he took the towel and wrapped it around his wound, knotting it using his teeth, and let out a pained scream.

Releasing the knot, he felt weak and disoriented. Tired, unable to think, all he remembered was a fog of darkness surrounding him.

His eyes flew open as he woke. The familiar itch and slight pain of his missing right arm tingled his senses. The pain from the gunshot wound in his left shoulder was gone, as expected.

"Damn it," he sighed, getting to his feet. Scanning the area, he was surrounded by rows and columns of red metal pillars, beams, fences of criss-crossing support rebar, cardboard walls, and sparse wooden plank flooring. A couple of gas lamps hung under the beams, spread out in such a way that there would always be corners of shadows. "Where the hell am I this time?"

The gaps in the floor showed there were multiple levels of the same environment that stretched down to what seemed like forever. From what he could see beyond the walls, there were what looked to be stars in the distant night sky. Overall, the place looked like a building in construction, yet it had no tools, materials, machines or anything else that even remotely tied it down as such a place.

Zut. Zoon. Zut. Zoon.

A hair-raising sound. He spun in place, looking for the source.

Zut. Zoon. Zut. Zoon.

The sound of the saw, back and forth, back and forth.

He backed up against the wall so he would have one less direction to cover. His eyes darted between the two corridors that connected his small piece of open space.

Zut. Zoon. Zut. Zoon.

The beating of his heart was almost as loud as the sound of the saw. The sound got louder, closer. He could now hear the Sawman's footsteps. Soft knocks for a thing of such size.

Zut. Zoon. Zut. Zoon.

He was ready to run to the opposite of whichever corridor the Sawman came from.

Zut. Zoon. Zut. Zoon.

"Come on, you son of a bitch," he whispered, jaws clenched.

Zut. Zoon. Zut. Zoon.

"Come on." He thought back to the line of the song *Que Sera Sera* and whispered, "Whatever will be, will be."

A flash of white appeared in the corner of his eyes and he was lifted off his feet by the white cloth that had wrapped itself around his neck. He wanted to shout, to scream for help, but the noose tightened around his airway, not letting a single puff of air in or out. He twisted, turned, kicked his leg, and flailed his arms, but could not get released.

Stars filled his vision and a distant part of him wondered if they were they same ones he saw earlier before his vision started to fade to white. It felt as if his eyes were about to come out of their sockets, his head dunked into water and pulled 1000 feet into the sea, about to burst from the pressure.

Then it was over.

Sister stood on the higher beam of the construction building. She had just hung Timothy Kleve, killed the teen in the dream to save his life. Below her, standing within the labyrinth corridor of cardboard walls and plywood floors was the man in the straw hat. The Sawman. The Father. Deprived of his prey.

She said to him, "Tim will stop you."

In a growl akin to that of beasts, it croaked, "I know what you are trying to do." Its voice was low, slow, and rough, like what a bulldozer would sound like if it had vocal cords. "There will be no happy endings for you."

"I don't expect one," she replied. "Happy endings are for people who are alive. I am dead. Just like you. There won't be a happy ending for you either."

The world dissolved around them, the bars and beams melting like molten metal, swirling and reshaping itself into a different shape, colour, and even material. What was once a metal beam she stood on turned into the large root of a mangrove tree. What used to be ground made of wood slowly flooded with muddied water. Trees sprouted out from the support pillars, and slowly, their surroundings transformed fully into a dampened, muddy swamp. Behind The Father, a giant whirlwind spun, the epicentre of the portal, stretching miles into the distance.

"You know our powers don't work on each other. You can't kill me." Sister stepped off her perch, floating down to the level of the water, her dress shrinking up to her shins, her feet never touching the mud. Starting out seductive, she continued, "So be a good boy. Get out of my way." She hissed the last part, her eyes glowing white as tendrils of cloth extended from her dress.

The Father, knee deep in mud, stepped onto and above the liquid surface as easily and as if it was walking up a stair. Saw in hand, it stared down at the girl, and without warning, charged in with blade raised. She readied herself for the impact. Her cloth shot outward at it like spikes. The creature dodged them with ease, fading uncannily before each hit could connect.

From the side, in unceremonious shorts and sandals, feet splashing against the surface of the mud, a trail of grey powder streaming in his wake, the white haired Clay came flying, his black hood flapping behind as he swung the steel pipe at The Father's face. The Sawman was caught off guard, catching the outsider's attack completely with the corner of its jaw. Supernaturally enhanced, the hit sent even The Father flying away into a tree.

Surprised at the arrival of her aid, Sister exclaimed, "You are—" However, the name evaporated from the tip of her tongue and memory. "Brother."

"I am," Clay replied, panting heavily from his rushed attack. "This power though, gonna take some getting used to."

Remembering, she added, "You should get to Tim! He knows your name. He can save you."

"The kid? I already know his plan. Had a lot of time to figure things out here." His pipe hung limply in his right hand as he stared at the tree The Father had crashed into. The dust, yet to settle, blocked Clay's view. "Go find his dad. I'll buy you some time."

"But what about you? You can't kill him!" She walked up to him in worry. "And without your name, you can't go back!"

"I know that. But I had a sister, didn't I? I know that much. And I know I loved her very much too." The powder that trailed from him gathered around his left hand, slowly spinning and condensing itself into his palm until they formed the shape, and eventually, the texture of another steel pipe. "She'll be here soon. I'm not leaving her alone."

The Father's figure stood up from within the cloud. Slowly, menacingly, he stepped back out of the crevice made in the large tree and back onto the field of battle.

Sister looked at their opponent and realising she was not going to have another chance like that, simply said, "Thank you." She rushed over towards the spinning whirlwind, gliding over the mud.

As she sped, the sound of clashing steel echoed out behind her. Even if The Brother had abilities, he was still new to them, and would not be able to hold back The Father for long. She had to hurry.

The nearer she got to the whirlwind, the green spectres appeared. Blobs of energy, formed from the souls of those killed and held hostage by The Father. They floated around aimlessly, barely forming the outline of humans. Ghastly after-images of the dead. Even at a hundred meters away from the whirlwind, there was no wind.

"Joshua!" she shouted, hoping that the spectre of the man had managed to retain its sanity. Time flowed differently in the dream world, and it could have easily been months since his spirit was ripped away from his body. "Joshua Kleve! Your son needs you!"

There was no reaction from any of the ghostly figures. Flustered, she reached her hand out to the nearest figure. A soft, white glow emitted from her palm and she placed her hand on the 'face' of the spectre. The translucent figure slowly took form, its head slowly returning to the looks it had in real life, albeit still see-through. The red headed teen that took the spectre's place was definitely not the man Tim had described to her. The bullet wound through the forehead was also a gruesome sight.

As she removed her touch from the figure, the face of Joseph Camein Price also melted back into green. For a moment, Sister thought of individually checking each spectre, hoping to get lucky. But the presence of literally millions of them surrounding the mile-wide whirlwind meant such an action would require luck even beyond supernatural.

"Joshua," she muttered desperately. Frustration settled in. And for the first time in a long, long afterlife, she felt hopeless. "Joshua!"

11:56 P.M.
Present day

Tim, stirred, the blood from his wound had slowed to a crawl and the towel-bandage seemed to be doing its job far beyond expectations. He looked to the digital clock next to the bed, midnight closing in and blinking at him in a ghostly green. The songs returned to plague his mind, even away from the dream world. He did not mind them, as he had long since figured out what they were. Precognitions. A glimpse into the future.

The Mist will come, and darkness spreads.

He got to his feet, wobbling slightly, but held firm to his stance. Doing another check on his revolver, still fully loaded, he finally went to remove the cabinet against the door. However, the cabinet proved harder to remove than it was to place, requiring him to yank the furniture out. He soon found out why. Behind the blockade was an emergency fire axe with its red head lodged deep into the door, the bladed portion stuck in the cabinet. Apparently, someone had tried to raid the room while he was unconscious, but couldn't do much since it was barricaded and their breaching equipment was stuck.

Hold the line, the world will end.

Breathing a sigh of relief, but still wary, he readied his revolver in his one good arm, a practice he had gotten used to in the dream world. Knowing that inching his exit would give anyone on the other side more time to react, he flung the door open with all his might, quickly sweeping the corner down the sights of his gun from the cover of his room.

Descendant, he will walk alone.

The corridor was empty, but the lights were all turned on and most of the rooms towards the elevator had been broken into, some with the violent destruction of their doors. The ones further down the hallway were intact, likely from the axe having gotten stuck and the looters giving up after. He contemplated taking the weapon, but could not convince himself that his arm would be able to wield it decently and left it in the door.

Watcher runs, as the verses clash...

Following a gut hunch, he headed towards the elevator instead of the stairs. Indeed, it was functional again, with the LED screen showing the last known floor being the first, meaning the looters that had taken it up had probably left the building. Feeling confident, he hit the button and called the elevator just at the song finished off in his mind.

"The world will end."

CHAPTER FIFTY-TWO

The End

*"Fear is a poison produced by the mind, and courage is the antidote
stored always ready in the soul."*
-Dean Koontz, One Door Away from Heaven

12:10 A.M.
Present day

Tim knew he was a lightweight and had half expected himself to be
swept off the roof by the high altitude wind, but when he stepped out of
the service exit and onto the skyscraper's rooftop, he encountered not one
breeze nor drops of rain. The portal floated menacingly above the centre of
the roof, just waist height above the 'H' of the helicopter landing pad,
purple and blue Mist swirling around and above its bus wide diameter,
spewing gas like a fountain. It was like a tear in the universe, someone
unplugging a drain in the sky and the water was travelling out in reverse.
He watched as the gas spun on the outskirts of the edges of the building,
just out of reach from the parapet, wind swirling outside of his little bubble
like a tornado.

"Eye of the storm," he muttered to himself.

He had confidence up till that point. Balls of it, in fact. But faced with
the whirling portal, it occurred to him that he had no clue of what to
actually do to close it. He climbed onto the helipad platform and carefully
walked up to the portal. Raising his hand to it, he focused, squinted, tried
to close it with the power of his mind.

It did not work. He waved his hand over his view. Nothing. Once
again, movie logic – of magic this time – had failed him.

Beyond the centre of the portal, he saw what he could only describe as
the universe horizon. Similar to what he learnt in science class about the

event horizon of a black hole, where not even light could escape, there was an image, sharper than anything around it, curved and distorted as the world would seem through a droplet of water. Within it, there were figures, clear entities of green, moving around in a pattern aside from the chaotic whirl that happened within his world.

"Is that..." he squinted, trying to get a clearer view. "The dream world?" He concluded that he was starring at the barrier that separated reality and the worlds between.

He paced around the portal, thinking of how to close it. He wondered if he needed physical contact to even interact with the energy. But just as he contemplated going closer, his left hand raised itself instinctively towards the direction of the portal.

Some of the veins in his forearm began to glow white, though disjointed and few, they spread upwards towards his elbow almost like a circuit, blooming like a flower.

"I don't know what you're doing," he calmly said to his arm, feeling silly as he did so, though quickly concluded that it might be the most normal thing he had done in weeks. "But I hope you have a plan."

Another spectre slowly returned to its physical form. Sleek black hair, drooping eyes, a bullet wound to the forehead. Adam Pearlman was not Joshua Kleve, and Sister frustratingly released the dead back to the realm of incorporeal.

She was running out of time, with Brother's hard earned extra seconds ticking away for her. There were literally billions of the dead. Even though the group she stood in seemed to be of those who were killed in Ridge Valley, that was still hundreds of thousands of spectres to comb through. She had barely covered the first hundred.

"Come on girl, think!" she yelled out loud, as if screaming would allow her to trigger some ideas. "If I was Tim, I'd think of something smart. Okay, my powers are based on emotion and personality. Mine is lust, Father is rage. So what? Think angry thoughts?" She felt plenty of anger as she was, yet nothing seemed to be happening. "Lust. Lust is...lust is!" She slapped her forehead in realisation.

She closed her eyes, her mind drawing up the image of Timothy. The maroon hair. The focused, determined green eyes. The rare smile. The missing arm? No. He had an arm before coming to the dream world. She felt a breeze pass her and opened her eyes to a green spectre floating mildly before her.

"Love," she said to herself as she placed both hands on the face of the

266

spectre.

Slowly, the gas peeled away, revealing the face underneath it. The hair was almost golden, and his build was muscular. Despite the polar contrast, she knew, without a doubt, that she had found Joshua Kleve, for his face was a splitting image of his son.

"Come on, old man, time to wake up." She focused even more energy into him, moving her hands down his body until she held him by the hands. The spectral form broke off like the shell of an egg, the green ghastly outer layer spinning and dispersing into their surroundings. Body still dressed in the white shirt with the fateful cut that killed him, blood dried across his chest, the man was physical once more.

Tenderly, she whispered, "Joshua."

His eyes flickered open, his fingers twitched as life after death flowed back into him. For a moment, he stared at her drowsily, almost as if he were a baby who had just woken from a nap, trying to make sense of the world around him. A glint then rushed back into his eyes as they wandered the landscape.

"Where am I?" he asked. He turned his attention back to Sister, looking her up and down as he struggled with pulling something out of his fragmented memory. "Who are you?"

"My name is Sister," she told him. "Your son asked me to find you."

Memories of his death at the hands of The Father seemingly flooded back. He looked down to his shoulder, still dried red. "I was dead. It was so...quiet." His eyes flew wide as his brain wrapped itself around the situation. "Tim! You said Tim sent you? Is he okay? Where is he?"

"Hang on! Hang on! He's fine, but he needs your help," she said pleadingly.

"I'll do it," he replied without hesitation.

She had expected some resistance. "Aren't you going to hear what it is first?" From what Stella had told her, Tim's relationship with his father had been rocky for years.

"He's my son," Joshua said, a conviction in his eyes the same as that during Tim's moments of strength. "If he needs my help, not even death is going to stop me."

She nodded understandingly. His love for his son was proof that the method she had used to locate him had not worked out of coincidence.

She explained, "He's trying to stop The Father from tearing into your universe. Basically, Tim's trying to kill him." She noticed his shock and eagerness to reply, but stopped him with an understanding nod. "I know it's dangerous, but there's no other way here."

He must have held his breath through that explanation for Josh let out

267

a loud sigh in resignation. "Okay. What does he need me to do?"

"When Tim kills The Father, someone needs to take that place, otherwise, The Father will just resurrect again." She saw a flash of defeat in his eyes as he grasped the situation. "I'm sorry," she solemnly said.

"No. It's not your fault. Tim's always been selfish."

She chuckled, "Yeah. He's the most selfish selfless person I've ever met."

Zoot. Zun. Zoot. Zun.

Sister spun towards the sound. Standing just a hundred meters away was The Father, apparently finished with his battle with The Brother.

Joshua exclaimed, "Back for round two, asshole?" He made a step forward but Sister held him back. "No! If you break contact with me, you'll lose your consciousness. You've been away from your physical body for too long, you'll just become one of these ghosts again!" She gestured at the spectres around them. "If that happens, you won't be able to help Tim!"

"Then what do we do?" he asked, The Father stepping ever closer. "We're sitting ducks like this. He'll just pry us apart!"

Sister stared down The Father, once again cornered by the man with the saw and straw hat. Uttering a rare curse, she prepared to buy enough time for Tim to get to them, despite knowing her combat ability not matching up to that of her opponent's. But just as she readied her cloth for battle, a gentle hand placed itself on her shoulder.

She turned, and Tim, in his real world white shirt and brown cargo pants, both arms intact, stood beside them. Behind the teenager and at the base of the whirl of energy, a tunnel was cut clean through it. In the middle of the passageway, past the universe horizon, was the crystal clear, albeit inverted image of the rooftop of Hotel Alexandria.

"Tim?" she exclaimed. She could sense that he was no longer an entity in the dream world. She was speaking to Timothy Kleve, in the flesh.

He smiled to her, "I got this. Go close the portal."

"Wait! You can't–"

But before she could finish, he said, "I love you, Sally Sparrow," and with the blink of an eye, the girl in white vanished from the dimension.

"Tim!" Josh grabbed his son by the arm before the former could run off. "I know what you're thinking, and I'm not going to let you sacrifice yourself, you hear me?" The slime-green gas began to wrap itself around the man's body, slowly engulfing him once more. "Screw the world, I am not letting you die!"

268

"Sorry dad," he smiled back, with all the love he could put behind the gesture. "Say hi to mom for me."

He yanked away from his father just as the man faded completely, before making a mad dash for the tunnel home. Tim could hear The Father speeding towards him, slashing through the air with the same ferocity and whistle as a jet across the sky.

"Let's end this!" Tim yelled back. The Father closed in, its saw raised, just a second away from slashing. "Vashmir Commons!"

The Father bleached away from the dream world, reappearing right on the opposite end of the portal, its weapon cutting through the empty air in front of it. Pulling out his revolver, Tim jumped just at the edge of the whirlwind. He glanced left, and a flash of strawberry blonde caught his eyes, Stella's last smile forever burnt into his mind. The girl, as The Sister, dashed towards Joshua Kleves lingering spectre. Shoulder first, he crashed through the universe horizon and slammed down onto the helipad.

He could not afford the time to cry in pain, settling for a grunt of discomfort as he quickly shot back up to his feet. Revolver out, sights aimed down at the figure at the edge of the roof and beyond the helipad, Vashmir Commons turned just in time to see the first flash from the muzzle and felt the bullet ripping through his shoulder. Tim fired two more rounds in succession. Still with his supernatural abilities, Vashmir brought up his saw, moving at a speed fast enough to block them, the bullets clanking and sparking off the blade.

Tim rushed in. With just three bullets left, he could not afford to miss. He aimed at his opponent's face and fired two more rounds. The sawman raised its weapon again, blocked the shots before they could reach him. For the split second that his own weapon covered his line of sight, Tim leapt wildly from the helipad, landing both his feet firmly onto the creature's chest. One hand holding The Father by the head, he jammed the barrel of the gun into the gap between the saw handle and The Father's finger.

The trigger clicked.

The firing pin knocked in.

The bullet exploded out of the chamber.

Smoke rose. Dismembered fingers, smashed and disintegrated, burst apart from the hand. The saw dropping to the floor.

Tim jumped back and landed on his feet. He threw the emptied gun at The Father, who swatted at the projectile. But without his weapon or his fingers, missed completely, and the firearm simply smacked him in the eyes. Vashmir swiped the weapon away, the blood from his hand smearing across his face, no longer the shadow of a nightmare, but that of a human, twisted with anger.

He lost track of Tim, and could only watch as the helipad moved further and further away as Tim tackled him square in the gut with the full, desperate force of his body. He was lifted off his feet, arms flailing in desperation as the two of them toppled over the parapet.

As Tim fell off the roof, watching The Father plummet away from him towards the ground below, the adrenaline of death by fall shooting through his veins, he could vividly see the faces of his best friends, Clay and Stella. His father and his mother, the day before she died. There were images of birthday parties and outings. Sleepovers and dinners. First day of school and last days of summer. He willed himself to skip all those memories. Life would have another chance to flash by his eyes when he dies of old age.

He reached towards the outstretched hand above him, grabbing it just before he was out of reach. Tim swung back to the building, slamming face first into the steel wall. His nose bled, but he did not care. One hand held up, he kicked desperately against the wall to prevent himself from falling and pushed and flailed against gravity. He swung his free hand, found the edge of the parapet, and with his saviour's help, pulled himself up, over, and back onto the rooftop, collapsing onto the ground in a final heave.

Lying on his back, staring up through gaps in the dispersing Mist, the stars wrinkled in the night sky. Tim panted to his rescuer, "Thanks."

Sister knelt beside him. After a moment however, she decided to lie down instead, his arm stretched out as a pillow for her. "Don't ever make me do that again," she huffed out, curling into his shoulder.

He could hear her heartbeat, the steady thumping as she tried desperately to calm it down. From the corner of his eyes, he could see that the portal had been closed. The purple gas no longer spewing, the wind no longer twirled, the world was no longer crazy. He could finally feel all the aches in his bones and creaks in his muscles.

"Sally?" he asked the girl in white.

It took awhile for her to answer, "Yeah?" Her own name must have contradictorily sounded both foreign and familiar to her.

"I'm gonna take a nap."

"Okay," she turned to face Tim, but his eyes were already closed.

His chest rose steadily with each breath, his heart no longer beating at death's door. The moon peeked out from the clouds. She kissed him on the cheek. He slept in evening's gaze.

Epilogue

Howard Galloway rummaged through the dark living room, circling the coffee tables' fruit platter in search of food. There were no cookies to gobble nor milk to drink, which suited him just fine, as he had no presents to leave behind either. His footsteps clinked and thumped without an ounce of finesse, knocking into the wooden furniture and scrapping the ground noisily.

The lights flickered on and the man froze on the spot. He turned slowly to face the ragged judgement of his old friend.

Timothy Kleve stood at the bottom of the flight of stairs in a ruffled shirt and boxer shorts, maroon hair greying from years, skin hardened from age. At fifty-four years old, he was a head taller and better built than the scrawny teenager that had once saved the universe.

Timothy greeted, "Old man." Though Howard looked three decades younger. "What are you doing here? And would you keep it down? Milton's still sleeping."

Howard held out an apple, "Do you have any bananas?"

"No."

"Well you should. Good source of vitamin B."

"I'll make a note of that." Tim stretched himself as he moved to sit on the long couch.

Howard sat on the lone recliner. "So, where were we?"

"Last I saw you, you came to tell me how my powers worked. That was what? Five years ago?" Tim sank into the cushion and yawned. "What about you? What have you been doing?"

"I just came back from your future," the time traveller replied. "Your future self says today is the day you made the prediction."

"Yeah. Who knew the whole Sin thing would give me the power to predict the future. But through song lyrics though, that's so stupid," Tim admitted, though with a tone of remorse in his voice. "One hundred and thirty nine years to the end of the world. That's what Leah translated it as."

"Smart girl."

"I know. That's why I hired her."

"I thought The Forum made you."

"Same difference." Tim stretched again, his bones creaking like the rusted hinges of a door. "Where are you off to next?"

"End of the world. Going to check out what's causing all these problems. Hopefully I can knock it right this time." The librarian got to his feet. "Just dropping in on old friends. Saying goodbye and all that."

Tim asked, "Last time I'll be seeing you?"

"Last time *I'll* be seeing *you*," Howard corrected.

Tim nodded solemnly before following to stand. "Wait here, I've got something for you." He headed back up the stairs and disappeared onto the landing. After a couple of minutes of feet tapping and show tune whistling, Tim came back down with a camcorder in hand. He passed the device to Howard.

"What's this?" Howard asked.

"It's a recording of everything that happened. I thought maybe you could put it to some use. Maybe write a stupid book with all your stupid quotes."

The man laughed. "Okay. I'll see what I can do."

Tim bobbed his head in approval. "Listen, Howard. The number one-three-nine, it has been popping up this whole time. Vashmir wrote it as the days to the end of the world, and now Milton has a hundred and thirty-nine years. I don't think those are coincidences." Howard gave a nod of agreement. Tim continued. "Days and years. Time between here and the dream world. It definitely have something to do with time. If there's anyone who could figure this out, it's you. You're the time traveller after all."

"I know. That's why I'm awesome." In a rare moment of seriousness, the librarian said, "Don't worry, I'll figure this out. I promise you."

"Good. Too many people died from this bullshit. Even more are about to come."

"You have no idea."

From upstairs, a woman called out, "Tim?"

Tim turned away from Howard and to the voice, "That's Sally. She'll want to–" he turned back, but Howard was gone.

"Asshole," Tim cursed the man one last time.

Prequel
Bleached

Wispy smoke filled the room and the stench of tobacco lingered forever in the air. Sixteen years old Sally Sparrow sat naked on the bed, her onyx eyes fixed blankly on the wall before her. Her light golden brown hair stretched messily to her waist. Bruises and lashes marked her otherwise unblemished, pale white skin. Her small, petite frame, coupled with her unresponsive stare, gave her the look of a porcelain doll.

From the hallway, the cries of a baby erupted. The shrill wail cutting through the quiet afternoon. Though she could not tell if it was lights out as every blinds were drawn and windows closed. She was forever trapped in the dark along with the odour of beer that had long seeped into the walls. The baby continued to cry and Sally managed a weak remnant of a smile at the sound.

A loud violent crash came from the bathroom, followed by a man shouting, "Sally! Go shut your sister up!"

Monotonously, she replied, "Yes, father."

"And go finish the sheets."

"Yes, father," she said again, the sentence now an automated answer in her daily life.

She got to her feet and reached for the tissues on the night stand. Going through the motion that she had repeated countless times, she reached down with the paper, wiping in and out of her vagina as clean as she could. There was once, a long time ago, where she felt shame and pain at the act and would break down in tears for hours, or until her father scolded her or started to rape her again. But after the years of abuse, something in her closed. A door that slammed shut and could not be opened. She threw the dirtied paper into a small plastic bin filled with burnt out cigarette buds, other tissues, and emptied cigarette boxes and beer cans.

From the footboard of the bed, she grabbed a thin, white, cotton one-piece dress. Even after putting it on, the clothing showed off far more skin than she would like. The skirt circled just below her thigh, the string-held low-cut revealed too much cleavage. The lack of sleeves froze her skin. Though she hated the dress, it was all she ever wore. It was all she was allowed to wear, and her entire wardrobe consisted purely of it. She missed the days of shorts and t-shirts, of sandals and shoes. She felt that the only colour she ever saw in the mirrors these days were the white of bones and sometimes wondered if the figure in the reflection was death greeting her early.

The baby continued to wail, and the man from the toilet shouted again, "Why is that little shit still crying?"

"On my way, father."

She headed for the door. As she passed the bathroom, a burly hand shot out at her, grabbing Sally tightly by her shoulders and pushed her against the wall, fingers sinking into her skin.

"When I tell you to do something, you had better do it quick!" the man growled, completely naked.

Craig Sparrow was her father. He was a large, pot-bellied man with dark, thinning brown hair. His arms were the size of her thighs, made mostly of fat, and his thighs were twice the size of his arms, made mostly of beer. Big, lumbering, and towering to the door, he threw his weight around like a thug, and his attitude shot off like a shotgun. His face was heavily scarred from years of brawling, half of his teeth chipped and all of them were smoked yellow.

Sally looked away from the revolting face, "I'm sorry father," she apologised insincerely. She wondered if she scratched at his face, would his skin peel off like scales on a lizard. "I was just getting dressed." As if reading her sister's trouble, the baby's cries died down to a lighter sob.

"What's the point of that?" he asked, pushing his face into the nape of her neck, taking in a deep breath, his hand moving up to caress her small breasts. "No one here will mind."

"I'm sorry, father," she apologised again. She had long since gotten used to the odour of smoke that reeked from the man, but could never completely get the smell out of her nose when he was close, and a part of her hope she never will, if just to keep some semblance of her individuality. "I'll be quicker next time." She wondered if she would get lung cancer simply from standing next to him.

She wondered about a lot of things. It was a good way to pass the time. It was a better way to distract herself from events that unfolded around her.

He moved his lips to her face and she readied her nerves for the revolting kiss. However, she was saved by her baby sister, whose renewed crying snapped the man out of his lustful fog.

Angrily, he stepped away and backed into the bathroom, punching the door in frustration. "I said go shut her up!" he yelled.

"Yes, father." With renewed haste brought on by the slight joy of being a step away from the man, Sally left the room.

The house was always kept dank and dark, with the only place lit being the second floor corridor, but only by a single lamp at the end of the path. She thought the scene was a strangely fitting metaphor for her life.

Down the corridor she went, her footsteps echoed as loudly as a jackhammer within the empty house. Light seeped out from the gaps of the last ajar door. From it, the baby cried. Sally entered.

The walls were dull grey, unpainted with any form or colours that might give the impression of joy or life. Yet, somehow, despite the sad wail, the despot atmosphere, the darkness from the drawn curtains, and the lifeless canvas walls, to Sally, the room was the most hopeful place in all of existence.

A cradle was placed in the middle of the room. No toys dangled above. No cuddly bears guarded the babe.

With a soft smile and gentle hold, Sally picked up her six months old baby sister. "Hey, Stella." She cradled the baby in her arms. "It's okay. It's okay. Everything will be fine." As if her voice was a lullaby, Stella quickly quietened down, sniffing the last of her sobs.

The baby girl had never met their mother, and Stella was all that remained of her that Sally had. A short puff of golden hair, a set of gentle glowing eyes. Stella was hope incarnate.

She carried her to a table where with one skilled arm, she opened the can of milk powder, mixed the solution in a bottle of warm water, shook, and twisted the lid shut. It was a strange set of skills Sally had developed over the six months since her mother died giving birth to Stella. She often found herself having to do multiple chores simultaneously, and soon, each action came to her as naturally as a step in her walk.

"Here you go, baby sis," Sally said, bringing the bottles' teat to Stella's lips.

Stella smiled at the sight, small arms waving in excited anticipation before clumsily grabbing a hold of the plastic bottle in her tiny hands. She put the bottle to her mouth, drinking in the grimy concoction that only toddlers could enjoy.

Sally smiled at the act, a pure bliss, untainted, even by the darkened events of the house. Slowly, she twirled on the spot, dancing slowly, rocking the baby into a gentle slumber. She hummed a soft tune, *Que Sera, Sera*.

She stepped around the cradle, the image of a classic cartoon princess, dancing and singing her life away, awaiting the fated day when a prince would knock on her door and sweep her off her feet. Away from her sexually abusive father. Away from the memories of her dead mother. A modern day Cinderella. A gritty reboot of the classic tale.

Somehow, in the short minute, Stella fell back to sleep, her bottle barely half emptied. Sally had expected this. Her younger sister had always been easy to care for. It was as if the toddler knew how hard her big sister's life was, and only ever called for the daily necessities.

She laid the baby back down into the cradle, pulling the blanket over her sleeping body. "Little sister, I promise you. Nothing will ever happen to you," a mantra she had repeated countless times over.

She kissed the baby on the forehead, the little ball of flesh and blood that was all that was left of their mother. She kissed her again before heading for the door.

Out the corridor. Down the dark stairwell and into the living room. How long has it been since they sat together as a family? Five years? Ten? There was a memory that lingered of her as a child, sitting at the dining room table with her parents, laughing under bright lights and coloured worlds. Before the drinking. Before the abuse. Though it was such a distant time ago it was but a faint spark in her mind.

Like the rest of the house, the curtains were drawn. The coffee table was heavily dusted with cigarette ashes, the couch worn with its leather tearing. The television screen cracked down the side from her father throwing a beer bottle at it when his team lost the big game. They crossed ten thousand dollars into gambling debt that day and lost half a TV screen.

The kitchen, unlike the rest of the house, was spotless. That was only because Craig had not cooked anything for himself in half a decade. Sally used to think of the kitchen as a sanctuary, a place where only she would go to. That changed when he raped her on the sink three months ago. It used to be that she would look forward to cooking, as that was one of the few times when her father would refrain from trying anything, less he ends up tasting his semen on his food. But since the first violation, it had become another part of her day where she looked over her shoulder.

Another set of stairs around the corner from the fridge stretched down into the basement. She descended into it, the air getting danker and the atmosphere darker with each step. A gas mask and work goggle hung on the wall on the way down. She swiped them and placed them on.

At the bottom of the steps, she faced a large basement, filled with dozens of industrial sized stainless steel 'pots' for cloth dyeing, and a larger, bed-sized one for bleaching. Craig ran an outsource service for dyeing and bleaching cloths and clothes. Even though the pots were tools of her father's trade, she was the only one who ever worked on them. He merely collected and delivered the shipments. She was sure that if he was less lazy and taught her how to drive, he would have made her do the deliveries as well. Of course, she thought such a thing was too fatherly an act for the depraved man.

She went to the container for the bleached clothes. Even with her mask, she could still smell the chlorine. She opened the metal lid and leaned over the solution. Grabbing a tongs from a stand beside her, she pulled out a bed sheet from the container, bleached completely white, and dragged it over to a clothes line across the back wall to dry.

"Is it done?" She spun around and saw her father in his stained boxers, standing at the landing.

"Yes, father," she acknowledged, a robotic tone in her voice.

"Good. Good," he said softly. His tone like that of a teacher praising a student. Words of sincerity with some condescension. "Stay there awhile."

She knew that tone for something else however. It was the voice he took before 'trying something new'. Craig slowly walked towards his daughter and she could only look down at her feet, obediently following his last command.

She thought of Stella, and daydreamed of a world where she would escape with her baby sister. But she had no job. No belongings. No friends or family on the outside. Not a penny to her name. The daydream quickly dispersed.

He closed in on her, cupping his hand around her chin and lifting her head to face him. His grin reminded her of a goblin from Saturday morning cartoons. Yellow. Misshapen. Tantalising to punch but too creepy to do so. He took off her mask and goggles. The smell of alcohol from him was overwhelming. The chemicals in the room burnt her eyes less than the sight of her own father. He leaned in for a kiss, tongue and all, whirling inside her mouth.

Sally had long since learnt to control the retching. Her emotions becoming something akin to a knock on the door, where she could choose to answer or ignore. It helped her carry through the more grotesque of his acts.

He moved down, pecking her neck. Between breaths, he said, "You know, I thought you would have ran away by now,"

She had wanted to. Initially, Sally stayed for her mother. When the latter died giving birth to Stella, she ended up staying for her sister. But that did not mean she had not tried to escape. Sally had once gotten as far as the front lawn with baby Stella in her arms, but was caught and locked in the garage together for three days. She never tried anything again after that, for fear of what Craig would do to Stella.

The man continued to move down her body, "I can't wait until your sister is all grown up as well."

Something in Sally snapped awake. Her eyes, watering from the nauseating chemicals, managed to fly open. "Don't you dare touch her," she growled.

He drew his hand back and punched her in the gut. She coughed hard, blood spewing. Before she could recover, he pushed her against the bleaching container, violently pressing her spine against the sharp metal edge. She tried to scream, but he reached out at her throat, gripping it till her bones hurt.

"You are my bitch!" he yelled, eyes glinting madly. "You and your sister belong to me! And I will do whatever the fuck I want with you!" He spun her around, bent her over, and shoved her face into the bleach solution.

Her lungs filled with the chemical as she struggled to breathe. She could feel the man pulling aside her dress and shoving his manhood into her. He rocked her back and forth. She struggled, tapping the metal container in submission. The liquid spilt out of the container and splashed onto the ground. She lost her footing, slipping on the bleach. Her head bent aside and Craig lost his grip as she fell to the ground. The man tipped forward head first into the side of the container, a loud smash as his head bashed into the edge.

She couldn't see. Her vision corroded by the bleach. But she took the chance and swiped blindly forward, managing to grab the man by the legs. With all the strength she could find, she lifted the heavy rapist off the ground, leveraging his weight against the container. She heard the man's head splash into liquid behind and she held her ground. His overweight body meant he did not have the strength to push himself back up.

He smashed the metal, kicked desperately. She held stead. A warmth ran down her back as the man lost control of his bladder. She was sure he had shat himself as well, but her nose were too burnt by bleach to smell anything distinct.

The kicking slowed. The splashing softened.

He stopped moving.

The only sound left was her furious coughing. She had not even realised she had been coughing that violently until the silence of the room engulfed her.

She dropped the dead body into the container and stumbled away, exhausted and in pain. Guts burning, blinded, coughing blood, lungs tearing, stomach churning with bleach, she took two steps forward and walked right into another dyeing container. Giving up on moving through the pain, she sat down on the floor. Stella's crying echoing through the house.

She could not recognise the burnt voice from her lips. "Stella..." she let out in a mutated croak.

She reached to the side and found Craig's pants. Following the stitching on the pants, she found the front pocket and the cellphone within.

Tracing the buttons, she dialled 9-1-1 and almost immediately, the operator picked up. But the voice on the other end was mumbled. She could no longer hear what they said. She could not even hear the silence of the world.

She bought the phone up to her lips and croaked out, "Help...her..."

Sally's arms fell to the ground. Her last thought as she drifted out of consciousness was of a sunlit past of long gone days, where the world was bleached white with innocence, and the worst that could happen were bad dreams.